In Advance
of the
Broken Justy

In Advance
of the
Broken Justy

A NOVEL BY

John Olson

QUALE PRESS

ISBN: 978-1-935835-17-2
LCCN: 2016931154

Quale Press
www.quale.com

CONTENTS

for Toby
August 2001 – September 14, 2015
best friend I ever had

An Impromptu Visit to the Hôtel-Dieu

On our first night in Paris Ronnie woke me at 3:00 A.M. with a black eye. The left eye was so discolored and puffy the folds of skin covered her entire eyeball. She looked as if I'd slugged her.

Hard.

We didn't hesitate. We needed to get her to an emergency room.

We got dressed and took the elevator down to the lobby. We explained the situation to the concierge, a solidly built man in his forties who appeared a trifle perplexed but otherwise nonplussed. I worried that he would think we'd had an argument and that I'd struck Ronnie. Or that she had pinkeye, a malady with implications of questionable hygiene.

The concierge got out a telephone book and laid it on his desk. It surprised me that he didn't use a tablet or smartphone, which were ubiquitous in the United States and had usurped the yellow pages almost a decade ago. The French had electronic gadgetry (there were abundant boutiques selling sparkly covers for smartphones) but didn't use them as often as people in the States.

The concierge told us that the nearest emergency room was at the Hôtel-Dieu de Paris, in the Île de la Cité next to Notre-Dame. Founded in 651 by Saint Landry, it is considered to be the first hospital in the city and the oldest worldwide still operating.

The concierge phoned a cab and within minutes one appeared. He led us into the courtyard near Saint-Sulpice cathedral and explained the situation to the cab driver, a large black man in his fifties with a West African accent. We said *bonjour* and got into the cab.

There was no traffic. It amazed me how quiet and still the city was. If I went running at this hour, I'd have the city to myself.

The driver circled the ancient building. It was huge and surrounded by a tall, iron gate. There were a pair of high blue doors at intervals that appeared to lead into a courtyard. The building appeared to be dead. There were no lights, no visible activity.

The cab driver did not seem at all surprised by the building's bleak appearance. He told us that there was a doctor's strike in progress. I was already aware of this. I'd seen the news report at home on TV5MONDE, our French cable station. I also knew that some doctors were still treating patients. They wore armbands that said, MÉDECIN EN GRÈVE. The doctors were objecting to the payment system in which the patient had to pay first then was refunded by the state, and wanted their hours cut to 48 per week. We were hoping that there would be at least a skeleton crew servicing the emergency room. The cab driver did not seem inclined to drive us all over Paris looking for a hospital that might be open. Certainly something must be open somewhere. Where would all the victims of car accidents, knife wounds and drug overdoses go for aid?

The driver stopped and gazed into a narrow, open corridor where he was certain he spotted a light. I could see nothing, but there was no point in arguing with him. My French isn't that great and his English wasn't much better than my French. I could read French with very little problem, but speaking and hearing it was a difficulty for both Ronnie and me.

Là, à la derriere, he said. There, in the back.

I understood that. I looked, but still couldn't make anything out. We would have to take his word for it. Ronnie got out, and I paid the fare. I wasn't sure if cab drivers received tips. Waiters didn't receive tips. The tip was included in the bill.

Do you receive tips? I asked. *Oui, monsieur*, he said. The fare was 12 euros. I handed him a 20 euro bill and asked, *Trieze?* He didn't appear to be happy with that. *Quatorze?* He seemed ok with that. He gave me six euros in change and I got out.

Ronnie and I walked the length of the narrow corridor and came to an office with a light on. We could see a woman sitting at a desk. We entered and the woman looked up, surprised to see us.

I explained the situation in my awkward, halting French.

Ma femme a une infection mauvais de l'oeil. Son oeil est gonflé. Nous sommes venus des États-Unis. Je suis désolé pour mon français. (My wife has a bad infection of the eye. Her eye is swollen. We come from the United States. I am sorry for my French).

Vous devez aller à l'entrée, she said. You need to go to the entrance.

Où est-ce? I asked. Where is that?

C'est dans cette direction, she said, pointing. *Vous la verrez. C'est une grande porte bleue.*

Did you catch that? I asked Ronnie.

She said it's a large blue door, in that direction.

Merci, I said to the woman.

We left without feeling very hopeful. All we had seen had been a series of large blue doors.

We returned to the street. It was freezing cold. My ears burned. I glanced to my right and saw Notre-Dame cathedral looming above, dark and silhouetted against the night sky. It startled me. I'd been so preoccupied with Ronnie's eye that I'd forgotten we were in Paris. There was an immense Christmas tree on the parvis ornamented with blue lights and bulbs. The blue was solemn, soothing and dreamy.

We followed the wall around the building. Each time we came to a pair of blue doors I gave them a shove. They were immovable. I found one that appeared to be open a crack and gave it a shove. It wouldn't budge.

We came to a pair of blue doors where there was an intercom. We pressed a button and a staticky voice came out: *Qu-est-ce que vous voulez?* What do you want? At least, that's what I thought he said.

Salle d'urgence, I said. We are looking for the emergency room.

The voice came back out but neither of us could make out what he was saying.

We returned to the office. The woman was still there, but this time there were two cops, a man and a woman. They all looked perplexed when we entered.

I'm sorry, I told the woman, too tired to keep speaking French. We couldn't find the emergency room. All the doors are locked.

She got up from her desk and led us to a door which opened into a dark corridor. She directed us to follow the corridor to the end (*tout droit*), then make a right (*aller à droite*).

We followed the corridor, made a right turn, and entered a huge room filled with darkness. There was just enough light to make our way through this space. Then we suddenly heard a man's voice. *Quel cherchez-vous?* It seemed to be coming from above. I looked up and saw a man sitting at a high desk. He could've been God. That is, if God were a middle-aged man with thick black curly hair.

Nous sommes à la recherché pour la salle d'urgence, I said.

Tout droit, he answered.

We came to a large door by which a small sign was posted with a handwritten message: "*Sonez 1 fois et quelqu'un sera venir.*" Ring once and someone will come.

We pressed the button and heard a bell ring. A young woman with reddish blonde hair came to the door and led us in and directed us to the desk where she and another man who appeared to be of Indian or Pakistani heritage sat by her. The young woman, who had a very shy and gentle manner, gave Ronnie a form to fill out. Ronnie filled it out and handed it back to the woman, who asked what was meant by "drive." Drive is like street, said Ronnie.

I noticed a sign listing the symptoms of Ebola taped to the desk. There were few words, mostly just simple line drawings of a man vomiting or bent over in pain with heatwaves over his head to indicate fever. I wondered if anyone had been there recently with Ebola symptoms and removed my elbow from the counter.

The young woman invited us to sit at a wooden bench in the hallway and wait for the doctor. I noticed another sign on the floor that said, "*Seuil de discretion à respecter.*" Threshold of discretion to respect.

We didn't wait long. A tall, handsome man in his thirties appeared. He wore a lab coat and had thick wavy black hair and glasses. He apologized that his English was bad and led us into an exam room. I sat on a chair while he administered attention to Ronnie's swollen eye. He examined it with an ophthalmoscope and had her read a sign that featured a constellation of letters. I could barely see them myself. Ronnie tried reading from the top but could see nothing at all with her bad eye, and as she continued farther down as the letters grew smaller she could not identify any of the letters with either of her eyes.

The doctor led us into another room in which he further examined Ronnie's eye with a keratometer, a diagnostic instrument that measures the curvature of the cornea's anterior surface.

When he finished, he led us back to the other exam room and delivered his diagnosis. It amazed me that he came up with a diagnosis so fast. Ronnie had had a swollen lymph node under her chin which — after a blood test, ultrasound, and a visit to an otolaryngologist — still did not have a diagnosis.

The doctor asked if Ronnie wore contact lenses. She said yes, she had for many years, but had not worn them in the last several months. The doctor said she had parietal keratitis, an inflamed cornea, that may have been caused by wearing contact lenses and keeping her eyes open in the dry air of a plane for ten hours. He made out a prescription for six items: Dacudoses, an ophthalmic solution for rinsing the eyes; Vitabact, an antiseptic solution of picloxydine hydrochloride used in the form of eye drops; Vismed, a solution of sodium hyaluronate also to be applied as eye drops; Optive, more lubricant eye drops; Levo-free (levocabastine hydrochloride), yet more eye drops; and Vitamin A Dulcis (cicatrisant oculaire), a pomade of vitamin A. He reviewed the prescription with Ronnie and stressed that one of the items must only be used once. The prescription was written in French. Later, Ronnie tried to remember which one must only be used once. I told her it must be the pomade. That's a cream. Certainly you wouldn't want to apply that during the day, but just before going to bed.

The doctor returned to wherever he'd come from and the young woman at the desk called a cab for us. I thought that was a particularly kind thing to do. The young woman struck both Ronnie and I as being very sweet and fragile and we wondered how she coped working in an emergency room where she must witness daily a stream of bloody fractures and injuries and people screaming and groaning in pain.

The young woman led us to an elevator that was lined with some sort of silvery metallic substance. I felt I'd been given an opportunity to practice some of my French. *Un ascenseur de l'argent*, I remarked, putting theatrical emphasis on *"argent."* The young woman smiled.

The young woman led us to a hall and to a huge window overlooking a courtyard. The courtyard looked medieval. I imagined the scene in *Macbeth* in which the porter is awakened by Macduff knocking at the door. Thomas De Quincey has an essay about this scene, "On the Knocking at the Gate in *Macbeth*."

I wondered, since the gate was closed, how we would know if the taxi had arrived. I looked more closely and saw that there was just enough space beneath the two blue doors to discern someone's feet. And so we did just minutes later, a pair of feet going back and forth. The young woman led us down to the courtyard, opened one of the doors and greeted the driver and explained that we needed to go to an all-night pharmacy. There was one on the Champs-Élysées. The driver was familiar with it. We said *merci* to the young woman and got in the cab.

The driver was an alert, chatty, cheerful soul from Bangladesh who had lived in Paris for twenty-six years. Ronnie told him that she had once worked as a line cook in a swanky Seattle hotel with a man from Bangladesh who had taught her how to say *tumi kemon aacho* (how are you?). The cab driver perked up at this, genuinely surprised. Wow, he said, you know a little Bengali! That's the extent of my knowledge I'm afraid, Ronnie answered.

The driver said he loved living in Paris, but that it was very hard, very expensive.

We arrived at the pharmacy quickly, noting all the make-shift sheds set up on both sides of the Champs-Élysées for Christmas shoppers. It seemed very strange to see the kind of festive booths that might be set up at any little town in Midwest America on the legendary Champs-Élysées. But then, filling a prescription on the Champs-Élysées was also unusual.

The pharmacy was located at the far end of a mall corridor whose windows were filled with chic clothing and luxury items. Right in the middle of the glitzy corridor was a mound of fecal matter, dog or possibly human. It was a hard call. The janitor would not be pleased.

We went to a window marked PHARMACIE and a bald man in his sixties appeared at the window. He seemed appropriately dour for a late-night job filling emergency medications, took Ronnie's prescription and went to fill it. He returned minutes later and said that one of the items — the Levofree — was unavailable and that we would have to find it later at another pharmacy.

The pharmacist spoke English, as did everyone in Paris, which I found disappointing as I was unable to practice my

French. The French are very particular about their language and if they sense you're American — and Ronnie and I both look quintessentially American, very Western — they begin speaking English right off the bat. Head you off at the pass, as it were. Mispronunciations drove them crazy. There appeared to be a lot of anxiety about their language, the seepage of English words into their vocabulary, for instance, was a continual source of chagrin. But French is not like English. English is a supple, highly flexible polyglot language that can take a lot of abuse. The more abuse, the better. It thrives on slang and mispronunciation. Not French. French is more like fine crystal. Careless handling shatters it.

I tried asking the driver, in French, what he liked best about France but the phrase came out garbled and he didn't understand what I meant.

We passed a group of people messing around in the street. It appeared to be a fight. The driver slowed, ostensibly to evaluate the situation and see if anyone required help. It flashed through my mind that I might need to get out and enter the fray in order to help quell tempers. It was evident from the sloppy, highly unstable movements that this group was pretty drunk. If they were fighting, they were too drunk to cause much bodily harm. They could barely stand, much less throw a punch. We continued on our way back to the hotel.

I paid the driver and we entered the hotel, still very quiet, picked up our key at the desk from the concierge who discreetly refrained from asking questions about our visit to the hospital, returned to our room and — after Ronnie applied several of her solutions — we crawled under the sheets of our very large canopied bed and fell instantly asleep.

This was our second visit to Paris in less than two years. The first had occurred August before last, in 2013. Ronnie had been there many years before, and so had I, during my first marriage, forty-three years ago, in 1972. These two visits were remarkable not just because we had both returned to this magical place after an interruption of several decades, but because we each felt an attachment that had become deeply emotional, like a drug. We had become addicted to this city. It inhabited us, as Ronnie put it.

It was hard to remember the exact circumstances that had prompted our visit in 2013, but it had had something to do with a broken Subaru Justy.

SEATTLE

R onnie and I live in Seattle. Ronnie has lived in Seattle her
entire life and I've lived in Seattle since age twelve, though
I spent ten years living in the Bay Area of California in my
twenties.

I've never really liked Seattle. It's cold, damp, gray and
gloomy most of the time. Electric cords get easily tangled
because of the constant humidity, which penetrates to the
bone. Summer lasts two weeks, beginning July 5, the day after
everyone has come out to watch the fireworks in their ski par-
kas. My dislike of Seattle evolved over a period of time, like
an allergy that starts out with a minor rash and then grows
into strange secretions and the constant application of topical
ointments.

There was something darkly Protestant about Seattle.
Within a year, even the most jubilant and outgoing of people
from California would grow petulant and moody, serious
about their work, hard as oak, their driving habits occasionally
deteriorating into moments of languid, spiritless *non compos
mentis*, their car swerving from the lane and slowly coming

to a stop at the side of the road while they sat drooling on the steering wheel in a coma.

I grew up in Minneapolis and my father brought our family out to live in Seattle in 1959 after getting hired at Boeing as an illustrator for their aerospace program. I didn't hate Seattle at first, I didn't think that much of it at all. As a kid, one place was as good as another. Life consisted of school, playing, watching TV, mowing the lawn and doing chores around the house. What made it difficult was my parent's divorce. I spent the years between ages twelve and fifteen shuttling back and forth between my father and mother while they battled for custody in the court, always being the new kid in school and always — since I developed very slowly and was small for my age — getting picked on by bullies. It wasn't until my brother and I went to live with our father on a permanent basis that I began to blend into something like a social life. At age fifteen, I also discovered alcohol. That was a boost.

At age eighteen, I left my father's house and struck out for California, following the scent of sex, drugs and rock 'n' roll. I was into Dylan and the Rolling Stones. I liked The Beatles, but they remained a bit too wholesome for my rebel-without-a-cause setup. And after reading Aldous Huxley's seminal essay on mescaline, *The Doors of Perception*, I had a raging desire to experiment with psychedelic drugs.

My mother had remarried a used car salesman and moved to San José, which allowed me to go to a community college for free and provided another incentive for my relocation program.

I had spent a semester at the University of North Dakota in Grand Forks after getting beat up at a New Year's bash in Burien, a suburb a few miles south of Seattle, and felt that moping around in subzero temperatures *à la* Hamlet at Wittenberg might do me some good. It got me started into the college routine, but apart from that, those subzero temperatures did little else but foster a keen appetite for sunshine and thrills, and it wasn't long before I made plans with my dorm mate to head out to California, which we did in the summer of 1966.

California did not disappoint. I loved it. Everything said about it was true. The people were jubilant and friendly, heady intellectual ideas galvanized that sweet salt air. Literary luminaries such as Jack Kerouac, Allen Ginsberg, Philip Lamantia and Michael McClure were all associated with the Poetry Renaissance of San Francisco, a mere 60 miles north of San José, and garage bands such as The Count Five, The Seeds, Love, Jefferson Airplane and The 13th Floor Elevator were countering the rich treasures of the British Invasion with lush new sounds.

I got married in 1970, divorced in 1972, and headed back to Seattle in 1976.

Why?

I still ask myself that. I must remind myself that San José turned into Silicon Valley. The affluence that converted the fragrant orchards of San José into the sterile, futuristic buildings of the computer industry pushed out struggling artists. There were signs of conversion as early as 1972; my ex-wife got a job at National Semiconductor. Talk of integrated circuits — bytes, RAM, chips and floppy disk drives — filled the air, especially at parties. This was the death knell of the Poetry Renaissance. People who once got excited at parties talking about William Burroughs or Bob Dylan or Janis Joplin now were more prone to discuss diodes, capacitors and memory chips. It was about this time I shook my head with disgust and left.

I got a job with the mailing service at the University of Washington and remarried. I drank heavily. I continued to write, but there were fewer people with which to discuss literary topics, and I felt increasingly isolated. The isolation fed the drinking; the drinking fed the isolation.

I got divorced again in 1987. I was still employed at the mailing service, part-time, and still pursuing something akin to a literary fulfillment of some kind, although by then that literary career I looked forward to in my twenties was now a nebulous cloud of utter social irrelevance. I liked to float on that cloud from time to time, but it felt absurdly romantic, giddily utopian and utterly useless in an anti-capitalistic way that I still find spiritually reassuring.

Those were the Reagan Years. John Lennon had been dead for over five years, Dylan was singing some form of Christian rock, and the Boomer Generation was now stuffing their noses with cocaine and their wallets with money, though not necessarily in that order.

To the east of Seattle, a little start-up company called Microsoft grew into a giant, which — like the earthquake in the Indian Ocean that generated the tsunami that destroyed Indonesia — created a tsunami of affluence that destroyed Seattle. A gray, wet, gloomy city of eminently livable and affordable communities seasoned with generous amounts of eccentricity and funky coffeehouses and wonderful old used bookstores with creaking wooden floors, disappeared. It became another soulless Silicon Valley of money-grubbing developers and clueless software engineers. The only people able to afford living in this city now are lawyers, developers, business moguls and chief surgeons. Everyone else has to commute a minimum of fifteen miles from one of Seattle's dreary satellite communities. And real estate prices are skyrocketing even out there. Seattle proper, at last count, now has a population of around 625,000 people. Metro Seattle is significantly larger at 3,600,000.

I met Ronnie in 1993. I had stopped drinking and started attending AA meetings. One of the young men in my AA meeting with a keen interest in poetry nominated me for a shot at competing for a coveted reading spot at Bumbershoot, Seattle's annual arts festival that occurs over Labor Day weekend. The competition was held in a tavern in Seattle's Belltown. I did well, and won. Two other readers were chosen from a reading held the following week, one of whom was Ronnie. I had spoken with her briefly during the competition in which I'd read, and I managed to coax a phone number out of her. Now I had a good reason to call. We traveled to Bainbridge Island by ferry on our first date. It was our first expedition.

The rest, as they say, is history.

ZERSTREUTHEIT

Before I continue, I need to make a confession: I hate noise. I mean really hate it. Not dislike it. Hate it. Cannot abide it. Cannot, for that matter, even define it.

It's like pornography: I know what it is when I hear it. Perhaps that's what noise is: the pornography of sound. Naked, voluptuous sound. Sound with its waves spread. Sound with its frequencies in seductive disarray.

But no. That's not noise either.

It's complicated. There are situations in which I rather enjoy noise. Coffeehouses, mainly. I like the sound of tinkling glass, voices in conversation, paper rustling, traffic going by, music emanating from a strategically placed speaker. So why does noise of any kind bug me at home? I can't say. It's a puzzle. When I hear noise at home, I go ballistic. I can't concentrate. I stick earplugs in my ears and if that doesn't work I squeeze my head with both hands hoping the noise is gone when I remove my hands from my ears.

And here's an even stranger part: I have tinnitus. Ringing in the ears. Constantly. I've learned to live with it, so you'd assume — I assume — that if I can adapt to that, why can't I adapt to noise? Not noise in my head, but external noise. Saws, hammers, shouts, barking.

Some neurologists have theorized that tinnitus in some cases is a neurological rather than audiological problem, that the neurons in the auditory cortex are hyper-activated, doing double duty and creating a phantom sound, a noise that isn't actually there. That makes sense to me. If my neurons are supercharged, there is going to be a sensitivity to the noises outside of my head as well as the ones inside my head.

Which aren't actually there.

Hence, my conflict over issues having to do with construction are fueled by one thing and one thing only: noise.

The condition — this supersensitivity to sound — has a name: hyperacusia. It has a powerful bias on my ability to get along with other people. People with power saws especially.

There are contradictions. On occasion, I like listening to music when I read. Sometimes I put on my Bose noise-cancelling headphones and put Pandora on shuffle and listen to music as if I were sitting in a coffeehouse with a tape of music playing. It distracts me from my tinnitus and helps me concentrate.

But here's the weird part: if I'm sitting at home and someone else is playing music — you know? that *thumpety thumpety* of drums you can hear through the plaster walls and ceiling in apartment complexes — I go into a fury. I can't stand it. Even if it's music I like. I don't like it if someone else is disturbing me with it. What's up with that? Go figure.

It's hard to explain. It defies logic. What is it, exactly, that makes noise so infernally, frustratingly noisome? What makes noise a noise?

It's largely a matter of context. A quality of attention I'm trying hard to maintain in which silence is necessary. The mind is fickle. It doesn't take much to trip it up. That elusive, vapory phenomenon called thought is notoriously difficult to coax into definition. It's a matter of attention. That lens of the mind called focus.

"Everyone knows what attention is," said William James. "It is the taking possession by the mind, in clear and vivid form, of one out of what seem several simultaneously possible objects or trains of thought. Focalization, concentration, of consciousness are of its essence. It implies withdrawal from some things in order to deal effectively with others, and is a condition which has a real opposite in the confused, dazed, scatterbrained state which in French is called *distraction*, and *Zerstreutheit* in German."

That's what noise is: *Zerstreutheit*. It's everything inimical to nuance and subtlety and delicacy and charm. It's a supervisor's sour gaze. It's mandatory overtime. It's having to work for a living. It's the buzz of an alarm clock dissipating a pleasant dream. It's a playground bully. It's a motorcycle gang at a rock concert. It's a cop spraying capsaicin in an elderly woman's face. It's a loud party next door when you're in bed and have to get up early to go to a job you hate. It's a toddler in a movie theater talking over the dialogue and his big hairy dad asking you point-blank if you've got a problem because you had the unmitigated gall to turn around to give him and his obese trailer park slob of a wife the stink eye. It's endless war. It's the nagging ever-present worry about climate change and corporate predation and the death of value. It's cancer. It's chemotherapy. It's Syria and Gaza and Israel and wrecked Iraq. It's smartphones and iPads and the obliviousness of one's fellow citizens. It's rudeness and insanity and fascism and a boot in the face. It's a neighbor's power saw ripping a quiet afternoon in half.

Or am I just being melodramatic? Is this what you call overreaction? Overreaching? Overindulgent? Ok, then, so be it. Guilty as charged.

The tinnitus and quite possibly my ultra-sensitivity to noise is the result, in large measure, of an LSD trip gone horribly wrong. I dropped some acid in the winter of 1966 with some people, strangers for the most part, sitting on pillows in the high-ceilinged room of a Victorian house in downtown San José. The trip went well for about an hour, then, with the suddenness of an electric switch, it became a horror: I felt an overwhelming unreality about my body, my being, my sense of self. I felt like I was nothing more than a cloud of molecules. Remember the transporter aboard the Starship Enterprise on *Star Trek*? Crewmembers such as Captain Kirk or Spock would stand on the transporter platform, dematerialize into glittery atoms then rematerialize on the surface of whatever planet they were visiting. If something went wrong, the crewmembers would remain in a molecular state until the computer could read their signals properly and reconstitute them, hopefully in recognizable form. That was me. I was a transporter malfunction. I awoke hours later in the padded cell of a local hospital, brought back to familiar bodily form thanks to a heavy dose of chlorpromazine. I've had the tinnitus ever since, and a philosophical disposition slanted toward the underlying unreality of existence.

I spent ten years living in California and then headed north to Seattle in 1976 to regenerate myself. Seattle was a far more appealing place in the 1970s. Rent was cheap, Starbucks had begun selling coffee but had not yet become a corporation, there was an abundance of bookstores, movie theaters and coffee houses, hardware stores outnumbered nail salons and the humidity and moss appealed to my aptitude for brooding and rumination.

Yet, even in the 1970s when Seattle's many amenities outweighed its disadvantages, I felt somehow constricted, cramped, claustrophobic. Why did I stay? Why did I continue to live here all these years? Fear of quitting my job and trying to find work elsewhere had a lot to do with my inertia. In any event, I stayed. Seattle, meanwhile, morphed into the monstrosity it has become today. Forced out by escalating rents, the old population of students, bohemian outcasts and middle-class families has been replaced by a population of highly affluent technocrats and real estate developers. I'm reminded of the futuristic dystopia in the 1992 movie *Freejack*, in which the rich hire "bonejackers" to snatch youthful bodies from the unpolluted past to replace their aging, decrepit bodies in the present and attain a shabby immortality in a substitute body. If I felt ambivalent about Seattle before, I now felt trapped and alien. Ronnie felt the same way.

We could move. There was that. But I didn't really want to move. No sane person wants to move. Moving is a nightmare that lasts a week of not knowing where anything is and then settles into the more natural rhythms of your life. Old habits are resumed. Boxes emptied and loved books put back on the shelf.

Noise doesn't bother Ronnie. She could sleep through a hurricane. Earthquake, tornado, war, tsunami, freight trains colliding, volcanic eruption or neighbors screaming at a football game would not cause even a minor disturbance in her sleep. She often finds it difficult to get to sleep, but once asleep, nothing outside of a boat horn can wake her. She does not understand my hatred of noise. Noise is noise. For her, there is nothing harmful in it.

Ronnie's nemesis is clutter. She hates clutter. She wants more room. We do need more room. We're two people in a modest 500-square-foot, one-bedroom apartment. Our bookcases overflow, the closets overflow. It's like living in a space laboratory except that we're not weightless, we do not float, we maneuver gingerly among the furniture, chairs, sofa, coffee table. There's a geography to it, a topography, a cartography. One plans one's moves or suffers the consequences, the unhappy products of spontaneity, a bumped shin, a broken toe. No toes have actually been broken as yet, but it's worth mentioning, it could be, could happen, a metatarsal, a distal phalanx, the tuberosity of the fifth metatarsal could fracture, could crack, could send shivers of pain screaming up and down the nervous system, you never know. Clutter has a magnetic force, its augmentations have a certain intrigue, a certain peripheral sedimentation, forms deposits secretly, mysteriously, so that before you know it you've got a mess, a jungle, a procreative drive of tropical proportions building stories of perplexity and confusion around you, preposterous contingencies, stunning entanglements, monumental agglomerations, a boundless capharnaum a lot like this sentence.

Wires and plugs and magazines. Books and disks and gadgetry. Boxes upon boxes upon boxes upon boxes.

Resistors, cenotaphs, minotaurs, muskellunge, pylons, fulgurations, Hagiographa.

Escarpments rags bumboats goiters flashlights lap joints pizza boxes tsunamis wave mechanics ommatophores pemmican pepperwort resonant circuits shofars auxiliary verbs crispations sponges spools sporozoans euphemisms generalities and Rayleigh scattering.

What clutter is to Ronnie, noise is to me: anathema. Noise is head clutter. Clutter of the skull. The clutter between the ears that prevents two thoughts from coming together to form a concept or idea. But clutter, literal, non-metaphorical clutter, the clutter of socks and shoes, the clutter of magazines and junk mail, the clutter of words in a sentence like this one, the one now under development, that kind of clutter I can live with. I'm not particularly happy about it, but I can go throughout my day stepping over things if there are other activities on my calendar of a more appealing nature. I have made amends. I have learned to accept a certain amount of clutter as a given, as an inevitable consequence of living. I will not say it has been an entire success, but if life's melodies are often off-key, it is dissonance that makes a piece of jazz light up a room. It is syncopation — the rupture of a fixed metrical pattern — that gives life to a piece of music. Too much harmony is dull. Too much bareness is barrenness. It is the aberrant, the perverse, the eccentric that holds our interest. Show me a messy room, and I'll show you an interesting person.

Why then not adapt to noise? Isn't noise the very breath of chaos? Isn't noise the tinsel that brings light and sparkle to the silent night of the Christmas tree? Are not stars the tinsel of oblivion? Isn't noise the colloquy of color on the canvas of time? Isn't that what noise is?

I have no defense. Yes, noise is a welcome sign of life and an antidote to the mortuary silences of a mute eternity. I wish I could argue myself into an appreciation of noise. But I cannot. I hate it.

My sensitivity to noise has grown lately, along with my anxiety, and chronic tinnitus. I'd been diagnosed with GAD, as in gadzooks, or Generalized Anxiety Disorder. I'd been taking an antidepressant called imipramine for over twenty-five years and it had ceased working. I tried going without any medication for a while, believing that my long distance running would sufficiently buoy my moods and bolster my mind against the abyss over which I teetered, but my mood slowly deteriorated and the abyss loomed larger than ever. Darker and deeper than ever. I was now on a par with Poe's Roderick Usher, whose acute sensitivity to everything had a morbid, preternatural caste to it, the smell of the swamp at midnight when strange speckled creatures crawl forth to feed and reproduce. The Gothic echo of phantom realms stirring the nerves into fever dreams, strange ecstasies and shadowy terrors.

I'd begun a new regime of antidepressants, the SSRIs as they're called. So far, they hadn't been helping. It takes a long time for an antidepressant to kick in. Months, in fact. Meanwhile, the drone of a neighbor's fan or bang of a car door slamming is enough to set my nerves on edge. I feel like a Van de Graaff generator shooting megavolts of raw irritability.

A Voyage Around Our Apartment

In the spirit of Xavier de Maistre's wonderful journey around his room, a journey that encompassed the forty-two days of his house arrest for dueling, I have decided to embark on my own journey and describe the chief sights and interesting customs of our native habitat.

Our journey begins in the bathroom, for that is where I begin my day. Here, it is the mirror that most engages the attention. It's a large mirror, taking up a great portion of the southern wall, reflecting the towel rack and towels and a print of André Derain's Fauve rendition of the Thames, with its constellation of tugs and boats in red and black, the yellow of the river and sky lightly mottled with touches of burnt orange, a vigorous blotch of bright red smoke emerging from the stack of one of the tugs. It is that red smoke that I find so exhilarating. It is the smoke of paint, of art, and has little to do with the actuality of the real world, in which smoke is characteristically white or gray or black. This smoke is demonstrably, aggressively red.

It tumbles into yellow like a tongue easing into naked color. It makes me happy to see this red smoke when I'm drying my hands on one of our new towels of lemon chiffon.

Above the toilet hangs Duchamp's *Nude Descending a Staircase, No. 2*, and to the immediate left, on the east wall facing west, is an early painting by Picasso depicting a naked woman giving herself a sponge bath in a shallow bathing pan of blue enamel, an enormous mound of white and patches of pale blue describing a bed enveloped in the gentle, voluptuous folds of blankets and/or bedcover, the length of it coming to an end just behind the woman's derrière. Off to the side and just below a bedroom window is a large green rectangular object swathed in regions of red rounding out a curved top. The object looks like a cross between a steamer trunk and a treasure chest. The scene is that of a bedroom garret, rough but sensual, restful but full of energy.

Our next stop is the kitchen. If our apartment could be compared to the United States, the kitchen would be Delaware. It's a small galley kitchen. The cupboards and drawers are relatively new. The dishwasher is old and soon to be replaced. Ditto the refrigerator. The wooden sill at the base of the window is comparatively new and the blinds will also be turned in for brand new ones. The food is generally new, because if it weren't generally new, and belching strong odors of mold and decay, it would not be considered food, but garbage, and summarily removed and deposited into the compost bin. This never happens. We buy our food economically and eat it robustly. Right now, the refrigerator is host to a full gallon bottle of grape juice, jars of Grey Poupon, strawberry preserves, mayonnaise, milk caramel, sweet marinated olives and chicken base. A quart of milk, two bottles of root beer, one bottle of barbecue sauce and two pints of heavy whipping cream. Two cartons of large grade AA eggs, a box of Philadelphia cream cheese and a big cube of medium cheddar cheese. Packet of provolone. Little jar of Louisiana hot sauce and a big jug of organic maple syrup. Five cans of V8 juice and two packets of Cajun-style Andouille. Container of crumbled feta cheese and a container of sour cream. The freezer is full of frozen bread, buns, ice cream and beef pot pies.

Just north of the kitchen is the large home computer and desk where I sit like a human jukebox trumpeting vowels and consonants in a pantomime of jubilant orchestration.

To the north of the computer is the table my brother built four decades ago based on an award-winning design that makes dismantling and reassembling it a breeze. On top of the table is a large Tiffany lamp with two pull chains, one of which sticks a little, and requires a slightly harder tug. Somehow, loosening the bulb makes it tug a little better. Graham's pillow (oval in shape with a paisley print) sits under the lamp, and Graham (our Siamese cat) sometimes sleeps there. At the far northern end is a Christmas cactus potted in an earthen pot with a sheet of cellophane under it to protect the table from water, a section of today's newspaper just to the side, a French dictionary, George Perec's *W ou le souvenir de l'enfance* and Cervante's *Don Quixote* stacked in a pyramid at the center front of the table. In the chair just west of the table sits Ronnie, sucking a lollipop the bank teller gave her this afternoon when she went to deposit a check for the dryer duct cleaning earlier this morning.

This has been an exhausting trip so far. It's time to lie down on the couch with a copy of George Perec's *La vie mode d'emploi*. Feel free to continue the journey in your imagination, or take a coffee break...

Ok, I'm back. Ready? Let's go.

Our next stop is the TV, which sits in front of two book-cases in a rather indecorous manner, blocking the bookcases and sticking out like the proverbial sore thumb, but our apart-ment is small. If our apartment were a country, it would be Liechtenstein. But without the wealth.

Ronnie and I are book lovers and most of our reading is in books and magazines rather than the internet, though I do a robust amount of reading there, too. We use our TV mostly to watch the programs on TV5MONDE. We're trying to learn French and the programming is excellent. Our favorite shows are *Thalassa, Des racines et des ailes, Le grand tour, Question pour un champion* and *Épicerie fine*. The cabinet below the TV is full of DVDs, movies such as *Sideways; Wings of*

Desire; What Happened to Kerouac; A Hard Day's Night; It Might Get Loud; Orpheus; Paris je t'aime; Gladiator; Jackie Brown; Up in the Air; As Good As It Gets; two versions (Joss Whedon and Kenneth Branagh) of *Much Ado About Nothing; Stones in Exile; Into the Wild; Stranger Than Fiction; Midnight in Paris; O Brother, Where Art Thou?;* John Ford's *The Searchers; Twelve O'Clock High* and *Braveheart* that we've viewed (and continue to view) numerous times.

In back of the TV is another bookcase with a silkscreen print by Jim Dine of a pair of blood-red riding boots on a black background. The intensity of the red is gleefully incendiary. It is the red of midnight bonfires on tropical shores. Red like Bach. A red hungry for skin. A deliberate red. An unappeasable red. The red of vertebrae and vivacity and planets in rain. The red of consonants on fire and vowels on fire and life hemorrhaging the truth of space.

To the left (or east) of Jim Dine is a ceremonial dancing belt from Cameroon. It is long and composed of thousands of beads, green and red and deep blue, depicting a snake and three birds — one blue, two red — and two masked and grinning faces, each face composed of contrasting patterns of red and blue and green. The belt is edged with little cowrie shells.

To the west of the belt is Matisse's *The Sorrows of the King*, one of his large gouache cutouts depicting a large figure in a black robe constellated with green flowers, two white hands above an orange guitar, a green man with arms upraised to his immediate left, the green man's arms raised and ready to come down on an orange drum, both figures surrounded by sparks from a fire, bright yellow and deliriously buoyant, a ghost-white figure in ecstatic dance just in front of the king.

Below *The Sorrows of the King* is another bookcase and to the right (or east) of that is a small end table with a watercolor by my dad under glass, a depiction of a rural landscape, upon which rests a leather valise and a Canon PowerShot digital camera. A towel covers the glass to protect it. There are also a few CDs stacked there: *There's a Word!* (Ray Manzarek and Michael McClure); George Kalamaras and Alvaro Cardona-

Hine, a reading at Acequia Booksellers; *I Like Your Eyes Liberty*, Terry Riley and Michael McClure; *The Dream Life of Cléo de Merode*, a film by Julian Semilian; *Claude Royet-Journoud, entretien avec Alain Veinstein (diffusé le 24 décembre 2007 hors de l'émission "Surpris par la nuit/Contresens" sur France Culture)*; *Crazy Heart*; *Firesign Theatre Presents Radio Now*; *Métamec* by Léo Ferré; *Le mot de passe* and *Sexe fort* by Patricia Kaas; *Room to Dream: David Lynch and the Independent Filmmaker*; and Gustav Mahler's *Symphony 2 in C minor*.

No journey is complete without a mobile. Such a mobile hangs from the ceiling, a squiggly abstraction of wire and little metallic triangles, located a few feet above the telephone, which we have nearly stopped using since Ronnie prefers the use of her smartphone. She gave me her old Blackberry to carry periodically so that she can reach me if I'm out on a run, or placed within convenient reach of the computer because we keep the ringer off the home telephone to protect our quiet from the assault of telemarketers, but apart from that my relationship with the Blackberry is tentative and awkward. I barely know how to work it. Hence, I do not think of myself as a full-fledged member of the mobile phone society. I'm peripheral to it, a tourist, a yokel sampling pie at the county fair.

Next to the couch at its northern end is a standing lamp with a pole of rubbed matte steel, a framed print of *Three Peaches* by Man Ray and a small flowerpot out of which bristles a bouquet of pens, pencils and an American flag. The flag is there in case anyone gets confused about which country they're currently visiting.

Next to Man Ray's peaches a man holds an umbrella over a cello in the rain on Montmartre in a photograph by Robert Doisneau, and just to the south of that hangs a woodcut titled *Rising on Sticks* by Peggy Murphy, a highly geometricized rendition in black and white of leaves with their nervure and tree limbs and bark.

On the other side of this particular wall and round the corner of the hallway leading into the bathroom is our bedroom. Our bed is a metal frame structure, the metal rods curlicuing round in merry arabesques, a gathering of pillows at the head of the bed and another Matisse print — *Interior in Yellow and Blue* — above the bed, the black lines of the wrought iron chair and table base harmonizing nicely with the lines of our bed's metalwork.

On the left (or west) side of the bed is an end table with a CD player, clock radio and lamp. On the other side of the bed is another end table, this one featuring a cabinet and a marble slab upon which rests a large lamp and a small digital alarm clock.

Several feet from the base of the bed, abutting the west wall, is an old oak desk that once belonged to my paternal grandmother, and is where she kept a diary of her activities on her farm in North Dakota, listing temperatures and incidental facts, such as the arrival by train of her ten-year-old grandson (me) arriving for a summer visit. The desk has a slant top that pulls down for writing and a space inside that once housed a Philco radio. The grain is varnished and dark. The desk has a serious demeanor and gives the activity of my writing a rather dignified air, although the writing itself may not be remotely dignified. Just the activity of it, not the actuality of it.

There is a giant bureau with a huge mirror and a small bureau whose drawers keep breaking and I continue hammering the nails back into their bottoms. The smaller of the two bureaus contains hundreds of letters, many of them from the poet Ted Enslin, who passed away a few years ago.

It would be more to the point to say that Ted entered the bourne from which no traveler returns, and a journey we will all have to make sooner or later. It will be our final journey, though who knows? Perhaps not so final at all, but the beginning of another journey no one could possibly envision. Hamlet doesn't call it the undiscovered country for nothing. He uses the word *undiscovered* advisedly.

If one proceeds to the hallway, one notices a closet to the left which is full of coats and jackets and running clothes (the running clothes have a section to themselves at the southern extremity of the closet, the Mississippi of the closet, which is where your strong humidities and earthier odors are to be found, and a vacuum cleaner, two folding chairs and a small tabletop ironing board). To the right, is another large print of Matisse's *Les poissons rouges*, and an abstract painting by Olympia artist Debra Van Tuinen, who uses an encaustic process to bring out tones of atmospheric light, *à la* Joseph Turner and Mark Rothko.

The large thick door that opens into the building hallway and stairs leading outside and to the two upper units has a tiny peephole in it. When I'm lying on the couch facing the door the peephole looks like a star since the lights are always on in the outside hallway, and it is generally dark in the inner hallway of our apartment, so the light shines through the peephole. The peephole comes in handy if I hear voices or some commotion in the hallway and want to see who it is or what's going on without having to stick my head out, I can put my head up against the peephole and peer out through its magnifying lens. It's rather a nice, voyeuristic feeling, almost like being invisible, to gaze at people without being detected.

Let us retreat back into the apartment for the present moment in order to complete our journey. But how does one complete this journey? Was there ever a real destination? Was there a schedule to keep? An itinerary? A route? A plot?

No, there was not. No route, no plot. This journey around our apartment has no real end to it. It is a circular journey, a Möbius voyage of continuous digression, and when we retreat from the hallway the sound we hear is that of a washing machine entering its spin cycle in the laundry room, accented by the hum of the dryer and the click of zippers and buttons in the dryer drum, a symphony of soap and suds and clothes tumbling in fugal disarray.

NEIGHBORS

Neighbors is a subject upon which I must wax philosophical, though I needn't elaborate. Philosopher Jean-Paul Sartre summed it up rather nicely: hell is other people.

Neighbors are not people we willing choose to share our domestic environment. Neighbors can be bad, good, sociable, unsociable, noisy, quiet, affable and nosy or retiring and cranky, gracious and agreeable, leering and nasty, personable and charming or brooding and sarcastic or hundreds of combinations of personality characterized by age or background. But whatever their makeup, it's vital to realize that these are people with whom we must, one way or another, adapt. We choose our friends and romantic partners, we do not adapt to them. Not at first, anyway.

Living in close proximity to people is inevitably taxing, particularly when the ownership of the property is shared and the maintenance and upkeep of the building necessitates costs that in turn necessitate discussions, discussions that can swiftly lead to the splenetic and touchy or inoffensive and congenial. One hopes for warm, spontaneous affability but most often one must settle for cold, contrived, begrudging civility.

Our building is strong, it has survived two 6.0 magnitude earthquakes, but lacks soundproofing. This situation is not conducive to forming good relations with one's neighbors. The space between the ceiling and floor acts more as a resonator, amplifying sound, rather than muffling sound. The walls are for decoration, a place to hang pictures and calendars. Other than that, they're useless. They provide the illusion of privacy, no more.

Ronnie and I are on the lowest floor. Half of our apartment is underground. Our front window looks out on a garden and a sidewalk. I recognize the tenants in the building by the shoes that they wear. Moccasins, mules, sandals, pumps, slippers, boots. Usually, it's flip-flops flapping by on a pair of hairy legs, or the occasional dress shoes, wing-tip Oxfords or bike toe loafers. The most outstanding footwear are Cindy's black leather knee-high boots. They look like dominatrix boots. I can see her in fishnet stockings cracking a whip over a crouched, begging man. Cindy has a walk to go with them: she thunders by in brisk aggression like a female locomotive in a pleated cupcake skirt.

I never think of myself as anyone's neighbor, which is a good thing. In general, I do not like neighbors. But there are exceptions.

Sam Adams is one of the nicest people I have met. He lives in the apartment across the hall from us. He is a large, heavy-set Black man who is easily the most courteous person in our building. He shuts the entry door quietly and walks gently down the steps to his apartment. I think he may have social anxieties. He always gets a pained expression when I see him, I know the feeling myself, when you don't want to encounter another neighbor, but I try to be as friendly as possible and he sometimes opens up a little. He likes a good laugh.

Sam rents from his friend Guy Manning, a tall, quiet, good-natured man who cares about little else other than his wife, his daughter and the Los Angeles Lakers.

Sam, as a renter, has the luxury of remaining far outside condo politics. I respect that, and never draw him in. That would be cruel.

Guy avoids condo controversy, especially if it's something that doesn't immediately concern him. He doesn't live in the building. He rarely joins in on any email discussion relating to condo policies and conflicts. He keeps a jovial distance. If, during a condo meeting, there is a divisive issue under careful discussion, he is careful not to become too vocal. If he expresses an opinion, he does so laconically, and with little show of emotion. When a vote is taken, he raises his hand with quiet aloofness.

Guy's detachment is a continual frustration for me because of all the condo members he's the only one I really trust. He is the least acquisitive, the most approachable and the least judgmental. I was, however, a little hurt when, at a recent condo meeting, he voted against my request for a certain percentage of hardwood flooring to be covered by some form of rug or carpet. This was in reference to the apartment directly above us. One previous tenant, a young single woman with a busy social life, liked trying on shoes. I'm guessing she would put the shoes on then parade around in them for a while until she decided whether to commit to them or not. It sounded like a clog dance every afternoon and early evening. This was when we had dinner and watched a movie. It drove me nuts. There had been many other instances of shoe clomping, dropped cutlery and chair legs scraped on the floor above our heads. Many other condos had had similar problems and had mandated some form of floor covering for hardwood floors. It did not seem like an unreasonable request. But Guy went, as usual, with the majority vote on this matter, which was totally against us. We were denied our request for some form of compulsory floor covering. Whoever tromped around upstairs would be free to keep the hardwood floor as bare as they wished. Ronnie and I would have to suffer the consequences. There would be nothing in the condo bylaws to help protect our quiet. We were at the mercy of a pitiless hardwood floor inches above the soft white vulnerability of our ceiling.

There are two one-bedroom apartments on the second floor. One to the south, one to the north. The one on the south has a fireplace. The one on the north does not.

Cindy and Lyle Dawson live in the apartment on the second floor on the south side of the building. They are in their early thirties. Lyle is a stonemason who is also skilled in tile, terrazzo and intricate mosaics. He is an athletic man with a bold disposition, dreadlocks, tattoos of snakes and dragons on a trim, muscular body with a prominent bristly jaw. His hobbies include yodeling and extreme ironing. He has ironed shirts while water skiing and dangling from a helicopter at an altitude of two thousand feet, in the middle of I-5 during rush hour and while bog snorkeling in Wales.

Cindy is a business analyst at Amazon. She is tall and shapely with long, flowing light sandy hair and favors jeans and cowboy boots when she isn't working but otherwise goes about in a smart wardrobe of tailored skirts and jackets. Her eyes twinkle with trout and mountain brooks. She is what you call outdoorsy. She grew up on a ranch near Anaconda, Montana and shared a love of the outdoors with her husband, Lyle. This love extends to the exotic, locations such as Sumatra and the Amazon basin, as she also has a passion for orchids and once won a prize for a Dendrobium King Dragon hybrid. This was no small accomplishment, as orchids are not easily grown. Their natural environment is the branches of a rain forest where humid air circulates around the roots. The potting media has to be very carefully attended to. A jellylike slime can form in the potting mix and restrict airflow. Standard potting mix consists of rotting humus, though orchids will grow in chopped tires, gravel, coconut-husk fiber, bark chips, peat/perlite mixes, eccentric membranes, junkyard fog, gingery regrets, weird reflections, drugged alphabets and New Zealand sphagnum moss. It is always amusing to visit Lyle and Cindy's apartment and view their assortment of irons and ironing boards and orchids.

Cindy does not share Lyle's enthusiasm for extreme ironing, but she does like doing wash. It surprises me that someone who loves the outdoors so much would take an equal pleasure in washing clothes, if it is the pleasure principle that may be assumed to be the driving motivation, and not some other more peculiar inducement.

Cindy is a virtual laundraholic. She washes everything. If it isn't nailed down, she washes it. Outboard engines, peculiar feelings, dominatrix boots, metaphors, simulacrams, stepladders, old maritime proverbs, fuller's teasels, lunar craters, fipple flutes, fourth-century Roman mosaics, NASA pressure suits, Vatican statuary, maidenhair and crisp salutes.

Chimeras, binoculars, epistemic dilemmas, rooftop views and blemished staccatos.

Synonyms, obscurantisms, obscenities, obsessions and Gilgamesh's T-shirt.

Claw hammers, dip needles and iconographic fortune teller towels.

Good intentions, bad intentions, spurious biographies, Hollywood scandals, chiaroscuro armchair reflections, timeless Parisian insults, anonymous allegories, mosquito mosaics, chapped lips, Arctic scars, highway rattlesnake charms, TV antennas, coppery vespers, antediluvian calliope screws, cemetery emotions, sly Caravaggio appeals, hissing eyeballs, winter bells, ancient cures, popped balloons, Elizabethan gloves, icy problems, sawdust mutations.

I once pulled a women's high school basketball team out of the washer. They thanked me and stumbled off dizzily, unsteadily, but very, very clean.

I try seeing the relationship between Cindy's compulsion to do laundry and her love of orchids. It's an amazingly delicate yet enduring and adaptive flower. It has powerful associations with love and violence. Orchidaceae, the family to which all these flowers belong, derives its name from the Greek legend of Orchis. Orchis was a passionate youth whose mother was a nymph and whose father was a satyr, the genetic engine from which he derived a raging libido. During a celebratory feast for Bacchus, Orchis attempted to rape a priestess. The Fates were swift to deliver punishment: Orchis was ripped apart by wild beasts. Orchis's male parts were transformed into the nether parts of the orchid, its tubers, which bear resemblance to testicles.

Is there a relationship between laundry and testicles? With Fate? With the forests of Madagascar? With *Dendrobium bigibbum*? *Disa grandiflora*? Narrative continuity? The hinged and gently rocking lip of *Bulbophyllum lobbii*? Is that the clue I'm looking for? I don't get Cindy. Her inner life remains as mysterious to me as the *Laelia albida* that favors the western side of the cordillera of Oaxaca in Mexico and whose crimson dots and bright yellow lip are found growing on old oak trees, and which — domestically — does better mounted on cork or hardwood than potted in good warm dirt.

Cindy does not impress one with passion. Far from it. She seems very contained, utterly guarded. She isn't shy. She isn't demure. She's assertive and athletic. She's full of energy and resolve, but she keeps her inner life completely to herself. Her communications are amiably upbeat but only in a superficial deportment of scripted small talk. There is no spontaneity or openness to what could be a more genuine exchange. You would need a crowbar at the very least to pry anything resembling an actual conversation from those lips. An encounter in the hallway is civil but abrupt. She appears to be full of conflicting impulses. But here is where I must stop. Because I don't really have a clue as to what's going on inside her. And who knows? Maybe among her friends she is an utterly different person.

Lyle is a little easier to figure: he's so outdoorsy he doesn't seem to have an interior at all. He rarely, if ever, expresses an opinion. I can't remember if he ever gave an opinion.

On anything.

Not just politics, *anything*: food, sports, news topics, rock stars, music, movies, books, Amazon, Google, Microsoft, Starbucks, all the companies that have a high profile in Seattle and color (and dominate) its life.

These companies piss off a lot of people. But not Lyle. He seems happily disposed toward everything. It's a little maddening. Especially when I'm trying to enlist some support in my dealings with Cal and Pamela (more about them later) and their constant encroachments. If any degree of contention is expressed, he smiles. He muses. He hovers. He appears bemused. He makes it abundantly clear that conflict is not his forte. It is beneath his dignity. He will not soil his brain with conflict.

Has he, I often wonder, reached some form of Buddhist enlightenment? Have his extreme sports led him to a satori of some sort? Is doing a highly demanding physical job good for the soul? Does lifting heavy dusty slabs of marble and mixing cement and pressing stubborn metal strips into mortar and smoothing and polishing surfaces with heavy whining machines all day conducive to a temperament of molybdenum equilibrium?

Is he a stoner? In all the years they've lived in the building, I've never smelled marijuana in their part of the building. My guess would be no.

Or is he just an idiot? Is he a holy idiot like Dostoyevsky's Prince Myshkin, or is he a true idiot like Jerzy Kosinski's Chance in *Being There,* a sweet-natured cypher whose hollowness is mistaken for wisdom?

His favorite word is *awesome.* But then, these days, whose isn't? Can you judge people according to how many times they say awesome in a single day? No, not fair, really.

But if everything is awesome, is anything awesome?

I can sometimes hear Lyle yodeling. Are his opinions expressed that way? Is his *Weltanschauung* vocalized in his yodeling? Yodeling sounds hysterically ebullient.

Stranger yet, Lyle had been attempting to develop a style of yodeling based on the bouncing rhythms of ska, commonly referred to as skank.

One would have to conclude that Lyle is one strange duck.

Like Guy, Cindy and Lyle are so freakishly agreeable about everything that I sometimes want to check and see if they have panels on their backs for opening to see if their circuitry is in order. It wouldn't surprise me to find lithium batteries and robotic components stowed away in their closet. Rod Serling in the background. Cue in *The Twilight Zone* theme song.

Ronnie worries more about social relations than I do. She has a giving, charitable disposition. She isn't naïve. She knows that our neighbors are less than perfect. But she has tolerance and patience on her side. Tolerance and patience do not come naturally to me. I would have to inject them, like heroin. Benzodiazepines are often highly useful. If I can't find forbearance and equanimity via the abundant self-help literature available, I swallow it in the form of lorazepam. Two milligrams of lorazepam equals a temporary, chemically induced feeling of composure. I prefer Valium and rum. But I can't get Valium, and I quit drinking twenty-four years ago, after pounding the doorjamb out of frustration because I could not stop drinking and drinking was the sweetest most wonderful thing in the world, next to sex. I hated to give it up. But the hangovers had become so excruciating that codeine couldn't lighten the black, bone-crunching malaise. And I didn't have cable. I was stuck nursing a hangover all day watching musicals like *Hello Dolly* or *Paint Your Wagon* while moaning and groaning in a fetal position.

Running also helps. Running is the biggest help. Four miles equals one hour of equilibrium. I could probably learn from Lyle's example. If Lyle had a philosophy. Is it possible that Lyle has a philosophy? Is there a Loch Ness monster? Have there been empires on Mars? Is there an afterlife? There are greater mysteries than Lyle's blank composure. But not many.

When Cindy and Lyle go out of town for a spell Ronnie is asked to care for the orchids. She does this with great delight. Ronnie loves to water plants. She loves sprinklers, and caring for delicate things, and the contour of spoons.

The top third floor is by far the largest and borders on luxury with chrome appliances and a spectacular view. The people living there now are named Cal and Pamela.

Cal Hartley is a marketing research analyst and art collector in his early fifties and a Harvard graduate. He had moved to Seattle from New Orleans. He is genial, quiet-mannered and bears a strong resemble to Kevin Spacey.

Cal is married to Pamela Pryor, who was originally from Oxford, Mississippi. She is a social media manager and has traveled a great deal. She is petite and energetic and something of a mystery since she rarely puts in an appearance anywhere, whether parking lot or condo meetings. She does, however, write energetic and detailed letters about changes to their apartment that affect the building, and researches these projects with an equal amount of vigor and conscientious endeavor.

Cal and Pamela are the aristocrats of the building. They evince the kind of charm and affability associated with mint juleps and grace and the unhurried elegance of the Deep South, although the current pace of their lives is more congruent with daylight than daydream, the demands of business rather than the romance of the Southern Gothic. Their speech, however, is unsullied by the coarsening exigencies of industry and remains happily laden with the opulent syllables, the fetching rhythms and love of words that lure you into lush conversation. Their speech is like honey, measured and easily paced, as if each word has a delicious contour and each sentence a unique perception. Each time they speak the room fills with wild bergamot and magnolias. One imagines oneself sitting on a Gothic arcaded porch shaded from the sun, chimes tinkling in a breeze scented with jasmine and sweet olive.

What they produce in me, however, isn't the sweet scent of Southern Romanticism but stress. Chronic anxiety. Ever since they moved into the building they've been making huge changes and sending a volley of emails detailing proposals for more projects, some of which made sense, others not so much.

We wondered why a couple like Cal and Pamela with their considerable income and financial resources would want to live in such an eyesore as our building. The building went up after the 1962 World's Fair. It had the look of an early 1960s style building with roughcast walls, cheesy balconies and a flat tar roof more suitable for sunny San Diego than rainy Seattle.

It aroused some suspicion. We live in a cynical world, to quote Jerry Maguire. It could very well be that Cal and Pamela happened to move into our building during a critical phase of entropy, when things that had held together all these years have reached a point of ultimate decay and need prompt attention.

Holes and craters *have* begun to appear in the parking lot, this is a fact.

It might well be that Cal and Pamela are best thing to happen to our building. If they hadn't moved in, the entire building would have fallen into irreparable neglect and ended up costing everyone a whole lot more money.

Or so we think. We like this narrative, because it makes their intrusions less painful. It is, we like to tell ourselves, their ambition and care that is infusing the building with new life. They're helping to bring about a renaissance of concrete and rebar.

Remodeling, which has become all the rage among Seattle's newly affluent population, offers a cornucopia of catalogues, materials, supplies, choices and alternatives, ample resources for the individual craving a little more meaning in life. The well-off may not find meaning, but they will find cathedrals of hardware. Home Depots dot the land the way Lutheran churches once dotted the plains of the Midwest. Real estate is the new religion. Remodeling is a sect, a denomination of that new religion. God in a toolbox. Salvation in sheet rock. Redemption in vanities. Baptism under a brushed nickel showerhead with a massage spray and integrated three-way diverter.

Cal and Pamela tend to go about things with righteous impatience. There was the matter, for instance, of the holly tree. Ronnie and I happened to notice that our bedroom was much brighter than usual. Our bedroom is mostly below ground. There is a high narrow window with a lovely view of a window well. I'd just painted the window well with some sealskin paint — "lazy day blue" — which had the effect of making things a bit brighter. But not that bright. Not like now with the full sun splashing its way into our little den.

Our little subterranean chamber had become bright as a hotel room on the French Riviera. Was that paint that magical, that strong, that highly reflective?

Then we noticed what had happened: Cal and Pamela had chopped down the holly tree growing in the midst of the laurel hedge with the assistance of the next-door neighbor. There was now a gaping hole where the holly tree once flourished.

And a sizeable stump.

It was a small matter, but the decision to make a notable change in the building landscape without consulting anyone worried us. I wrote to Cal and Pamela and asked what had happened. Did the man next door chop it down? Was the tree on his property?

They wrote back that they'd seen fit to remove the holly tree because it was a mess and a nuisance with a dead vine that was crowding out the laurel and evergreens, and cleaning out the dead leaves and trimming back its branches was a pain.

We hadn't looked that closely at the tree. It seemed to be doing fine whenever we happened to be in that area. The leaves were glossy and green and the shrub had an appealingly asymmetrical balance to it that inspired feelings of joy.

One instinctually moves toward feelings of affability toward one's neighbors, if anything because it makes sharing a space with other people less strained, less antagonistic. But in the case of Cal and Pamela, this is difficult: they're highly aggressive, highly acquisitive and highly motivated to take possession of a space. Even these are things that one can learn to live with harmoniously, so long as one's neighbors don't encroach on one's privacy.

Maddeningly, many of Cal and Pamela's projects do have merit. If bad electrical wiring or plumbing is discovered, nothing can be said to stop them from going through yet another remodeling project that will take weeks to complete since contractors and sub-contractors all have to be scheduled separately.

But isn't that a good thing? Am I making sense? Shouldn't we be grateful that such a conscientious and motivated couple are living in our building?

It baffles me how hideously unfair I am to these people, how petty I'm being. Chalk it up to the tinnitus. To the constant ringing in my head. I've always been far from being that stoical, tight-lipped cowboy with an Olympian ability to tolerate pain and discomfort, sitting in a saddle during a thunder storm gazing Buddha-like into a herd of nervous cattle. I'm not that guy. Not a John Wayne. I'm far closer to Woody Allen on the stoicism scale. I don't just complain. I make an art of complaining. I flourish in it.

Not that my complaints aren't entirely without merit. I'm not the only one who is disturbed by noise. Lyle and Cindy had once complained that they'd been awakened by hammering at two in the morning. The noise was directly above them, in Cal and Pamela's kitchen, in which cupboards were being installed. Cal said that this must have been a contractor who'd decided to go late into the night.

Was this true? A contractor working at two in the morning? What kind of dedication is that? Was he desperate to finish the job because he had other commitments? How could anyone be so oblivious to the noise they were making, to the people trying to sleep just a few feet below? Or had this been a fiction? Perhaps Cal and Pamela hadn't been so spotless after all and I'm not entirely without an ability to forbear and forgive.

Cal and Pamela bought their third-floor apartment from an elderly couple named Jay and Mabel Bellamy. The Bellamys had lived on that spacious third floor of our building for twenty-nine years. They were here when I moved in. They were a gregarious couple with two toy poodles. The two toy poodles drove me nuts. They barked constantly. Every time there was a change in wind direction, the poodles barked. Every time a squirrel farted, the dogs barked. If a maple seed twirled to the ground and slid to a halt on a mound of pine needles, the poodles barked.

And barked and barked and barked.

The dogs were kept indoors, but Jay Bellamy had converted the balcony on the backside of the building into a small office space that hung over the back parking lot and provided a small space to display his numerous trophies. I don't know what the trophies were for. He wasn't athletic. They probably had something to do with business achievement. Jay had been an insurance actuary. He could tell you with bald, unflinching accuracy how many years you could be expected to live. He was a man of logic. He lived a life of eminent sanity and stability. And he was a likable and sociable man. He liked to put outdoor block parties together at the nearby park. He would invite people to bring some snacks, he and Mabel would always bring something good to eat, sandwiches and fruit, and he would bring labels and marking pens to make name tags.

Except for occasional shopping excursions, Mabel busied herself at home. She had raised three children when they still lived in Dallas, which is no small task, but when the children reached adulthood and went their separate ways, Mabel assumed a life of quiet domesticity, and busied herself with grandmotherly zeal when her children and grandchildren visited. We always knew when the grandchildren were visiting because the little tykes would spend hours chasing the poodles around the apartment, so that we on the lower floors would hear a constant *thump thump thumpety thump thump thump*.

Jay was retired. He liked taking the poodles for walks. He enjoyed meeting people and the poodles provided opportunities for him to say hello and shake somebody's hand and invite them to the next block party or even to their apartment to look at slides or photographs.

It was a blessing, for me, that the Bellamys liked to travel. They went everywhere: Russia, Kenya, Cambodia, Cameroon, Singapore and Seoul. Once they even visited, via helicopter, an isolated part of Kamchatka. They would leave their poodles in the care of, I assume, some sort of pet hotel. The quiet afforded by the absence of the poodles was nothing less than heavenly. When the Bellamys and their poodles moved and put their apartment up for sale, it sat on the market for over two years. Two very sweet years. I got very, very spoiled.

Ronnie and I occasionally thought of moving elsewhere to a place with more square footage and an extra room or two, preferably a house rather than another condominium, but never pursued the idea with earnest intent. We oscillated between whimsy and emphatic. Now our discussions acquired a real urgency. We really needed to move. Things had become too aggravating and tense. As two people who describe themselves unreservedly as homebodies, people who truly enjoyed being at home, the new situation was now bordering on the unendurable.

The couple in the apartment on the second floor to the north side, above Ronnie and I, are from Detroit. They're renters, the third set of people to rent from Clark Pruitt, a young IT specialist with a shy disposition and a growing family who longed to sell his apartment and get it off his hands, but since he'd bought it before the crash in 2008, he could not afford to let go of it until he got a matching price. I didn't have the heart to tell him that in all likelihood we were far more likely to experience an even more devastating crash than a slowly recovering economy. He was slated to be an unwilling landlord for a long time to come.

The newest tenants are not a good match. Rocco Radmacker works a swing shift as an airplane mechanic at Sea-Tac, which means that he gets home after midnight and his partner, Terri Dettweiler, who spends her day in front of a plasma TV screen, or pedaling some sort of gym apparatus she ordered through Amazon, which, as it happens, she does in front of the TV.

She also likes baths. The water will run for fifteen or twenty minutes as she fills the tub, occasionally making *swish swish swish* sounds in the water, for what reason I can't even guess since it has nothing to do with cleaning the tub, the pipes meanwhile making a loud hushing sort of sound, whispery but loud, followed by quiet when she soaks in the tub. The intimacy of this procedure is noticeable as it occurs directly above my head when I sit at the computer. As does the sound of Rocco's pissing. He pisses like a mule, a long thunderous flow of urine that lasts a full minute or more, followed by a resounding flush.

It was Rocco's scraggly beard that first caught my attention. Some men look good with beards. Rocco is not one of them. His beard looks like it was drawn by a cartoonist. Matt Groening's Groundskeeper Willie or Al Capp's bloated McGoon, neither of which are all that bad compared to the extraordinary facial hair corkscrewing out of Rocco's cheeks and chin. It looks like a hair explosion, a face hidden in a wilderness of follicle chaos. He is not a bad-looking guy, not a George Clooney but modestly handsome, and I had to wonder why he hid his face behind that wacky facial hair. Maybe it had something to do with a religion, or a dare, or a hatred of razors.

Rocco is casual by manner and good-natured and Terri, who is quite pretty, is guarded and secretive, a quality she tempers with a serene, almost regal graciousness. When I first began to make complaints about the noise in their kitchen at night, the two responded with sincere concern. There was, at first, what appeared to be strained attempts at being quiet, but either they didn't understand my description of the hollow between the floorboards and ceiling as acting more like a resonator than a muffler, or they thought I was being humorous. I am not. When they do dishes at night, it sounds as if I were lying in bed right next to them.

Did they think I was kidding when I told them I could hear a fruit fly fart in their butter dish? They must also have thought I was kidding when I said that we went to bed at 10:00 P.M. because beginning at about midnight Rocco and/or Terri will begin to assemble what appears to be complicated gourmet meals while watching TV until four in the morning. Meals that require a lot of chopping, stirring and cutlery dropping on the hardwood floor.

I can tell that they're trying to be quiet. But, paradoxically, the more they strain to be quiet the more sensitive I become to the little creaks and scrapes and bumps. I would almost prefer it if they could be louder. Is it better to hear cutlery drop to the floor, or wait expectantly for cutlery to drop to the floor?

When, after trying to adjust to their noises and I could no longer endure it, I went and did my diplomatic best to complain about the situation. I tried to make them understand that it wasn't so much their error as the fault of the insane architect who designed our building and put their kitchen over our bedroom, that the building was constructed like a cheap motel whose ceilings and walls were so negligible that one did not live *next* to another so much as *with* another. Much to their credit, they didn't respond with the usual entitled arguments and dig their heels in and refuse to make any changes. They appeared to empathize.

So what went wrong?

The noise in the kitchen continues. Utensils are dropped. Floorboards creak. The refrigerator door slams shut. The microwave hums and dings. Drawers groan and clatter as they're opened and closed. Water howls in the pipes like banshees.

Ronnie works as a barista, making cappuccinos and lattes for Seattle's bustling citizenry, though her duties also include packaging and pricing rolls, pies, tarts, croissants and other sundry items and making sure all the products in the display counter at the grocery store's bakery department are fresh and appetizing. Rocco and Terri's swing shift hours coupled with Ronnie's insane o'clock bakery hours are a bad match. More complaints have ensued, and will no doubt continue to grow increasingly strained and ugly. Not surprisingly, they do not like getting a knock on their door, and so gave me their cell phone numbers for texting. This gives me the opportunity to frame my complaints in more detail. A few adjustments have been made, more cookies and pies have been offered to us in the spirit of appeasement, but nothing solves the ongoing problem. They are intent on continuing their dining habits no matter what.

Though maybe it's not obstinacy so much as terminally poor judgment. Good people making bad decisions.

Recently, I was awakened by the outdoor faucet. It was four in the morning, dark and frigid, the ground covered with heavy snowfall. The washer on the outdoor faucet has worn down so that when someone gives it a twist it squeaks quite loudly. I wondered who in the world would be washing their car at that hour. I got out of bed and dressed to go and investigate. I found Rocco squatting by the front tire of their Honda Fit attempting to put chains on while Terri stood nearby, a silent shadow with crossed arms. Rocco had tried driving up the easement and lost traction. The car was at a sharp angle. He was willing to go through the trouble of putting on chains in order to go a few more feet to park his car in his driveway rather than park it in the street. I felt awkward and embarrassed to be out there investigating at four in the morning and explained that the squeaky faucet had awakened me and asked if everything was ok, which constituted a rather tepid offering of help. He said everything was ok so I returned to bed. I waited to hear the sound of his car inching the rest of the way up the easement and worried about him crashing into our car but I heard nothing. Had he changed his mind and backed down to the street? I finally went back to sleep and discovered the next day that, yes, he'd given up and parked in the street, which would have been the practical thing to do in the first place. Rocco's manner of thinking was unique, to say the least.

It is Rocco and Terri's habit to sleep late into the morning. As soon as they moved in, Cal and Pamela's demolition team began. They had my sympathy there. Damage was done to Rocco's car. Plaster and wiring went flying out of the windows with little care as to where it landed. The demolition team seemed to be a crew of pirates and ne'er-do-wells, one of whom hired a group of Mexican-American mechanics to work on his truck while he was busy swinging his hammer at the walls and tearing the plumbing out. The mechanics kept revving his truck, which vomited thick billowing clouds of black smoke, and were constantly talking loudly in Spanish. I wondered how the guy had managed to finagle these guys into doing on-site work in such abysmal conditions. Our mechanic required an appointment and had as much willingness to pay a house call as a highly paid surgeon.

Cal and Pamela gutted the entire apartment. The demolition went on for two solid weeks. When it finally finished, there was nothing left but the exposed wooden beams and planks that held the building together. In my view, it would have made far better sense economically to just buy everyone out, demolish the whole building and begin anew.

There were actually two demolition teams. The first one got fired. The whole bunch of them. I do not know the ultimate infraction they committed to get themselves bounced from the place, but they were sent packing and were followed by a seemingly more legitimate crew (their trucks were at least newer and shinier and did not require a team of Mexican-American mechanics to work on the site), but who were just as noisy, and worked just as late into the evening.

Then came a pair of electricians who were louder than the demolition team, drilling and pounding and stomping and dropping heavy equipment on the floor.

My first meeting with Pamela did not go well. Cindy and Ronnie and I had been invited up for a consultation on one of the pipes that connected with a drainage system on the roof. There was a roofer there and what was essentially a construction site, a chaos of wires and ducts and splintered wood.

Pamela was having words with the electricians, who looked like stagecoach robbers who had just stepped out of a silent movie Western to do some electrical work while eluding the law. Pamela apologized and let us all know how exasperated she was, stressing how unanticipated all this ruin and mold had been. She was truly sorry for the disruption. But I lost my cool and delivered a jeremiad. Chalk it up to the Prozac. I was new to this antidepressant. It wasn't going well. The Prozac tended to aggravate rather than ameliorate my anxiety. It made me grouchy and aggressive. I pointed out that we were living under a construction site. I was desperate for quiet. I had begun looking for a hotel room. We agreed on some set hours for construction, and she went off in a huff. Work would not begin until nine in the morning, and go until seven at night. If these hours were trespassed in the slightest, give her or Cal a call and report it.

Which I did. The work went on well past seven one night. I called. Cal answered the phone. Yes, he knew the workers were still working. He was answering on his cell phone. He was up there, too, doing work. He promised they'd be done soon.

And so the days went.

Bang! Bang! Thud, thud, thud. Bang! Bang! Bang! Squeak, squeak, squeak. Whir, whir, whir. Whackety whackety whackety whack.

It took roughly six months for that work to be completed. It dissipated slowly, erratically, spasmodically. I continue to worry about more projects: swimming pool and sauna, helicopter pad, musical fountains, hall of mirrors, bronze elevator doors, a central aedicule of veined Breccia Oniciata marble, terra cotta Roman roof tiles and a luxurious aviary for the raising of peacocks.

The tensions that have accumulated over the last few months continue to seethe and bubble in the recesses where noise and irritation circulate in brooding hyperacusis.

Last night Cindy was babysitting two brats — five and seven years old — who buzzed our intercoms repeatedly and tried to get into our apartment. I sought sanctuary in the bedroom, heard scraping noises outside the window, lifted the blinds, and there sits Pamela. Hi, she says. Hi, I say, somewhat embarrassed. She was gardening.

At 8:00 P.M.

We feel trapped. The only solution is to move.

I contacted an old friend, Ben Shapiro, who is in real estate. He came out with his new iPad and began making calculations, running his finger up and down the screen, moving kitchens and living rooms and bathrooms and closets (some with clothes still in them) as if they had the virtual ephemerality of bubbles. It was hard to realize that to each a mortgage of hundreds of thousands of dollars would be attached, looming above one's life like the sword of Damocles.

Ben had made his living in real estate for many years. He was sixty-eight, and had done well in his work. But his real passions were ornithology and poetry. He liked to study bird song, and was fascinated by the range and variety of sounds produced in the avian realm. When his cell phone rang, it was the song of a cardinal. *Richmondena cardinalis,* said Ben.

Ben wanted to give us a sense of the market, an idea as to how much money we could expect to get for our apartment. Ronnie did not believe we could sell our apartment for any amount above $100,000. It was partly below ground and subject to moisture and mold problems.

I was eager to go look at a townhouse we'd found in Green Lake on the internet. I was so intent on living there that all I wanted to do was race to the bank and sign the mortgage and begin to move in. It was keeping me sane, what with the endless construction and bald chicanery of Cal and Pamela.

Ronnie had, in fact, already filled out the bank's pre-approval documents. We'd walked them down to a FedEx office where, at $1.49 per page, we waited for them to go through while visiting with several FedEx employees Ronnie knew through her job as barista in the grocery store below the office. The process finally finished and we paid a bill of $56 dollars.

Several days later, I got a call from a woman at the bank. She cheerfully announced that we'd been preapproved for the hefty amount we required to procure the townhouse.

Ben dropped by the next day to take us out to look at it. We found it, and I saw right away why it had been on the market for a month already. There was a huge construction project next door. Also, the place was distressingly small and cramped. Much of the square footage was taken up by the steps. The bathroom was small and filthy. No one had bothered to clean it. The kitchen looked like a motel kitchen, a casual setup for temporary stays.

Ben drove us back home and Ronnie and I hardly exchanged a word. We were utterly crestfallen.

We decided to compromise, to begin looking at some condos, and to concentrate on getting our apartment ready to sell. That in itself was a formidable task, but bounded, circumscribed and doable.

BANGKOK

The day we decided to move, our car died. It was a 1994 Justy, a car we had grown to love as if it were a pet. Ronnie had owned a blue 1989 Subaru Justy when I first met her, but we lost that one to an accident. We had been on our way to visit one of Ronnie's friends when she realized she'd forgotten a flyer for a reading we were going to do. We returned and parked in the driveway in front of our building, which belongs to Sam, and connects directly with the street. Sam was at work so his driveway was free. We parked there as a matter of convenience. Our driveway is entered by an easement in the back of the building. The grade there is very gentle, but we didn't want to lose time driving around the block to reach it. The street in front of our building is extremely steep. Driving to the top is like taking off in an airplane. I sometimes worry that the angle of the car is so acute going up that the car is going to tip back on its rear wheels and slide to the bottom of the hill on its roof. The driveway, however, has a very slight grade sloping to the street. Ronnie got out of the car and went into the apartment. At first, I was content to sit and wait. But for some reason, I decided to get out and join Ronnie in our apartment. When we returned to the driveway, the little blue Subaru was gone. My heart sank. I knew what had happened. And yup, there it was, sitting at a sharp angle a few feet down, smashed into the back of a neighbor's car, pieces of taillight scattered on the ground. Apparently, Ronnie had failed to set the hand brake properly. It had managed somehow to roll out of the driveway, swerve down the street and collide with a neighbor's car, a middle-aged IT specialist from New Zealand who had already appeared street-side to vent his rage upon our heads, shaking his fist like King Lear, berating our negligence and the general unfairness of the universe. This was the second time this had happened to him. Ronnie's insurance covered damage to both cars and, luckily, no one had gotten hurt. It had only taken us a week to purchase a new Justy, the last of a line. Subaru ceased making the Justy in 1994, the year of our purchase. The new Justy was a bright red five-speed manual hatchback, nimble and economical. We were lucky to get one. It had served us faithfully and well for nineteen years. This sad drama, this moment of doleful frustration occurring in the here and now, on the Bangkok level of the Pacific Place underground parking lot, this last sign of automotive life, this last shift into reverse, this last failed maneuver of hopeful mobility, was its death knell. Less and less mechanical life had wheezed from its bowels with each turn of the key. Now all that was there was a click. A sad dead click. The Justy would not respond.

Would not start. Would not go.

I know what you're thinking. Why doesn't he get out of the car and look under the hood? I could do that. I could get out and pop the hood. But what would I see? Nothing. A black shape. Wires. Little labels with indistinguishable writing, which I wouldn't be able to read without a flashlight, and we did not have a flashlight. But even if we did have a flashlight, I would be looking at a car engine of which I know absolutely nothing. Its valves and hoses and wires and caps would be as much of a mystery to me as the anatomy of a humpback whale. Not to mention the fact that in order to pop the hood I would need to roll the car back away from the wall so that its back end would be partially obstructing the driving lane.

So if that's what you were thinking, that's why. Why I sat there. Befuddled.

I have no idea what you're thinking. And this is my story.

This is the story of not knowing what you're thinking, but of what I'm thinking, of what I'm thinking you might be thinking, of whatever it is you might be bowling in the lanes of your mind, or assembling carefully into meaning, word by word, which is what I do when I want to think something, mean something, bounce something, dangle something, escape something, unearth something, spawn something about a car that won't start. These are the kind of thoughts that go through your head when your car doesn't start.

I tried again. It chuffed and chuffed, the pistons turned over, the starter struggled to put life into the engine, but the pivotal moment in which the car assumes fire and wings and self-sufficiency did not come.

There was no spark. Nothing to turn the car into a concertina of power and music, the music of gears, the music of oil and grease, the music of acceleration, and so back out of the parking lot, and maneuver up the ramps and slide our paid-for ticket into the thin little slot of the parking lot ticket machine and wait for the barrier to go up and permit us to issue from the cave of the parking lot with the little robot voice saying "careful pedestrians approaching" or whatever it is that robot voice says and enter the chaos of one-way streets, erratic traffic lights, anarchic bicyclists, incoherent traffic lanes, Bluetooth androids in leviathan SUVs, tweeting attorneys in sinister sedans, balding assholes in Jaguar convertibles, tattooed hotties in unpredictable hybrids and zombie pedestrians that is downtown Seattle to get back home.

I tried again.

Nothing.

And again.

Nothing.

And again.

Nothing.

Ok. It's official. The car is dead. Fucking goddamn shit-ass dead. It was time now to become philosophical. To allow philosophy a place in our lives. To cook that anguish and frustration into the roast beef of thought.

Ronnie tends to be calmer than me in general, so she was probably already there, comfortably ensconced in the realm of Plato and Seneca and feelings of Stoicism and resignation.

Ronnie is eleven years younger than me. She grew up when Neil Young had morphed into the Zuma Beach Neil Young. I grew up with the wacky Buffalo Springfield Neil Young. The young Neil Young. The "Mr. Soul" Neil Young. The "For What It's Worth" Neil Young.

Ronnie and I looked at one another.

How the hell do we get ourselves out of this parking lot?

This underground parking lot.

The Bangkok level of Pacific Place.

Which is the deepest level. Except for the underworld. That would be the Cerberus Level. In which ghosts step forward begging for forgiveness and the keys to your car.

Pacific Place is an upscale shopping center located in downtown Seattle. It has five floors of glitzy, chichi shops selling jewelry and candy and women's apparel that surround a gigantic open space that is dizzying to gaze out into and an escalator that rides from the first floor to the fifth floor, where a cluster of restaurants and an eleven-screen movie theater appease tongue and eye with Cajun pasta or Brad Pitt, Adam Sandler's latest piece of dung or pan-seared miso mahi-mahi. We took the elevator, which was jammed with people because it was a Saturday afternoon, down to the concourse level to pay for our parking ticket, descend farther into the parking lot and be on our way. The floors in the parking garage are named after world cities to help you remember where you parked your car: Sydney, San Francisco, Hong Kong, Bangkok and Shanghai. What we didn't discover until later, on this one ill-fated and inauspicious occasion, is that there are two parking garages.

We'd gone to see the Steven Soderbergh movie, *Side Effects*. I was eager to see it because antidepressant medication played a pivotal role and I've been taking antidepressant medication for over half of my life. I'm taking an antidepressant now. I'm taking it so that I don't get swallowed by the abyss again. Or get crushed by the tsunamis of panic and chaos and sheer freaking terror that are modern life. Without that medication, I felt like an astronaut losing an umbilical connection to the ship and drifting off into space to spend days in total isolation before dying miserably of thirst and cold. Thanks to modern medicine, I was able to function, watch movies, eat food, take elevators and try to figure out how to get a dead Subaru out of an underground garage.

"Each monad," said Leibniz, "makes a living substance with a particular body," and "like a mirror of God, or indeed of the whole world which it portrays... is like a little world which expresses a great world... and represents a multiplicity in the unity, or in the simple substance" and "is nothing else than what is called Perception."

The monad in Ronnie's hand was a dead cell phone. We were underground in a parking lot where she could not get reception. We would have to surface. We returned to the elevator, rode back up to the concourse level, and Ronnie made her call. We connected with the rest of the universe. We connected with our savior, AAA. They would send a truck. They would text us when the truck was on its way. We returned to our underground space and Subaru. As soon as we arrived, we realized we would have no way to receive the text messages coming from AAA. Ronnie would have to go back up. On the way back up, she spotted a AAA truck. But then it disappeared again. She continued on her way. I hoped for the truck to reappear.

It did not. I waited. I had a copy of André Breton's *Poisson soluble* in my coat pocket, and thought about getting it out to read, but decided against it. I needed to keep out a watch for the AAA truck. Which eventually arrived. A smiling, middle-aged Asian man clambered out of a small pickup truck and explained that he was going to tow me to the surface by attaching a strap to the bumper. We would have to descend first before going back up the ramps. This would require me to apply the brake from time to time to keep the strap taut, or it might wrap around the wheel of the car. He shoved the car while I steered and backed into another slot. Then he tied his strap to the front of the car and we took off. I tapped the brake lightly as he pulled me and I kept a close eye on the yellow strap. Then we began to go up, and all I had to do was steer. We came to the surface and there stood Ronnie, who then followed us the rest of the way to the street, where a huge man and a huge tow truck awaited us. The man in the pickup sped off with an amiable wave and the other man went to work on getting our car pulled aboard the flatbed of his truck. When he finished, Ronnie and I climbed into the cab, which was surprisingly high from the street. The man was a cheerful soul and we began to talk about Saturday night towing jobs. He said Saturday night was surprisingly slow as a rule. I found that strange. I searched for a reason, but could think of none. His busiest time was during rush hour, during the week. There are a lot of breakdowns during gridlock.

I had last Saturday off, he said. I went up north to the Muckleshoot Casino.

My brother did the electrical work for them, said Ronnie.

Really? No kidding, said the tow truck man. Man, that must have been a ton of wiring.

Yeah, said Ronnie, and you've got to follow a lot of codes. It took them quite a while to do it, but in the long run, it was a lot of money.

Did you win any money? I asked.

Naw, he said, I lost about $200. But that's all right. It was fun. Hell, if I had a million dollars I'm not sure what I'd do with it. Money isn't going to make me any happier. I'd just blow it on gambling, or buying a bunch expensive toys I don't really need, silly sports cars or a ruby-encrusted cell phone. I'm fine with my job. I like my job.

I disagreed about the money not making you happy thing, but I didn't want to run contrary to his views, which were far nobler than mine. I believe money does make you happier. It would make me happier. Ronnie and I could afford a larger, soundproofed apartment. Just give me a space where I can work without the world intruding on me in the form of noise and I'm an extremely happy person. Wealth isn't just about objects. It has to do with options. Quality of life. You have choices. Alternatives. Don't like your neighbors? Want someplace quiet but within the city with all its amenities? You can move. You can afford soundproofing.

They also say health is wealth. I won't argue with that. But wealth also buys health these days. You can afford medication. You can afford to see a doctor. You can afford health insurance. A short stay in the hospital won't leave you bankrupt or with a crushing debt.

A robotic female voice gave the man directions from a radio speaker. It was my first time hearing a GPS at work. I told the man as much, who was surprised, and I explained that I was from another century. Which is true. Except for my fluky relationship with Ronnie's old Blackberry, I don't carry a cell phone. I don't understand them, and I don't really like them. I concede that they have their place and they can be very useful in tight spots like the one we were in, and may have saved some lives considering how a car might break down in subzero weather miles away from the nearest town, but the way people seemed obsessed about them and constantly fussed with them was disturbing and evil, the death of solitude. No one spends time in their own head anymore.

Rumination is extinct. Rumination is the woolly mammoth of the new millennium. Those times when people were phoneless and walked the streets alert to their surroundings and might be available for conversation or the humble acknowledgement of another human being and were free to muse and daydream as they ambled past shop windows or waited for a bus or taxi or friend to pick them up were gone. I missed that world. I missed that world of people who still had curiosity and passion and spoke with confidence and clarity. Who were familiar with Poe. Who pondered the hairs and aggregated drupelets of a blackberry. A *real* blackberry. Not the kind you Twitter, the kind you put in your mouth and savor.

A young friend tells me there is a term for this phenomenon of people glued to electronic screens: *screensuck*. I like that word. I could see the person disappear from the dramas and birds of the real world and, hunched over in a private impenetrable trance, focus all their attention on a tiny world of hastily written text messages and cute little cat tricks on You-Tube. I was out running once and as I ran between two sixteen-year-old boys hunchbacked over their smartphones, each in a trance, stepping forward without bothering to look where they were going, both jerked upright stunned with surprise as I, a sixty-five-year-old man, whizzed past.

The tow truck driver arrived at our block. It remained to determine whether he would be able to get his leviathan truck up the narrow easement leading to our parking spot. I got out of the cab and ran up the easement and shouted directions while the driver maneuvered his truck around and up the easement. He did it. He was a skillful driver. He lowered his flatbed and rolled the Subaru onto the asphalt. I got in and rolled the carcass of our old Justy into our allotted spot. And that was that.

I tipped the driver a twenty, and we went into our apartment, without a functioning car for the first time in twenty years.

THERE WILL
BE MOISTURE

Ronnie and I hit our first big snag in our moving plans a day or two after Valentine's Day.

The Godzilla that stomped on our dreams was not a giant rogue reptile, however, but a little thing called moisture.

Our apartment, which was partly below ground, tended to be damp.

I hired a home inspector to come out and go through our place and let us know what we would have to disclose to keep ourselves out of any legal problems.

He was a middle-aged man with the rather perfunctory demeanor of a state patrolman pulling you over for a speeding citation (in our case, ostensibly, a speeding apartment), and a handheld thermal leak detector. He put his palm on the wall then held his leak detector to it and showed me the image of his hand in the little screen: it was phantasmal and red.

He went into our bedroom to examine a tiny protrusion surrounded by a small patch of mold that Ben had noticed on his tour. His thermal leak detector detected a leak. He showed it to me. There was large thick band of blue at the top of the screen that faded into a deep red at the bottom. It looked like an abstract painting by Richard Diebenkorn, irregular fields of red and blue which might be titled "Imminent Disaster" or "Don't Let These Pretty Abstractions Fool You, There Is Havoc and Destruction Lurking Behind This Wall."

You have a leak here, he said.

A leak? We've never seen any water trickle down there. I think it's just the dirt on the other side of the wall soaked in water.

Trust me, he said, there is something going here. Water must be collecting at this spot and is soaking the wall. Eventually, it will begin to seep through.

We went outside. I pointed out the area where our bedroom and leak would be. It was under a boardwalk and three big pots of plants. He suggested removing the plants, as they attracted moisture. He also suggested getting a contractor to remove a section of boardwalk, dig out the dirt by the wall, and see what was going on. If there wasn't an obvious leak, he recommended cleaning the area with muriatic acid and applying sealant.

We went back to our apartment. He recommended a GFI (Ground Fault Interruptor) for the outlet next to the kitchen, which the computer was plugged into, cleaning out the ventilation fan over the bathtub (he turned the fan on and held a small square tissue to the overhead grill which demonstrated a lack of suction when the paper floated down), getting a new kitchen faucet and hood range and caulking the kitchen sink, and cleaning the mold from the aluminum window frames and getting the apartment freshly painted. He charged $175 for this service. I wrote a check, we shook hands, and he left. I pondered the list of recommendations as if it were a ticket citing gross negligence, reckless insouciance, and aiding and abetting an area of insubordinate moisture.

Ben kept remarking on the smell of must in the entry hallway. He strongly recommended that we get the Home Owners Association to do something about it. This would not be easy. Cal and Pamela's repairs to the third floor had depleted the HOA budget, albeit it could be argued that their exertions improved the value of the overall building. Nevertheless, the others would be reluctant to spend more money, especially on something as ephemeral and insignificant as the smell of must. But if we didn't, Ben insisted, it would deter potential buyers. This thought was reaffirmed by two contractors.

By now, I had begun feeling overwhelmed. These tasks could be done, but it would mean weeks of interruption. Waiting for contractors to arrive. Then sitting around trying to make conversation, the way one does when catching a taxi. You feel the obligation to speak, to have an exchange, to fill the void with humanity, and combat the depersonalization that seeps into the crevices of the social construct when money and service is involved.

I became quite animated and annoyed with the moisture problem. We're selling our apartment, not the fucking hallway, I said.

I emailed the situation in the hallway to several HOA members. They wrote back expressing reluctance to spend more money. I could understand this, but it was frustrating, and felt unfair.

Cindy, meanwhile, scheduled a condo meeting for March.

One of the contractors had suggested leaving our windows open a crack to relieve the moisture. Ronnie immediately put this suggestion into action, cracking each of our windows open a sliver of space. The bedroom went from a nicy cozy warm place to repose and read a book into becoming a refrigerator where street sounds came in raw and uncensored by the mitigating graces of glass. I wasn't entirely happy with this, and shut the windows tight when I wanted to read and opened them again to avoid the moisture problem. The sad slow trickle of water pooling onto the sills and runnels creating narratives of rot and ruin.

Water (which I happen to like very much) is a central fact of existence in the Pacific Northwest. Everyone knows this. Everyone concedes to this phenomenon — the terminally gray, Cimmerian gloom, the ubiquitous damp that penetrates right down to the marrow of your bones where it clings like Antarctic fungi, days of endless rain that culminate in sometimes lethal mudslides — and some succeed at making an agreeable adaptation. Some achieve a kind of peace with the rain and drizzle and manage, even, to derive a felicitous equanimity out of the ever-present gloom. Others do not. They try. And try. But then their artificially contrived acceptance collapses into unabashed hatred. When this happens, they do the sane thing, and move. But if funds are lacking, and they (like me) are marooned here, they must live out their days with an acute sense of resignation. For the rain it raineth every day.

And yes, let me repeat that parenthetical remark, I am one of the marooned. I moved to Seattle thirty-nine years ago to find better and cheaper digs and amend the trajectory of my life, find a good job, buy books, read books, write books, browse books, comb books, smell books, breed books, bleed books, heed books, heave books, suffuse diffuse and inhabit books. On a trip to Seattle that same year to visit my father the old man took me to the Elliott Bay Bookstore in Seattle's historic Pioneer Square district and it was love at first sight. I loved the look and smell of the place, the creaking wood floor, the old red bricks, the thousands of books peopling the abundant, enticing shelves. Seattle offered what San José was fast ceding to high tech. By 1975, San José and environs had already begun to morph into the sterile dystopia that is today's Silicon Valley. I remember spending an afternoon with some friends drinking wine and walking home past a cannery that produced a powerful fragrance of processed pears and peaches. That had all irrevocably disappeared and had been replaced with futuristic buildings that looked like props from Woody Allen's sci-fi comedy *Sleeper*. The move was initially a big success. I found a large studio in Seattle's trendy Bohemian Capitol Hill with a fireplace for $125 a month. I found a sixteen-hour-a-week job at University Hospital folding hospital gowns and linens and still managed to pay rent, buy food and have a few bucks left over for movies and books.

But then Bill Gates happened. The same thing that devastated San Francisco and the Bay Area devastated Seattle in the early 1990s. Microsoft's absurdly generous wages had a direct effect on Seattle real estate. It wasn't long before I found it necessary to work forty hours a week for a small one-bedroom apartment, and even then I truly wasn't making it. I was kiting checks and paying a lot of overdraft fees.

According to a recent Economic Policy Institute Family Budget Calculator study, a Seattle household with one adult and one child must take in at least $52,611 per year to live comfortably. I realize that "comfortable" can be very subjective, but this figure bears out what Ronnie and I were beginning to discover.

Ronnie bought her one-bedroom condo in the late 1980s, the final decade in which Seattle was affordable for people whose jobs did not fall within a professional category and commensurate wage. This included a lot of artists, writers, actors and other creative people who were forced to move from Seattle if they were still renting. Rents had gone through the roof.

In order for Ronnie and me to find the kind of townhouse or apartment that would more or less guarantee the kind of quiet we were hoping to find, we would need to win the state lottery. As it was, we were hoping to find digs that were notably improved but with a mortgage that wouldn't weigh heavily on us each night as we tried to sleep. We were, in essence, searching for a chimera.

Claws enter the sleeve of my right arm as I sit in front of the computer. It is Graham. When Graham gets on his hind legs and taps me on the arm with his outstretched paw, or uses a little more assertiveness and sinks his claws past the fabric of my cardigan and shirt to the skin of my arm, it means one of two things: he wants attention, or he wants to eat. In this instance, he wants to eat.

I get a can of cat food out of the fridge and dollop out some "turkey formula" cat food onto his plate, then rinse off the fork under the kitchen faucet, running a stream of warm water over the tines of the fork. The bits of food disappear and I wipe the fork off on a towel. I refresh his water, rinsing his bowl out and refilling it with cold water. I bump the bowl as I set it into the little tray that holds his bowls in place and a little water splashes out, forming beads on the carpet. I soak up the beads with a paper towel and think about water. How clear and pure it is, how it beads up and looks like jewels.

DANCE OF THE ACCIDENTALS

This whole business of moving and getting our apartment primped and proper for sale began to border on the metaphysical.

Age doesn't matter. As soon as we decide that it's high time we make a change in our lives, do things differently, stop procrastinating, alter our circumstances, get out of our rut, the first thing we encounter is that ugly, merciless, sandpapery thing called reality. Reality is always invoked when we dream of aspiring to new heights, get rich quick or (more likely) try to get someone else to do something. Fulfill an ambition, take on a new responsibility.

But what the hell is this thing called reality? Is it internal, external, a product of the mind, something totally separate from the mind, an objective medium standard for all people or a wobbly gestalt skewed variably according to our culture and disposition?

What is consciousness? What is essence? What is being? What is existence?

Reality consists of pins and walls. Heliotrope and hemoglobin. Consciousness is more congested. It drips morals and opera. Consciousness has wings. Reality has friends. People in important places. Who write history. Who make history. Who are history.

But is this reality, or a disguise?

True reality is a truly pure experience. Keats's strenuous tongue bursting joy's grape against the palate. But that's Keats, not me. I'm dodging my own proposition. Did I have a pure experience today? I had many. The first was the feeling of the floor beneath my feet when I got out of bed this morning. The second was noticing the feeling of the feeling of the floor beneath my feet when I got out of bed this morning. The third was giving the feeling of the feeling an analysis and a history and sublimating it into a cumulonimbus in the cloud chamber that is my mind.

Pure experience is what we experience before the experience is clouded with judgment and words. Before we make a history of it. Before we paint it, describe it, sculpt it, post it on Facebook or incise it in copper. Before we sprinkle it with notes and blow it out of a horn.

History is to reality what rhythm is to melody: a C major in flames, the inconvenience of different pitches for organs, a polyphonic composition stuffed with accidentals. Jack LaLanne pulling a tug. Tommy James singing "Mony Mony" for Hubert Humphrey.

When consciousness meets reality the result is milk. Traffic lights blossom into prayer wheels. Laundry folds itself into armies of tide pool angst and marches around like generalities of floral chambray. Rain falls up instead of down. The acceptance of frogs liberates bubbles of pulp. Time sags with basement ping pong tournaments. Garrets ovulate glass bagatelles. Realism percolates prizefight sweat. Details sparkle like crawling kingsnakes in the mouth of a Mississippi attorney.

Reflection reveals that the most direct, primordial facts are in fact the phenomena of consciousness, not utility belts.

It is not that consciousness is inside the body, but that the body is inside consciousness. In other words, consciousness is a cocoon in which scintillas of meaning evolve into anatomies of potential flight. The end result is a recruitment of facts, paint and carpet samples. Martian butterflies invade the capital of a clank. Hats turn to airplane crashes for inspiration. Their brims flap. Their crowns flop. Their bands burst.

Thus the reality and enduringness of hats is assured not only by the transformation of profane space into a transcendent space but the transformation of retail into geese. Every construction is an absolute beginning — that is, tends to restore the initial instant, the plentitude of a present that contains no trace of history, or haunted house. The push must entail a pull. Pullulations of words float empires. Meanings get entangled in description. In the obscurities of form, infinity gives birth to a railroad, and time is nailed to space.

The relation between the phenomena of consciousness and the stimulation of the brain is identical to the relation between what one senses in the ear as a glockenspiel and what one senses in the eye or hand as elephants on the rampage, circumcision or initiation.

Incense suggests something entirely different. Incense insists on texture, the theater of experience, which employs dialogue and glucose. There is no circumcision. There is only shouting and dermatology.

A cat enters the room seeking affection and repose. The law of causality is thus a habit of thinking that derives from velvet. With reflection, we see that the materialists put the cat before the repose, and so lose an important distinction between real estate and the astronauts lost in the catacombs of a harmonica.

Esse est percipi: to be is to be perceived. But what about dark matter? Dark matter is perceived through its gravitational pull on the more familiar normal matter of stars and treasury bonds, while dark energy is perceived as poetry, a raging monsoon of pajamas and hogs.

Why does consciousness imagine the existence of such a thing as flavor? Because The Blob had none. It ate everything. And was a B movie of moderate success. And starred Steve

McQueen. Who would go on to play Doctor Thomas Stock-mann in Henrik Ibsen's *An Enemy of the People*.

Flavor is an invention of the nose, which detects goose-berry pie, and tingles with toast, which is salutation, and dusky with butter.

The black sticks of writing, which we call letters, create Calibans, crustaceans and free will. Deep reflection inevitably brings us to Boise, Idaho, where giant potatoes tempt us into restaurants, and eggplants exceed their dimensions in arbitrary vectors of regret and exile.

The gist of my argument is that true reality is a table. It is not separate from the mind, it supports the mind, stands on four legs, and can be extended with leaves, or the frolic of whales.

THINGS AS THEY
REALLY ARE

I slide my CD toward Eric Burdon who sits, smiling and gracious and fatigued from Seattle traffic, at the table at Silver Platters, where I have just purchased *'Til Your River Runs Dry* and stood in a line of old gray heads to have him sign it. I remove my hat and ask him to sign it, "To Ronnie and John." Don? He asks. No, John, I say. I point to Ronnie and say this is John and I'm Ronnie. He laughs. I see a black elastic bandage on his wrist and worry that he suffers pain there, some form of carpal tunnel syndrome. I remark on it, but he doesn't appear to understand my concern. I realize later it's a protective sleeve that all guitarists probably wear. Oh well, I think, he probably didn't know what I was talking about anyway.

He finishes signing the CD and I go around to the other side of the table so a fellow with a camera can take our picture. I smile, feeling ridiculous. I am sixty-five. Eric Burdon is seventy-one. I still harbor strong memories of getting drunk at age fifteen listening to "House of the Rising Sun" over and over again. I never tire of that song. Never. The picture is taken and Eric invites Ronnie to come around for a picture. Another picture is taken and I feel buoyed by Eric's evident amiability and graciousness.

We exit the store and head to Crow, one of our favorite restaurants. Crow serves the best lasagna I've ever had, the best arugula salad I've ever had, and the best pumpkin soup I've ever had. It's a bit pricey, but worth it.

We go in. It's dark. People are seated at booths and tables, candles flickering, conversations in progress. The hostess comes to her lectern and I tell her we were just passing by. She looks at the reservation list on the lectern and tells us we can sit at the bar overlooking the cooks at work in the kitchen, but there are no tables available. The place is crowded. I look at Ronnie and ask how she feels about that proposition. She asks me how I feel. She always does that. It drives me crazy. She will never tell me what she wants. It is always deferred to what I want. I decide no. We sat at the bar once before when we couldn't get a table and it wasn't comfortable. I couldn't lean back in the chair because it wasn't a chair, it was a high stool, and it felt awkward to watch people at work. I thank the hostess and say, we'll catch you another time, and we leave.

Ronnie made fettuccine Alfredo with sausage and we watched *Up in the Air*, with George Clooney, Vera Farmiga and Anna Kendrick. It's one of my favorite movies. I love the speech about the backpack. We both love the speech about the backpack. Especially now. Especially after all this fuss over a mortgage and trying to figure out what we can afford. Imagine, says Ryan Bingham, that you're carrying a backpack. I want you to feel the straps on your shoulders. He invites the audience to pack it with all the stuff they have in their life. That anyone has in their life. Little things, he says, the stuff in drawers and on shelves. The collectables and knick-knacks. Feel the weight as it adds up. Now, start adding the larger stuff. Your clothes, table-top appliances, lamps, linen, your TV. Go bigger. Your couch, your bed, your kitchen table, your car. Get it in there. Whether you have a studio apartment or a two-story house, stuff it into that backpack.

Now try to walk, he says. And waits for this image to pen-etrate.

Kind of hard, isn't it? This is what we do to ourselves on a daily basis. We weigh ourselves down until we can't even move. And make no mistake, moving is living.

He invites his audience to imagine a backpack with every-thing in it gone.

It's kind of exhilarating, isn't it?

The movie turns an ironic corner when Ryan Bingham gets involved with his sister's wedding in upstate Wisconsin. This is where Bingham's former message gets messy. This is where the movie tells us we need these things in our proverbial backpacks because life is ultimately about sharing.

But I liked that first message, about the empty backpack.

There was a time in my life when I lived that way. I shared a bunk for a while on a Blue Bird school bus a pot dealer had driven to Peru and back and installed with four bunks and rented them out at $10 a bunk. He let us use his bathroom and kitchen facilities. My bunkmates liked smoking dope and so spent nearly all their time in the house. I did not like smoking pot, I preferred reading books, and so I spent most of my time alone in the bus. Until one crisp October morning the four of us arrived at the front door, towels and toothbrushes in hand, to find the door locked and a note attached: we all had to be out by the end of the day. We had no idea what had brought this on. Had one of the others made a pass at his wife? Stolen some of his dope? There was no reason given.

Then there was the month my first ex-wife and I spent hitchhiking in Europe. We started out in London and made our way south, to France. We spent a month living in tents, sleeping bags, hotel rooms and once, in Perpignan, a taxi driver spot-ted us late at night walking in from the train and kindly drove us to his brother's house, who gave us a bed. He asked for a little money the next day, which wasn't much. I was frequently amazed at the kindness of the French.

I had lived in many apartments over the years, rarely staying at one place longer than a year or two. The apartment on Queen

Anne was by far the longest I've lived in one place. I've lived with Ronnie in the same apartment for almost twenty years now. I know almost every crack in every street and sidewalk, eaten at all the restaurants, rescued stray dogs, given directions, made some friends, and watched houses come down and new, bigger ones go up. McMansions, they call them. The trend on Queen Anne has been a Brobdingnagian splendor of unchecked wealth.

Which is strange. Ronnie and I feel like those little mammals skittering around the legs of dinosaurs. We don't really belong here. The hill is for the wealthy. Cal and Pamela are the tip of a new demographic. People who have never had to make a tough choice between medicine and food.

Don't get me wrong. I have nothing against wealth. I wouldn't mind being wealthy. *Pas du tout.* My dream home is a house in Nevada, fifty miles distant from the nearest town. I own a helicopter for doing our shopping in Reno. It's just Ronnie and me and the wind and the sage. The rest of humanity can go fuck itself.

I know. I'm an asshole. But I'm not. Not really. Not really an asshole. I'm conflicted. What was it Whitman said? "I am large, I contain multitudes."

This is why putting a life into a narrative with momentum and structure does something to betray the truth of it as it happens. As a person lives it. Things happen too quickly. The truly significant things are elusive. They don't always have momentum. Sometimes it's just a trick of light, peripheral sounds and odors. A distant siren. A certain feeling to the air late at night when all I can hear is the faint whirr of the computer, and Ronnie has left the kitchen window open a crack, so a bit of cold comes in and contrasts nicely against the heat from the electric baseboards.

The kind of narratives that feed into a life like the thousands of tributaries that feed into a river never occur with any kind of symmetry or regularity but swell and diminish and tumble and spray, sometimes collecting in deep green pools of inner reflection and sometimes crashing over rocks and canyon walls in a brilliant menacing foam of spectacular turbulence.

But how do you combine the past, present and future in a continuum that best represents the actuality of a life that is being lived? Change tense. Flow freely. Improvise. Because every moment is created. Every perception is created. Every memory and sense and mood and mania is created, brought into being by a dynamic of interrelation. The only thing that separates our interior lives from the external world is skin, and skin is an organ, a living membrane, not a wall but a porous, actively engaged medium, saturated with nerves and cells and affiliation.

"Thinking is a wave on the surface of a great intuition," observed Kitaro Nishida.

I love that image, thought as an emerald wave, wild and salty out on the colossal Pacific, fathoms of unbelievable incomprehensible darkness below, strange delicate creatures bioluminescing over the rippled sand of the ocean's bottom where Neptune leans on his trident dreaming of his return to the sky one day.

Words are magnets. They draw everything to them. Histories, fables, thoughts, speculations, beliefs. Moonlight illumining a dream of water, jellyfish flowing into themselves, the roar of a chainsaw severing the ears from their slumber, summer awakening the colors of L'Estaque. The eyes climb into the words of a seminal rumination and so escape the impenetrability of mass. The fork is a dollar of air. The biology of the comma anticipates the hem of a pronoun. A cardboard vagina insinuates feathers. How can impressions that are not needed by the intellect be jettisoned from all relation to the rest of consciousness? Adjectives float in a pool of English, the heat of another moment shines in a shovel full of coal, the consonants whispering mutability is a virtue, pay heed to your pain. The wind demonstrates its meaning in the trees.

Baudelaire sits down to breakfast. Constancy fulfills the morning light. Elegance is a muscle in the sorcery of being.

I venerate the sticks of a calamitous gyration. The angels of contrast ride the dragons of art. I have constructed this emotion with tinfoil and stilts. A contagion of nerves escorts the cauldron of an ancient heat to a bank of sea wrack where the sand defers to the surf.

The constellation of little white dots on my jeans is where the cat's claws have penetrated. Perception has this ability to circumvent the coffee table and blur distinctions between inside and outside. Experiences create me. I am soaked in ambiguity.

"It is true that storytelling reveals meaning without committing the error of defining it," observed Hannah Arendt. Instead, it brings about consent and reconciliation with things as they really are.

Things as they really are is this: we all die. No one gets out alive. That much we know for sure. Some age into common maladies, treatable maladies, usually back problems, pain hard to manage, and their twilight years are spent moderating pain and watching TV reruns and visiting grandchildren until a final week in an adjustable hospital bed surrounded by family and hospice workers giving you liquid morphine drops until the lights go out.

There are those who die suddenly of a heart attack. Car wreck, bullet, bomb, avalanche, fire, shipwreck, slip on a puddle of grease.

There are those lucky few who age into wrinkles and wisdom and stay busy in the garden or attending the occasional conference and go quietly into the night, slide away into sweet oblivion, fade into nonexistence as gently and sweetly as a sugar cube in cup of hot chamomile tea.

Not entirely gone though. No one is entirely gone. Not disappeared totally. Not as long as friends and loved ones survive, not as long as things you once treasured still live, still produce actualities of sensation and movement and shape. Then your life continues, continues outside of your body, like this, like these words, sounds with meaningful shapes, resonances, ramifications.

Snow falls gently through the night. Individuality sparkles like Christmas. Mahogany speaks to the endurance of form. This is why I stopped worrying about my hair. What's hair? Hair is a group of syllables impersonating a paradox. The restless fathoms demand gold and submersion. Hair does no good there. My eyebrows have become scrapyards. It is in ramification that affinities embark on a voyage of unknown destination. Ramifications that make the jigsaw jig. Ramifications that shine like money in a dish of candy. Ramifications that predispose the symmetries of summer to excess. Once I was fat but now I'm bizarre.

My thoughts are extended by crickets. Detours are marvelous. Detours are where the dead linger and flag us down. Give us directions. Urge us to continue until the horizon bristles with sunset. Even the river hints at something larger than itself.

Ramifications that remedy the relics of a failed rationalization. Ramifications that ransom the random and randomize the rainbow.

I ache to believe such things. And then listen to Bach and discover that money is immaterial. And that I am a spell. And that the orchid has a frivolous solemnity. That the knees are angels and the nose is a star. That I jingle when I walk gaping at the antics of summer.

It is in ramifications, these endless associations that move through the mind like rivers, like those luminous colors we find in clouds during winter, the coldness of the air making colors more vivid, that's where death meets life, life meets death, in a crepuscular cabbage of folds and convolutions, a gulp, the eyes bursting open, parameters broken down, that we find our souls, our true selves, that thrilling sense of being alive and not just brushing our hair in the morning as usual, but jumping a fence. Redeeming our bones in a life above hills and dirt.

A Rubble of Words

On a Saturday morning in late February I wake up listening to *Eat the Airwaves!*, a weekly news program devoted to covering items that haven't been covered properly, if at all, with Geov Parrish, Maria Tomchick and Mike McCormick. They segue from their winter fund drive into a discussion of the surveillance cameras the Seattle Police Department put up on the Seattle waterfront, Alki, the Fremont and Ballard bridges and the Ballard Locks, and a wireless mesh broadband network created by 160 wireless access points, without informing anyone of their decision to do this, or formulating any policy about how the cameras will be programmed to respect the privacy of residents, whether the cameras will rotate or remain in a fixed position, who will operate them, whether they will include sound, what kind of data they'll be collecting and what happens to the data long term. This, like the drone program the SPD tried to launch without public discussion, got a lot of public outcry. SPD backed off and promised not to activate the surveillance system until City Councilmember Nick Licata drafted some legislation governing the acquisition and use of surveillance technology.

I pour some coffee and sit down at the computer. Graham leaps up on my lap so that I can't reach the keyboard. I can click the mouse so I go to France Culture, an online French radio channel, and listen to a discussion of *La coeur de la jeune Chinoise*, by Eric Marty, on *Le carnet d'or*. This is a novel written in the style of a thriller, full of death and desire and a cruel satire of contemporary French culture, a corrosive humor and flair for violence akin to Quentin Tarantino.

I give the window a hard shove with my hand (there is a dog squealing in Bhy Kracke Park) and condensation rains on my hand.

I sit down again at the computer and listen to Carole Bassani-Adibzadeh read *Traité de la réforme de l'entendement et de la voie qui mène à la vraie connaissance des choses*, by Baruch Spinoza, and translated *par* E. Saisset. Translated from what, I don't know. What language did Spinoza originally write in?

Spinoza writes about the good that people desire. He begins by saying that the events of his life have shown him that the ordinary attractions of life are vain and futile and that no objects or events are good or evil in and of themselves, but that their character comes from the way in which they've touched our soul. He decides to devote himself to the quest for an essential good which might be communicated to people, a good which can fill the human soul so thoroughly that after that frivolous and vain and superficial things will hold no attraction and the soul will be satisfied with that one good thing alone, that eternal and supreme sense of well-being, which he is sure exists, but is as yet undetermined.

He goes on to describe the three main attractions to people, the three main things that cause people to slip up and make life worse for themselves. These are wealth, reputation and what the French call *la volupté*, which is pleasure in all its forms, sexual, intellectual or purely sensual.

Spinoza asks himself if it is possible to attain this higher level of well-being without giving up the things he likes, without altering his habits. The answer is no. The quest for pleasure is the greatest obstacle, since after its realization, which is inherently fleeting, comes sadness, and a spiritual flaccidity. Reputation, by which I believe Spinoza means fame, is equally unsatisfying and toxic. The quest for fame coarsens the soul because in order to obtain fame one must do whatever is necessary to please other people, to seek what they seek and avoid what they avoid.

Spinoza sounds a lot like Buddha. What he urges is a form of Buddhism. Attachment to worldly things brings sadness and coarsens the soul. Detachment brings us closer to the infinite, to eternal well-being.

I go write. I hear the upstairs neighbors making breakfast. Their kitchen is directly above our bedroom, where the desk I use for writing is positioned against the wall, facing west and facing a window well. I put in ear plugs and remind myself to tell Ronnie that we need ear plugs and *Hamlet*. I want the *Hamlet* with Sir Laurence Olivier. It's the only one I really like.

I'm disturbed by the sound of a power saw. I look up, out of our basement window, and see a large, heavyset man with a chestnut mustache sawing a section of hardwood. I get pissed and go put on my shoes to complain. There's no reason for these men to be working outside on the porch, inches from our window. Why aren't they doing their sawing on the worksite, inside Cal and Pamela's apartment? I try to calm the fury within with arguments of latitude and prudence. I don't want to say something I will later regret. But I have no more patience. The patience tank is empty. Dry as a bone. I'm ready to go do some serious bitching. As soon as I get my shoes on, the noise stops. I figure maybe the guy was only sawing a bit of molding, and go back to my writing.

I go for a run. I take the recycling and garbage out with me and the drywall guy sees me and apologizes about the day before. He turned the water to the building off when I was taking a shower. I could hear him in the laundry room, on the other side of our bathroom. I was so full of rage, this being the fifth time in the last several months our water has been turned off, that I almost stomp into the laundry room nude to give him a piece of my mind. Instead, I poke my head around the door and shout, what the fuck! The drywall guy appears and apologizes. And now, today, he is apologizing a second time. I tell him I survived. It's ok. I hope he didn't have his three-year-old daughter with him when I put my head out the door yelling at him. It seems odd that he would bring a toddler to a worksite with him. I figure he's divorced and this is the only time he gets to see his kid, or maybe his wife has a job at Walmart or something.

Litter. I spot a scrap of paper in the parking lot and pick it up and examine it out of idle curiosity (it's a receipt for coat hangers and a box of candy from Bartell Drugs), and toss it into the emptied sack, which I hang on the doorknob to our apartment. I'll bring it in on the way back. Ronnie doesn't like me wearing shoes on the carpet.

My legs are still going strong into my third mile, on Tenth Avenue West. The man I frequently see out riding his bike turns round to say hello. This guy waves at me every day and I wave back and I don't have the faintest idea who he is. He appears to be about sixty. It's hard to tell because he wears a helmet. He's fit, I know that.

After I shower and dress I hear the guy outside with his power saw again. I try to contain my rage. I phone Ronnie at the grocery store and ask if she wants to take the bus down to the central library with me. She isn't sure. She was thinking of going for a run. But she calls back minutes later and says yes. I tell her to meet me at Caffé Vita, at the bottom of our hill.

Caffé Vita is crowded, as always. It's a tiny coffeehouse and always packed. I order a raspberry Italian soda with whipped cream on top. The woman behind the counter prepares it for me and I ask for a spoon. She gives me a spoon, I drop a dollar in the tip jar, and sit at a table by the window. There is music playing. I like the music, though it's hard to identify what's going on with it, over the hubbub of the coffeehouse. A soft woman's voice sings over a background of other women's voices, all in high melody, all echoing over a flute and drum. It's joyful and otherworldly and helps calm me down. I sip my raspberry Italian soda and imagine all the ways I could disembowel, decapitate or dismember Cal.

I pull out a copy of *Le parti pris des choses* that I stuck in my coat pocket on the way out. I read a piece called "*Natare Piscem Doces*," in which Ponge wonders if the author can remain at the interior of writing and deduce the reality of a reality. He compares it to being in a cave, as opposed to liberating the sculpture within a block of marble. But then he asks, is the book the chamber within a cave, or the rejected material from digging into a rock? Does writing penetrate reality, or does it create a rubble of words that are only peripherally related to the subject, automatically dissociated once they've been written down? Ronnie appears and we leave Caffé Vita to catch the bus for downtown.

We find two audiobooks at the library. One is a collection of short stories by Melville, Hawthorne, Chekhov, Cather, Joyce and de Maupassant. The other is *South with the Sun: Roald Amundsen, His Polar Explorations, and the Quest for Discovery*, by Lynne Cox.

We take the Number 4 bus home, eat dinner and watch Part 1 of *Lonesome Dove*. I finish out the evening immersed in *Tristes tropique*, by Claude Lévi-Strauss, in which he beautifully elaborates his preference for the mountains to the ocean, and I dream of Georgetown, in the Colorado Rockies, where I once heard a French woman sing "La vie en rose" in a cowboy saloon, hemmed by the mountains of Clear Creek Valley.

Adventures in Installation

A kitchen installation company sends out a guy as big as a truck to install our new stainless steel Kenmore dishwasher. He has a tattoo on his left forearm of what appears to be barbed wire or thorns and a man on a horse who might be Don Quixote. He is robust and hardworking and adamant. He is exactly the kind of guy you want your dishwasher installer to be. He puts down a sheet of plastic and goes to work undoing screws and plates and begins working the old machine out of its berth under the kitchen counter, a niche it has occupied for forty-nine years, since 1964, when our building was built. Johnson was president. "She Loves You" by The Beatles, "I Get Around" by the Beach Boys, "Don't Let the Sun Catch You Crying" by Gerry and the Pacemakers and "House of the Rising Sun" by The Animals were all hits. They were all on the radio, which was AM, stations everyone listened to, when they weren't listening to sports, society was so much simpler, everyone knew who Ed Sullivan was, everyone knew Mr. Magoo and *Hullabaloo*.

The installation man has the old dishwasher out and I ask if I can help him lift it out to the truck but no, he says, he's got it all under control. A few minutes later he returns with the new one. He immediately goes to work on removing four screws from the kickplate so he can get to the wiring on the other side. But one screw refuses to budge. He tries again. And again. It's a Phillips-head so he doesn't want to force it too much and destroy the little grooves. He goes to his truck for some Rust Off, which he says is WD-40 on steroids. It's a penetrating lubricant that works partly by spraying cold on the stubborn part and making the molecules contract. He sprays some on and waits and I ask what's in it and he hands me the can. I read the ingredients. I can't pronounce any of the chemicals, much less have an inkling as to what they are. Kentucky white lightning, ammonium nitrate, rattlesnake venom and methamphetamine, I joke.

We talk while waiting. I ask how long he's been doing dishwashers. Five years, he says. And before that? I asked. I was in the merchant marine. Really? I say. So you've seen the world, I bet. Not really, I worked a tramper that supplied small villages in the Aleutian chain. I'm in a book, he says, but I was a green-horn, and it's embarrassing to read all the blunders I made. What's the book? I ask. *Tramper*, by George Lowe, he says. I'll look for it. Which, later, I do. I find it on Amazon and Google Books, but no preview, alas.

He goes back to work on the little screw. He's as frustrated as we are. A whole brand new dishwashing machine held up by a stubborn little screw.

He calls some coworkers for advice. They suggest doing what he's already been doing.

He talks about the sense of entitlement a lot of his customers have, how they stomp the floor and shout and demand results even after he explains the impossibility of doing something due to mechanical, or sometimes legal, reasons. I can relate to what he is telling me. Ronnie gets customers like that where she works in the grocery store's bakery, and the chronicles in *Waiter Rant* by Steve Dublanica have plenty of stories of adults acting like six-year-olds when they can't get the table they want, or a certain item on the menu is no longer available. The United States is over and done with, that's for sure. It's become a nation of cry-babies and whiners except when it comes to killing people with drones or bombing Middle Eastern cities into the Stone Age. Nobody seemed to mind that. Draw attention to this barbarism, and people often respond with a barbaric reply: better to kill them over there than over here.

This is the pathology of empires as they begin to crumble.

Meanwhile, back at the kitchen, our man has decided to give up. He calls the unit in as defective. I ask him how we can go about setting up a new installation time if Sears has another model ready for pickup and he gets on his cell phone and navigates his way through a labyrinth of people, each time repeating the circumstance with the screw. He manages at last to get the right person to write the correct information down. He tells us they may be able to send someone out tomorrow. I thank him, and he packs up his things and leaves.

He meant well, but that doesn't happen. We wait a few more days. He returns on Wednesday of the following week with a "new" new dishwasher. He gives me a call first, minutes after I get out of bed, at 9:00 A.M.

I overslept. I couldn't sleep the night before, and after listening to a reading of James Joyce's "The Dead" on audiobook, I got out of bed and went to the cupboard for some ibuprofen. I had a small headache, quite possibly from the lavender oil supplement I took earlier in the night. I'd begun tapering off the lorazepam and sought a more healthful substitute on the internet. An orally administered lavender oil called Silexan was recommended as an effective anxiolytic, and so Ronnie took the bus to Whole Foods where they sell such things — they actually have a section called Mood Enhancers — and also to get some Virgil's Root Beer and Earth Enzymes Drain Opener for the bathtub, which is clogged again. There's a QFC close to us, but they don't carry any of these items.

Ronnie was now in the habit of keeping our windows open a crack and I could hear the soft sound of rain through the kitchen window, which is one of the best sounds in the world. It's a celestial sound, exquisitely subdued, soothing and peaceful. As soon as I began running water into a glass the sound was broken by the footsteps of Rocco Radmacker coming home from his shift at Sea-Tac. Rocco was a nice enough guy, but clumsy. Whenever he was home it sounded like he and Terri were moving in all over again. Thuds, scrapes, groans, crashes and the *boom boom boom* of Rocco's heavy steps on a hardwood floor intruded on one's consciousness until he got his boots on and left the building. Terri, who started out being quiet for the first few weeks, worked part time at a downtown taphouse serving artisanal beer, but she quit her job and began throwing impromptu parties for a coterie of mothers and their babies and toddlers, and she began doing housework with the worried aggression of a homeworker commando in a dust bunny war. These blitzkriegs could occur at any time during the day — three in the afternoon or two in the morning. It sounded like she was sorting coat hangers one night at about 1 A.M. — metallic objects periodically hitting the hardwood floor to produce a crisp *clackety-clack*.

I lay down on the couch a while and read a few paragraphs of *Un amour de Swann* until I got drowsy and returned to bed. It sounded like Rocco was going to be up for several hours as usual, walking about the apartment to and from the kitchen to the TV in the living room so I stopped to put some ear plugs in. What's the matter? asked Ronnie, who must have just awakened. I'm putting some ear plugs in, I said. Rocco is thumping about upstairs as usual.

The lavender oil must have worked because I'm usually awake by 8:00 A.M. and lie in bed listening to NPR and wait till nine to enter the world. The phone rang and it was the dishwasher guy informing me he was on his way. I rushed to get my clothes on, pour some coffee and clear a path for the dishwasher guy. I noticed a mound of dust or dirt and a couple of small pieces of wood in a crevice where the old dishwasher had stood and decided to clean that out. The debris must have been sitting in there since 1964. I got a dust pan out of the storage closet in the entry hallway and went back to clean the debris out. I put the two pieces of wood, one of which still had nails in it, off to the side in an empty plastic bread bag. Then I grabbed the flashlight from the top of the refrigerator to get a look at what I was dealing with. I put my hand down on the floor and I felt a nail go into my palm. I looked at my palm and saw a little blood begin to appear and so went to wash it immediately. I feared another infection like the one I had during the summer from swimming in Lake Washington at a crowded beach, which put me in the hospital for twenty-four hours while they pumped me with every antibiotic known to humankind. I was told that pathogens had become much stronger because of global warming. The emergency room had seen a spike in infections.

After everything was ready I sat down to rest and sip some coffee. Then I got the vacuum cleaner out and did a little vacuuming and just as I was putting the vacuum cleaner away the dishwasher guy appeared with the new dishwasher. I hope we don't have to screw around again, I joked. He laughed.

I watched as the dishwasher installation man maneuvered the new dishwasher in and performed a number of tricky maneuvers, lying on his side, working his arm and hand into cramped little spaces to attach a hose or put in a screw. It looked unbelievably complicated to me. I told him we'd had a neighbor who thought he could install a dishwasher on his own, with no prior experience. He couldn't, of course, and had to get someone out to give him a hand. I couldn't believe this guy's hubris. It's like saying, geez, think I'll perform some heart surgery on myself today. The dishwasher guy laughed.

He finished and I signed some papers and he packed up and left. I tore off a sheet of paper towel, sprinkled a little dish soap on it, soaked it in water and rubbed the face of the dishwasher down. I tossed the paper towel into the wastebasket under the sink and watched as a tiny bubble floated toward me, caught a gleam of light, drifted to the floor and popped.

Graham had not yet reappeared, so I went looking for him. I peeked under the bed and saw his two black ears, returned to the kitchen, and started breakfast. Scrambled eggs, toast, and some grape juice. I got hooked on scrambled eggs from my stay in the hospital. They say hospital food is awful, but that particular morning it was pretty damned good. And now I've learned to make it even better. I use lots of butter. It's the butter that makes it better. Butter and salt and a sprinkling of pepper.

THE MEETING

The annual condo meeting was scheduled for a Monday in late February, at 7:00 P.M. Ronnie and I dread these meetings all year long. The only time we don't dread these meetings are the few minutes after the meeting, when we have an entire year ahead of us before the next meeting.

Why did we dread these meetings? Conflict. Lies. Shenanigans. Sly maneuvering. Subtle politics. Bankruptcy. Blows to our self-esteem. The carefully maintained illusion that we all liked one another. And which kept out of view a seething hive of angry little wasps.

Conflicts are bound to emerge in a situation where ownership of property is shared with a group of people. First begins a volley of emails: disagreements over asphalt or concrete for a parking lot, grate or fencing for a window well, whether to pay for a neighbor's awning based on an argument that it is destroying a nearby hedge, the percentage that a hardwood floor should be covered with carpeting in order to prevent noise, whether to incorporate our Home Owners Association so that it can take out loans or pay for projects out-of-pocket based on a percentage of ownership calculated by square footage, whether a neighbor's chimney or balcony should be covered by capital funds because (technically and technically only) it is part of the building, whether to permit a neighbor to build an addition to their unit or install a helicopter pad on the roof, what gardening service to hire, who is willing to meet with contractors, whether to permit dogs or cats or boa constrictors as pets in the building, whether to paint lines in the driveway or let it go another year, whether to power wash, when to power wash, how to power wash, why power wash, what are Aristotle's thoughts on power washing, etc., etc.

Feelings get bruised, egos injured, personalities exposed. Hostilities are muzzled. Emotions seethe. The illusion of neighborly affability feels tighter and tighter until it begins to choke.

Remarks sting, complaints spill, jokes to alleviate the heavy atmosphere fizzle or offend.

The spirit dies a slow death as minutes of unrelieved boredom asphyxiate the mind and crush the heart. In other words, it's just like having a job. Another job. A job on top of your job.

My chief bugaboo is, as always, the fearful announcement of future construction or maintenance projects, days in which I am driven from home and work, exiled to coffeehouses where high-tech geeks plunk away at laptops and twinkly twentysomethings jabber on smartphones, evenings spent trying to eat dinner under somebody's hammering and sawing, nights awakened by a contractor trying to finish a job at two in the morning.

Nor do we feel particularly well liked or respected at these meetings. That may be mutual, I don't know. Hard to discern anyone's true feelings amid such contrived politeness. This perceived hostility could be just that: imagined, not actual. Or maybe partially true, partially untrue. There is no truly identifiable reason that indicates visibly and unambiguously that we are unliked or disrespected. It is a feeling, and the both of us shared that feeling, that sense of unease, that sense of being unvalued undesirables.

Which, I repeat, could have been the product of our mutual insecurity.

Or not.

But where does the feeling come from, this dogged, persistent, souring insecurity?

Who knows?

Multiple sources. The source of our individuality and personal demons is as murky as the origins of the moon. What makes our emotional lives so complicated has to do with events that have long since been repressed, wounds that never fully healed, things that happened in childhood, high school, the soccer field, football collisions, teasing in the shower, the way one carries oneself, the manner one dresses, any personal effect whatsoever that differs from the norm and so makes us the target of mockery and rebuke. People can be heartless and mean. I had the good fortune to attain adulthood in the late 1960s when there was not only a tolerance but a ringing endorsement for eccentricity and free expression. It was sweet while it lasted. It all reversed in the mid-1970s. The search for transcendence, growth of the intellect, freedom from bondage to the material world and enchantment of hallucinogens transformed into disco, mirror balls and meteoric careers fueled by chicanery and cocaine.

Humans are hungry animals. Always seeking, never satisfied. And it certainly isn't just food that we're looking for. Love, fame, recognition, respect, power, sex, money, beauty, luxury, truth, immortality, freedom from pain, enlightenment, the beyond, the list is endless. Some get entangled in politics and crime, seeking worldly power and possessions and others lead bleak, Spartan lives in order to support an addiction to writing or art. You can't escape desire: even the desire to escape desire is a desire.

And all the while we are shaped by phenomena we do not see, or glimpse dimly.

"It is not that experience exists because there is an individual, but that an individual exists because there is experience," observed Japanese philosopher Kitaro Nishida.

Our thoughts and perceptions frequently get in the way of our contact with the external world, distorting and obstructing the purity of our experience. Social cues might well be misinterpreted, or exaggerated. When you lean toward the negative as I do the results (not surprisingly) are generally negative.

And I can't speak for Ronnie. She's very sweet and charitable and doesn't have my negativity. Her negativity is humble and apprehensive. My negativity is deep and huge and solid as interlocking polygons. This colors my interpretation of events with the dark tints of despondency. I should disqualify myself right now and begin quoting Ralph Waldo Emerson. This philippic is unbecoming. But the reason I lean toward the negative in the first place is due to a lifetime of betrayal and disappointment. Which means that my emotional algebra isn't entirely cockeyed but based in real polynomials with non-negative integer exponents.

I can cite a few things, insignificant but wounding little events such as not being thanked for helping out with a condo project and feeling taken for granted, or arriving home and seeing your neighbors hurry to get into their car so that they don't have to talk to you.

Or the unsettling fact that we had the smallest unit in the building and so our vote, calculated by the percentage of property one owned in the building, had the least weight and so put us at mercy of the other condo members. Things like whether to remove window security bars, what color to paint the building, what contractors to hire, what work truly needed to be done as opposed to vanity projects, what was considered a common area and what was private, what additions or repairs the condo would have to be paid for collectively and what fell within the purview of one's own finances, who was available to meet with contractors, whose responsibility was it to contact contractors, all these issues were voted upon, and since Cal and Pamela owned most of the property, they generally got their wishes.

I frequently objected to proposals on the basis that they were unnecessary or vain. This did not make me popular. I told Ronnie I continually felt like Doctor Thomas Stockmann in Ibsen's *An Enemy of the People*.

I know. This all sounds petty, not to mention a trifle melodramatic, now that I've dragged Ibsen into the picture. And it is. It is petty. It is a trifle melodramatic. In my own defense, I'm going to wade a little deeper into a nasty pool of cynical conjecture and see what I can fish out of it to make this splenetic exhibition a little less paltry.

I do have one theory in support of my malaise that has sociological underpinnings. The meetings are a compression of that one central immovable fact rampant in American culture: you are evaluated according to the amount of money you have. The amount of property you own, the model of car you drive, the number of bathrooms in your house. It doesn't matter how stunning your insights are, how extensive your knowledge, how beautifully you construct a sentence, how disciplined you are in the arts, how self-sacrificing and Spartan you have deliberately chosen to live your life in order to achieve certain artistic or intellectual goals, unless you command a robust sum of money you are not thought of very highly. If your income is modest, it must be because you have somehow failed. You must have a defect. You're perceived as a feckless bohemian or malcontent whose bitterness, antisocial behavior and pessimism have crippled and prevented you from achieving the American dream. Which is, simply, to own a lot of shit.

In our condo association, this egregiously misguided and mean assumption takes a very concrete form: the amount of square footage you own in the building. With volume comes power. Why bother to attend at all, we always ask ourselves. Not only does our vote count for the least, but I had quickly developed a reputation for being the building grouch, a curmudgeon whose observations are tainted by a splendidly perverse and splenetic disposition. This tendency (which I do not entirely disclaim) is counterpoised by a stifling predisposition that runs through these meetings: the meme of agreeableness. Agreeableness is somehow tacitly acknowledged as a sign of wisdom, of maturity, as the premium value to uphold at these meetings. Grouching is infantile. Grouching is obstructive and contrary to the social equilibrium of the building. And maybe it is. Of course it is. But I'm a touchy guy and if things get under my skin, I'm not modest about holding back and letting people know. It's one of the reasons I chose writing for a profession;

when you write, you've got lots of time to frame your complaints in seething, glittery prose.

I hold back at the meetings. I try to be civil. Mostly, I'm just bored out of my skull. But there are undercurrents of feeling that make it harder than it needs to be. It could be these undercurrents are completely imagined, that the perceived slights and subtle affronts that we sense are utter distortions, born of deep-seated insecurities, but the truth is that Ronnie and I have never felt accepted by the people in our building. We feel a diminishment of self-esteem. We are the ones with the smallest unit in the building, which Jay Bellamy jokingly and wrongly announced had once been a storage room, and that the previous tenant, an elderly Welsh lady who enjoyed doing needlework on her pillows while watching wrestling matches on TV, could hear the male tenant upstairs piss in the toilet. That part was true. One was never far from the melodies of micturition.

Whether Jay had intended his remark maliciously or if it were, as I more suspected, simply a product of gross insensitivity, I'm not entirely sure, but it did serve as a more outward sign of the perceived disregard the other tenants had for Ronnie and me. One can never gauge authenticity of feeling in a social environment so manifestly — and necessarily — counterfeit.

"Politeness is organized indifference," observed Paul Valéry.

The meetings are business-oriented and horrendously dull. It is all about figures, numbers, expenses, accounting details. The meetings are sanitized of any real human emotion.

I do not do well in such staid circumstances. I lose my sense of balance. I teeter. I brood. I ruminate. Which I do most of the time anyway; it's just that, at these meetings, I am on a tightrope. I tread very carefully. If there's one thing I'm good at in life, it's generating and juggling a brood of insecurities.

There was a time I could effectively handle awkward social environments with bourbon or beer, but those days are past. My only resort now is lorazepam.

What is it that I'm afraid of? I can't say. That's the difference between fear and anxiety. With fear, you know what you're frightened of: a hungry bear, an angry bull, a Spartan warrior coming at you with a sword. With anxiety, the fear is nebulous, theoretical, ontological.

The meetings are unsettling because they deter any outlet for getting an emotional bead on the immediate environment. It's like walking in a field planted with landmines. The threats are all hidden, invisible and quite possibly entirely imagined. Not real at all. No landmines, just gophers and worms.

But how do you know what people think of you, and why does that even matter? It's a puzzler. I always try to imagine the stoical face of Clint Eastwood in those early Spaghetti Westerns, the ones where his face looks like chiseled mahogany. Nothing in his eyes but mystery.

There is an unspoken, unofficial but very real taboo against showing too much authentic emotion. This was partly a matter of civility; things could get out of hand very easily, and two people would be at one another's throats trying to strangle each other. You can't live in this kind of proximity to people without going slightly insane.

Casual banter and banality are encouraged. Authentic feelings are nitroglycerin. What is desirable is a breezy cordiality.

Underneath my skin darker emotions simmer and boil. The mask I present to the others is one of decorous affability. It is the same mask the others wear. Who cannot get by with a mask in modern society?

Perhaps I speak for myself. Perhaps it is me alone who struggles with these conflicts and keeps everything hidden. Maybe what I mistook for breezy cordiality was, in fact, breezy cordiality. It could be that the constraints I imposed on myself à la Lon Chaney, Jr., in *The Wolf Man* were necessary for personal conflicts, frictions I alone harbored.

"Everything that is profound loves the mask," observed Friedrich Nietzsche.

I remember the masks I wore as a kid during Halloween, the smell of the rubber and the little slits for eyes. I could barely see where I was going and never got a good look at the candy I was collecting, which was considerable back in the 1950s when kids covered a lot more terrain going door to door and it was a much safer world. The joy of occupying another identity, particularly a monster such as Frankenstein or Dracula was wonderful and I can see what drives actors to continually seek roles. The kind of disguises I now wore as an adult were not the monstrosities of classic horror movies but the cool, calm demeanor of civil affability, the veneer of a liberal, democratic spirit.

Disguise is a form of hypocrisy, of hiding one's true thoughts and feelings. It is also indispensable.

Disguise is a form of fiction. It feels dishonest, and it is dishonest, but the fiction is maintained partly as a mode of self-enhancement or self-protection, but also to make others feel they are more liked or appreciated than is the actual case. And in many instances, one does not completely understand one's own emotions, or perceptions. A dislike can easily become an affection, an assumption can be proved wrong, a rivalry, a revelry.

"In deceiving others we deceive ourselves," says Martin Heidegger. "This concealment is dissembling. If one being did not simulate another, we could not make mistakes or act mistakenly in regard to beings; we could not go astray and transgress, and especially could never overreach ourselves. That a being should be able to deceive as semblance is the condition for our being able to be deceived, not conversely."

I like these words of Heidegger's. I especially like the part about overreaching ourselves, and the paradox of finding revelation in concealment, the capacity for error, for wandering, for erring, and the need for making mistakes in order to arrive, eventually, in a fuller reality than the one we formerly inhabited. No wonder actors have such a passion for acting, for losing themselves in other identities. Not only is it liberating, it's a crucial antidote against the static, the stable, the inert.

The word *mask* derives from Medieval Latin *masca*, which variously meant "mask, specter, nightmare," and has powerful associations with both the repression of an instinctive self or soul and its opposite, a mode of release, a vehicle by which a repressed identity can feel at liberty to let loose, get down, get dirty, allow themselves the freedom to do things they're ordinarily prohibited from doing.

Adam and Eve used fig leaves to cover their nakedness after their fabled transgression of eating an apple from the Tree of Knowledge and falling from a state of innocence into a state of sin, but in the Greek Bacchanalia and the Dionysus cult, masks were used not to hide, but to allow release, free the psyche from the controls of society. The ordinary controls on behavior were temporarily suspended and people caroused and capered outside their ordinary rank or status.

The False Face Society of the Iroquois used masks in healing rituals, invoking the spirit of an old hunchbacked man named Ethiso:da', our grandfather, a great healer also known as Old Broken Nose who was not suitable for children's eyes and lived in underground caves and great wooded forests. He could only leave when called upon to cure or interact through dreams.

Ronnie and I went up the steps for the condo meeting at about 6:55 P.M. Clark opened the door for us. Clark is a young man in his early thirties, thin, edgy, alert, with brown hair and worried eyes. He was in the information technology industry and always appeared besieged. He had a warm side that counterbalanced his more guarded nature.

Guy brought his wife Rochelle, who we met for the first time. She was a woman in her mid- to late-thirties, zaftig and four months pregnant, pretty, well groomed, with diamond studs in her earlobes and a reserved, self-contained disposition.

I had known Guy a long time, but only very superficially. He was not much given to conversation, unless the topic was sports. He was devoted to the Lakers and the Jacksonville University Dolphins, but I wasn't into sports at all, which left us with very little to talk about. Guy owned the apartment across the hall from Ronnie and I, which he rented to his friend Sam.

Cal was the last to arrive. He brought wine and a relaxed, jovial disposition. He seemed to have an inexhaustible supply of charm, which I simultaneously enjoyed, distrusted and admired. Pamela had chosen, ostensibly, to stay home. I took this as a certain aristocratic disdain for these dull proceedings, and I respected it. They were astoundingly tedious, and since they focused chiefly on financial issues, I only understood half, if that, of what was being communicated. This left me feeling more of an outsider than I already felt, which was considerable, since I had easily cornered the market on Building Grouch, Building Weirdo, Bohemian Poet and Aboriginal Oddball. I attend these meetings to support Ronnie, who has similar feelings of alienation.

Lyle's gusto and wildman appearance was somewhat reassuring, but there was little that was truly rebellious in his nature. He wasn't a rebel at all. He liked to go to extremes, but these extremes were the extremes of wind and weather, not philosophy and art. He was fundamentally gregarious, not the least bit antisocial. He loved excitement but was not excitable. I envied his calm.

Cindy had made grilled scallops wrapped in prosciutto. I appreciated that. I wasn't fully on board with the idea of eating during these meetings since I was eager to get them over with as quickly and painlessly as possible, but I did appreciate the fact the food was prepared and ready to be dished up. It wasn't like most dinner party buffets where nothing is ready and you have to wait an interminable time to eat. There were also fruit and brownies and Ronnie brought a tray of gruyere chive popovers.

Lyle appeared from the bedroom, and our quorum was complete.

The meeting proceeded with remarkable harmony and was altogether unremarkable in its business-like and sober appraisal of our budget and work that needed to be done in the future, including the condensation of moisture by the exterior wall near our bedroom and the dampness and must of the entry hallway. Some good suggestions were made, including getting the carpet cleaned and cleaning the rubber rim around the sideway-loading washer portal more routinely.

However, Item IV.D. was odd. Cal wanted to "Establish more specific criteria for renters/rental units."

Ronnie and I couldn't imagine what this was about. We weren't even sure whether Cal and Pamela had moved in yet. We had not seen any furniture delivered or Cal and Pamela come and go on a daily basis. Were they sleeping on cots? Cooking meals? We couldn't say. Their unit still seemed more like a union hall for plumbers and electricians and carpenters to come and practice their skills than a place where people might actually live. Like all the other affluent people in the neighborhood, Cal and Pamela's fussiness was extreme.

But what was up with the renters? Why was that a concern? It was so unashamedly patrician, which I both marveled at and shared, despite its flagrant elitism, and was happy that Cal brought it up. We'd had renters with dogs, big dogs, one of which had the nasty habit of pooping and pissing in the hallway. There had been a young couple from upper Michigan with a Rottweiler puppy that not only shat in the hallway but pissed on the shale floor by the mailboxes at the entry of the building and the couple never bothered to clean it up. I would let it sit there for hours to see if one of them would eventually discover it and wipe it up. But they didn't. They'd jump over it. I finally got fed up and wiped it up with a paper towel.

Cal was anxious that we might get someone in the building who would be a source of perturbation and friction, which I totally agreed with. We live in a culture of self-aggrandizement, the Golden Rule turned upside down: treat others as if they didn't exist. The majority of people living in these United States were notoriously rude, selfish and megalomaniacal if not downright sociopathic, loud as a Harley and belligerently entitled. I explained that I'd run past a townhouse currently up for sale where a rock band practiced in the garage. I had to wonder how that went over with the neighbors. I also said I had had a neighbor who played electric guitar at three in the morning and who didn't understand why I was complaining about that to him.

An incident flashed through my mind, a grotesque conflict that occurred in a poor part of town, a place of rundown hotels, the stench of whiskey and beer, cigarette butts on the sidewalks, the drabness that accompanies the forced asceticism that is being down and out. The night before I had posted an excerpt from a prose poem by Susan Sontag concerning cutlery on Facebook. The excerpt I posted was about the spoon:

The spoon is the utensil of childhood, the friendliest utensil. The spoon is childlike. Yum-yum. Scoop me up, pour me in. Like a cradle, a shovel, a hand cupped. Doesn't cut or pierce or impale. It accepts. Round, curved. Can't stick you. Don't trust your child with a knife or a fork, but how can a spoon harm? The spoon is itself a child.

Everyone's comments were appropriately benign concerning spoons. But not Matt Roper. Matt Roper was a local poet who made a living doing handiwork and/or managing apartment buildings. He had recently moved back to Seattle after settling for a short time in the Rust Belt back east, a little town near Rochester, New York. Roper's comment was shocking:

When I was living at the Ambassador Hotel, a guy used one to scoop out the eye of a neighbor who refused to turn his stereo down. So there, Susan Sontag.

It gave me pleasure to think of Roper. This sudden digression in my mind was a welcome relief from the monotony of going over the year's expenditures for water and garbage and maintenance and electricity. The cold reality of numbers, which in their own very abstract condition do have a certain curious appeal, particularly when thought of as a form of language and what they might have to say about our more ideational relations with the universe, but this group of numbers was pedestrian in the extreme. Roper's situation as a poet in contemporary American society was of far greater interest to me, especially at a time, such as the condo meeting, when my own feelings of alienation became so acute. I knew poets who had jobs that paid quite well, several of whom worked as software engineers, but Roper was the kind of poet for whom poetry came first, jobs second. Dedication to poetry as a career means that the jobs one takes in life rarely rise above the most menial conditions. Roper had managed to secure a position managing an apartment building, but still required odd jobs to make enough money for food and clothing and other incidentals. He led a life identical to the one I led before I met Ronnie and got married and began living in a condo and attending annual meetings. Roper had gone to make T-shirts in the Rust Belt of upstate New York but the enterprise hadn't worked out the way he'd hoped and he returned to Seattle where he had to stay for a while in the few flophouses remaining in Seattle. Places such as the Ambassador Hotel in the Chinatown-International District, a chiefly Asian neighborhood which had not yet been subjected to the gentrification of Seattle's Capitol Hill, which transformed from a Bohemian zone of tolerance and liberality and low-rent apartments into a glitzy dystopia of overpriced apartments and tanning salons. The Bohemian element was still in evidence, but these were bobos, bourgeois Bohemians, with high incomes and bank accounts bulging with disposable income.

These neighborhoods are fast disappearing. Seattle's Chinatown-International District was one of the last places where someone with a meager income could find spartan but respectable shelter.

The Ambassador Hotel was but a step away from the missions that housed the homeless. It offered a bed, a sink and four flat, thin surfaces of flaking, discolored paint for walls. They afforded very little in the way of quiet or privacy. You could hear a cockroach crochet a sweater.

I admired Roper and others like him who heroically dedicated themselves to an art form that offered so little in the way of income or even recognition. Most of the literary awards went to poets with high degrees and prestigious positions at universities. They constituted a club, as it were, which excluded those still at the frontiers of poetry, those margins of society where beats and surrealists hunkered down in the rain on their way to a job, or library, and existence was raw and its estrangements were auditions for the afterlife, for otherworldly explorations in the oceans of consciousness unheralded by grants and academic fellowships. They did not have résumés. They had revelations.

Society can be tough. Unforgiving. Especially now that society had become so much more aggressively mercantile, grimly financial. Those whose values flow in a direction contrary to the tenets of profit can easily find themselves alienated and excluded.

Poets are the most vulnerable. Musicians and painters have at least a shot at financial security. Poets do not. There is nothing under the sun more contrary to the capitalist impulse than poetry.

As the French philosopher Axel Honneth recently communicated in an interview, if the possibilities of self-fulfillment have been enlarged (with education, travel, free time, consumption, etc.), they have ever since been diverted for the profiting of that managerial ideology grounded strictly and aggressively on economic performance. One can, in this regard, speak of moral regression. The principle of self-realization thus instrumentalized gives birth to new pathologies — feelings of inner emptiness, uselessness and chronic anxiety. The enormous pressures of neoliberalism constrain individuals to think of themselves as products forever for sale: it is ceaselessly necessary to present oneself as hyper-motivated, flexible, adaptable, subservient. Everything is team this and team that. Individual wants are scorned as frivolous and contrary to the needs of the group. It is no longer the capacity for inner dialogue and solidarity that finds itself privileged, but whatever contributes to ruin this aptitude: the extension of a rapport more and more mercantile and strategic for oneself and others.

I was convinced of the truthfulness of this statement. One only had to step outside to see it in action. But the way it colored my attitude toward my neighbors, which are in many ways similar to coworkers in that we do not choose who our neighbors are going to be, could be eminently misleading. I always tried to bring that into consideration.

Judgments make me nervous. But don't get me wrong: the ability to judge character is crucial. One can get into serious trouble by not being able to assess someone's character or motives. But it's equally important to maintain at all times a certain reservation, a mode of uncertainty. A negative capability, as Keats put it. A lot can happen in that space.

The real challenge of condo meetings was to remove from myself all assumption and try to see reality. Bare, unadorned reality was what? I didn't even know what it looked like I was so caught up in my preconceptions. The world visits us through our five senses. That's a beginning. But things are far more complex when it comes to society, to the masks and ceremonies that hold people together, or keep them apart.

The world is always taking down its tent. We whirl through space round and round the sun and wonder why there is something rather than nothing. There is no way to answer that unless we somehow invent a telescope powerful enough to see through the tremendous heat of the primal Big Bang and see what was there before the Big Bang. The Big Bang that led to trilobites, to brachiopods and bony fish, to cephalopods and crustaceans and echinoderms, to conifers and dinosaurs and cycads and ferns, to mammals and birds and grasslands and forests, to neckties and needlepoint and factories and condo meetings.

Why is there something rather than nothing?

Why do we wear clothes when there's no need to wear clothes?

Why do we dig for metals and gold and adorn ourselves with rings and necklaces?

Why do we stuff our wallets with credit cards and identification and money?

Why are the sports departments of colleges so gigantic and lucrative but the philosophy and art departments are so constantly challenged and threatened?

Why do we so ardently insist on having one romantic partner for the duration of our lives but obsess and fuss over the infidelities of movie stars?

Why is it so easy to lie and so difficult to tell the truth?

Why do some people transform so radically during their lives while others remain the same?

Why did Bob Dylan do a Chrysler commercial during the Super Bowl?

"The silent rage scribbles on the wall inward," says the Swedish poet Tomas Tranströmer. "We living nails hammered down in society! / One day we shall loosen from everything. / We shall feel death's air under our wings / and become milder and wilder than we ever were."

The subject of hardwood floors came up, and my attention returned to the meeting. This was the flour that thickened my bile. Ronnie and I had long suffered deep regrets about our final surrender to allow the installation of a hardwood floor. We'd been promised that the underlayment would reduce noise with the equivalent muffling of a carpet. It did not. I had read numerous postings on the internet about other people undergoing the misery of living below a hardwood floor, some of whom had arrived at a partial solution by making it mandatory to cover a minimum of eighty percent with some form of rug or carpet. I put that forward, but it met with utter indifference, and Clark's immediate and vocal objections to the percentage, which he felt was somehow arbitrary. Eighty percent did not seem arbitrary to me, it seemed very specific, but it was clear he did not want to impose that on future tenants. The hostile indifference of the others left me no other choice but to back-pedal and relent.

This is why I hate these meetings. One's self-esteem drops like a hammer on a small toe.

The hardwood floor issue was the last item in the minutes to be discussed. If indifference were a measurable entity, I still would not be able to measure the indifference of the other board members to our ongoing misery living under a hardwood floor listening to the constant footsteps of the neighbors above walk back and forth ad nauseam *clomp clomp clomp clomp clomp* because that indifference was too large, too dense, too imponderable to be calculated as cubic inches or pounds or stones. It would have to be weighed like a planet. Planets are weighed by measuring their pull, their gravitational force. But the nature of indifference is the opposite: to push away. It would have to be measured according to the force of its repulsion. I would roughly estimate the weight and size of the board's indifference to, say, the density and force of the supermassive black hole at the center of galaxy NGC 1277, which is estimated to be

17 billion times the mass of the sun (our sun), making it the largest black hole ever detected. But this analogy confers far too much romance and interest on what can only be characterized as numb aloofness. Black holes suck things in: indifference does nothing. It has no reaction at all. My analogy collapses on itself. I can give it no image or empirical correspondence. Indifference is the ultimate hostility, the hardpan of Death Valley, admitting no seed, no root, nothing but the shifting of dust, the sour breath of alkali to burn the nostrils in the heat of a blistering sun.

You see? I cannot write about indifference without wanting to attack it, hit it again and again with images, keep punching until it bursts and some kind of ugly pus issues out of it, anything other than that awful asphyxiating apathy that gives it its lethal venom.

Suffice it to say, the HOA could care less about our noise issues. Mandating the use and size of a carpet on a hardwood floor was not in the cards.

The meeting segued into small talk and tepid affability and we went home, relieved to have another meeting behind us rather than in front of us, at least for another twelve months. It took a day or two for the toxicity of repressed feelings, bruised scruples, frustrated desideratum and other assorted injuries to my self-esteem to dissipate. For the pall of indifference to fall from my being and allow my pulse to recirculate blood and warm my body. I would have a full year to brace for another meeting, but for the time being, I could feel the cells in my body recess into sweet repose.

It Is I, Hamlet,
King of the Crabs

I get up at nine, pour some coffee, and sit down to check our email. There is nothing from the contractor who came out to look at the wall on the west side of our building where, according to the home inspector, a high concentration of moisture was flirting with impending doom and destruction. I pictured the wall giving way to a torrent of water and creating an apocalyptic flood like the Christmas tsunami of 2004 that slammed into the palms and hotels of Indonesia, the two of us gripping the rails of our bed as we rode a wall of churning water and debris all the way to Spokane.

The contractor, a clean-cut guy in his thirties, surveyed the situation with supreme confidence and rattled off an itinerary of things he would do to remedy the problem, including the surgical removal of the planks in the boardwalk blocking access to the dirt by the foundation. Two days later he emailed us an estimate, which I in turn emailed to the members of our HOA. They in turn responded with a barrage of emails querying us in short bald phrases of hostile skepticism, "was any of this truly necessary or urgent or cost effective or *blah blah blah.*" Each member of the HOA suddenly became an expert in hydrology, soil and foundation construction.

Clark, the young Turk in the IT field, who was no doubt highly competent at math but seemed seriously challenged when it came to literacy, or the ability to focus on the written word, selecting four or five words out of a paragraph to cobble together a meaning that reflected his line of thinking rather than the carefully worded argument presented in the letter, inquired about the surgical removal of plants. Why was this necessary?

Surgical removal of plants? I wondered. Did he envision a callimammapygian beautybush dense with ventricles and veins? Or that a team of horticulturists in hospital gowns would be grouped around a potted hellebore in heavy concentration as they delicately maneuvered the shrub to a nearby bed of soft, sandy soil?

Then I realized his error. He had mistaken the word *plank* for *plant.*

Other more pertinent questions had to do with the actual repair: there was no mention of flashing or sealant, and no mention of what this guy was going to do with the dirt he excavated. Was there a charge for that? Was he going to remove the dirt? Cal Hartley, who was the owner of the big potted plants on the boardwalk, wanted to know why they were considered a source of wall-eroding moisture. I wondered this too. I sent these questions to the contractor. So far, he had not responded.

I did get an email from the novelist Valerie Delain, who was in Marfa, Texas. She wrote that she'd just seen Jeremy Irons play psychotic twin gynecologists in a pocket movie theater with a cowboy wearing red long johns.

I close out my email and sit back to listen to a French woman who goes by the username Saperlipopette read the opening chapter of Balzac's *Illusions perdues.* I like this title. It fits my present circumstances. Age, maturity, lost illusions. I don't like the word *maturity*, it makes me think of Robert Young in *Father Knows Best,* which you would only know about if you were my age, and once fostered illusions of social adhesion and people striving to do what is best for the good of all because compassion and valor and honesty and beneficence are innate and to do otherwise is to stray into the darkness and become foul and ugly. I don't know whether it is the age in which we live, or my age in particular, but to discover that people behave contrary to my youthful assumptions is an understatement.

But enough of that. Let's get back to Balzac.

The novel begins in a printing house in Angoulême, France, in the early 1800s. Angoulême, which is situated on a plateau overlooking a meander of the Charente River in the southwest of France, is a town full of paper mills and printing presses. The presses are still very crude. Balls of wool covered in leather are still used to dab the ink onto the characters. Jerome-Nicolas Sechard, a journeyman pressman in his late fifties, and who is referred to as a bear in compositor's slang because of his great size and continuous pacing to and fro during the operation of the printing press, can neither read nor write. In an extended flashback that occurs in 1793, during the Reign of Terror, his business is on the verge of extinction when he is hired by a "Citizen of the People" to print the Decrees of the Convention and is given a master's printer's license. He becomes the only printer in Angoulême and his business prospers. He marries and his wife gives him a boy before she dies. The boy is named David. He returns home after receiving an education in Paris, and it isn't long before he and his father are arguing about replacing the old equipment with a new Stanhope printing press, which has a printing capacity of 480 pages per hour.

I can tell that the woman reading Balzac's novel is elderly. She doesn't pronounce words as crisply as the younger woman I listened to read Jules Verne's L'île mystérieuse, but she does read smoothly and attentively.

I have a hard time concentrating because of my frustrations and anger over finding a contractor. It's like trying to find a date for the prom. I can never get a definite answer. I get equivocation. I get intricate, convoluted reasons for why a particular man or outfit cannot do this job.

I call Lucas Spratt, another contractor, the one who originally looked at our problem by the wall. He answered on his cell and seemed irritated by my call. He asked to send him our email and address so that we could set up a time to meet and do a formal estimate. I will not hear back from him either.

At 11:30 A.M. I go do some writing. Several hours later I get antsy and decide to go for a run, even though I shouldn't. I have a chronic pain on my left heel. It's probably a heel spur, a symptom of plantar fasciitis, a diagnosis I've made based on all the internet podiatry sites, running forums and advice columns I've read. Plantar fasciitis, and anything associated with it, sounded nasty. The term sounded mean and refractory.

I watch a number of treatment solutions on YouTube, including taping. The taping videos never tell you where to go for the special tape they're using. And all but one show a man taping someone else's foot. Where is anyone supposed to find someone to tape your foot before a run? I mean, someone other than, say, Mick Jagger or David Beckham?

I watch the one where a young woman tapes her foot, beginning with an X across the bottom of her foot, and encasing that in swath upon swath of athletic tape. I follow her instructions with the tape I bought at Bartell Drugs. I'm not sure it's the right kind of tape. It's called Comfort Tape. I stick the Comfort Tape to my foot like the woman in the video, get into my running clothes and take off for a run. The heel continues to hurt. By the end of the run, I'm limping. I realize I'm just going to have to take time off. I dread the ensuing depression. Running is my favorite medication. It's more effective than the lorazepam. It keeps my head above water until I go to bed and with the help of 1.5 mg of lorazepam, I can get some sleep. I'm not sure the antidepressant is being all that effective. It works, but not that well. Worries never cease visiting my skull or barging in like a SWAT team. I'm always at war with the world. Braced for conflict. Braced for disaster. Wild fires, tornados and earthquakes. Buildings toppled by giant lizards in a frenzy of rabid destruction, their tails thrashing, cars flying, their jaws crunching military jets like crackers. Such is the palette of my mind: all dark browns and lampblack and steel gray and madder red. The colors of war. The colors of scorn and abhorrence.

I don't like confrontation, but when it happens, I tend to get off on it. It's a dry drunk, as they say in AA. The free-floating antagonism is related to the decay of our society, the corporate hegemony and how it erodes the social membrane. There is something wrong when lawyers and contractors and people of other ilk and profession don't reply to queries, voicemail messages or email. It's not just a lack of respect. It goes deeper. It's a lack of recognition, a loss of reverence for life in general. It's symptomatic of an epidemic anomie, a malignant narcissism fueled by a self-serving cynicism and apathy. I wonder what it is that is still holding the society together. It looks like the only thing people care about is vanity and money. How do you fight vanity and money?

After my run, I put my sore heel up on a pillow and watch a show I recorded about French cathedrals, *Les cathédrales dévoilées*. It is said that the cathedral is essentially an experience of light. Light is the most important architectural element. The rose windows of Chartres Cathedral, for instance, celebrate the passage of light through a material, metaphorically transmitting a message of divine passage through the human body while telling the story of David's triumph over Saul, the birth of Jesus, the Last Judgment and Christ with the twenty-four Elders of the Apocalypse. The delicate stone tracery that holds the stained glass in the rose windows of the cathedrals is due in large measure to the quality of the stone itself. Most of the cathedrals are clustered near what were once quarries of calcareous stone. Notre-Dame de Paris benefited from two nearby quarries, one at Charenton and one at Val-de-Grâce. The deeper into the quarry the workers went, the higher the quality of stone was discovered. This allowed for the finer stone tracery and sculpture. It was also crucial that the quarry was near a river for transport. An expert in Gothic architecture named Arnaud Timbert showed how the blocks were sculpted and initialed by the sculptors for payment at the end of the day.

A thirteenth-century artist from Picardy in northern France put together a portfolio of 33 sheets of parchment containing 250 drawings intended for sculpture, ecclesiastical objects, architectural plans and mechanical devices, such as a perpetual motion machine, a water-driven saw, lifting devices, and a machine for straightening the struts of a leaning house. The book survives and can be found in the Bibliothèque Nationale de Paris.

Ronnie comes home carrying two sacks of groceries, one including a four-pack of Virgil's Root Beer. This is heavy stuff. It amazes me she is able to carry these items up our steep hill, nearly a mile in distance. I watch the news on our French cable station while she makes fettuccine Alfredo. It's all about the new pope, Jorge Mario Bergoglio, who will be called Francis, after Saint Francis of Assisi, and who had been archbishop of Buenos Aires. He appeared at the white balcony overlooking St. Peter's Basilica as thousands cheered below, and said, "I would like to thank you for your embrace." The crowd cheered back: "*Habemus papam!*" waving umbrellas and flags.

I don't get any of it. I fail to understand how one man can get so many people excited. I find their beliefs touching, it's moving to see that so many people find faith in something, in anything, when the world seems so overwhelmingly in the grip of Mammon, of war, of evil. But I can't understand it. This man is just a man. How could one man have a direct line to God? And is there a God? Is there a single intelligent being responsible for moths and grass and oysters and diphenylamine? For human beings? For dinner theater? For mathematics and matrimony vines? One guy? With omniscience? One single supreme being who can hear the pleas of a banker in Athens, Greece, create storms of ammonium hydrosulfide on Jupiter and attend to the birth of a star trillions of light years distant, and do all this simultaneously, including the trillions of other events and traumas and prayers and tragedies occurring throughout the known physical universe? An omnipotent being? A being who is responsible for good and evil? For epilepsy and polio? For facial hair and opium? Who created hawks and ladybugs and geraniums? Who created silence and space and tumefaction?

Who also created whatever extraterrestrial beings use for eyes and ears and mouths and whispers?

Whispering seems so quintessentially human. It is what human beings do when they want to say something without disturbing other human beings, or make an unflattering observation about someone in the same room, or issue a piece of provocative gossip. But is this trait really all that anthropocentric? Do extraterrestrials whisper?

Do extraterrestrials have popes?

Do extraterrestrials have countries and borders and trampolines?

Do extraterrestrials, any extraterrestrials, make movies about their planet being invaded? Or suffer xenophobia and racism? Dance? Pin nude pictures to the wall? Do extraterrestrials have a concept of nudity? Or drama? Do they act? Make speeches? Thunder invective? Carouse in gay apparel? Wallow in illustrious sorrow?

Or is the phenomenon of being human so uniquely and profoundly human that it is impossible to even envision what life for an extraterrestrial intelligence might be like?

And what, exactly, is intelligence, anyway? Most of the time, I don't feel intelligent. I feel stupid. I might be intelligent, but I don't feel it. Would visiting the Pope alter my attitude about anything? Would I feel a sense of holiness in his presence? I wish I could share in the emotion all those people in the Vatican rain shouting *Habemus papam* were feeling.

During dinner, we watched Episode Six of season two's *Enlightened* on HBO, the one that ends with Amy (Laura Dern) glancing back through the passenger seat window at Levi (Luke Wilson), standing in the driveway, looking utterly incredulous and stupefied, as she and Jeff (Dermot Mulroney) go off on their dinner date. We watched *Questions pour un champion* during dessert, then got ready to go see the Seattle Shakespeare Company's presentation of *Love's Labour's Lost* at the Center House.

It was warmer outside than I expected, and colder. I wasn't sure on the entire way to the theater if I was feeling warm or cold. As soon as I was sure I was cold, I'd suddenly feel uncomfortably warm, and regret wearing too many layers of clothing. But as soon as I removed an article of clothing, I'd be shivering again. March is like that. It is full of ambivalent weather and so makes the mind ambivalent, flowering and crumbling in irrational equivocations. On the way, Ronnie told me that March 14 is Einstein's birthday, and that the number 3/14 is the number for pi, 3.14159265359, which is an irrational number.

This production of *Love's Labour's Lost* was set in the 1920s, which I initially found off-putting. It has become such a cliché. Why, I asked Ronnie, do directors like staging Shakespeare in the 1920s so much? Maybe it's because everyone drank so much. It was a time of brassy extravagance. Frivolity, enterprise and tragedy. Extremes of behavior burned in luxurious disregard. Everyone spurned the obligations of the future. Doom stood outdoors in the midnight banishment of raffish soirées, austere and inexorable, an ominous spirit amid falling snow.

The Center House stage is a semi-thrust stage. There was a white piano to the left of the stage, and a chaise lounge which appeared to be upholstered in AstroTurf off to the right. As the audience entered and looked for their seats and shifted their weight and adjusted their arms and legs and visited with their companions or played with their cell phones, the male actors stood on the stage drinking cocktails and conversing, all dressed in formal dinner wear, tuxedos and tailcoats. A constellation of mirrors hung above, just below the stage lights.

The presentation was terrific. The audience laughed heartily throughout. I had tears running down my cheeks. I've never paid much attention to this play. I've always found it tedious and confusing. But this time I really got it. There isn't much plot to it, it's all language. Shakespeare really let go on this play. It's full of flare and wit and surprisingly meaningful lines, streaks and flourishes of provocative thought, elegantly delivered. Considering the overall vanity and studied superficiality of the characters and situation, lines such as

Make us heirs of all eternity,

It adds a precious seeing to the eye,

As love is full of unbefitting strains,
All wanton as a child, skipping and vain,
Formed by the eye and therefore, like the eye,
Full of straying shapes, of habits, and of forms,
Varying in subjects as the eye doth roll
To every varied object in his glance,

surprise the mind with pith and scope. I realized that this play is a feast of language. The story is negligible. It is the words, hot and prodigal, that make the play a play.

In bed, we talk about the play. I ask Ronnie what character in Shakespeare I most resemble and she tells me Hotspur because I'm grumpy, quick to lose my temper.

I ask about Hamlet. Doesn't Hamlet qualify as a notorious grump? If you were younger, she says, you could be Hamlet. But Hotspur was a young guy, I correct her. That's true. I guess you could be Hamlet if Hamlet lived and got to be older.

You mean if Hamlet lived to be sixty-five, and lived in a one-bedroom condo apartment, and collected Social Security?

Yes, Ronnie answers.

So that would be a viable Hamlet?

Yes, Ronnie agrees.

A contemporary Hamlet of existential angst vilifying cell phones and computers and Bill Gates and belligerent baristas?

Yes, Ronnie concurs. Ok, I'm going to sleep now, she announces. Good night, sweet prince, and flights of angels sing thee to thy rest.

What keeps me from being a total asshole? I wonder as I lie in the dark.

I'm not sure. I *am* an asshole, I know. I possess asshole qualities, though it might be something of an overstatement to say I'm a total asshole. I'm not a total asshole on the scale of, say, Dick Cheney or Donald Trump. I'm not a sociopathic, megalomaniacal asshole with a golf iron and a country club. I've been horribly unfair and unfairly unpleasant to a lot of people a lot of the time. I've been stubborn and willful and selfish and narrow. My attitude about life tends toward the dark. My head is full of morbid soliloquies and the tangle of cypress vines draped with the kind of sickly moss that is nourished by gloom and swamp gas. I am frequently given to making howling declamations anathematizing the stink of humanity and the futility of life. This is me. This is *what* I am. This is *who* I am. It is I, Hamlet, King of the Crabs.

BLACK MALIBU

Early Saturday afternoon a young Chinese-American man named Glen Ling appears at the door. I emailed him earlier in the week. Our realtor, Ben, recommended him. It's a bright chill day. I lead him down the hallway stairs and into our bedroom and show him the spot where the inspector's thermal leak detector had registered the deep Diebenkorn blue on its small handheld screen. The blue that has been the cause of so much anxiety and frustration.

We went outside and I led him around to the other side of the building. Cal was getting a power tool out of his car. I said hi, and he said hi back.

Glen and I stood on the wooden walkway, looking down at the section of wall. The part that needed attention was hidden from view by the walkway, and three big potted plants. Cal came walking by and said that he had a few more cuts to make for the cupboards upstairs. I introduced him to Glen. He paused to listen to Glen tell me that he could not see what needed to be done. He could not see a problem. I said that had it not been for the color blue popping up on the inspector's leak detector, he would not be there now, looking down at a mysterious wall. What if we do nothing? I asked. Cal said he didn't do everything his inspector advised him to do. Which I found amazing, considering the fact he gutted his entire apartment, and was fanatical about anything related to real estate — contractual, structural or legal. But it was also a relief.

The inspector said we were obligated to do something about this problem. Cal said you just needed to mention it as a matter of full disclosure. He suggested Glen put his observation in writing. Glen did not respond to this. I could tell by his facial expression that this was a worry he did not want. I decided not to push it. I suggested instead that he get in touch with Ben, who had recommended his services. He said he would. It sounded like he and Ben had a working relationship so I believed he would.

Consequently, Glen's would prove to be the best estimate yet. Which was to do nothing. This was my favorite philosophy in life. If it ain't broke, don't fix it. It was sound, it was Taoist and it smacked of wisdom.

Glen left and I returned to the apartment. A few minutes later Graham came out from hiding. He walked to his favorite toy, a circular track with a white ball that rolls and rolls around when Graham swats it with his paw, and sat down and gave me a look. The Look. The Look that means "time to come and play with me." Time to sit by his side and rub his head when he swats his ball and the ball rolls round and round. So I did. I sat down and Graham began purring and swatted his ball and we got into the old familiar mode of rubbing his head and swatting the ball and rubbing his head and swatting the ball. We did this for a few minutes and then I got up, slowly. Age and the antidepressants cause me to get dizzy easily. I don't mind it. I like being dizzy.

I got into my running shorts and shirt and slipped an elastic band on over my left foot, the one with the injured heel. The previous Thursday I'd gone to see an orthopedist. X-rays were taken. The woman who took the X-rays positioned my foot this way and that and fussed with a giant machine. I guessed she was in her fifties by the grayness of her hair and texture of her skin. I joked that I wished I could go shopping for a new young body like that episode in *The Twilight Zone*. She looked old enough to remember *The Twilight Zone* but she did not remember that particular episode. I tried to remember it for her but didn't remember it that well myself. I remember the couple could only afford one body and it was the old man who bought the new young body, the idea being that with a new young body he could go out and get a job and earn enough money to pay for a new young body for his wife. But I couldn't remember how it ended. I think it ended sadly. I think the man got interested in a lot of new young female bodies and forgot about his aging wife. But I could be wrong. In any case, the doctor appeared, a young man with short brown hair and dressed in the standard white lab coat, and examined the X-rays of my foot and pointed to the heel and said, there's the money shot. I had insertional Achilles tendonitis. He said there was no sign of plantar fasciitis, which surprised me. In fact, my feet had great flexibility, and the prognosis looked good. I could keep running as long as I didn't overdo it and stayed at my three-mile distance until the heel began to feel better, and do some drop-down exercises, which I'd already begun doing. I watched a muscular young surfer-looking guy with spiky blond hair and earrings in both ears demonstrate it on YouTube, putting his foot on a step then literally dropping down, putting all of his body weight to bear on that foot and tendon. The doctor said that tendon is like a rope and it doesn't get much blood there, that's why it takes so long for the heel to heal.

On Monday, we decided to rent a car to take care of some chores that involved long distances and heavy items.

We needed cat litter. We needed Gatorade and light bulbs and chocolates and coffee and cheese. We needed paper towels and *Love's Labour's Lost* and the power of prayer. We needed Walter Benjamin. We needed autonomy and socialism and soap. We needed a combination smoke and carbon monoxide alarm. We needed guns and lawyers. We needed conviction and cashews and a CD player for Eric Burdon. Some of that stuff was heavy, some was not. But there was also a house and a townhouse we wanted to look at. So we rented a car: a black Chevy Malibu.

We caught a Number 3 bus to Virginia Street. My ORCA card registered "out of funds" and so I slipped two dollars into the pay machine and plunged my left hand into my left pocket for a quarter and came up with a bunch of change and a nickel, at least I think it was a nickel, fell to the floor and rolled somewhere in the vicinity of the bus driver's feet. He was a large Black man with large thick work boots. He looked momentarily puzzled by the dilemma but I joked "consider it a gratuity" and he laughed and I went to join Ronnie who found a seat midway into the bus.

We got off the bus at First and Virginia and walked the rest of the way in chill March air to the car rental office on Westlake. The staff was made up of young men, all with short bristly haircuts and eager-beaver personalities. I wondered if they were that way naturally. I don't remember a single time in my twenties when I beamed such zest and cordiality. If this was an act, I was impressed. If not, if these guys were truly that full of vim and vinegar, I was equally impressed. How had the heartbreak and sorrows of young Werther not yet stricken them down and made them appear at least a tinge forlorn? Did they not know these were post-apocalyptic times and Obama was a fraud and Wall Street banksters had corrupted what was left of Western civilization? That they were working hard for wages that had been frozen since 1970? Was their innocence to be trusted? There was, I had to admit, something very appealing about their zest, however surreal it appeared to me on the surface.

I filled out the necessary forms (there are always forms), which never fail to confuse me. I do not do well with forms, but I got the pertinent information down however illegibly and signed my name and promised to give them my firstborn child in case I lost the car, or fail to return, because I don't know, I've driven it underwater to Siberia via the Aleutian chain.

There was also the matter of insurance, which I hadn't really thought about. It was expensive, the same price as the rental per day. But I could easily see myself at an intersection amid broken glass and looks of stupefaction wondering why the fuck didn't I buy insurance when I had the chance? Now I am in fealty to the car rental company for the rest of my adult life.

So we paid for insurance.

A chipper young man in a suit and tie disappeared into an underground garage and reappeared with the black Chevy Malibu. He got out a disk of cardboard about the size of a silver dollar for measuring scratches. Any scratch that exceeded the circumference of his disk merited attention and registration on his form. That way, we would not assume blame for the scratch. We all went around the car looking for scratches, dents, contusions, cuts, graffiti and signs of early man. The scrutiny went deep and felt archaeological. We completed our journey around the car, and the young man handed over a set of keys. The keys were attached to lumps of plastic on which little icons represented their function as lock openers and secrets to the wind and grave.

I got into the driver's seat and Ronnie clambered into the passenger seat. It felt strange. I was used to our old Subaru, defunct and donated now into the possession of the Humane Society. The Subaru had a stick shift, and it was small and easy to look out the windows. It had a great turning ratio. The Malibu felt intimidatingly large and cumbersome and I could not see out the back. I had to rely on the sideview mirror to the right rather than look out the back window as I was used to doing. The Malibu was an automatic, which is good, but once you've gotten accustomed to shifting gears, it feels funny to slide the shift knob into drive. My left foot felt idle. It feels natural to me to step on a clutch at the same time I shift into gear.

I had a difficult time getting my seat adjusted. I found the button that made the seat go up and down or lean back but nothing for releasing the seat so that I could shift it forward, closer to the dash. I don't like sitting far back from the dash. Ronnie got the manual out of the glove box and said that there was a bar under the seat that could be raised for moving the seat back and forward. I reached under the seat and felt the bar, but it wouldn't budge. I was stuck with the seat as it was. I would have to get used to the additional space between me and the dashboard. It felt like I was piloting planet Earth from a balcony in Naples. I don't know what made me think of Naples. Whenever I get confused or disconcerted I think of Naples. I've never been to Naples. It just looks like a confusing place.

Now for the emergency brake. The boys back in the rental office must have been wondering why we hadn't left yet. Maybe they thought we just wanted to sit in the car and listen to music. Ronnie checked the manual again. You put your right foot on the regular brake, then press down on the emergency brake with your left foot. I did so, and voila! The emergency brake released.

I entered the traffic on Westlake. Here I was again, back in the saddle, part of the automotive world. It felt good. Good to be in control of something this big. And scary. It felt simultaneously exhilarating and intimidating and dynamic and daunting. That's what makes driving so addictive. It gets all those emotions going. And then we slid the new Eric Burdon CD in and the sound came out like gangbusters: "This world is not for me, I'll make a new one, wait and see..."

When one rents a car one divides one's time carefully so as to maximize the use of the car. I begin imagining an hour as a slice of meat I must carefully dice into minutes. Tasty little minutes, spicy little morsels of time, ticks, tocks, seconds, scruples of time, thin sillinesses of time, delicacies gleaned from the clock. One thinks in terms of: How fast can I do such and such? How much time to do such and such? Until it makes you dizzy and you collapse from the fatigue of options, or go racing madly through the city, honking at the imbeciles in front of you who won't let you pass, who seem to move with the slowness of quadrupeds under the influence of powerful barbiturates. Time becomes king, and you, laboring to achieve some semblance of expedience, some bang for your buck, you become the fool of time.

Which makes music essential. It is music that redeems you from time, from the nonsense of time.

A rental car is a time-consuming enterprise (it takes well over an hour to get the forms filled out, check the car for dents and scratches, figure out where all the devices and levers are), but, ah, the luxury! After the days spent waiting for the bus, breathing the second-hand smoke of someone's cigarette, or brood of cigarettes, taking in every detail of the immediate neighborhood out of a spirit of marooned curiosity, while simultaneously trying to find that one spot free of cigarette smoke, chiding myself for being such an elitist Puritanical prick and reminding myself that I was a once a clueless smoker poisoning the local air then forgiving myself for thinking of myself so harshly and allowing myself the luxury of feeling unjustly abused, spinning those contradictory impulses around *ad nauseam*, fretting, chafing, stewing, riding crowded buses smelling of sweat and urine, swaying back and forth holding onto a smudged stanchion trying not to end up cradled in somebody's lap, watching a populace lose itself to mobile phones and other electronic gadgets, thumbs and fingers working with insect-like dexterity, disembarking from the temporary respite of the bus and trudging heavy bags of groceries up a steep hill, bottles clanking, arm muscles aching, time leaking out of that brief little dream called life, after that, after all that, however whiny and trivial these ordeals may in reality be, a rental car is magic. It is truly magic. Suddenly, *kawham*! You're at the store. Then *whammo*! you're home again. And all the while your ears have been swilling the sounds of the Rolling Stones or Eric Burdon or Otis Redding, music swirling around in your brain with voluptuous soulfulness, wonderful engorgements of bittersweet soul, jukebox apples of shiny sorrow, joyful defiance, prodigal disclosures, unapologetic lusts, distillations of universal woe embedded in heady rhythms and hot emotion, Mick Jagger jubilantly declaiming time, time, time is on my side, yes it is!

THE FOOL ON THE HILL

April 1, 2013. 9:05 A.M. I drink five mugs of coffee purchased the previous week from an herbalist in the Chinatown-International District, which is strong as cast iron and proves to be a fine substitute for personal existence.

9:20 A.M. I'm being followed by pillows. Big, paisley pillows and cushions the size of kangaroos. I shoot one with a double-barreled wheellock, a gift from Charles V, and the pillow drops to the ground, hemorrhaging xenogenetic Slinkys.

10:17 A.M. There can be no question of easy faith. I study the plants at the window and realize that there is no empirical method for determining the molecular velocities of horripilating zithers. Even if I grant James Clerk Maxwell some justification for the Clausius virial equation that holds for macro-particles in an enclosed vessel will also hold for molecules, any zither matted with hair such as the one I used in my experiment will naturally tend toward cashmere. This includes the complicated charges and currents employed in the Chicago-style metaphor, particularly those employed on the South Side, where the field of magnetism tends toward the space-time formulations of

Buddy Guy. Transcendence is crucial when the scientific method fails. Here is where faith becomes an emancipation from the tyrannies of empiricism, and flexes its resistance to the banality of fish like a bicep on the arm of a Russian Bolshevik.

10:47 A.M. I notice my watch is upside down. The world is upside down. The kitchen and cat and bookshelves and neighbors and exhalations and exhilarations and napkins are all upside down. The floor is now the ceiling and the ceiling is now the floor. I revert to modes of perspective and horizon to stabilize my sense of hygiene. I turn upon the poles of incarnation and invocation. I try to distinguish between what is true and what is apparent. As soon as I collapse into sheer arbitrariness, the raging discord between art and truth thereby seems to cease. But how am I related to my body, is that not a continuing problem? It is. This is what I do. I move my arms, I move my legs, I turn my head. This releases the unconcealment of Being. Being itself is determined by Being itself. If Being is allowed to reign in all its Questionableness, the roots draw up more water, and a fragrance reminiscent of hyacinths will pervade the atmosphere.

11:15 A.M. I drink more coffee. This is the way I see it: the world of experience is a standing invitation to deny or ignore my transcendence. But I will not do it. I will not deny my transcendence. I will not ignore my transcendence. I will, instead, seek attainable felicities, and pull meaning out of the world wherever and whenever time and space may permit such inquiry.

12:03 P.M. It is wonderful to talk to Mick Jagger in his hotel room. He is absolutely charming, and the women filling the room seem as natural as the sound of rain or the play of sunlight. We discuss the dynamics of gas, and confess a need to discover within our actual world a primal other world of ideality. Mick says he feels the same way, and begins singing "You Can't Always Get What You Want," and points directly at me. I blush. We converse until late in the afternoon, after which I stop at QFC, and pick up two four-packs of Virgil's Black Cherry Cream Soda. This is a new flavor, and a deviation from my usual root beer, but I like it a lot.

12:22 P.M. On the way home, I hear the singing of millions of ants. Or is it laughter? I cannot decide. Sometimes it sounds like singing, sometimes it sounds like laughter. It is ants who built the hill on which I live. Millions of ants toiling millenniums to create a hill of sand, grain by grain. Their laughter is an alloy of sand and plurality. It's the laughter of ants. It's the laughter of the marvelous.

1:01 P.M. The rest of the day is open, and serves as a common pasture for my thoughts. There are those who gambol, those who wallow, and those who suddenly take wing, and fly to other lakes and ponds and places of sweet reverie. Many dark and sleepless nights have I been a companion for owls, separated from the cheerful society of men, scorched by the summer's sun, and pinched by the winter's cold, an instrument ordained to settle the wilderness. But now the scene is changed: peace crowns the sylvan shade.

1:05 P.M. How fleeting is the peacefulness occasionally afforded us? My quiet is broken by Bronson, the heavily-built, crew-cutted sexagarian who owns the duplex next door, a blue and white two-story Queen Anne style house built circa the 1920s. Bronson rents out the upper and lower units and drops by frequently for maintenance and landscaping and other problems. He was engaged in a cell phone conversation which was well within my hearing, pacing back and forth, *blah blah blah blah*, presumably dispensing information for his next tenant. His face was frowned, per usual, which made him look like a general in the midst of a crucial battle.

2:02 P.M. I feel peculiar sensations, like many creatures on Earth at the approach of violent atmospheric changes. The atmosphere is evidently charged and surcharged with electricity. My whole body is saturated; my hair bristles just as when you stand upon an insulated stool under the action of an electrical machine. It seems to me as if my cat, my fond companion during these convulsive and ominous afternoons, the moment he touched me, would receive a severe shock like that from an electric eel.

3:05 P.M. I go for a run around the crown of Queen Anne Hill. The view is a majestic. I see an airship hover over Elliott Bay, and what appears to be a giant squid, a marine organism of tremendous size, its tentacles reaching for the airship, as the people look down photographing this anguished monster and its frustrations with their smartphones. A man leans too far out from the railing of the gondola and is snatched by the creature's beak and instantly swallowed. The glimmer of smartphones recording this for later YouTube viewing maddens the creature further. It crawls up Pier 57 and attaches itself to a giant Ferris wheel, rides around five times, then slithers up Seneca Street eating pedestrians and leaving a trail of black, viscous bile. News at 11.

4:30 P.M. Ronnie returns home and we sit down to a dinner of veal soup, veal collops, and bacon and a brace of partridges, roasted, and apple dumplings. We watch a demonstration of skill on television, in which a man riding a Harley-Davidson motorcycle around the walls of a cylinder, lets go of the handlebars and leans back, wrenching the handlebars at the last moment to prevent a crash at the bottom. This is followed by a lobster quadrille, in which the lobsters, having been well fed, take their partners by the claw and daintily maneuver themselves across the floor.

7:05 P.M. I retire into my laboratory to do research on the effects of metaphor and magnetism. The existence of a pervading medium, of small but real density, consisting of nothing but sounds and letters, capable of setting the mind in motion and transmitting ideas from one part to another with great velocity, is irresistible in its application. Inasmuch as this medium can transmit undulations with exquisite power and invisible force, it is useful in a literary context, though not that of minimalist prose, which has become the norm in writing, the byproduct of Facebook and Twitter and a generation of people for whom literacy has become anathema. Today's poet must learn the hermetic discipline and approach of the medieval alchemist. The transmutation of base metals into gold occurs in solitude. There is no support. There is sometimes persecution. There is often mockery. But the process is worth it. And it is a process. One learns to think in terms of energy flux rather than Newtonian matter. Intensity of feeling provides the furnace. Clarity of intellect provides the alembic. Eventually a concrescence of words takes form. A nexus of possibilities pulses with vision. Experience starts as an emulsion of intuitive perceptions — colors, smells, textures, taste — and becomes a recognizable image or condition. Art has the capacity to exalt such experience into an entity greater than the sum of its parts, the master perspective which initiates all possibilities. This is the alchemical part. This is where something is started which is larger than definition. But no, this isn't quite what I'm trying to say either. What I'm trying to say is that the most essential core of any project is to open. Open, open, open. Create a state of total nakedness, an *anima mundi*, a connection with the world soul that is non-judgmental and quick to excite. It's not always pleasant. The intelligible world, the world of the familiar, the world in which life is predictable and we feel safe, is annihilated. We're set loose, like Rimbaud's drunken boat, to be plunged into a state of "is-ness." Unadorned being. In his essay on French philosopher Gabriel Marcel, H. J. Blackham writes: "Philosophy, as Jaspers said, can nerve the thinker by reflection upon the conditions of thinking to dare to think that there is a reality which cannot be thought. In that case, Being can be experienced, indicated, attested, but not represented and possessed." It takes a little while for Blackham's statement to digest. It's galvanizing to think of a domain (if one can think of it as a "domain," a location, which seems silly on the face of it) of consciousness that has not as yet been realized, articulated, sculpted or painted. Perhaps not even dreamed. But if the philosophy is good enough, strong enough, bold enough, the mind can dilate into entertainments with no limitations, no defining features. The very opposite of what most people strive to possess: assurance. Not that I'm a fan of anxiety, or Kierkegaardian dread. I'm not. But I do like mystery, the kind of enigmas we find in carnivals and back alleys and certain blues chords.Uncertainty lacks the comfort of religious faith. It does not have the elegant simplicity of binary digits nor enjoy the viscous pliability of vocal fold mucosa, but a state of uncertainty can, with the application of the right metaphor, bubble into metaphysical hyperobjects, each one populated with tiny animalcules, and elves.

    11:00 P.M. We retire to bed, and linger there in the dark until sleep arrives, and folds us into its easeful realm.

CHAPTER
ENDING IN BLUE

Suddenly it's spring and there are cherry blossoms everywhere, flurries of them like snow, so much like snow I think at first it is snow, whirlwinds of whitish pink, empires of spume. Everything is a Japanese haiku. Squiggles of oil ribbon down the gutters. Sweet perfumes of rain or drizzle charge the air with the imagery of heaven. There are greens so intense I can't believe my eyes and have to rely on my other senses to take it in. I need to smell green, hear green, taste green, my eyes are insufficient, there is so much greenness to the greens of moss and newly emerged leaves that implicate space with sororities of shape. I near the end of my run, begin a descent down Highland to Bigelow and see Ronnie walking down the sidewalk, returning home from work dressed in black — black pants, black jacket, black purse. I think about coming up from behind and surprising her, pinch her butt, then think otherwise, it might not actually be her, then what? But it is her. She turns round and bends over, I imagine to pick up a dime or penny, heads up, which she considers good luck. But I get close, she sees me, I look down, it's an earthworm. She's trying to maneuver the earthworm back to the dirt at the edge of the sidewalk. But she can't get a grip on the creature without hurting it. Maybe it could use some mouth-to-mouth resuscitation. Maybe we should take it to an animal shelter. Maybe we should X-ray it, check it for dropsy, lethargica, pernicious anemia. What can be done?

There is nothing to be done. We leave the worm to its destiny and continue on our way home.

Ronnie discovers via computer that *The Seattle Times* is running an article about Seattle's severe housing shortage. People are paying cash for houses. Where in god's name are all these people getting so much money? Ronnie thinks it's investors with all the cash. I think it's drug money. I don't know what it is. Seattle's affluence has been a stupefaction and an enigma to me since the 1990s. At first it was obviously IT people, Microsoft employees and their derivatives and subsidiaries and whatnot, young people getting rich thanks to high math competency and skills at pushing a cursor around on a computer screen. But it continues, mounts, gets crazier, it can't all be people involved with computers. So where the fuck is it, I wonder, this fountain of money? I see dollars squirting out of the ground like Old Faithful in Yellowstone and gangsta hedge fund managers in baggy hip-hop pants collecting it in their baseball caps.

The article explains why we've had such a hard time finding places to even look at. The few places that we've actually gone out to see have been dismal. The nicest was a townhouse in Ballard, but it was smack-dab on a busy street, no end to the traffic except perhaps by ten or eleven at night when it thins to four or five cars per minute. But there it would be again in the morning at your bedroom window, the rat race, the eternal *whoosh whoosh whoosh.*

We ride the Rapid Ride D Line out to the north end of Seattle, a cul-de-sac near Carkeek Park where the lawns are riddled with kid's toys and junked washing machines, it reminds me of the scene in *Sideways* when Paul Giamatti is discovered in the bedroom snatching Thomas Haden Church's wallet and the huge trucker man who is otherwise preoccupied with fucking his penitent adulteress wife discovers him just as Giamatti tiptoes out of the room and gives chase, Giamatti running full out now, the trucker Cyclops right behind totally naked, his dick swinging as Paul Giamatti closes the door and starts the car and the trucker rushes up so fast his dick and ballsack get mushed up against the car window. I remember the mess of the trucker's house and the impressive attention to detail, it was totally authentic, and then this cul-de-sac pocketed next to Carkeek Park and its drab bare winter trees brings it back afresh. It seems like the kind of neighborhood where, in the summer, people sit outside drinking beer or work on their cars or wash their kids down with a garden hose.

We enter the condominium, which is part of a duplex, and feel its interior inspissate around us. Years of domesticity ancient as old Jerusalem enter our nostrils and penetrate our pores. I know immediately it is not for us. There is something oppressive about it.

It looked so promising on the internet, private and wooded and sedate and serene, but the reality is hilariously different. The realtor, a man in his forties with thick black hair and a dark Mediterranean complexion, gets up and seems genuinely pleased to see us. He lets us go round and check the place out. It has a very thick carpet, unusual in this day and age in which the hardwood floor has become as popular as tattoos and smartphones, and the people must have just recently moved, or were still in the process of moving, since there were still a few framed photographs and books on the shelves.

After dinner we watch *Faut pas rêver*, a documentary about Bhutan, and I nod off. I come awake just in time to see a yogi stupefy a dragon by displaying an enormous, iron-hard erection. What's up with this, I wonder, pun intended.

The yogi is a legendary figure in Bhutan Buddhist folklore named Drukpa Kunley. He was a great master of Mahamudra in the Buddhist tradition, a poet of great reknown, and is often counted among the Nyönpa, a group of saintly madmen noted for their unusual practices. He is the yogi credited with bringing Buddhism to Bhutan. A consequence of this man's influence is the prevalence of phalluses: they're everywhere. Huge as murals. Each one is a testament to the male organ. Big hairy testicles from which rockets a colossal dick with a glans so pronounced in shape and gleefully alive and colorful and blatantly hedonistic it provokes unabashed elation. Among the men, at least. I can't imagine what the women of Bhutan make of these monstrous dicks everywhere. Do they arouse feelings of giddy spirituality, or is their ubiquitous tumescence just an annoying and wish-fulfilling sign of male domination?

The host of the program, Tania Young, does not seem especially offended, nor do any of the women in Bhutan who she interviews. Everyone is as used to seeing giant cocks everywhere as if they are ads for shampoo or toothpaste.

But what if, instead of the phallus, the dominant, mural-sized depictions on Bhutans walls was that of the vagina? What if their chief avatar had been female? A cosmic nymphomaniac?

What if the people of Bhutan wore penis pendants like Christians wear the cross?

I fell back asleep.

At noon the following day, a Monday, we take Graham to the local animal clinic. I carry him. Ronnie is worried and thinks about taking a cab. But I convince her it's a very short walk and won't be a problem. Which, as it proves, it is not. Graham is much calmer hanging at my side than he is riding in a car. He ain't heavy, he's my brother.

I put Graham, still comfortably ensconced in the thick black carpeting in his carrying satchel, onto the chrome exam table. He begins to growl. He knows the smells of this room. He hates it. I can feel his hatred. I can feel his hostility. The growls get louder. I sympathize. I hate bringing him here. He doesn't have a clue. He doesn't get that we're bringing him to this place to be cared for. From his point of view, we've gone insane, we've brought him to a place where strangers pick him up and restrain him and poke him with sharp objects. I think dogs and cows and horses have an understanding deep down that no matter how uncomfortable they're made to feel during a medical procedure they know they're being cared for. Cats do not. Graham, in particular, most certainly does not.

The doctor arrives and Graham's growls continue, punctuated, now and again, with a cobra-like hiss. The doctor is a middle-aged man with a calm demeanor. He explains several of the things they'll need to do and then calls for some assistance. Three women arrive, all dressed in hospital gowns, and Ronnie and I exit and go into the waiting room where an older, very nicely dressed and poised couple sit with a puppy they just acquired. The dog, a Maltese, is trembling, but otherwise completely manageable and trusting. We begin talking about the differences in behavior among dogs and cats and hear Graham crying and yowling from the exam room. He sounds remarkably like a baby. I tell the couple how frustrating it is to bring our cat here. He doesn't know what's going on. He probably thinks his owners have gone insane and brought him for torture. Turned him in like some terrorist to Guantanamo Bay. I think this is funny but the couple with the Maltese do not.

After the vet and his staff finish with Graham I carry him outside in his cozy tote bag. Once outside, he calms immediately. It's warm, but laced with a certain invigorating chill. Spring chill is different than winter chill. Spring chill has the vigor of life in it and wine and perfume and blossoms and fresh new leaves. Winter chill cuts to the bone. Flattens you with heartache and headache and gloom. Christmas lights are an antidote. Christmas itself could be an antidote, might, at one time or another, have been an antidote, but is not now an antidote. Quite the opposite. Christmas has become capitalistic and toxic. Christmas is a fraud, a shamble of nauseating movies and stress. Raw nerves crowded parking lots unspoken resentments veiled threats bullying miscarriage predestination crowds elbowing bumped shoulders bruised egos emotional blackmailing savage arguments and the perpetual cycle of obnoxiously cloying music.

But how did I get hung up on Christmas? It's spring. Graham is calm and hangs from my shoulder. I can feel the warmth and occasional squirm of his body nice and serene in its black furry cave with mesh on either side to smell all the smells and hear all the sounds and wonders of the world in its wedding gown of spring and tea garden rhododendrons. Ronnie steps out from the animal clinic after paying our bill and we begin a slow easy walk homeward. I marvel at all the houses, porches and peaks and gables and wonder if there was ever a time when average people with average salaries could afford such things but not now these houses can only be afforded by lawyers, doctors, bank investors and computer wizards. They're way out of the reach of people with regular jobs checking groceries or slicing meat or fixing cars or teaching mathematics to high school kids. Ronnie points at a bush with red flowers on it and says that's hellebore. Hellebore, I say. That's hellebore. Now there's a word. Hellebore. It comes from Greek *helleboros, ellos* meaning *fawn* and *bora* meaning *food of the beasts*, so that hellebore translates into something like "plant eaten by fawns." It was once believed to cure madness. In Greek mythology, the ancient physician Melampus of Pylos used hellebore to save the daughters of the king of Argos from a madness induced by Dionysus who caused them to run naked through city, crying, weeping and screaming.

After we get settled at home, we put on our running clothes and go for a short run, return home, shower, get dressed and walk to the bottom of the hill to catch a Number 4 bus and ride to Denny Way with a crowd of high school kids who poured out of the Seattle Center. We walk down Denny to Whole Foods where we find two packets of CalmAid left. They're having a sale on these things, lavender extract which brings on a state of calm. And it does. It's pretty mild, you can barely notice it, but it's there. It affects you a bit like a drink, a soft euphoric moment that might lead to considerations of redemption and space travel. I like the way it's arranged, thirty little red tabs in little bubbles that you press and they come out the other side of the card. They're easily swallowed and diffuse into the blood within minutes, bringing the fragrant hills of Provence and warm Mediterranean breezes into your nervous system and brain cabbage.

I get a craving for beef ravioli so we catch the 13 to the top of Queen Anne and go to Athena Pizza. The waitress, a young thin girl in a black sparkly blouse who's grown familiar with us, asks if I want my usual root beer and I say, yes, and then she asks if Ronnie wants her usual chianti and I say, yes, but I'm not entirely sure. Ronnie is in the bathroom washing her hands. We make it a practice to wash our hands after riding the bus. I've just returned from washing my hands which, for some reason, feel big and clumsy, as if they belonged to someone else, someone larger than me who might drive a truck. The body can feel alien at times. I don't know what brings it on. Too much poetry maybe. But there are times when everything feels strange, defamiliarized. Being suddenly feels odd and singular, as if your consciousness has overflowed its banks and mingled with the cosmos and everything that normally went unnoticed is now weird as a rooster's wattle: fingers, thumbs, palms, the little lines crisscrossing and mapping the inner part of your hands, the tiny grooves in your fingernails, the food on the menu and all these Italian words, *fettuccine, tortellini, rigatoni, penne putanesca,* the smoothness of the vinyl and rotundity of the booth and shape of the glass and cutlery, it's all immensely wonderful and foreign as if experienced for the first time. Added to this is the acute feeling of being in relation to other things and beings, so that it is symphonic, a clatter of plates and cutlery and trays. And delicate Rembrandt browns imbued with the heat and light of the time and creams and ointments to soothe the bruises and abrasions that come with living and letters that are sent out into the world with your feelings and thoughts, pale vaporous entities of thought and idea that balloon and evaporate like they do in the comics. Steam billowing up from a pot and disappearing for example or Beetle Bailey dreaming of an Hawaiian beauty in a grass skirt.

I finish off my beef ravioli and Ronnie is still working on her tortellini when the waitress arrives with the check and asks if we want the bread boxed and Ronnie says, yes, and can you box this, too, I'm finished eating. Sure, says the waitress and moments later returns with two boxes in a paper sack. We love this bread. They always serve it just before the meal so that we rarely get around to eating it. We're too full. So we ask to have it boxed. Ronnie freezes it and sometime later makes a delicious dinner out of it.

We get back home and watch a documentary on our French cable station about the organs of Wallonia. There are thousands of organs in Wallonia. Their immensity and complexity is staggering. The organ of the Church of Saint-Jacques in Liège is a restoration of an organ originally built in 1599. Concert organist Jean-Baptiste Monnot describes the counterbass of the newly restored Saint-Jacques organ as having a very warm sonority. Even though he's a young man, and wearing a white hardhat, he talks elegantly and has the enthusiasm and demeanor of a musical aristocrat, a prince of the pipes.

I get up and put our dessert dishes into the dishwasher and press the button for "normal cycle," which isn't actually a button but a little iconic square you press, and close the dishwasher door and it starts making its hushed sounds of water running and circulating and spraying.

When the dishwasher finishes, it sets a round patch of blue light on the floor. It's a very pretty blue, otherworldly and pure and hypnotic. It's not the kind of light you would associate with anything as pedestrian as a kitchen appliance, which, of course, makes it all the more wonderful. I think of it as a haiku in blue. But a haiku in which the words are still in embryo. Still in space. A potentiality of words. A glitter of syllables in the mouth of a constellation.

COLD RAIN, WARM LATHER

I go online and discover British poet Tom Raworth has posted on his blog a picture of Gregory Corso's marble burial slab at its location in the English Cemetery of Rome. A friend sent it to him via smartphone. It's rather amazing that pictures can be sent that quickly, or taken that easily.

Corso is buried near Shelley and Keats, the way he wanted it. The inscription on the stone reads:

> Spirt
> is Life
> It flows thru
> the death of me
> endlessly
> like a river
> unafraid
> of becoming
> the sea

"Spirt" is, of course, meant to be "Spirit." But I like the typo, and I think Gregory would have liked it, too. His spirit was all spurt, all huge ejaculatory *élan vital*. He even made brooding look cool. He didn't brood quite like Hamlet, the master of brooders. Gregory's irritabilities had dash and impishness in them. He was a wise old fool like King Lear's companion, speaking truth to power in jokes and sparkling wit. Corso was a fool in the tradition of the Sacred Clown, the Native American Contrary, but did not suffer fools — the truly foolish, the stubborn, the obtuse, the pretentious — gladly. He could be exhilaratingly honest. He was full of mischief. But he was also tuned in to the sublime, the divine. He was like Shelley's twentieth-century incarnation, wild hair and trenchant vision, cutting through the bullshit of the age, the stuffy academicism and snickering, postmodern irony of the intellectual elite. He fully, unflinchingly recognized the pain and frustration and tragedies of life, but just as fully counterbalanced it with waggish, spirited philosophy and jingly bells of an ineluctable goofiness, a wonderful sense of the absurd, a carnivalesque ribaldry *à la* Rimbaud's "Parade" with its collection of ragtag carnies that ends with the line *"J'ai seul la clef de cette parade sauvage."* His work possessed a marvelous comedic energy, yet as bizarre and giddy as his lines could be he could just as easily slide into great cosmic epiphanies, or the imponderable treasures of reverie and dream. "I learned life were no dream," he wrote. "I learned truth deceived / Man is not God / Life is a century / Death an instant."

Impulse and perception are the stuff of life. There is a kind of fever we tap into when we're exposed — and sensitive to — the possibilities of art. Art is synonymous with possibility; it dilates consciousness the way amphetamines and hallucinogens dilate consciousness. It is all the stronger when we discover the underlying fusion of art and life, that perception isn't passive at all but creative in and of itself. The underlying absurdity and sadness of existence in daily realities, soap bubbles, warmth of a cat on our lap, wrinkles, suitcase SNAFUs, hope, rubber bands, giddy inspirations, honey luminous and amber in a glass jar, orange peels on a gray sidewalk, gropings in the dark for a light switch or clothes, veins of rain down a sad Sunday window, brandy twinklings, star breath on lunatic glimmers of wilderness lakes, are what flavor the dishes of this spectacular movable feast, this endless highway, that ever alluring horizon in the sweet trickle of twilight.

I go for a run in the afternoon. It's mid-May and raining heavily. It's cold. If there weren't so much foliage on the trees, I would think the date to be closer to Thanksgiving or Christmas than Memorial Day. I curl my hands into a fist. They feel cold and sting a little. The sensation is simultaneously pleasurable and painful. My pants are soaked. How can a sensation be painful and pleasurable at the same time? It's the intensity of it. Anything intense has qualities of both pain and pleasure. And sometimes a pain is pleasurable and a pleasure is painful. Though I think it's mostly the former. Sometimes a pain, if it isn't too lasting and intense, can feel strangely good, perhaps because it's a feeling, plain and simple, and nothing makes you feel more alive than a mildly painful sensation that mingles itself in the nerves with electrochemical impulses, little stabs of lightning with no clearly identifiable quality good or bad and it all flows into the brain where it gets processed and sublimated into thoughts about it, rumination and speculation and wondering how and why and what is all this business about and why is it so cold and rainy this far into May? The robins sing. The sidewalks are littered with seriously green samsara.

I get home. I take a shower. The shower feels terrific. They always do. The body blossoms. The body opens its pores to little tongues and trickles of hot water. I grab a towel and dry myself and take the new can of shaving lather and press it a little too long and vigorously because I'm still used to the old can of shaving lather that I had to press long and hard to get the last little squirts and splurts of lather out of it, lather that turned wet and drooly, like cream. I now have a large mound of lather that I smear around my face and rinse the rest of it off. Who invented lather anyway? How did lather work its way into human civilization? I've used soap before when I ran out of lather and the soap worked out ok so what's up with lather? Is lather rather unnecessary? I'd rather lather than soap and soap is hope and rope and dope and ropey dopey soap. Soap is great in its own way, neat and cubed bars of olive oil and canola, slippery ingots of liberated glycerol, pellets combined with fragrances Amazon lily baby rose chamomile bergamot black amber and lavender.

I read Kitaro Nishida on will, then "Angoisse" by Rimbaud, which fascinates me. The two seem related. There is a connection. Will often takes action as its goal and accompanies it, but will is a mental phenomenon, which is distinct from external action, and action is not a necessary condition for will, writes Nishida. Rimbaud's "Angoisse" presents a highly complex figuration. He makes reference to ambition, which is an expression of will, as "continually crushed" (*continuellement écrasées*); *i.e.*, unfulfilled, and in a spectacular manner. The poet begs his anguish, personified as the She of the poem, for pardon, for an affluent end that will compensate for the ages of indigence, that a day of success will lull him and his anguish-inducing ambitions to sleep on the shame (as if shame were a mattress) of "our" fatal incompetence. It's a strange attitude, simultaneously disparaging, suppliant and conciliatory. There is a sharp sense of personal failure and deep frustration running beneath, but one that seems alloyed with a kind of sanguinary expectancy, of compensation for the heroics of being a poet in a world where only material, quantifiable attainment is the measure of success. I'm not sure that I fully understand this emotion, but I know that there have been numerous times in my life when I've felt acutely disappointed in fulfilling certain ambitions, wallowed in foolish obsessions, tirades, and bitter self-recriminations, and fallen back on the knowledge that higher awards are obtainable to the imagination. "We have a tendency to think of will as some special power," Nishida writes, "but in fact it's nothing more than the experience of shifting from one mental image to another. To will something is to direct attention to it." One minute it's soaked pants, stinging hands and the dribble of cold rain down the shin, the next it's a mound of happy lather and a room full of steam. Warm water and open pores. A razor across the skin.

Looking Back at
Don't Look Back

R onnie sends me an email from work. She heard an interview with Karen O on NPR before leaving for work. She
had to go in at 6:30 this morning.

I write back to tell her I have a headache because our
upstairs party revelers, Rocco and Terri, woke me up at 3:00
A.M. They're up by 10:00 A.M., a Sunday, which is rather amazing, considering how late they went to bed, clunking around,
thumping bumping clumping, dropping objects on a hardwood
floor, making the planks crack, scraping chair legs or bed legs
or table legs across the floor. Despite our urgings and the urging of the owner of the apartment, their landlord, they do not
get a rug. I have dreams about rugs. Big thick dark Persian rugs
in all the rooms right up to the wall. Essentially, a wall-to-wall
carpet without actually being a wall-to-wall carpet. Relative
quiet resumes and our need to move to other lodgings ceases to
be a vital concern. Really, it's the only reason now that we feel
any need at all to move.

It's not that Rocco and Terri are deliberately rude or malicious. They cannot be blamed. Rocco is simply a clod and Terri is an eight-year-old girl in a woman's body.

There's also a point where expressing complaints to your neighbor does more harm than good. It's best to get most of your complaints out in the open early on before resentments have time to congeal. Early in your relations with a new neighbor a presumption of innocence prevails and the complaints, if expressed diplomatically, seems less provocative and more like telling a driver, hey, do you see that sign up ahead, it says something about falling rocks.

Or, maybe you should slow down. 100 MPH is considered a bit gauche in a school zone.

Or, you're on the wrong side of the road. This isn't England.

Or, you know, when you drop anvils on the floor and they crash through the wood and plaster and hit the floor in our apartment while we're watching TV, it's a bit distracting. Perhaps you could do blacksmithing elsewhere.

Or, you know, when you rev your Harley-Davidson at five in the morning, I know you're eager to get to work, and it's exciting to rev a Harley-Davidson, but if you could wait until you and the motorcycle are outside of the building to do that, it would be greatly appreciated.

One thing all psychologists love to tell you when you're in the midst of a personal conflict involving other people — and what personal conflict doesn't involve other people? — and that is this: you cannot control other people.

I repeat: you cannot control other people.

Much of my frustration stems from trying to impose my wishes on other people. My desire to see them behave with an equivalent amount of courtesy that I extend to them, to enter the building a little less like a SWAT team, to conduct their neighborly behavior with a view toward serenity and quiet so that I don't hear their every emotion during a basketball game, or the vigor of their lovemaking, or the gallons of water used in such interesting and original ways while practicing their daily hygiene.

Later, in the evening, we search HBO for something good, or at least watchable, or something that we haven't already seen a gazillion times. I get down on the floor and go digging through our collection of DVDs in the cabinet beneath the TV. I create four big stacks next to me before I get to the far back and fish out *Don't Look Back*. Hey, I said to Ronnie cooking dinner in the kitchen, how about this? Yeah, she says, that'd be good. We haven't seen that for a while.

And right off the bat the movie gets me excited again. It's astonishing what energy it still has, though now it's a different energy, not the revolutionary energy that galvanized me when I first saw the movie in 1967, that revolution had long ago fizzled out, but the dynamic flux of a singular event caught on film in a manner so raw and natural that it doesn't seem so much modified by time as intensified by time. The movie hasn't lost any of its freshness or pizzazz. It's not like looking at something that occurred decades ago where everything is quaintly dated and irrelevant but looking at something in a parallel universe where the events are occurring simultaneously, a bit like the time disruptions in Chris Marker's *La jetée,* and still have the thrill of consequence.

I get that sense from the way Dylan is marketed in general. And, in many ways, it is Dylan himself who appears to be the marketer, such as his ludicrous appearance in a Chrylser commercial during the Super Bowl. I have a strong feeling he was more interested in selling records than cars. It was always easy to imagine Dylan as a huckster, as one of those barkers I used to encounter in San Francisco's North Beach district in front of all the topless dance clubs, or one of those pencil-mustachioed guys at the carnival trying to lure the rubes in to see a bearded lady or a mermaid comprising the torso and head of a juvenile monkey sewn to the back half of a fish. The poet as P. T. Barnum.

It's not uncommon to enter a music store (if you can still find a music store) and see the array of Dylan's image as it morphed and mutated over the years, beginning with the tousle-haired fresh-faced Dylan of Greenwich Village when he was first starting out and modeling himself on Woody Guthrie to the saggy-faced pencil-mustachioed Dylan in his mid-sixties with his louche carnival huckster foxiness, one part hustler, one part desperado. There is no sense of linear progression to these images, they all seem to be occurring at once, as if time doesn't matter, as if time were a malleable, unstable element in the cosmic roulette wheel. Wherever that little ball randomly plunks is the Dylan you're going to get. They're all the same man, or are they? Even Dylan is mystified by his transformations.

The movie kicks off with the energetic "Subterranean Homesick Blues," defiant, witty, provocative, Dylan holding the lyrics to the song on cards he lets drop as the song progresses. He is standing in an alley of what appears to be lower Manhattan; off to the left margin a bearded and rabbinical Allen Ginsberg stands under a rig of rickety scaffolding in a heavy overcoat engaged in conversation with Bob Neuwirth, who walks jauntily on screen as the song ends and the conversation ceases and Neuwirth and Ginsberg each go their separate ways. Dylan himself looks frail and androgynous but also curiously diamond-hard and indomitable. You wouldn't want to mess with him. He is wearing a pale, long-sleeved shirt, black vest and a pair of slacks. His hair is thick and wild, exploding from his head as if from too much amphetamine, or sheer excitement. It's an odd nineteenth-century look, a nod to Whitman and post-Civil War America.

"Subterranean Homesick Blues" is the only electric number in the movie's songs. The other songs, most of them from the very early stretch of Dylan's career and rooted deeply in folk tradition and the intensely original poetry that was the core inspiration for these songs, are performed solo on stage in black leather jacket, harmonica and acoustic guitar. This is Dylan just as he was beginning to morph into the Warhol Factory cosmopolitan Dylan of *Blonde on Blonde* with its uncannily vivid imagery and intense amphetamine surrealism. He had already begun to play with a band and electric guitars but for this concert he was willing to appear as the Dylan people had grown to recognize and beleaguered him with labels such as prophet and protest singer. This is apparent during the scene in which some very young girls with the heavy accents of northern England question him about his new way of performing and Dylan responds with good-natured, non-condescending wit and tells them, "You know, I have to give some work to my friends, you know. I mean, you don't mind that, right?"

What amazes me throughout this movie is Dylan's frailty coupled with his abrasiveness, his confrontational style. His movements seem odd and out of balance, are heavily concentrated in some self-conscious manner that causes him to move awkwardly and affectedly when he's without his guitar, coupled with his diminutive size and overall delicacy. It did not seem at all strange to see Cate Blanchett play this phase of Dylan's career in *I'm Not There*. He was truly that androgynous, that good looking in a dark, defiant, electrifying Jean Harlow kind of way. There is a mystique to it. It's exotic and freakish and thrilling to watch, though it amazes me he doesn't get the crap kicked out of him, considering his open mockery and disdain for a lot of the people he encounters outside his immediate group. I mean, I was eighteen the year this movie was filmed, and far more muscular than Dylan, and far more amiable to boot, and I got the shit kicked out of me for being a trifle too flirtatious at a basement New Year's Eve party my buddies crashed while dragging me along, so drunk I could barely stand or see straight.

So how did this little guy get away with it?

There's the famous scene in which Dylan goes ballistic over some broken glass in the street outside his hotel and gets into an argument with a drunken man roughly his own age. The rage appears real, and you've got to wonder if he isn't exploding out of the tension of a grueling performance schedule and the demands of a very sudden and colossal fame. The other point of interest in this scene (besides Donovan; in fact, contrasting heavily with Donovan) is the old folk singer Derroll Adams, who looks down and out, a true hobo, rider of the rails, the real deal. Adams willingly takes a backseat to Dylan's brassy spotlight, sits on the floor and settles back against the wall in the crowded hotel room and comes across as genuinely humble and raggedly authentic and not a little drunk. He had, in fact, taken Donovan under his wing and seems better aligned with Donovan's evident innocence than Dylan's edgy surrealism. Perhaps in actuality he wasn't all that destitute, but you can see the aging man needs dental work and new clothes and wonder how he's managing to get by. He seems to be eking out an existence and earning just enough money from busking and doing gigs in the hubbub of England's pubs to feed himself and buy a little booze. And you realize this is the true fate of someone who takes up a guitar and sings songs for a living. It is a fate far closer to the life of a poet, struggling to get by outside the sheltering walls and income of academia. This would have been Dylan's, and Donovan's, fate had not the weird moment in time that was the 1960s made it possible to reach a giant, highly enthusiastic audience in at least two continents, if not all of the Western world.

The question that always goes through my mind, and grows larger as I age each time I see this movie, is: what happened to this guy, this particular Bob Dylan, the iconic Bob Dylan? Where'd he go? The body of songs Dylan composed up until *Nashville Skyline* is stunning. The poetry is incandescent. The songs on *John Wesley Harding* are not as intense or nearly as expansive but they're still intellectually appealing, simple yet enigmatic in the way William Blake's *Songs of Innocence and Experience* are deceptively simple parables about social injustice, hypocrisy, oppression and the moral fiber of the universe. The music and lyrics since then are spotty. There will be, occasionally, a work of genius like "Blind Willie McTell" circa the 1980s or "Not Dark Yet" from the late 1990s, but by and large, take the music away and the lyrics on their own are often quite bland and cliché-ridden.

I'm fascinated by an interview Dylan gave to Ed Bradley of *60 Minutes* in 2004, in which he admits that he can't write with the same quality of poetic intensity now as he did back in the day. "Those songs seem almost magically written," he confesses. "There's a magic to that... and it's not the Siegfried and Roy kind of magic, it's a different kind of penetrating magic, and I did it at one time." "And you don't think you can do it today?" Bradley asks. Dylan mumbles no. "I can do other things now, but I can't do that."

I don't know what he means, exactly, by "other things," but although his more recent songs lack the lyrical ferocity of his early years, there is still something often very quirky and fascinating about them. The lines taken individually are sometimes flat as can be, neutral in tone, bland and prosaic as a bag of nails or a cotton swab, but the way the songs are structured they can encompass a very broad and evocative range, evoking a terrain not unlike a short story by Larry Brown or Raymond Carver. For example, in "Duquesne Whistle," are the lines "Can't you hear that Duquesne whistle blowin'? / Blowin' like the sky's gonna blow apart / You're the only thing alive that keeps me going / You're like a time-bomb in my heart." It isn't great poetry, but taken as a song, these lines are pretty damn interesting. They have a timeless quality; they could be a song from the late nineteenth century. But they're also modern, quietly eccentric. Nobody really talks like this anymore, and the very name Duquesne, with its French-sounding syllables, seems to reference a time and place more akin to William Merritt Chase than Oprah Winfrey or Jon Stewart. But the outrageousness of a sky blowing apart, as an image of goofy urgency, romantic crisis in a cockeyed mode, suggests a milieu of colorful distortion like the work of Red Grooms.

So, no, the Dylan of *Don't Look Back* didn't disappear entirely. But he did get old. Old in a funny way. There is still that unmistakable gleam in his eye. The often cocky, arrogant prick of *Don't Look Back*, openly mocking and insulting people, is now the strange old man police officer Kristie Buble had sitting in the backseat of her cruiser one rainy New Jersey afternoon in July 2009, picked up for vagrancy, for being an old man in the rain, an eccentric-looking old guy wandering around in somebody's front yard. He gave her his name as Bob Dylan, but this was far from the iconic Bob Dylan we've all grown accustomed to seeing, the man with the penetrating eyes and hair exploding out of his head. And he wasn't carrying any ID. She took the guy in black, soaking wet sweatpants, floppy rubber rain boots and two separate raincoats, one with a hood pulled over his head, to be a crazy homeless man. A complete unknown. With no direction, or home.

GOING TO THE DOGS

The apartment next door has been for rent and it appears that the crazy fuck who paces back and forth in the driveway talking into a Blackberry loud enough to be heard two blocks away is our new neighbor. He talks money and real estate and big plans for the future. He seems pretty confident and utterly obsessed about money and real estate. His parade seems to be intended for the world to see what an important jerk he is.

Meanwhile, upstairs, Rocco and Terri have been taking one shower after another. It's uncanny how many sounds that they're able to elicit from the plumbing. Sometimes it sounds like splashing, as if she's trying to get some kind of surf going in the bathtub — I can tell it's Terri since her footsteps are a little lighter than Rocco's *thump! thump! thump!* — and other times it sounds like a robot wrestling a boa constrictor. A sloshing splashing slopping swamping gurgling gargling squirting spattering clattering chattering shattering robot versus boa constrictor match.

I close my eyes and begin imagining a life on Mars. I envy Curiosity, the NASA rover that spends its time rolling around the surface collecting soil samples and analyzing them.

The solitude is sweet. I'm in motion. I've got six wheels in rocker-bogie suspension and each of them is independently actuated and geared for climbing soft sand, rocks, whatever terrain the random proclivities of the universe put in my way: rills, hills, folds, rifts, hollows. Dips, divides, depressions, drifts. I can tilt 50 degrees in any direction without tipping over. I can whip up a dune and arc like a duck on Benzedrine.

I open my eyes. I'm back on Earth, sitting on a chair, looking at a computer screen, a desktop image of Ronnie blowing out the candle on a chocolate birthday cake. This would mean the picture was taken in mid-July, and is a fairly recent photo, uploaded shortly after we bought our new computer, which has since aged two years, the equivalent of twenty human years. Ronnie's cheeks are puffed out, her neck muscles are taut and her eyebrows are raised in excitement and anticipation. The flame still burns, so her breath has not yet left her mouth. She is wearing her usual clothes when she relaxes at home, a light blue velour jacket with metal snaps, a pair of loose-fitting flannel pants, and a low-cut blue blouse. Graham walks across the computer desk, his tail in an upraised curve. *The Human Condition*, by René Magritte, hangs just behind Ronnie's head.

Everything looks the same, except that our old dishwasher is gone, replaced with a new one of stainless steel, and the stack of letters on the upper shelf of the computer desk is higher. I corresponded for many years with the poet Ted Enslin and after he passed away I collected all of his letters, some of which were in a bedroom drawer mixed in with a lot of other letters, and the ones interspersed in the stack above the computer. Then I put a rubber band around them, and put them on top. I don't know why I left them there, though I like seeing them. I miss hearing from Ted, who lived a somewhat hermetic life on the coast of Maine, deep in the woods. He loved classical music and had once entertained ambitions of becoming a composer. He became a poet instead and his music went into his poetry.

I change my clothes and get ready for my usual afternoon run. I remember yesterday, and cringe a little inside, embarrassed that I'd yelled at a man in Kinnear Park for letting his dog go unleashed. I don't know why I get so enraged with that. The potential for being bitten is partly why, though I think the general attitude of the scofflaw comes into play and gets mixed up however irrationally with the general arrogance and sense of entitlement I see in so many people these days, as if everyone sensed the truth deep down, which is that the planet is dying, or certainly altering in a very dramatic way that will make life for us bipedal mammals nearly impossible, and as a bizarre consequence to this overwhelming sense of powerlessness and lack of control is this new phenomenon, this all-too-human human behavior, this ironic manifestation of entitlement and unabashed narcissism, this mania for getting one's nails done, with spas and pedicures and body wraps, as if we were Roman demigods, or the kings and queens of some twenty-first–century feudal empire.

I've done this before, yelled at people about unleashed dogs, and feel acutely embarrassed and silly afterward.

I've got to stop it, I think to myself as I tie my shoe. It didn't used to be this way. In the past, my encounters with dogs and dog owners were far more infrequent.

What's up with dogs all of a sudden? Why does everyone suddenly seem to have a dog?

I like dogs. I think dogs are marvelous creatures, loyal, unconditionally loving, playful and full of life and expression. It's unleashed dogs that make me go ballistic. Their owners don't understand that dog bites have nothing to do with their dogs being mean or aggressive. Dogs see runners in the same way they see sticks and stuffed toys, as something fun to chase, and sink their teeth into.

I've only been bitten once. I was running through a small business district I would normally try to miss because I don't relish the time I spend dodging zombie pedestrians, but I've incorporated this little bit into a three-mile run. My insertional Achilles tendonitis in my left heel limits my run to these three measly miles. I do enjoy one little spot that I run by, a Mexican restaurant serving mostly burritos and tacos, a very casual little hole in the wall place with a table and three or four chairs outside on the sidewalk. I enjoy the rich smells of food emanating from within and just the general vibe of this place. And recently they've taken what used to be one of Seattle's last public telephones, not an entire booth but a boxy encasement where a big black public phone once offered itself with a fat phone book hanging from the ledge of a cheerless aluminum shelf by a metallic cord, and which has been an empty shell for the last several years after the phone company pulled it out but left the shell, so someone in the restaurant thought to put a doll inside and surround it with flowers, irises and roses and tulips and sunflowers. The doll is androgynous, I can't tell if it's a male or female, but the figure is very angelic and curiously blonde and dressed in a robe and wearing a big gold crown. I think the doll is intended to represent a saint, Saint Christopher, maybe. It reminds me of the doll the gypsies in Saintes-Maries-de-la-Mer in the south of France near Arles installed in the subterranean chamber of a fortress cathedral, a black doll representing Saint Sarah, the gypsy saint. I still remember the heat of that chamber with all the candles burning and the deep sense of reverence that hung thick as candle smoke in the chamber. So it gives me a happy feeling and what a delightful use to make of an empty metal box formerly occupied by a cheerless black public telephone. This particular afternoon there is a dog tied up outside, a short-haired mutt of some indeterminate breed with spots of gray and black. He looked friendly enough and he was, after all, tied up, so I thought what the hell and went running past and the dog leaped and took a bite of my ass. He didn't get to my skin but he did grab hold of the bottom of my jacket and scared the shit out of me. I continued but then stopped and it occurred to me, wait a minute, what if some woman goes by with a toddler and the dog takes another leap and this time grabs hold of some baby flesh. It worried me, so I went back and popped my head into the restaurant and said, hey, the dog outside here just tried to bite me. I had to repeat myself because nobody seemed to register what I was saying, they just looked at me like I was a crazy person. A middle-aged Asian guy sitting on a stool by the window going to town on a burrito suddenly looked anxious and said, it's my dog, and got up to go outside and do what he needed to do with the dog. I didn't stick around, but since he didn't ask, I thought I should tell him the dog didn't hurt me, or tear my jacket, and I held my jacket out to show where the tear would have been if the dog had torn my jacket. He didn't seem very interested, so I left.

There's a leash law with a fine of $140 though I have yet to see it enforced. Nevertheless it's the law and the anger I feel at the people who let their dogs go unleashed is intense. I've read stories about people getting mauled to death. It happens. So I get pissed. And I can't stop yelling. As if I, too, were some sort of dog. Barking and barking and barking. In front of a cave entrance, thousands of years ago, when the threats were a little more obvious, and people paid attention.

And Now for Something Completely Efferent

The sound of the rain can be heard through the cracks in the windows. These aren't actual cracks. There are no cracks in the glass. The windows are open a crack. This prevents condensation. But there are cracks. There is a crack in the drywall of the window frame, and another in the northwest corner of the bedroom. I will fix them later.

We decide, once again, not to move. This isn't the first time we've discussed moving and then came down with a serious case of cold feet. It wasn't that we were fickle, or insufficiently motivated. We truly were desperate to find a little more space and get away from condo politics. But the world was a very different place then the one to which we'd grown accustomed in the 1970s. There were much greater risks involved. The volatility and rapacity of Wall Street had spread throughout the entire culture. The signs at this juncture seemed particularly ominous. The triumph of neoliberalism had weakened all the safety nets. It would be relatively easy to get a mortgage, but doing so would lock Ronnie into a job when she hoped to retire early, or at least work fewer hours. She wanted to pursue her writing and felt cramped and exhausted by a grueling work schedule. Nor did we trust the banks.

Ronnie adds an article in the *New York Times* today to our "favorite" list. The banks are at it again, creating dubious financial products, such as "collateralized debt obligations," which evade the few regulations imposed after the collapse in 2008. The old excesses are creeping back into the market.

I will have to do the best I can to adjust to Rocco's thumping and creaking around late at night, Terri's peculiar showers, Lyle and Cindy's nerve-wracking aggression, the insane man next door blabbing away into his Blackberry, and the clutter that is the interior of our apartment. I have fantasies of buying a fold-out couch and putting it in the living room, then moving a good number of our bookcases into the bedroom, which I create into an office, a quiet place for the distillations of the brain and the dilations of the soul.

But a fold-out couch won't work: Ronnie has to get up early and have breakfast. It would feel awkward to have me lying in bed next to her while she tries to enjoy her breakfast. Other strategies will have to be incubated, consolidated and hatched.

Meanwhile, there is our old friend indeterminacy.

I escape into language where the words sag with hope and valentines. I boil the vapor of appearance in the spongy mass of a wool piano. The syntax squirts. Palominos rip the sod. Gravity hammers a stone guitar.

What paradox that the art of manipulating objects with signs that are exterior and alien to them! And of which even the correspondence with them is altogether arbitrary! It's necessary that each thing be doubled by a phantom where the sign attaches itself, another phantom. The signs combined, combine the phantoms — and a special machine permits the return of phantoms to things — and by their imposition on things, awaits the same fate that the accommodating phantoms have endured in that bizarre location where they're slaves to the signs. So writes Paul Valéry in his *Notebooks*.

Syllables: everything is syllables. For instance, here is an emotion: it tastes of clairvoyance, but looks like a stew. There are no monotonous odors in our house. This is why I prefer wearing denim. I write for the sheer pleasure of folding my opinions into quadrilaterals and bagpipes. For the exploration of nothingness. For adapting my grammar to the grammar of the world. Or not. I press my ear to the blood of a cat. The biology of a consonant glides through the anatomy of a dollar and gets hooked on a murmuring phantom. This results in insemination.

I move my hand across a sheet of paper. Words come out of my hand. An elevator arrives and its doors slide open revealing a shepherd and his flock. I scrub the distance between a bistro and an explanation for light. The definition for twilight is warped by fatalism. The flowers all thrive in a sulky anonymity. I search for your caress as aggressively as an asterisk in a liter of swallows. The waves unroll their scripture of foam on the absorbing sand. A sense of autonomy collides with a stain of adjectives spread across the giant nipple of an acoustic emotion. Faith runs across the Mediterranean and delivers a granite baby. You might think that none of these sentences are connected but I assure you that they are. I'm braced for anything. The death of a planet. The strain of a glockenspiel. A pile of words writing themselves into rooms and embassies.

MEETING REMBRANDT

It's a Saturday morning and I wake up pissed. Rocco had once again awakened me during the night, shortly after I had fallen asleep. As an insomniac, I treasure sleep. Falling asleep is no small thing. I did manage to make it back to sleep, but it wasn't that smooth, deep, healing sleep that leaves you feeling refreshed and refurbished. It was that fitful sleep of grotesque, violent nightmares and howling storms and Nazi Martian vampires that leaves you feeling choleric and cantankerous the next day.

Rocco and Terri had been entertaining some guests, which is irritating when you're trying to read and the sound of voices cuts through your meditations and deforms your concentration, but it's nothing to legitimately complain about, it is, after all, a Friday night, so what the hell. That's what people do. They have their friends over for drinks and TV and laughter.

I'm arguing constantly for the legitimacy to make a complaint. I hate my reputation as Building Grouch. But as a wise man once told me it's better to be a pain in the neck than have a pain in the neck.

Kelly, the previous tenant of the apartment above us, worked as a physical therapist and had normal hours, going to bed at about the same time we did, so that it was quiet when you needed it to be quiet.

Not so with Rocco. He came home about midnight from his swing shift and clunked and bumped around until two or three in the morning, stopping to take a shower at about 1:00 A.M., which he did with the maximum amount of noise. He did not seem to have a grasp of the plumbing. He induced sounds from the plumbing I did not think were possible. He was like a John Cage of the bathroom. He elicited an array of exotic noises. He must have been carrying a load of dishes into the kitchen when he woke me up. It was the clatter of porcelain and cutlery and something hitting the floor that did it. I woke with alarm. And in the morning I was still pissed.

I composed an email. I modulated its tones. It went from outright belligerence and incrimination and bald, seething anger to a gentle invocation for quiet. I strategized. I unfolded my plans to contact soundproofing contractors to come and help with our noise problem. I used the word *contractor* repeatedly, and calculatedly, because he will understand what that means. He will know that contractors lead to noise and disrupting during the mornings he will be trying to sleep. Most importantly, he will know how serious I am about the whole thing.

I don't send it. I put it in draft form so that I can continue to work on it and make some decisions. I fuss with it as I would a prose poem, making sure the tone is firm but not too shrill, making sure my argument is sound and fully reasoned and legitimate. I want to be diplomatic. I want to preserve good relations. I urge Rocco and Terri to buy a rug. A large thick rug. It's the easiest, most cost-effective solution to the problem of noise caused by a hardwood floor when you're the party who has to live beneath it. I even offer to pay for it. I Google a few rugs to price a few. They're not that much money. I also mention, pointedly, that putting down a rug was discussed at our condo meeting when Cal was campaigning for his hardwood floor. Everyone, including Clark Pruitt, Rocco's landlord, agreed that a rug was the best way to muffle hardwood floor noise.

But is the offer to pay for a rug such a good idea? I can't make up my mind. I waffle and waver. The email sits like a missile in its silo. I want to make sure it will make its point without causing bigger problems. It makes me nervous having it there. It's also reassuring to have it there. I consider sharing a nuclear launch code with Ronnie, to make sure I don't fire it during a moment of anger and later regret it.

I go online and post a paragraph on Facebook, an excerpt from an essay by Walter Benjamin titled, "Experience and Poverty," in which he refers to the joyless properties of glass: "It is no coincidence that glass is such a hard, smooth material to which nothing can be fixed. A cold and sober material into the bargain. Objects made of glass have no 'aura.' Glass is, in general, the enemy of secrets. It is also the enemy of possession."

I add a photo of Dale Chihuly's Garden and Glass exhibit beneath it to underscore Benjamin's point. But just to be sure everyone gets the connection, I add, "That this aura-less, cold, sober chapel of bourgeois vapidity has replaced the ebullience of the Fun Forest is an injury to the spirit. It speaks to Seattle's sea-change from an affordable, art-friendly city to a cheerless, affluent dysphoria of clueless bobos."

I loved the Fun Forest. This was a carnival-like zone left over from Seattle's World Fair in 1962, the identical place where a ten-year-old Kurt Russell kicks Elvis Presley in the shin in the movie *It Happened at the World's Fair*. There were rides such as a jeweled Borrelli carousel, a Windstorm roller coaster offering a smooth fast ride laid out in a multiple figure eight configuration, Wild River log flume, bumper cars, the Kiddy Galleon, the Rainbow Chaser, and an Orbiter which featured a cluster of cars mounted on arms radiating from a central axis that lifted into a 90 degree horizontal position when the ride was spinning. There were games of skill offering stuffed animals as prizes, stands selling hot dogs and cotton candy, and a Flight to Mars ride whose interior décor was studded with black lights and glow paint. It's all gone now, replaced with the cheerless Chihuly exhibit with its strong commercial appeal and shabby pretense at art.

It's a bright, sunny afternoon and the temperature is starting to rise into the lower 60s. Ronnie and I decide to hop on a bus and go to the art museum to see Rembrandt and a few other Dutch masters. I love seventeenth-century Dutch art. Alas, there will be no Vermeer, but there will be some canvases and techniques similar to Vermeer.

And there are: I'm transfixed by *A View of the Maas at Dordrecht* by Aelbert Cuyp. The delicacy of the ships, the beauty of the clouds, the feeling of reality in the serene water. The effects of the light are like sweet soft theorems of illumination in paint. He has distorted reality to depict reality. He has obscured reality to illumine reality. Cuyp was skilled at altering the direction of light in a painting, bringing it to a diagonal position from the back of the picture, so that the viewer faced the sun more or less directly. The light appears to be emanating from the paint. This also gave a greater feeling of depth to the space. I could dwell on this one painting for an hour. But I continue. The gallery shines with seventeenth-century light.

I see *Family in a Mediterranean Seaport* by Jan Baptist Weenix, *A Canal in Winter* by Isaac van Ostade, and *Old London Bridge* by Claude de Jongh. All the paintings on display are from the Kenwood House collection in Hampstead, London, on the northern boundary of Hampstead Heath. It must have been there when John Keats lived nearby. The collection was once owned by Edward Cecil Guinness, the first Earl of Iveagh, an Irish philanthropist and businessman. He died in 1927, bequeathing his home and collection to the nation.

The highlight of the show is Rembrandt's *Self Portrait with Two Circles.* I've seen this painting many times before, but the reality of it, and its immense size, is stunning. Rembrandt appears so astonishingly real and present and soulfully available for meditations on art or philosophy or just the dubious ritual of visiting an art museum that one's own presence becomes unavoidable and real. Whatever shadows and distractions have been clinging to you throughout the day dissipate. It is you and this old man.

And he is old, no question of that. His jowls sag, his nose has the bulbous fleshiness associated with heavy drinking, his hair is white and long, his body is corpulent and heavy, an effect heightened by the heavy fur-lined robe he wears, and the white nightcap is a clear signal that he has entered the night-time of his life. It will soon be lights out and sleep forever. But there is still great light and energy in his eyes and the way he holds his mahlstick and paintbrushes and palette is nothing less than regal. His face is highly expressive. There is great sadness and maturity there. He has experienced the inevitable losses and disappointments of this all too mortal life, and he is burdened with poverty and debt. But he is triumphant. He has his creativity. It's still going strong. This painting is proof of that.

After taking in nearly all the seventeenth-century paintings I entered the adjoining galleries which segued into the eighteenth century, featuring work by Sir Joshua Reynolds and Thomas Gainsborough. I've never been too excited about this phase in western European painting, but now that the same disparities of wealth and poverty that led to the French Revolution are in play again, it is particularly galling to see these aristocratic pricks and their progeny. The conventions of eighteenth-century painting with their values of harmony, cool elegance and casual grace, are pleasing to the eye and give one a sense of balance and meaning to the universe, but this is a reflection of aristocratic wealth, the people who employed painters such as Gainsborough and Reynolds. The work of poets and painters such as William Blake during this era give a very different view, a critical perspective that I happen to share. I feel like Jean-Paul Marat wandering these galleries.

My heels are dogged by a tour group that began at approximately the same time that Ronnie and I started our viewing. An elderly woman leads a group of some fifteen or twenty people of differing ages and genders, though few are younger than thirty. She seems to know her stuff and speaks with enthusiasm about the paintings, parenthetically inserting allusions to the

European collections and museums she and her husband have visited on their travels. Her group caught up with me at Sir Joshua Reynolds's portrait of Kitty Fisher as Cleopatra dissolving a pearl. According to Pliny the Elder, in an effort to impress Marc Antony with her prodigality, Cleopatra put out a great feast and at the end plopped a pearl into a goblet of vinegar and then drank it after the pearl dissolved. Reynolds chose this story for a particular reason, and I was eager to hear about it. I was listening to the story of Kitty on the little audio wand the museum provides at the entry to the show, how this remarkably beautiful and charismatic woman rose from a humble life as a milliner to become one of London's most notorious femmes fatales, known for her affairs with men of wealth, such as George William Coventry, the sixth Earl of Coventry, when the elderly woman with her flock of tourists intruded on me and began speaking as if I weren't standing there. I moved on, and went to find a painting that the tour group wouldn't reach for a few minutes.

This turned out to be one of the strangest paintings I'd ever seen. *Hawking in Olden Time* by Sir Edwin Henry Landseer presents a ball of feathers and fury at the center of the picture with a group of medieval hunters faintly represented off to the right margin, riding up a knoll, stunned to see the sight of their falcon bringing down a heron. I couldn't quite make out which eyeball belonged to which bird, so furious and energetic was this conflict. It looked like a whirling asteroid of feathers. I lingered long enough for the tour group to arrive and listened to the guide explain the nostalgia for the past people felt during the time this painting was achieved, in 1832, right at the beginning of the Industrial Revolution. I saw something other than just nostalgia. The birds were so engulfed in a frenzy of survival and predation I could not help but feel a high level of anxiety. One world was ending, another was beginning.

I did not expect to see Turner. I did not at first know that I was looking at a Turner. When I think of Turner I imagine dramatic atmospheric effects, black engines in radiant mists, imposing buildings engulfed in flames. Dramas of air and light in which the overarching mood is clear as a Wagnerian opera but the specifics of what is occurring are ambiguous. *A Coast Scene with Fishermen Hauling a Boat Ashore* was highly detailed and offered a very clear narrative: two boats have been run ashore and a third is at the mercy of breakers during a mighty tempest that is pounding the shore with unabashed fury. A group of men struggled mightily with muscle and rope to keep the two boats from being swept back out to sea. I could feel the wind. I could feel the wet salt air sting my cheeks. The dark mingling grays of the sky and the white gnashing waves were sublime and merciless. I was trying to make out the fish and detritus on the beach but the tour group engulfed me and the guide's opening words capsized my attention. I made for the exit.

When Ronnie and I arrived home Cindy was at work on the front porch, scraping it with a stainless steel palette knife and a wire brush. This was the third time in two years she was painting the porch. It's been a frustration for all of us in the building, but for her especially, since this has been her project. The paint keeps chipping and flaking, resulting in a calico surface of sour yellow cream and battleship gray. I offer to help. Ronnie and I go in, change our clothes, and return, each of us provided with a palette knife from my toolbox. It's hard work. We spend an hour at it. We tell her we visited the exhibit of Dutch art at the Seattle art museum. I tried to describe the power of the Joseph Turner canvas, since her Lyle is a fisherman. Cindy tells us she and Lyle visited the Chihuly exhibit recently. She didn't seem that enthusiastic. It occurs to me to share my recent posting on Facebook, and my opinion about Dale Chihuly's glass art, but decide to keep silent on the subject, and keep scraping away at the porch.

THE FUNNIES

I get up, pour myself some coffee, and sit down at the computer to check email. I hear noises coming from the hallway. I get up to see what's going on. I peek through the peephole in our door and see Cindy sitting on her haunches amid a bunch of gardening tools and paint cans which she has removed from the storage closet under the stairway. She must have a hair up her butt about cleaning the storage bin. It's 9:00 A.M. on a Sunday morning and she is within a few feet of where Sam no doubt lies abed. I assume this began when Cindy finished painting the porch this morning and was putting her supplies away when a bulb lit over her head and she decided to give the storage closet a cleaning. I hope she finishes soon.

I listen to a woman read *La bécasse* by Guy de Maupassant on *Littérature Audio*. A *bécasse* is a snipe, a wading bird with a long, needle-like beak for hunting invertebrates in the mud and water. The Baron de Ravots had, for forty years, been the champion sportsman of his province, but after being paralyzed by a stroke he has been confined to a chair for the last five or six years. He enjoys having his friends visit and shoot pigeons from the window or doorway. During dinner, they play a favorite game, which is to take the head of the snipe, attach it to a cork and needle, and set it atop a bottleneck in order to spin it round. Whomever the needle-like beak of the bird points to must tell a story. Such is the introductory story to a small collection of short stories.

After listening to the story, I get up to see if Cindy is finished with her work. I peek through the peephole. I see no one, and the closet door is shut. I open our door and pick up the Sunday paper.

Ronnie subscribes. I don't read it. The paper has an obvious right-wing bias and when I do read it, I get boiling mad and write letters to the editor that don't get published. So I've learned to avoid the news and go straight to the comics.

I like *Dilbert*. *Dilbert* is usually right on with its dig at corporate culture. This week is no exception. The boss, with his balding head and tufts of hair that point up like horns, giving him a devilish look, tells his employees that their bonuses will be based on the usual formula. Fifty percent is based on pure luck, and fifty percent is based on the performance of people they've never met. This year, he tells them, the luck factor was good and their industry experienced huge consumer demand. Unfortunately, the people that none of them have ever met did a horrible job of marketing and sales were terrible. This means the engineers, including Dilbert, must be punished. They will receive no bonus. But the boss gleefully announces that his bonus is based on how well he can convince "you idiots" (Dilbert and his coworkers) to work hard without receiving bonuses. "I don't like to brag," he says in the last panel, "but I'm fairly sure I'm nailing it."

I can't stand *Doonesbury*. Trudeau is usually so middle-of-the-road I don't understand his point, his gentle satire, and it doesn't help that all of his characters are now engrossed in digital media, laptops and smartphones.

Get Fuzzy is another favorite. Darby Conley's flair for zany black humor generally cracks me up. I love the way the cat is drawn with his two huge demonic eyeballs and black fuzzy head. He contrasts nicely with Satchel's amiable doofus-y clue-lessness.

I always read *Beetle Bailey*, but I don't know why. It's so intensely, flagrantly stupid. In all these years, Beetle has never gone to war. They occasionally have war exercises, but they're no more serious than a game at summer camp. Paintball conflicts have more violence. And Beetle's conflicts with Sarge, which are really that of an adolescent having conflicts with his father, are tiresomely repetitive and clichéd.

Martha Stewart, at 71, is on the cover of *Parade*. She sits casually on a kitchen stool, her hair nicely blonde and shiny, wearing a dark blue V-neck shirt and smiling. She leans forward a little, as if she were a jet approaching take off. I look at her hands: they're unusually rough, the hands of someone who works hard. I find this surprising, considering Stewart's considerable wealth.

Ronnie threw the universe away on Monday. This occurred on a very noisy day. The owner of the duplex on the east side of our building, an older house dating from the late-1930s or early 1940s, went to work remodeling the upper apartment, hammering and sawing away, windows open, so that we could hear everything. He had been asking $2,800 a month for the two-bedroom apartment, whose kitchen was modest and offered very little cupboard space. But the apartment had been totally remodeled less than five years ago. Rather than ask a little less rent, the owner, a man in his early sixties with cropped white hair with a squat muscular build determined and solid as a tank, decided to remodel. All the new material that went into the last remodel got gutted and tossed.

The universe was an inflatable black ball imprinted with the known constellations and galaxies. It was a mnemonic device for learning astronomy. It had become irredeemably dusty over the years. We kept it perched atop a pitcher and bowl I inherited from my grandmother. It nested perfectly there. The pitcher and bowl are porcelain and printed with blue flowers. The bowl reminds me of those scenes in Westerns in which the gunslinger or sheriff or cowboy stay at a hotel with pretty white curtains and dip their hands into the soapy water and splash it on their face and wipe it off with a towel. Then they go and get in a gun duel.

We were dismantling the bed frame so that a man could come on Tuesday to take it to his shop, sandblast and refinish it. It was an iron frame painted white, though a great deal of the white paint had flaked off and the dark iron underneath shown through. The finials were brass.

On Tuesday, my sinuses hurt. I don't know if it's an allergy, or a cold. I try to think if we have any medication for this, but can't think of anything outside of ibuprofen and morphine. I have ibuprofen, but no morphine. I ask Ronnie if she can bring some Theraflu home. But then we find that there is no Theraflu. The Theraflu factory in Lincoln, Nebraska, has been shut down for renovation. Until then, no Theraflu.

That night I discover that sleeping closer to the ground is not demonstrably different from sleeping a few feet higher. The clock is harder to see; I have to lift my body up to get a look at it. I also have to reach a little higher to press the buttons on the CD player.

Sleeping near the floor is like being on a raft. I think about Huckleberry Finn and Jim moving slowly down the Mississippi at night. Black water. Deep quiet. It helps to focus on these two people. I have an extremely hard time relaxing my mind at night and getting to sleep. I find it difficult to let all the perceived threats and monstrosities of a worried mind dissipate into vapor. I know they're not real. I know that worrying about things is like trying to solve a math problem by chewing gum. I get that. I just can't seem to do it. Let it go. The harder I try to let go, the tighter the worries grab and wrap themselves around my brain. So here I am on a raft, I tell myself. I'm Jim. I've just escaped from slavery. The night air feels good. But then the Duke of Bridgewater and King of France show up and ruin it all. I wish Mark Twain hadn't introduced those two characters. But then, where would the story be?

Thanks to the luxury of being able to take a little extra lorazepam, I get to sleep. Nevertheless, when I get up the next day my nose gets a lot worse. My body isn't aching, which is a good sign, nor do I appear to have a fever, but something is going on. The membranes of my nose and sinuses tingle with ultra-sensitivity. I start blowing my nose. The nose-blowing accelerates. Before long, the nose-blowing occurs every two minutes.

By Thursday, it becomes obvious I don't have a cold, I have an allergy. A humdinger of an allergy. My nose is running like a broken hydrant in Hoboken and every time I sneeze I blow the roof off our building. I blame the dusty rusty bed-dismantling operation. That, and going for a run with tons of early-May pollen floating in the air. The four-day Pollencast on the internet Weather Channel registers a very high amount of pollen.

I look up histamine on Wikipedia. Histamine is an organic nitrogen compound involved in local immune responses as well as regulating physiological function in the gut and acting as a neurotransmitter. Histamine triggers the inflammatory response. Don't I know that!

I write a check to renew our *Harper's Magazine* subscription. I blow my nose. I get a stamp to put on the envelope in which I have inserted a check. I blow my nose. I discover that the envelope has been prepaid. I don't need a stamp. I return the stamp. I blow my nose. I take the letter out to the mailbox in the hallway. I come back. I go to the bathroom. I blow my nose. I blow my nose into a paper towel. Blowing my nose into a paper towel is so much more satisfactory than blowing my nose in a Kleenix tissue. The tissue is soft and falls apart. I can really let go with a paper towel.

Pollen or no pollen I go for a run. It's too beautiful outside not to. Everything is dripping with haiku. I hear some wind chimes hanging by someone's door on a white porch, see buds beginning to appear on the chestnuts on Bigelow. Pink blossom on a green Corolla. A police cruiser passes me as I run down Eighth Avenue West, the street with a panoramic overlook of Puget Sound and the Olympic Mountains. The cruiser stops near the intersection of Eighth Avenue West and West Galer Street and a police woman gets out and goes searching for something in the trunk. I wonder what's up. I pass her and see a motorcycle cop giving directions to a driver. His motorcycle is parked nearby, on Galer. I try to make sense of this narrative. They must be preparing for something, but what? This isn't the place for marching or demonstrations. There are no banks to rob. Has there been a burglary? Was the suspect caught?

As soon as Ronnie gets home, she insists on using the computer. She's pissed. She saw a roofer on the way in and immediately wanted to know what Cal was up to, since he'd been squawking about getting another roof drain. It looked to us as if he'd just gone ahead and hired a roofer to do it without consulting the HOA. Before she sends her email, we see Cindy walk by. I run out and ask her if she knows anything about a roofer doing work on the roof today. She doesn't. Ronnie comes out and the two of them go out to the parking lot to talk to the roofer. A little while later, I hear laughter. Ronnie returns and tells me the roofer was just there to check the work the chimney crew had done. He said the roof drain done last January was a crummy job and we could expect to see that leaking in a couple of years. The roofer also lets Ronnie and Cindy in on a secret: contractors hate working for condo associations.

I also find out what was going on with the police I'd seen during my run. A thirty-five-year-old man got in an argument with a fifty-year-old man at the bus stop at the corner of Denny and Aurora Avenue. The thirty-five-year-old man assaulted the fifty-year-old man and the police were called. The police arrived. The thirty-five-year-old man somehow managed to steal a cruiser and the police gave chase. The man crashed into the retaining wall at Eighth Avenue West and Olympia Place. It must have happened shortly after I ran by. We look up an article about it online. There is the cruiser, hanging over the rise in the street, the railing smashed.

To Drive, or
Not to Drive

We were late. Taking the bus had consumed more time than we'd estimated. And we were still a good mile from our destination when we disembarked. We had to run down Capitol Hill's crowded Broadway, a sea of eccentric denizens in black leather, tongue studs and tattoos, stylish shoes with gargantuan heels, cigarettes or joints dangling from mouths, eyes deep in kohl, dodging same-sex couples and surly Sid Vicious phantoms with spiky hair and bony rib cages under ragged T-shirts. I was amazed at how easily I could run without straining my lungs. How was this possible? I had run this same street twenty years in the past, when I was slightly drunk and on my way to a video porn store, and had barely gone twenty feet before I'd stopped, panting, ready to faint, my heels already aching. I was clearly benefitting from twenty years of running and no smoking.

We were on our way to hear Natalie Nussbaum perform her artist diploma recital at Cornish College of the Arts. She was to perform a repertoire of mostly baroque chamber music, composers such as Virgilio Mazzocchi, Sébastien le Camus and Alessandro Scarlatti. We arrived in time to sit down and let the sweat trickle down our backs as we caught our breath and the performers assembled onstage.

Last time we'd come to hear Natalie perform at Cornish we'd driven and parked our car in the lot below the theater. We'd been able to arrive calmly, and with the comforting knowledge that our car, our little old Subaru Justy, would be waiting for us afterward to get us home within ten to fifteen minutes. Jesus, I missed having a car. I was having a tough time persuading myself that taking a bus was not only a viable alternative but lifted the stress and responsibility of private car ownership from us and replaced it with the altruistic euphoria of "going green," saving the planet from being choked on hydrocarbons, and allowing us the privilege to gaze dreamily out of bus windows rather than curse our fellow drivers for their inattention and general assholery.

But it wasn't really working out that way. There was a real rigor in taking the bus. There is walking, and waiting, and more walking, and more waiting. And you had to accustom yourself to a different mode of time. Car time is leagues different from bus time. Except for rush hour and gridlock, you can get places damn quick in a car. Not so with a bus. Because not only does a bus go slower, it has to stop every half mile to pick up a new set of people.

As the musicians readied themselves onstage, I shifted in my seat, tucked my shirt in, and reviewed our recent voyage on the Number 8.

We'd walked about a mile to catch the 8 to Capitol Hill at a stop on Mercer, near the grocery store where Ronnie's bakery was located. It was almost 7:30 P.M. when the driver of the 8 decided to take a small cigarette break. The driver returned to the bus, the air conditioning came back on and we were in movement once again. We may have time, I thought. But what we will do if we don't? Will Natalie notice if we bumble to our seats in a dark theater? The bus stopped at Queen Anne Avenue

North and one of Ronnie's coworkers got on and sat in front of us, a young woman from a village in southeast Turkey, which she said was located in the mountains, near the border. She didn't say which border, with which country. I tried to picture where her village might be in my mind, the countries bordering Turkey, but my geography of that part of the world is hazy, and I ended up saying (stupidly), that would be Persia, right? Yes, she answered graciously, not pointing out my blunder (there has been no Persia since when, the sixteenth century?), Turkey borders Iraq, Armenia, Georgia, Iran and Syria. My village is far to the east, close to Iran. Human settlement in that region goes back at least as far as 5000 B.C. Winters are harsh, but summers are dry and warm. I miss the summers there.

Iran, I think to myself, of course. Why the hell did I say Persia? I blamed the bus. The bus had nothing to do with my ignorance. I just felt like blaming the bus, because it wasn't a car, and I missed having a car.

We talked about the pros and cons of living in Seattle. She liked the city for the most part but couldn't stand the constant damp and gray. I agreed. I told her I spent a decade living in the South Bay area, mostly in San José, but several years in Los Gatos, which I loved. I tell her Los Gatos is like the village she described. It's a mixture of retail and residential. You can get anywhere by walking. It's one of the few places in California where you can get by without a car. Or bus, for that matter.

She talked about a beach in Turkey where you can wade out for a mile and the water doesn't come above your waist. I asked about jellyfish. There are no jellyfish there, but she did get stung once on another occasion, in the Mediterranean. It hurt like hell. It would go away, and then come back again. It took forever to heal.

I enjoyed talking to this person. She had a wonderful accent. She came to Seattle because of her husband, who grew up here. I confessed to her I really don't feel at home anywhere. Not anymore. I felt like I drifted into this century by accident. I don't understand the appeal of cell phones. It grieved me to see books disappear. Everyone has a dog and a mobile phone and a plasma TV. Hardly anyone reads anymore. I feel like an alien.

She appeared to understand what I said, but before this topic evolved any further, her stop came up.

She's really nice, I told Ronnie, who agreed. She's a pleasant person to encounter at work.

The group onstage began to perform, and my attention returned to the light and shadows of the theater. Natalie was accompanied by trumpet and guitar, theorbo and lute.

I was especially fascinated by the lutenist, a man in his early sixties, bald head with a fringe of short white hair, intelligent face. I cannot say why a face looks intelligent, but it does. I wondered with both curiosity and admiration that someone would devote themselves to an instrument and music of such rarity. How many lutenists could there be in the country? In the world? The lute is a beautiful instrument. We had just seen a lute in the play *Taming of the Shrew* by Shakespeare. Hortensio, played by Victor Spinetti in the Zeffirelli production of 1967, plays a lute for Bianca. The lute has a melon shape with a front teardrop-shaped soundboard of thin, resonant wood, usually spruce. The soundboard has a hole with a grille in the form of an intertwining vine or a decorative knot. The neck is made of light wood that has a veneer of hardwood (most often ebony) to furnish solidity and backbone for the fretboard beneath the strings. Renaissance strings were generally made of animal gut, typically from the small intestine of sheep. Modern strings combine nylon since gut is more susceptible to changes in humidity.

Natalie's voice was amazing. She seemed to have an almost infinite range. I marveled at the fact that someone could devote such time and discipline to an art that had long ceased to be part of the general culture, and reminded myself that the practice of poetry is headed in the same direction. The poet has become the equivalent of a lute player, though it's hard to imagine Charles Bukowski bent over a lute playing a baroque composition.

We met with her afterward in an area designated as a small receiving room. The other musicians appeared as well. Ronnie and I felt shy and awkward. Sparkling cider and bottles of water were available and there was a table-load of pastries. I went immediately to the water. I had a powerful thirst. When we got a chance, Ronnie and I went to say hello to Natalie, who was very pleased that we had come. I complimented her on her dress, midnight satin with a mermaid cut. Our conversation was brief, since Natalie had many other friends who wanted to congratulate her. Ronnie and I slipped away, and walked down Capitol Hill's Broadway to catch the Number 8 back to Queen Anne.

It seemed strange to walk down Broadway for a variety of reasons. One was that I used to live nearby. It was my old stomping rounds. I remembered vividly where I used to catch the bus to go to work at the University of Washington mailroom and sit on a retaining wall under a couple of flourishing golden rain trees by Jimmy Woo's Jade Pagoda, which was now a Lab5 Fitness center. The other thing that amazed me was how, after so many of the old funky buildings and stores had been replaced by glitzy chrome and glass luxury suites commanding astronomical prices for a minimal amount of square footage, the population of pinks with spiky mohawks and gay men and women with colorful dresses and personalities had remained the same. The dramatic change in price and architecture had had no effect whatsoever on the demographics. Did these people continue to live here, or did they drive here, or take the bus from one of Seattle's less expensive neighborhoods? These people gave me a happy feeling. They lived on society's margin. They had an aura and a manner of being in the world that gave one a feeling of freedom, tolerance, a carnivalesque warrant for weirdness and gleeful deviancy. It was a mystery to me how they could afford the rents of the surrounding apartments. Capitol Hill had Seattle's densest population of apartment buildings, many of which dated back to the early part of the twentieth century. They were brick structures with ornate cornices and leaded windows and marble lobbies. The newer buildings were handsome, but had a definite aura of costly modernity. A studio of less than 600 square feet typically rented for $1,200 to $1,400.

We arrived at the stop on East Olive for the Number 8. A handful of people were already there. It was a popular stop. Across the street, one of the newer apartment buildings looked quite inviting. One of the lower apartments was right above the Desert Sun Tanning Salon. I wondered if the person living above would get free tans from the rays permeating the apartment. Would it be warm? Would you be able to feel the heat of those ultraviolet lamps?

I did not like waiting for the bus. I am not a patient person. I'm definitely not into fascism, but I do share the Futurist's love of velocity.

There had been a time when all I did was take a bus. I got into the rhythm of that. Cigarettes helped. Maybe that's why so many bus riders smoke cigarettes. But I don't smoke cigarettes anymore, and I had long gotten out of the habit of waiting for buses. I used to be quite good at it. I could occupy a waiting period with ease and grace, particularly if I had a good book to go with my cigarette. I remembered the whole ceremony, peering down the street to see if a bus was coming, and if it wasn't I'd fish out a pack of cigarettes from my breast pocket and light it and kick back and wait, happy to suck smoke in and blow it back out, sometimes (if the air was still) in rings. There is a gentle ease in smoke, the way it drifts, or gets stolen away on a breeze. And the chemical taste mixed in with the tobacco seemed quintessentially urban, as if you were acclimating your mind and body to the rigors of industry, acquiring an immunity.

I hate secondhand cigarette smoke now. I try to move as far away from it as I can. I've frequently noted it's never the people who never smoked who are most bugged by secondhand smoke, but former smokers. It doesn't take much to awaken that raging addiction.

But what really upsets me is to see so many people, nearly everyone, utterly engrossed in smartphones. They truly seemed hypnotized. They were in a trance. It wouldn't have surprised me to see drool fall unconsciously from their mouths. Their eyes seemed empty. Their fingers went mad, scrolling electronic pages up and down. For what reason? It seemed frantic. What were they looking for? Conversations had ceased, even among friends. People would sit at restaurant tables and immediately bring their smartphones out and begin scrolling up and down, ignoring their friends. It was disquieting. Another sign of social decay.

Riding a bus put me into the public much more. When we had our car, we could dash to the store and back, or attend a poetry reading or lecture with minimal contact with the public, outside of the other friends and acquaintances attending an event. I really missed that.

It wasn't long before I really began obsessing about cars. I particularly had in mind another Subaru, a Subaru Impreza. I looked up compact cars in *Consumer Reports*. The Subaru Impreza received the highest marks for reliability, comfort, power and fuel consumption. We could, I realized, afford to buy one. I would have to take money out of my meager retirement fund, but we could do it. It was attainable. I could see it in the driveway, feel my hands on the wheel. I still had the key from the old anti-theft club Ronnie always made me put on the steering wheel. They're a lot of scoundrels in this neighborhood, she would say. Weirdly, as annoying as I found it at the time, I now missed that little ritual.

The main thing holding me back was principle. I'm against cars in principle. They pollute. They kill. They make noise and use up thousands of acres of valuable arable land in order to make parking lots where their hulks of steel and glass and rubber leave spots of grease and oil. Instead of soaking into the earth the way rain is intended to do, percolating down to nourish roots and worms and microorganisms, it flows into the sewage system and thence into Puget Sound where it creates a contrasting brown with the Sound's usual midnight blue of white-capped waves.

Highways and freeways on which to drive them scar and disfigure the earth.

Cars are destroying the planet. I do not want to contribute to that.

Will that change anything? No, of course not.

If I refuse to buy a car and continue to ride the bus, I will not change a thing, will not alter the course of the juggernaut that is warming the climate, creating droughts, destroying crops and burying the planet in concrete and asphalt. This action would strictly be for me. For the benefit of my self-esteem. For the sense of cohesion that gives me a sense of identity. But every time I get the image of a car in my head I feel unmitigated joy. I feel glee. It's an addiction. The yearning for a car is identical to my yearning for morphine, or bourbon or lorazepam.

My body misses the feeling of being in a car. I miss shifting gears, maneuvering in traffic, listening to my CDs at full volume, and subverting time and space with heady accelerations. There is the psychology of it, the feeling of having your options broadened, the world at your doorstep. I miss the convenience of having a car at our immediate disposal.

It's crazy. I can't defend this yearning rationally. I can't come at it with a full, inexorable need. The walk to the bus stop, the wait for the bus, the gymnastics of riding the bus, are effortful, sure, but really not that bad. And you don't need to pay insurance or get speeding tickets or parking tickets or search for a place to park. Yet I long for the complexities of a car, and cannot get the image of a shiny Subaru Impreza out of my head. The delicious curve of a steering wheel. The sound of a seat belt clicking together. The wistful glow of dashboard lights.

We sit down at a booth at the Nonesuch restaurant on upper Queen Anne. It's essentially a bar, but the food is pretty good. The meat loaf especially. We go there for meat loaf. We've just ridden the Number 2 to the top of the hill and are feeling quite hungry. We could pop in for some pasta at the local pizzeria, but we're hooked on meat loaf. We must have meat loaf. The Nonesuch doesn't begin serving dinner until four in the afternoon. It is now 3:30. We browse at the new bookstore. Ronnie was right: it's like an airport bookstore. All I see are trashy bestsellers. I can't wait to get out.

The glazed front wall at the Nonesuch has been removed, joining the interior of the restaurant to the exterior, where a few tables have been set up on the sidewalk, and a young man resembling Colin Farrell is smoking a cigarette. His smoke drifts into the restaurant so I gesture to the bartender if it's ok to take a booth deeper inside. He gestures back that it's ok. We find a booth and sit down.

The napkins have been folded into roses. It's quite spectacular. The art of folding napkins seems to be on the uptake. Napkins have become theater. They're folded so intricately, uniquely, into such a variety of animals and objects and patterns and shapes. A man talking into a microphone, a meat loaf, a soliloquy of cloth, a brain crawling toward a thought. It is astonishing what worlds can be created by folding a napkin. Jimi Hendrix strumming an electric guitar, a lost cat hiding under a hedge of laurel, Elvis Presley singing "That's All Right Mama" on the *Louisiana Hayride* show in 1954. One enters a restaurant and is led to a table and invited to sit down. You sit down. Everyone sits down. You all stare at the napkins. The swans, Ferraris and Impalas, Elizabeth Taylor shouting at Richard Burton in *Who's Afraid of Virginia Woolf.* I'm pretty good at folding towels. I'm not so hot at folding shirts. But the ability to fold a napkin into a suspension bridge or a scene from *The Wizard of Oz* is an impressive feat, and one that I do not take lightly when I take the convolutions of linen into my hands and spread it softly on my lap. And as I do so I surrender myself to reveries of folding and unfolding. The sun unfolds the day. The day unfolds the night. The sun itself is a fold of nuclear fusion. Fourth-dimensional space is folded into three-dimensional space, or vice versa. There are folds of gravity and folds of time. Folds of cerebral cortex, folds of philosophical meaning. Fold upon fold of overtones in the woodwinds of Bach's *Goldberg Variations.* How is it done? How are these things accomplished? How does one fold the phenomenon of distance? Of a propagating wave of light? How does one do that? Where does one begin? With the right corner, the left corner, all four corners simultaneously? How does one flip it, crease it, tuck it?

One begins with a periodic lattice in a higher dimension. Fold the lattice by taking one end and sliding it under the other end. Make your folds exciting and smooth. Make them subtle as the heart of a bubble. Make them as convoluted and many as the folds of the brain. As a golden mean convulsing in a glass of milk. Make your folds deliver tendencies of shape. Shorelines incidental to the memory of a dance. Storm waves, sea caves, columns of rock. Make your folds long and wide and cinematic. Make them glide and hover over a table of horsetail fern and browsing brontosauri. Make your folds balance a metaphor on a vacuum. If you can fold a sweater, you can fold a hemstitch cotton napkin into a telescope and hold the universe in a lens of incidental linen while you bring a mouthful of tender halibut to your lips and the room expands and the weight of a thousand shadows ripples through the rings of Saturn.

Now, doesn't that halibut taste good? Taste special? Taste different? Folds of flavor juggle sensation on the palate.

One afternoon, after getting off the Number 4 bus on Galer, we heard the wind whistle through the radio towers atop Queen Anne. There are three altogether. The third is farther to the west. These two rose high in the sky, humming the rough overtones of a tempestuous sky. Rags of cloud blew through the girders. These three radio towers, seen from a distance, have always given Queen Anne hill a regal look. The hill itself has an elevation of 456 feet, making it the tallest of Seattle's seven hills. The tower farthest to the east, the KING TV tower, is the one chosen to hang Christmas lights on every winter, the day after Thanksgiving. The tower was erected sometime in 1947 and made its first television broadcast on November 10, 1948. Seattle had six hundred televisions. A crowd gathered downtown at Frederick & Nelson's department store. In order to strengthen the fuzzy image within the studio, the crew applied white powder to their faces, which gave them a cadaverous look. For further contrast, and so that it might be apparent that mouths were moving and words were being shaped by animate skin, men applied brown lipstick, women blue. They looked like zombies. The more things change, the more they remain the same.

Ronnie signed up for a Car2Go. We haven't been able to use it yet. It takes days to get the card, or whatever they send you in the mail that will allow her to activate one of their cars. It's like applying for a passport. The Car2Go gives me a lot of anxiety. I've read less than enthusiastic things about their call center. And the range of things that can go wrong is quite formidable, including not being able to log off while the clock is still ticking and you're being charged by the minute and the call center has you on hold for an interminable amount of time, or being immobilized in Seattle's dense immovable traffic, or getting into a fender bender with a clueless adolescent with no insurance, or an attorney in a brand new BMW. What happens then?

Today the sky is a mottled disarray of blue and gray. The day feels neutral and vague. I make some scrambled eggs and slather some strawberry jam on a piece of toast and watch some people in Switzerland argue in French on TV5MONDE. I can only pick up certain phrases. The thin woman with the thick black shoulder-length hair appears to be in distress concerning some beach property that belongs to her family. She has a son with a mental disability. She talks to a young man full of hope and enthusiasm who tries to encourage her to take some form of action to defend the beach property, though I can't tell what it is specifically. Another man, who appears to be her husband, is a sourpuss. He appears to be in a lot of pain. He's never happy. He's always at work and when he's interrupted by the woman he gets angry. Abruptly, there is a scene in which she's swimming in the lake. The water must be freezing, but she appears very relaxed.

I will not be swimming in Lake Washington this year. I don't want to get sick like I did last summer and spend an entire day in the hospital having antibiotics dripped into my veins. I will go swimming in the imagination. I will twang and twinkle and dream. I will weave sensations of the outer world into inner worlds and roll the inner worlds into the outer world by way of language. By way of sentences. By way of a brain crawling toward a thought, a nuance as delicate as the odor of faded lilac in a sepia print. Is there anything more explicit than a human leg? There is meat loaf. There is a man playing a lute. There is the clash of cymbals.

Yesterday I saw a fire engine on fire. Black smoke billowed out of the cab. The fire engine was parked right in front of the station, a temporary station, which is a large white tent. I wasn't sure if this was intended as an exercise or not. The firemen were dressed in their firefighting gear and running a hose of water into the cab to the put the fire out. How in the world does the cab of a fire engine catch fire?

I think about fire. I think about words. I think about money. James Kunstler writes that the Federal Reserve intends to juice the financial markets with U.S. Treasury bonds and miscellaneous securities with the goal of putting downward pressure on longer-term interest rates and thus support economic activity and job creation by making financial conditions more accommodating. Which is a polite way of saying fake wealth. Smoke and mirrors.

There is often a kind of poetry to finance. Their operations are so delightfully abstract. And unreal. Money has no reality. Its value has no reality. You can't eat money. You can't eat gold or silver. Where does value come from? Who makes value? What is extrinsic value? What is intrinsic value? Intrinsic value is value that something has "in itself," or "for its own sake," or "in its own right." Its value does not derive from anything else. Thomas Hobbes believed the goodness or badness of something to be constituted by the desire or aversion one may have regarding it. David Hume also subscribed to the view that all ascriptions of value involve projections of one's own sentiments onto whatever is said to have value. This makes it the whole argument subjective and fuzzy. It does not help me decide whether having a car is of higher value than not owning a car. Neither Thomas Hobbes nor David Hume drove cars.

John Dewey, who did drive a car, at least once (he hit a tree), suggested that, since the world is always changing in such a way that the solution to one problem becomes the source of another, and that what may be an end in one context is a means to an end in another, it is a mistake to seek a timeless list of goods and evils, of goals to be attained for their own sake.

Which makes intrinsic value all the more elusive. This is all I know: rivers inspire reverie. Sunlight penetrating the foliage of a thick forest is beautiful. When a hedge of wild lilac loses its petals the sidewalk gets a thick coating of deep blue petals. A window without a dream is just a window. When an image crashes among its words the sentence convulses into a coat hanger. Removing a hinge pin and coating it with olive oil will quiet a squeaky door. Chaos gets our attention. Car rental agencies never give you the economy car you request but a much bigger car which also happens to be the only car available at the moment — take or leave it. Perceptions wander my skin when I shave. A horse is virtuous and paper when it is written in blue ink. Cézanne discovered a universe of cubes on a prominence of rock. There is a pivotal point in everyone's life when one's narrative trajectory alters quite dramatically and goes in a different direction. Nature is a riddle. There is a latent pterodactyl in all of us, and DNA is a helix.

Why is DNA a helix? I find that curious.

So are fingernails. They grow so rapidly. One day they're nicely trimmed and the next day they've gotten long and get in the way of your plunking on the computer keyboard. Hair, too, hair grows with a strange rapidity though perhaps not so much for a person who has just had a terrible haircut and must now go around like that for X number of days and months.

I like things that change, color and climate, I like flux, I like flow, but I also like enduring monuments and the feeling and look of marble, the feel of a freshly squeezed sponge and water rushing out and diminishing into a drip. Sensations are wonderful. There isn't anything to figure out. No calculation involved. You just feel things.

And here is a wonderful thing: my Achilles tendon has stopped hurting. It stopped hurting the exact same day I ordered an aerobic step bench to exercise the tendon and prevent it from hurting. It had been hurting each day for over a month. And stopped. The very moment the article I sent for was charged to our credit card. Some things are magic. Some things are not. They're not exactly magic. They're another phenomenon. One that involves coincidence, and credit cards, and luck.

And what is luck?

"There's always the same amount of good luck and bad luck in the world," observed Tom Robbins. "If one person doesn't get the bad luck, somebody else will have to get it in their place. There's always the same amount of good and evil, too. We can't eradicate evil, we can only evict it, force it to move across town. And when evil moves, some good always goes with it. But we can never alter the ratio of good to evil. All we can do is keep things stirred up so neither good nor evil solidifies. That's when things get scary. Life is like a stew, you have to stir it frequently, or all the scum rises to the top."

Luck is a lady. Luck is a tug at the sleeve. Luck is a goddess tapping you on the shoulder. Luck is a tactic that hardly ever works, but when it does work, it blows the top of your head off.

There is no luck. There is no moral fiber to the universe. But there are towns and highways and signs and garages with chuckling mechanics and calendars with pretty girls in skimpy little bathing suits. There are velocities and amplitudes and ontologies and parallels. There are nuts and bolts and gasoline and wheels. There is chance and randomness and probability and infinite sequence.

This inner philosophizing over value was camouflage. Bullshit. The upshot was: I wanted a car. I was jonesing for a car. I couldn't stand it anymore. I had to get a car. I went to the bank and took some money out of my savings, enough for the price of a car, called a dealer, described what I wanted, a Subaru Impreza in Venetian red with a manual shift, he said, sure, we can get that on the lot for you tomorrow, and waited for Ronnie to come home.

But when Ronnie came home and we were deciding whether to get to the car lot by bus or taxi the thought of a car sitting idly in the parking lot began to weigh on my consciousness with actuality. What if, I suggested, we used this money to go to Paris, instead of buying a car?

I'm all for it, said Ronnie. That sounds fantastic.

I'm still not sure how it happened, but somehow a Venetian red Subaru with manual shift turned into a trip to Paris.

We reserved a room for six nights at the Hôtel Récamier in the Left Bank and seats aboard Air France for a roundtrip to Paris. It happened so fast I hardly had time to blink and bam we were on our way to France.

I looked up the carry-on luggage rules for Air France thinking they might be different than the rules to which we'd already grown accustomed. Air France allows one standard carry-on bag per person and one accessory — handbag, notebook computer, camera, etc. The restrictions for the carry-on bag were given in centimeters so Ronnie jotted them down and converted them into inches and I got my black leather carry-on bag out of the closet and a tape measure out of my toolbox and measured it. Air France allowed 21.65 inches in length, 13.78 inches for the width, and 9.43 inches in height. All this included pockets, handles and wheels. My bag didn't have handles or wheels, but it did have a few pockets. Not to mention wrinkles, crinkles and history. The bag had been to San Francisco, New York and Minot, North Dakota, a few times. That's a lot of history, but whatever that history weighed was restricted to the vagaries of my mind. The bag measured in at 21 inches in length, 12 inches in width and 14 inches in height. I couldn't see a flight attendant making a stink over an excess height of four and a half inches. Unless we packed it to the bursting brim of its sad existence, it wouldn't fully distend to 14 inches anyway. There was also a maximum weight of 25.6 pounds allowed, but since it would be August, it's unlikely it would weigh that much. I hadn't any intention of packing an anvil or auxiliary jet engine in case one of them went out and I offered to hang another one on the wing for them mid-flight.

There were plenty of other details, but they could wait. We had a couple of months ahead of us. Meanwhile, we had Port Townsend to think about. That was coming up. Ronnie was off in a few days and we'd made plans to visit a friend in Port Townsend, a novelist named Valerie Delain. She was in her seventies, though she retained a very youthful aura. We had met for the first time last November, when she and I read together at Elliott Bay Book Company in celebration of a literary journal that had just come out called *Automatic Radish*.

Neither of us had been in Port Townsend in eighteen years. We went there in February 1995, shortly after getting married, as a sort of honeymoon. We stayed at a bed and breakfast that offered a variety of rooms whose décor and ambient spirit was intended to reflect the sensibility of an English poet. Robert Browning, Algernon Swinburne, Dante and Gabriel Rossetti, and William Butler Yeats. There may have been several others who escaped my notice, rooms decorated *à la* George Eliot or Edward Lear. We stayed in the Yeats Room, which was predominantly yellow and featured a clawfoot bathtub situated dramatically in the center of the room raised on a slab of marble with peacock feathers flaring out from the shower curtains. It seemed both decadent and beguiling in a *Celtic Twilight* sort of way.

I fantasized about other rooms mimicking the style and deportment of other poets. Charles Bukowski, for instance, what would his room be like? I imagined a scene of chaos, unmade bed, crushed beer cans, fake rubber vomit on the writing desk. Or Jack Kerouac. Bare, austere, with a crucifix over the writing desk and a 1953 copy of the *Railroad Brakeman's Manual* on the end table, next to an old Philco radio. I thought of Emily Dickinson, but her room eluded me. I gave it a shot, anyway. There would most certainly be flowers, and a closet full of delicate camisoles and Mother Hubbard dresses, and a shelf-load of books, and a Hindu elephant with his trunk upraised in a bedroom window facing east, toward a graveyard.

Yeah, I could see that. And Emily gazing out. Blinking, the light bright against the glass, not sunlight, no, but mother of pearl, the color of gauze, of gray going gradually into lavender, that kind of light, the light of diffusion, and the feeling of moisture everywhere, penetrating, piercing, the marble and granite tombstones glistening in the rain.

> And Oh, the Shower of Stain —
> When Winds — upset the Basin —
> And spill the Scarlet Rain —

WILD LILAC

We go for a run. As we finish our last mile, we pass a brick apartment building. I notice a chicken in the kitchen window of the first-floor apartment. It doesn't move. It's a stuffed chicken. Why would someone stuff a chicken? Was it a prize chicken? A pet?

A few yards farther Ronnie and I prepare to cross Queen Anne Avenue North, one of Seattle's busiest arteries. After many years of negotiating the crosswalk with only a little yellow light feebly flashing a word of caution to the motorists rocketing up the slope to pay heed to the pedestrians, which they mostly do not, we now have a full-fledged traffic light, a ponderous apparatus with a set of signals the drivers must take seriously.

The grade up Queen Anne Avenue North is quite steep. When it snows in the winter, it becomes a popular ski slope. The rest of the year drivers shoot up the slope with extreme aggression, which I believe has something to do with fighting gravity, or the anxiety of falling rearward if the engine of one's car suddenly gives out, or one's tires lose their grip, which sometimes happens. When it rained, the tires of our Subaru Justy used to spin and squeal like teenage banshees at a Justin Bieber concert. We would barely make it to the top.

The crosswalk is well-marked, but no one pays any attention to crosswalks in this city. It's just white fluorescent paint gobbed on asphalt in thick meaningless stripes.

The most worrisome aspect to this crosswalk are the drivers who, heading north up the steep slope, do not see that the car ahead of them is stopping for a pedestrian. They assume the car is stopping to make a left turn, or stopping for no reason at all, which is typical of Seattle drivers. Seattle drivers have a tendency to lose cognition of their function as drivers and stop, presumably to receive a sign from God or the unconscious to give them renewed purpose and direction life, or sink into the wax of their being and ferment in inanition. Until then, they're just going to sit in their car and gaze over the steering wheel as gobs of spit drool from their chin.

This is a common occurrence on the steep slope of Queen Ann Avenue North. The drivers behind, irritated and cursing, make a sudden strategic move to the right, thinking to pass the stopped car and re-enter the proper lane as soon as they crest the hill. It's a lucky pedestrian who notices this, and a lucky motorist who sees the pedestrian before creating another traffic fatality.

The new light is wonderful. There is a button to press that makes a little beep, or blip, and the light turns red almost immediately. Cars stop. One proceeds into the crosswalk feeling like a king or queen on the way to a coronation. The power to stop traffic with a color is a form of magic. The eyes moisten. The pope and court retinue await our arrival on the other side. The motorists gaze at this spectacle with seething impatience. But, perhaps, also with a little awe, as the court applauds our arrival and our heads bow to receive anointment and crowns.

We pass a high granite wall on Highland, where the street curves gently to the north, then straightens in an east-west direction. The big rocks are sparkling. I've never noticed this before. It must be the direct light of the sun creating this effect.

There is also a hedge. But I hedge on the hedge. I'm not sure this is a mass that you can call a hedge. What makes a hedge a hedge? Can flowers make a hedge?

Is that a hedge? I ask Ronnie. Yes, that's a hedge, she answers.

I never thought of flowers being a hedge, I remark.

I don't think of flowers constituting a mass, particularly one that creates a wall. Perhaps this is a momentary preoccupation, a perspective suddenly set askew, but it occurs to me that flowers make poor walls. I think of flowers as single items. Tulips in a bed or in a row might be viewed collectively, but I still see individual tulips growing by individual tulips. Flowers grow individually. Even roses on the same rose bush seem uniquely suited to be nothing else but individual roses. Roses sharing the same thorny branches, but in a way that makes it obvious and irrefutable that each rose is its own unique and inimitable rose. Hedges are a far more pragmatic branch of the ornamental lawn or garden. Boxwood. Glossy Abelia. Japanese Barberry. Holly. These are the shrubs that constitute barriers, walls, fences. They grow as a mass. They have a formal logic. They have opinions regarding private property.

So here was all this lilac. It was really my introduction to lilac. I normally don't pay that much attention to things having to do with gardening. I had come to associate it with punishment and pain. Days spent in the rain clutching a rake or a pair of pruning shears pretending to weed and garden for the satisfaction of my parents who believed that working outdoors in inclement weather inculcated a hardy perennial out of the prodigal narcissus of adolescence and taught valuable lessons of survival and adaptation forever ruined any inclination to garden.

But this lilac. It was crazy. There was so much of it. And it was so intense. So intensely there. So intensely alive and full of the energy of spring.

The petals were a deep blue.

An amazing blue. The blue of ecstasy and mystical elixirs. A blue to awaken the colors of heaven and unite the troubled air. Laugh at the pathos of change. Tread the turbulence of storms with the aplomb of a mountain. Pound sagas of rain into the mind and heart. Spin midnight out of rags. Guzzle the sky and gurgle the stars. Deliver the lost keys of paradise.

The color seemed, in fact, more than a little immodest. But that's the nature of flowers. They are, after all, reproductive organs. It is sexuality written large. Sexuality is intense. Like poetry. I think of Allen Ginsberg busy at a typewriter whacking out *Howl*. I don't think of *Howl* as sexy but it is intense, and anything that is intense is sexy. It just is. Even if a poem devotes its energies to ethereal phenomena its very intensity makes it sexy. Take Emily Dickinson for instance. Poetry, like blackberry and duckweed, like wild lilac, like fennel and houndstongue, has the intensity of things that propagate. Of things seditious and weird. Ginsberg's beard and hair. Ginsberg's eyes. What appeared to be his one good eye in particular after suffering a stroke. A deep, penetrating eye. The eye in a gaze of ecstasy and despair. The eye of the albatross as it wings over the wastes of Antarctica. The poet's eye, in fine frenzy rolling.

I think of all the poets of Egypt and America and Burma and Cameroon, poets at their worst, poets drunken and puking, and how thrilling and beautiful that is on this dying and terrible earth.

Like the ugly, poisonous toad that wears a jewel in its forehead.

How does one describe the hue of opal?

They say the hue of the opal changes color when it's in the room of a dying person. It's painful to see people age. It's painful to see myself age. To feel myself aging. Having an old body is like driving a used car. You're always braced for the inevitable. For that little rattle to turn into a complete breakdown somewhere in the middle of nowhere. Let's say Nevada. Nevada is as close to nowhere as I've ever been. There are mind-boggling expanses of alkali desert in Nevada, merciless bone-white dust, punctuated with brothels. Small brothels, usually just a house. But the signs for them are huge. You can see them from fifty miles off. You think you're seeing a gas station sign, the one with the Brontosaurus in particular, I think it's Sinclair. But as you approach the Diplodocus morphs into a Playboy Bunny. You look to the side and see a sexual worker outside in her britches washing a window. You smile and wave and she smiles and waves back.

The sky in Nevada is always blue. Bare and blue. Existence feels raw. Here in Seattle wherever you go you are surrounded by trees and hills and mountains and penetrated by humidity. Fog and rain and drizzle and damp. Constant, unrelenting damp. This is why I'm in love with root beer. It's such a cheerful beverage. An antidote for the blues. The blues which is begotten from the constant, unrelenting gray. Root beer is cold. This is true. Cold is an adjunct, an enemy to gray. But its evanescence and flavor make up for that cold. Pepsi and Coca-Cola are too aggressive. Too eager to please. Dr. Pepper seems somehow Nestorian, suggesting that pop has two natures, one of which is fun and frolicsome, the other of which is prudent and medical. No pop should be prudent, or referred to as a doctor. 7UP and ginger ale are too transparent, too tart. They seem more like axioms than happy, evanescent nonsense. Root beer is just right. But cream soda is where it's at, baby. Cream soda all the way.

MAGIC WANDS AND JESUS

Ronnie and I rent a red Impala for the day and do some grocery shopping. The young Asian man bagging groceries asked if we'd wanted a sack for the root beer. I was about to say yes, but Ronnie said no. I thought about it, and a sack did seem redundant. So we brought the soda down to the car with the other groceries and put it in the trunk. When we arrived home, and popped the trunk, we discovered the bottles had fallen from their cardboard cases and rolled and tumbled about. One of them had leaked. The pressure of the carbonation must have loosened the cap. We had to go out later with some paper towels and wipe it up before it got sticky and left a permanent smell of root beer in the trunk.

The bill came to $80. I'm amazed. I examine the receipt more closely when we return home. How is it possible that this amount of groceries could be so expensive? How do people manage? Are goods becoming scarce? Is it price fixing? What gives?

The coffee is the most expensive item. We got two one-pound bags of Starbucks coffee, at $14 each. $4.59 for whipping cream, $4.99 for a jar of strawberry jam, $5.29 for a hunk of Romano cheese, $4.49 for a two-quart bottle of Welch's grape juice, $5.29 for a container of feta cheese. $3.39 for spaghetti sauce, $3.39 for a dozen eggs, $20 for wine and root beer.

There is a sheriff's car in the underground parking garage when we arrive, the lights on the roof of his black-and-white car flashing. There is no immediate explanation for this. No one is being cited or arrested. The sheriff and his car are still there when we return with our groceries, the car lights still flashing. This worries me a little as I've always had a tendency to draw the suspicion of the police. Was I an outlaw in a previous life? Does my sense my alienation stick out? I don't know what it is but I swear every time I see a cop I get a panicky feeling, which in itself constitutes some form of guilt, or at least a look of guilt. Furthermore, I'm always ill at ease in cars I'm not used to driving. The newer the model, the more the doodads. I'm still not used to making windows go up and down electronically. Everything I did in the Justy was manual. I'm nervous as a hare in the Impala. But everything goes smoothly and we exit the garage without incident.

We watch a segment on *Thalassa* — a program on TV5MONDE featuring everything and anything to do with the ocean — about a fish in the Sea of Galilee called tilapia, or Saint Peter's fish, so-named because of the story in the Gospel of Matthew about the apostle Peter catching a fish that carried a coin in its mouth. It is assumed that the species was tilapia, though it is not so named in the Bible. It is also probably tilapia that appears in Matthew 14:15-21 (King James version):

> And when it was evening, his disciples came to him, saying, This is a desert place, and the time is now past; send the multitude away, that they may go into the villages, and buy themselves victuals.
>
> But Jesus said unto them, They need not depart; give ye them to eat.
>
> And they say unto him, We have here but five loaves, and two fishes.

He said, Bring them hither to me.

And he commanded the multitude to sit down on the grass, and took the five loaves, and the two fishes, and looking up to heaven, he blessed, and brake, and gave the loaves to his disciples, and the disciples to the multitude.

And they did all eat, and were filled: and they took up of the fragments that remained twelve baskets full.

And they that had eaten were about five thousand men, beside women and children.

The meat of the tilapia is white in color with a flaky texture that's a little firmer than that of catfish. It provides more protein than it takes to raise it (unlike farmed salmon or tuna). Tilapia are omnivorous, preferring phytoplankton or benthic algae. In the Sea of Galilee they love protein-rich duckweed and filter algae from the water using the tiny combs in their gills. The fish are highly adaptable, easily cultured and can tolerate low oxygen levels and a range of salinities. They're happy in ponds, rivers, lakes, canals, even irrigation channels. They have high reproductive capacities and quickly establish self-reproducing populations. The fish has an oval shape and is sometimes referred to as an "aquatic chicken."

Tilapia is known as *izumi dai* when prepared for sushi.

Water has been on my mind a lot lately as I've been reading *L'eau et les rêves* by Gaston Bachelard. I was struck by one passage in particular, having to do with Poseidon defending the daughter of Danaos from the attack of a satyr. Poseidon thrusts his trident into a rock and water gushes out, thereby discovering a life-giving spring on the otherwise completely arid island of Lerna. The story, gleaned from Charles Ploix, is referred to as a *baguette magique*, a magic wand. I find this interesting. The image of a stick thrust into a rock and producing water has an obvious sexual implication. This makes me wonder further about the phallic power of the magic wand. A conductor's baton, for instance, is shaped very similar to that of a magic wand, and as the conductor waves it rhythmically about, it seems to draw from the orchestra a world of sounds and timbres as if it were a form of conjuration as much as musical direction.

The pen, too, is a form of magic wand, a little stick full of ink from which words are conjured, worlds created.

There is similar imagery in the poetry of William Blake, as in this passage from the *Book of Thel*: "Can Wisdom be put in a silver rod / Or Love in a golden bowl?"

The first recorded instance of the word *wand* with reference to its magical power is (according to the OED) this passage in Middle English from *The Wars of Alexandria*, an alliterative poem surviving in fragments on what is called the Ashmole manuscript housed at Trinity College in Dublin. It was written sometime between 1450 and 1500 by an anonymous author: "On higt in his hand haldis a wand / And kenely by conjurisons callis to him spirits."

I discover another spring, this time in the pocket of my coat. But it's detritus, not water, that I bring forth from its depths: ticket stubs to *Safety Not Guaranteed, Prometheus, Man of Steel, Seeking a Friend for the End of the World*, and a receipt for four pillows from Fred Meyers.

The pillows are wonderful and have made a significant change in our lives, providing rest and sanctuary, a place that is soft and receptive for the weight of the head, full of the problems of life, and hungry for sleep and renewal.

Later that same week two young Mexican-American men returned our bedframe. The ends were enveloped in soft Styrofoam and the two men leaned the frame gingerly against the wall in our hallway where Matisse's goldfish normally hang but I had to move to accommodate the bed frame. The steel was now dark gray and the balls on the bedposts were a muted copper. It was quite beautiful. Ronnie and I reassembled our bed and it felt good to sleep higher off the floor again, the clock and CD player within easy reach. When I got out of bed, it was easy to swing my legs to the floor, rather than make that effortful rise from the floor, feeling like Lazarus risen from the dead.

BED

Bed is the most important piece of furniture in our lives. It is a place of healing when we're sick, a place of delicious languor when we're lazy, or meditative, or lost and inconsolable. We are born in a bed. We die in a bed. We have sex in beds. We listen to the radio in bed. We watch TV in bed. We stare at the ceiling in bed. We suffer colds and mumps and malaria in bed. We forget ourselves in bed. We amuse ourselves in bed. We explore shape and hair in bed. We climb into dreams in bed. We promise desperate change and forgiveness in bed. We toss and turn searching for sleep in bed. And when we find sleep we assent to it gladly and break from the world to go drifting God knows where.

I once visited Percy and Mary Shelley in Geneva in bed. I wasn't in bed when I got there. That is to say, my body was in a bed, but my spirit was sitting cross-legged on the floor of the cottage that Lord Bryon had generously offered the Shelleys during their visit.

During my visit. My oneiric visit.

"How vain is it to think that words can penetrate the mystery of our being," wrote Shelley in his essay, "On Life."

"Rightly used they may make evident our ignorance to ourselves, and this is much. For what are we? Whence do we come? and whither do we go? Is birth the commencement, is death the conclusion of our being? What is birth and death?"

We dissolve into oblivion in beds, and in losing consciousness, gain the consciousness of stars.

We discover the basements and underworld fantasies of our true selves in bed. We read in bed: magazines, journals, newspapers, iPads, books. Beckett in bed. Burroughs in bed. Beattie in bed. *Moby-Dick* in bed. *Ulysses* in bed. Guy Davenport of *Da Vinci's Bicycle* in bed. Proust in bed *à la recherche du temps perdu.*

Virginia Woolf's lighthouse sending its "sudden stare over bed and wall in the darkness of winter" floods my mind with light and shadow and the murmur of the sea in bed.

Rimbaud's *Illuminations* illumine my mind in bed: *J'ai tendu des cordes de clocher à clocher; des guirlandes de fenêtre; des chaînes d'or d'étoile à étoile, et je danse.*

Shakespeare in bed: "O sleep, O gentle sleep, / Nature's soft nurse, how have I frighted thee, / That thou no more wilt weigh my eyelids down / And steep my senses in forgetfulness?"

And what mimics the sweet oblivion of death better than sleep? Isn't sleep the rehearsal for that final sleep in which we exit the world permanently?

The memories of people who have passed enter our minds when we lie in bed and the mystic glitter of eternity permeates our muscles and relaxes and seduces us into something larger than our normal selves, the boundaries of our skin and limbs provoked daily by worry and the quashing chatter of remorse and frustration. We slide into simulacrums embarked on stars gluing raindrops together with the baked eyes of ravenous inner light and rise to our conscious selves in the morning wondering what is real and what is not real, what is it still stirring in us and will it crawl back into the night eventually or meet us again when our eyes close and we ascend, blithe and willowy, newly delivered to other worlds, other cities, other ecstasies thrashing in the linen of our secret sharers.

A bed is a sorcery of blankets and springs. Its suppleness bids us welcome. Its simpleness earns our trust. It is where we dream. It is where lips find lips and fingers find conceptions of skin that are smooth as the implications of cats, wicked as the trinkets of insinuation.

In France, if one goes bankrupt, the bailiff is entitled to take everything except one's bed.

I love to sleep. Sleeping is my primary mission in life, my preparation for death, for the final sleep, the sleep to end all sleep. The sleep from which I will never awake. The bourne from which I will never return.

I am a candle in sleep, a column of wax burned down to the bone of the plate, a pool of wax and a tiny black wick, the last flicker of a flame snuffed into gentle wisps of smoke.

I particularly enjoy the two twilight states that accompany sleep: hypnagogia, the twilight state that proceeds sleep, and hypnopomp, the twilight state into which we emerge from sleep. It is in those states that I do some of my most important work, achieve some of my most important insights.

Thought processes on the threshold of sleep differ radically from those of ordinary wakefulness. Hypnagogia may involve a loosening of ego boundaries, openness, sensitivity and a sweet, empathetic dissolution between the boundaries of the mental and physical environments. There is often a fluid association of ideas and a heightened suggestibility. Thinking turns supple. Pliant. Hypnagogic trains of thought turn abstraction into concrete imagery, or find abstraction in the concrete. Sudden *éclats* of insight and problem solving occur in these states between wakefulness and sleep. August Kekulé realized that the structure of benzene was a closed ring while half-asleep in front of a fire and watched molecules form into snakes, one of which grabbed its tail in its mouth, *à la* the fabled ouroboros. Visions, prophecies, premonitions and apparitions all emerge in this twilight world.

Once, on a trip to San Francisco, Ronnie and I had tea with the Surrealist poet Philip Lamantia in his North Beach apartment. When I described these two states of consciousness, he became very excited and told me that Edgar Allan Poe had devoted an essay to the subject. He went and got the book and showed it to me. It was in a section titled "Marginalia," and originally appeared in *Graham's Magazine* in March 1846. Here is an excerpt:

> There is, however, a class of fancies, of exquisite delicacy, which are *not* thoughts, and to which, *as yet*, I have found it absolutely impossible to adapt language. I use the word *fancies* at random, and merely because I must use *some* word; but the idea commonly attached to the term is not even remotely applicable to the shadows of shadows in question. They seem to me rather psychal than intellectual. They arise in the soul (alas, how rarely!) only at its epochs of most intense tranquillity — when the bodily and mental health are in perfection — and at those mere points of time where the confines of the waking world blend with those of the world of dreams. I am aware of these "fancies" only when I am upon the very brink of sleep, with the consciousness that I am so. I have satisfied myself that this condition exists but for an inappreciable *point* of time — yet it is crowded with these "shadows of shadows"; and for absolute *thought* there is demanded time's *endurance*.
>
> These "fancies" have in them a pleasurable ecstasy as far beyond the most pleasurable of the world of wakefulness, or of dreams, as the Heaven of the Northman theology is beyond its Hell. I regard the visions, even as they arise, with an awe which, in some measure, moderates or tranquilizes the ecstasy — I so regard them, through a conviction (which seems a portion of the ecstasy itself) that this ecstasy, in itself, is of a character supernal to the Human Nature — is a glimpse of the spirit's outer world; and I arrive at this conclusion — if this term is at all applicable to instantaneous intuition — by a perception that the delight experienced has, as its element, but *the absoluteness of novelty.* I say the absoluteness — for in these fancies — let me now term them psychal impressions — there is really nothing even approximate in character to

impressions ordinarily received. It is as if the five senses were supplanted by five myriad others alien to mortality.

Now, so entire is my faith in *the power of words*, that, at times, I have believed it possible to embody even the evanescence of fancies such as I have attempted to describe.

When I sleep I raise my antenna into the wavelengths of dream. I am transcendentally amused beneath the blankets. I bump into stars and yell about feathers. I lay my knife down in the midst of the lobster recruitment. My skin is leather; I am swollen and insoluble. I am soaked in railroads. The house is soft and unfettered. I do not deny my meandering. When we sew, we sew fire. I am literally mohair at the mailbox. And then I become music.

The piano agrees with a hit song. I dig it and strike it with my shovel. I personify myself with a hairbrush and include a little age which I shove into quarks. My glasses hit the glass of the window and it sparks a distortion of sound that tumbles through a voice shouting at a form of turret to enhance our collective memory. I float a bite of thunder in circles. I catalogue a moccasin behind the light. The ceiling convulses in exasperation.

I am your hirsute profligate palpable pronoun. The pronoun I, which diffuses into ink, and becomes words, these words, which are brightness and wheels. I ramble in the sky below the cemetery. It feels explicit. I cannot escape the brass or the punches of dirt beneath my feet. I push the snow and yearn for you across the river. There is a mink caboose there that is eager in its reality and murders the mineral earth with its steel and carbon. I sugar a philodendron and the philosophers all cringe. They drill through a wall of stars and arrive in heaven bleeding tinfoil.

My desires embarrass me. I space my beard until it coheres into sex. Life is sweetness and elation on the vagina planet. My alchemy is the glue of development. I flail anthologies at the birds. My incentives are vermillion, my book is the waltz I perform on water. I yank my throat out and scatter saga buttons at the taxi driver. My thumb is everything red that I lift to my sternum where it slides into vapor. A pair of friendly binoculars boils with Shropshire. I take my medication before I go to bed where it extrudes locomotives and takes me to places where I can scratch my emotions with hypnopompic straw.

The first thing I do when I wake is make the bed. What a curious expression — make the bed. It is a little like making something. I'm attentive to the chaos of sheets and blankets and strategize how to make it smooth and harmonious again. A bed that appears orderly is an invitation to sweet, restful sleep. I like to tuck the sheets in at the bottom. When I get into bed it helps to produce a cocoon-like feeling. If my feet stick out, I feel exposed. Vulnerable. I need to feel hidden, invisible, gone from the troublesome world.

The bed is a mode of transport. It is our vehicle, our spaceship into oblivion. It is where we welcome the bidding of our unconscious. It is where the sparkling cavern of our inner being lures us into its labyrinths. It is where we discover our secret selves, our shadow selves, old feelings that are suddenly and strangely renewed. Dead parents speak to us. Dead friends give us advice. When we wake, our eyes open and the light of day dispels the spell.

Car2Go À-Go-Go

Ronnie's Car2Go card arrived in the mail on Monday. I needed to go to the bank, so we thought it'd be a great convenience if we spotted one of the little white and blue Smart cars that make up the Car2Go fleet and drove it to the bank. There had been several Car2Go cars parked on our street or very nearby for the last several weeks. This sold Ronnie on the idea, but not me. I just figured it was a fluke. Which it turned out to be. That would be the last time we'd see any little blue and white Car2Go Smart cars parked across the street. I think the guy in the brick house was using them for a while. When a new car popped up in his driveway, a Subaru Crosstrek, the Car2Go cars disappeared.

I was, I must admit, a little irritated when Ronnie signed up because she did so without my input. I was sure it would be a waste of $35. I hate to waste money. Even $35.

I smelled smoke. Ronnie put a small slice of bread in the toaster that got caught and burned to a black smoky carbon. She dug it out with a butter knife. I was surprised the new fire alarm didn't go off. I opened our kitchen window wider and the living room window wider and started fanning the air with magazines. I also turned the overhead fan on over the stove but that unit is pretty much as useless as tits on a screwdriver. This all happened at the same time the gardeners went to work on our side of the building with saws and clippers. It was chaos. The noise was driving me to distraction. It was a big relief to get out of the house.

As I anticipated, there were no Car2Go cars parked across the street. As we began our climb up the cliff wall that is our street, some cirrus clouds caught my attention in an otherwise flawlessly blue sky. It seemed uncannily vivid and well-defined, accentuating the china blue sky with dazzling lucidity. It was so veiled and feathery it was difficult not to think of it as some form of sublime consciousness. Was this a moral universe after all? Was there truly a higher power underlying life's random brutality and unfairness with a mysterious order and angelic harmonies? Or were these just cirrus clouds, feathered by the deposition of water vapor in the thin air of high altitudes, measurable, gaugeable, knowable as anything else? That same day, 2,000 miles distant, a murderous two-mile wide tornado would devastate a suburb of Oklahoma City, leaving twenty-four people dead.

There but for fortune go you or I.

After I finished depositing a check, we went to go see the new Star Trek movie at the Boeing IMAX theater, which was just a short walk from the bank. We followed the ramp that spirals downward into the waiting area for the theater. I like this part of the ritual. It preserves that old sense of going to a movie, of departing from everyday reality and entering the realm of light and spectacle and imagination. The silver screen.

There was an area cordoned off for the movie line. We slipped under the rope and I sat down on the carpet and pulled out my copy of Bob Dylan's *Tarantula* that I'd brought along to help fill the time while we waited to be seated. *Tarantula* is one of my absolute favorite books. Dylan used Burrough's cut-up technique and Kerouac's brilliance for neologism and slang to create a series of wild prose poems with nutty titles like

"Guitars Kissing & the Contemporary Fix" and "False Eyelash in Maria's Transmission." I jotted down words and phrases of slang to look up later in Daniel Bismuth's French translation, "dumb hill bully," "minstrel peekaboo," "witchy," "bunch of backslap."

Ronnie continued to stand. She was debating whether to get some coffee at the concession stand. She was certain it would be terrible, yet she craved some coffee. She opted, finally, to sit down and forget about the coffee until later. Almost as soon as she sat down, the ushers began taking tickets and letting everybody into the theater. There was also someone on hand to hand out 3D glasses.

We enjoy the movie. The dialogue is crisp and witty, the villains are truly menacing, the special effects are eye-poppingly exciting in 3D and the story is full of suspense and spectacle. I've always liked the underlying themes of Star Trek: Kirk, who is all impulse and gallantry and threatened with having his rank removed for insubordination, is contrasted brilliantly with Spock, who is all reason and logic and at war with the emotions of his human side. There is always intensity and great friendship between these two characters despite frequent outbreaks of resentment and irresolvable ethical dilemmas when one of them saves the other from sure death but must break Federation rules in order to do so. Chris Pine assumes Shatner's old role with an almost seamless realization of Shatner's mischievous, devil-may-care sparkle and this astute casting coup is even more evident with the role of Spock; Zachary Quinto is totally convincing as a young Leonard Nimoy.

Boeing IMAX is the perfect location to see a Star Trek movie because it is located on the old Seattle World's Fair grounds. The theme of the 1962 Seattle World's Fair, which was called the "Century 21 Exposition," was a futuristic celebration of science whose evident intent was to demonstrate that the United States was in no way "behind" the Soviet Union in the domains of science and space but was, in fact, at the very forefront of stellar discoveries and technology. I was fourteen at the time, and remember it well. I saw the Space Needle rise out of the ground from the vantage point of my drafting class on the third floor of Queen Anne High School. As I attempted to draw precise configurations of screwdrivers and C-clamps (never to the satisfaction of the humorless prick who taught the class), I watched as a convoy of concrete trucks filled a thirty-foot-deep hole for the base and then, as the days and months progressed, the massive steel beams that form the legs and upper body of the needle were welded together by men too small to see. As the beams rose vertically toward the sky, it looked like a colossal gladiolus growing out of the ground.

There is great cruel irony for me in this now because the twenty-first century is thirteen years old, but I'm not here. I'm still in the twentieth century. I despise digital technology and its consequent undermining of intellect and literature and destruction of books and print media, and although I keep a blog, it is a headache-inducing inner conflict in which I simultaneously feel the empowerment of instant self-publication and the degradation of instant self-publication.

I see young beautiful women who will never be nude because every inch has been inked with tattoos. A few tattoos are cool, but tattoos all over the body? That's an enigma. I saw in it the stain of anomie, a kind of decay, the despair of innocence, the need to proclaim — or reclaim — a social identity.

I noticed other signs of social decay: rudeness, people jabbering on cell phones in public, intruding on other people's space with their private matters, people at restaurants staring at smartphones and ignoring one another, the difficulty of finding anyone reliable or competent to do handiwork or odd jobs, or the peculiar zoned-out zombie-like behavior of men dressed in the garb of toddlers in baggy pants and duckbilled caps worn at a cockeyed angle and women dressed like whores in stiletto heels and torn fishnet stockings that had become a staple of any journey into the public sphere.

Nobody, for instance, gave a flying monkey shit that the habeas corpus removed by the despised Bush administration has not only not been restored by the Obama administration, but other disastrous infringements on our civil rights such as the

National Defense Authority Act had been signed by Obama into law. It was disheartening and deeply perplexing to see people swallow these things with such baffling passivity. Was totalitarianism the inevitable dystopic mindset of the future? Was it the inevitable consequence of all this new technology? Money had become a strange, abstract, mathematical irreality that benefited a small plutocratic elite at the expense of the less fortunate. The ones who didn't graduate from Yale or Harvard and didn't know an algorithm from an aardvark. This expertise in reckless speculation and dizzying, algorithmic trading created daily and exponentially the suffering of millions of people.

The Occupy Wall Street movement, which had grown into a national movement of tents and young men with dreadlocks and Apple iPads and young women tattooed head to toe who gathered to maintain debates and discussions by vocal repetition and wiggling their fingers so as to do away with anything, such as a microphone or bullhorn, that would smack of "authority," had only proved to show how militarized and brutal the police in the United States had become. This was also true of Europe and Asia. It wasn't a national conflict but a class conflict. People making themselves heard in the streets of Athens were getting their heads bashed in just as much as the people in Oakland, California, or Springfield, Illinois.

The militarized, totalitarian culture of the so-called Federation was another aspect to the Star Trek series. It had always reflected a totalitarian structure of hierarchy and military rule. Everyone wore the same plain body-molded uniform. Everyone was following, assimilating, rehearsing or chafing against the rules. Ethical dilemmas were invariably involved with some form of disobedience to Federation rules. It had always been fun to watch because it was a culture that looked familiar but was also safely removed and distant. The distance was closing. That militarized totalitarian culture aboard the Starship Enterprise was starting to be seen in everyday life on Earth. On a planet which, like Krypton, was on the threshold of destruction.

As we walked up back up the ramp, a series of photographs caught my interest in the central lobby, an enormous room with a bright white floor and glass walls in which the world's biggest electric guitar was housed. The photographs, all handsomely framed, were part of an ongoing Nikon Small World competition and exhibit of scientific photomicrography. I gazed at several and was stunned at the power of the images: what appeared to be a cracked yellow sun with blood veins emanating into space was, in fact, a "3D lymphangiogenesis assay" of cells sprouting from "dextran beads embedded in fibrin gel on Bing." A membranous tornado of green and black peppered with luminous blue dots was a "single optical section through the tip of the gut of a *Drosophila melanogaster* (fruitfly)."

We hoped to find a Car2Go outside the Seattle World's Fair grounds. There were none. Ronnie uses a Samsung "dumb" phone. It does not have internet access, so there was no way we could obtain the Car2Go availability map and reserve a car. The bus proved the more convenient option. We rode the Number 2 to the top of Queen Anne and went to The 5 Spot café for dinner. The 5 Spot is a "themed" restaurant of "regional American food." Every six months or so they change themes from one U.S. location or event to another. The décor and food on the menu is a reflection of the theme and is often quite clever, and good. The current theme was "Blue Highway," a.k.a. "Highway 61," the highway legendary for its musical history because it drops down from Minnesota to run through Saint Louis to Memphis to New Orleans. A papier-mâché rat, spider and snail hung in the center of the restaurant and were occasionally animated by electrical device. I think they were supposed to be musicians in a band. I think the snail was the only one with a musical instrument, a guitar. I couldn't quite tell. Was that a guitar in the snail's hands? And what was a snail doing with arms and hands? Why a snail? Even for a papier-mâché puppet, arms and hands on a snail are an extreme anatomical anomaly. Shouldn't the spider be the one playing a guitar? The puppets weren't moving, so the illusion didn't really matter as anything other than the joke it was intended to be.

Paintings of blues and rock 'n' roll greats adorned the wall: Otis Redding, Etta James, Jerry Lee Lewis, B. B. King. Elvis

Presley, dressed in his over-the-top regal high-collar rhinestone-studded getup from his 1970s Las Vegas period, lunged flamboyantly in front of a pizza delivery man.

There were musical notes painted on the wall just above the cooking section. I wondered if the notes were random, or an actual song. I asked Ronnie, since she had once played piano, but she couldn't tell. It was an odd contrast seeing the chefs in their white jackets flipping and pouring ingredients and hearing the sizzle of meat and their voices as they shouted orders under the merry sharps and flats on the wall above.

I looked at the menu. I was torn between the slow-smoked Tennessee brisket ("dry rubbed & hickory smoked for ten hours; served with baked beans, spiced & blistered green beans & sweet 'n' hot Memphis BBQ sauce") and the St. James Parish bowl of gumbo with Andouille sausage (I love Andouille sausage), chicken and shrimp slow-cooked in dark roux and served over herb rice. I decided on the Tennessee brisket. Ronnie ordered the Crossroads pan-roasted chicken, topped with "habanero Voodoo sauce and served with Brussels sprouts & griddled cornmeal cake." I also got a Crater Lake root beer to wash it all down. They used to have Crater Lake root beer on tap and serve it in a big glass shaped like a cowboy boot but had since done away with that for some reason. Now you just got a bottle and regular-shaped drinking glass.

The meal was good. The pork was tender and juicy, the baked beans were sumptuous and spicy and the green beans were toothsome as the Jolly Green Giant's big grin, but I don't think it was worth anywhere near the $17 they charged for it. The portions were rather small and the humbleness of the food did not merit such a heady price. This was The 5 Spot, not the Café de Flores.

The next day, a Tuesday, we scored our first Car2Go. While Ronnie was at her doctor's appointment downtown, I Googled the Car2Go map for available cars and found several just a few blocks distant. I texted her the information, hoping the cars would still be there. Ronnie called after her appointment and I checked to see if those two cars were still available. They were not. I found another one on Columbia. It was still available when Ronnie got there, so she was able to drive that one home. We felt triumphant. We went for a run, and when we returned approximately an hour later, we showered and dressed and walked down our easement to see if the car was still there. It was. Hallelujah. Unfortunately, someone had reserved it. I wondered if you could do that, I told Ronnie, that it didn't seem fair, but I went no further and didn't bother to check. Ronnie explained that yes, you could reserve these cars from your computer or smartphone, but there's only a half-hour window to make it to the car before the time expires. That still didn't seem right. I mean, there you are in a hurry, your card awkwardly wrestled out of your wallet or purse while struggling to hold a recently purchased guitar or cherub lamp in your other hand, and the car smackdab in front of you has been fucking reserved. That sucks.

Back home, we checked the computer for more cars. There weren't any close enough to make it worth our while. We just wanted to go to the QFC at the bottom of the hill and get some grape juice and root beer and anything else cumbersome to lug up a steep hill. We checked again a few minutes later and the car Ronnie drove home was still in its same spot and had become available again. Maybe the person that had reserved it changed their mind, or got caught by a phone call just as they were leaving and their time ran out. Ronnie reserved it from our computer and we once again strolled down our easement to the car. Ronnie held her card over the reader in the windshield, unlocked the doors and got in and opened the door for me on the passenger side. I watched as she went through a series of moves on a little computer screen, questions about the condition of the car, etc. Then she put the key in and started it. There was a high-pitched electrical whine which died down in a few seconds as the car resurrected into mechanical life.

Ronnie described her driving experience: she said she felt a weird surge of power when she stepped on the accelerator, which was due to the fact it was electrically powered. Other than that, it was easy to maneuver. It had a radio, which seemed always to be tuned to KEXP, which was fine with me. I like their music, except for the occasional rap. We brought our juice and root beer down to the underground parking lot and resumed our ride in the Car2Go bucket. I couldn't get the trunk open so I had to hold two big paper grocery bags on my lap. Ronnie parked it on the street again and we walked the rest of the way up our easement. The total for that day's Car2Go driving came to $17.00.

We drove another Car2Go car the next day, on Wednesday afternoon after Ronnie returned home from work. Earlier in the day I'd heard a report on NPR that money in savings accounts was vulnerable to getting chipped away by inflation because interest rates were so low. That did it. That was the tipping point for me. The incentive to keep my money in an IRA just vanished. It wasn't that I believed this reporter instantly, I'm far too cynical and skeptical a person to do that. Everything the report said jived with my own observations. My bank statements were proof. The money in the accounts did not compound with interest. Inflation nibbled on its value like rabbits raiding a cabbage field in the dead of night. The NPR reporter advised making your money work for you, invest it in something that appears to be appreciating, real estate being the most obvious. A car is not an investment, it depreciates the instant the wheels leave the lot and hit the street, but it's enjoyable, it's fun, and it is a vital piece of equipment in a city like Seattle where the public transit system is barely adequate and is dying from lack of funds.

We went online on our computer (you really do need a smartphone when you're on the go for a Car2Go) and found a Car2Go at the bottom of the hill, on Valley. Ronnie reserved it, showered, dressed and we walked down to take command of the little tin can and drive it to the credit union where I could shift some money into my checking account. I was sure now that I wanted to buy a car. I knew I was giving into an addiction, a driving addiction, car addiction, listening-to-music-loud-in-a-car-addiction, but three months of bus riding, taking taxis, renting cars, and now using the costly and not particularly convenient Car2Go system had persuaded me that my recent headache-inducing conflict over whether to buy a car or not was leaning inevitably in the "buy a frigging car you dope" direction. I had made my choice.

I must also admit to some grieving for our old Subaru Justy, which I suppressed for obvious reasons. It was a machine, not a pet, not remotely a living creature. Yet the old Subaru had felt like a friend, a member of the family. I did feel bereaved. I just wouldn't admit it. Buying a new car would help with that hole it left.

Ronnie started the Car2Go and we headed toward Mercer, which used to be the easiest way to get to Fairview and Eastlake until Paul Allen began evolving his empire south of Lake Union. Half of Mercer was closed. It looked dicey, so we headed to Dexter. Traffic on Dexter was heavy and slow. I worried that we would be trapped there long enough to miss the bank being open, but eventually we made it to Fairview, made a left, and minutes later found ourselves at the bank. The transaction was quick so we kept the Car2Go and resumed driving it back to Queen Anne. We parked it on Queen Anne Avenue North and walked to Uptown China, a restaurant we used to frequent much more often when we still had our Subaru. We waited in the entry for someone to seat us. There is normally someone there. It was unusual to wait. The service is normally quite good at Uptown. While we stood waiting I spotted our old neighbors, the Bellamys, having dinner with another couple. We did not want to visit with them. Even a brief chat would have been painful. So we crept out before they caught sight of us and had dinner at Athina (that's not a misspelling, it was spelled with an "i" instead of an "e"), a little farther up the street.

Our trip to the bank had cost $13, roughly. That means that in two days our Car2Go use totaled $30. A taxi would have been cheaper. I looked forward to getting a new car. There was dread, and guilt, but mostly the relief of an addiction finding its way to wheels, acceleration and appeasement.

SHADOWS OF SHADOWS

Sunday, June 2, was a quiet day. There was some minor commotion as Cal walked by our window on his cell phone, going on about some new problem he and Pamela had discovered in their apartment, and Lyle and Cindy thundered back and forth, presumably loading Lyle's Toyota Tundra with ironing boards, camping equipment and mountain climbing gear for his next extreme ironing adventure.

Saturday had been loud. Cal and Pamela had discovered yet another leak in their apartment, this time in their guest bathroom, that required demolishing the wall for the plumbers to gain access to the pipes, which were represented as being close to bursting. Cal said that he and Pamela would do the work themselves, which would involve a lot of hammering, which would be loud, which it was. They started later in the morning out of courtesy to the others in the building, a building where sound travels so easily you could sit, as I am now, on the first floor of the building and still be able to hear a gastrointestinal anomaly transpire in a neighbor's duodenum two stories up on the third floor. He said the job would take four to five hours, so I suggested to Ronnie that we go downtown for dinner and watch *Frances Ha*, a new movie with Greta Gerwig. This woman fascinates me. Her body, which is shapely and well-proportioned but seems somehow overly large, giving her presence a strong fullness of being, unlocking the space around her and creating a delightful tension between balance and order. When she plays a character who is unsure of herself, as in Frances Ha, a woman who describes herself with self-deprecating humor as "undatable," and tries to pursue a career in modern dance, her occasional klutziness and anxious affability energize the screen like Buster Keaton's antics in the old silent movies. It's much more subtle, there isn't the same slapstick and burlesque, but she embodies everyone's awkwardness in social situations that must be carefully navigated, and never are.

We had dinner at Gordon Biersch. I ordered the jambalaya, which is really good, although they now put the rice to the side in a mound of virginal white, rather than mix it all up the way they had done in the past. Ronnie ordered the California Cobb — grilled chicken, bacon, avocado, tomato and cheddar cheese, finished with baby greens tossed in balsamic vinaigrette, served on a piece of crunchy flatbread. It looked more like an appetizer than a dinner and I kept asking her if she was sure it was listed among the dinner entrées. She insisted it was. I gave her some of my rice.

After dinner, we still had an hour and a half to kill before the movie, so we went shopping. I hate shopping, but in this instance, we were looking for items that we could use on our upcoming trip to Paris. Ronnie needed a purse. Her requirements for a purse exceeded my understanding. It had something to do with size and the number of compartments, their arrangement and disposition, the ease with which she could pull out cards and money and identity cards and books. I saw hundreds of purses that seemed like good candidates. But she had no interest in them. They weren't even in the ballpark of purse utility. I tried to picture the ideal purse, but it was like trying to puzzle together a contraption for capturing and analyzing atmospheric neutrinos.

I spotted a handbag with an adjustable padded shoulder strap that looked perfect for carrying books and a passport and maps and a compass. It was hanging from the shoulder of a manikin perched atop a small display table. I managed to reach up and pull it down, which impressed the young salesman who appeared minutes later. The bag had a fully lined, double gusset interior with a secure flapover closure, a padded main compartment, a front pocket organizer, three padded open pockets and a spacious rear open compartment for easy access. I really wanted it, but it was pricey. $185. I asked if they had any more in stock, since we were on our way to a movie, and I hadn't planned on spending that amount of money today. I need to brace myself for outlays of money like this. I need to get into a certain mindset. He went to his computer and said, nope, this was the last one. So I bought it. While he wrapped it, and waited kindly for me to get around to putting my pin number in the card reader for my debit card, he asked where we were going. Paris, Ronnie said. That impressed him. How long? he asked. Six days, Ronnie said. Have you ever been there? I asked. No, he'd never been off the continent, he said. He'd been to Mexico, but that's it. He asked if we'd been there. Yes, we said. Ronnie said she'd been there about thirty years ago. For me, it had been forty-one years. What in particular did we plan to see? I told him art. We were going to look at a lot of art. The Louvre, Musée d'Orsay, Centre Pompidou. And bookstores. It will be so nice to be in a real bookstore again.

What do you mean by a real bookstore? he asked.

A bookstore with a lot of books, I said. Titles in philosophy and poetry. Not just cheesy bestsellers.

You mean like Powell's in Portland? he asked.

Exactly, I said. Like Powell's. Powell's is a real bookstore.

The young man said he was from Portland. He'd only been in Seattle about a year. He said the restaurants in Portland were better, and the city was easier to negotiate, but he was getting to like Seattle. He said he was living in the South Lake Union neighborhood, Seattle's latest glitzy addition, the province of former Microsoft mogul Paul Allen, the same multi-billionaire who created the chaos and commercial rip-off that is the Experience Music Project.

The young salesman put my bag (its full description was a Columbian Leather Flapover Laptop Business Case) into a paper sack with string handles and we left. We traveled through Seattle's underground Metro station, a marble-clad Piranesian mezzanine of ceramic tile walls and granite benches, to Macy's to look at more purses and jackets. There were hundreds of purses, but none of them met Ronnie's rigorous standards. We thought AAA might be the place for us. Their bags are designed more exclusively for the anxieties and disasters of travel.

We went to the theater, a multiplex across the street from the convention center. I marveled at how crowded the streets were, and the variety of people. We entered the heavy glass doors and wound our way through the nonexistent ticket purchasing line, which was cordoned off in a wrap-around configuration. We still had over an hour to kill, so we rode the escalators to the third level where *Frances Ha* was playing and found a small round black metal patio table and matching chairs to sit down and while the time away. It was set up by a high glass window where we could look out on the adjacent buildings and crowded streets below. I read "Pieces," by Francis Ponge, his long poem about the sun, *"Le soleil placé en abîme,"* and Ronnie practiced using her new Android smartphone. I asked if she could get TV5MONDE's *Le Journal* and she could. It was amazing. The audio was negligible. I could barely hear it. But the images were clear, and if Ronnie had had earbuds, she could have listened to it easily.

My reading was abruptly interrupted by Darth Vader's booming voice and electronic swoosh of lightsabers coming from a Star Wars video game close by. I suggested we move. We found another table where it was quieter and lingered for our hour.

After the movie, Ronnie checked to see if there might be a Car2Go car nearby. There was one on Madison, about five blocks to the south, a walk of about a half mile or so. We pondered calling a cab, but I was still adjusting to an acute feeling of decadence after spending all that money on a leather bag, so we opted for the monorail instead.

It was 9:30 P.M. when we arrived home. I braced myself for another of Cal's email announcements about new construction that would have to be performed because they discovered a trickle of water running down a bathroom wall or a dust bunny under the bed. But there was none. This could be good, or bad. Cal might need time to describe in detail all the forthcoming construction.

I could hear the plumbers laughing all the way home. Their kids's dental bills and college education would all be paid for now, thanks to Cal and Pamela and their ongoing anxieties about entropy and nature's untoward intrusions into their domestic impeccability.

We watched *Questions pour un champion*. Ronnie fell dead asleep. I could hear her snoring. Graham got on my lap, but he was restless and agitated and tried to bite me every time I petted him on the head. He must think this is amusing. He likes these little bites because it makes him want to eat when he really isn't hungry, and he likes to eat. The bites must stimulate the neurons in his arcuate nucleus, that aggregation of neurons in the mediobasal hypothalamus that controls appetite. That was my theory anyway. Because the bites, which weren't serious bites, unless I started rough-housing back, in which case he'd get carried away and really take bites, were invariably followed by his claws digging into my thighs as he prepared to jump down and walk to his plate of food.

I started to nod off as well. I would awake and see people answering questions on TV then consciousness would once again dissolve, my head would nod and I'd be once again asleep. Eventually I came awake more permanently and found Graham curled up on my lap again, the warmth of his body imbuing my thighs with the pleasure of his being. He gazed at me with his blue eyes and purred.

Bubbles of
Soapy Dream

Bubbles of soapy dream float out of my mouth and drift around the room. I'm going to resurrect an irresponsibility, rub it shiny and bright with paradigms of elephant piss, and then restore the biology of the harpsichord. They say the earliest harpsichords came from Italy and were made of cypress and had a robust tone. The Italian builders were phenomenal, but it was the French who developed the performance practices of the sixteenth-century lutenists into ingenious quasi-polyphonic textures and a subtle use of arpeggiation, and made that cypress travel the light of heaven.

The trombone is an entirely different animal. It has a telescopic slide, an orotund tone and a gleaming pulchritude. The muscle of embouchure rides its reach of perfect metal to the birth of rapture. It is to the harpsichord and piano what the heron is to the estuary.

There is an ocean in me screaming to get out, a black dish on a white table, and a shore of black sand where a knot ripens in convolution. Persia is the dream I'm having now. Yesterday it was foolish lace and old barbed wire fences, a memory of snow blowing in a deviation across a highway in North Dakota. It was 1972 and pronunciation was slow as a sockeye salmon lazing under a winter sun. Later I thought of eels in an East Anglian slough. I am slender and uncontrolled. I hear a fluttering beyond the pigment, raw umber on a background of hope. I wear an empty hat and an empty sweater. They remain empty even when I am wearing them. This is their circumference. This is their delineation. Here is a feeling rendered in syllables: a coat on a hook in a barber shop. Feathers of a hawk. An alphabet of trees murmuring haiku into the night. An alphabet of broken violins below the skin gratifies the water word by word, healing the wounds of these things with thunder and ice and a bird of infrared feathers defining reality with a penumbral grace on a snowy street. I choose a brush and go to work on my hair.

I have conflicts around the creation of reality. I never deny a bud its blossom, but the language hints of an invisible structure like the hole in Noguchi's *Black Sun*. I hear it whirring round itself. The mind corrects the dark like a yo-yo. An adjective rips the air and yawns in a glass of water like a suitcase full of scarves and craters. There is a hurricane caught in my nerves. My other car is a bed in Paris. I'm a cemetery cat. I'm a tattoo nobody can decipher. I'm a finger pressing a button on a jukebox. I'm an immodest raw umber and soft as a ghost of hydrogen. I feel the creak of a staircase in a house that has ceased to exist.

I'm obsessing over personal injuries that I drag from place to place. The life we are in is invisible. My thinking is gray. It fulminates and whistles. I can feel a splinter beneath an old wooden bench in Montmartre. Audacity is its own reward. Metal is never introverted. It doesn't need to be. It twiddles an autumn leaf behind an arras in a Rocky Mountain dream. What amazement there is in typing. I see young girls busy with their thumbs making small messages and wonder what theaters we are when cartilage is so willing and supple and the presence of fish is so ruminative and driven. I can do marvelous things when the drums are pounding and the coupons have been well-perforated and the avocados are fresh and have the sound of drums.

I can move my finger along the rim of a bowl. I can create a subjunctive mood if I so wish. I can shape reality so that it looks like a bank teller or a hole in the ground. Europe weeps in its gloomy rain. I walk along the highway. I feel like a glass of milk shattered on the floor. There is milk and glass everywhere. The floor is light beige tile. I have made a hat of carefully chosen twigs and a ruffled collar circa sixteenth-century Holland. My mind plays with the dark like a big potato. Like Noguchi's *Great Rock of Inner Seeking*. My elbows are on the table. I'm eating the sound of a harmonica. I'm authorized to do this. It's my poem and I'll cry if I want to. Cry if I want to. You'd cry, too, if it happened to you.

What? Life, the imagination, poetry, chiaroscuro boxing, convocation, fabric softener, stirring anthems, rain and umbrellas, the umbrellas of Cherbourg, the umbrellas of Pocatello, Idaho, sensation and trembling and sexual Tuesday. The caresses of people buying things in thrift stores. If my palomino weighs two pounds, I can describe it better. But it will be a very small palomino. It will be about the size of a word. The word *palomino*.

Here is a real palomino. It is real because your mind is at work picturing a palomino. I write palomino and you see a palomino but who gets credit for the palomino?

What is a brown and ravenous muscle doing in my wallet wallowing around as if there were no tomorrow? Euclid gives it motion and presents me with a phantom key. He defines the line as a breadthless length. But why should a line have bread? I take his point as the end of a line. The edges of a surface are lines. These are lines. This line has an inclination to cry. This line has an angle and is called rectilinear. This line is waiting for a hotel clerk. This line is perpendicular and standing on its head. This line is running parallel to a phantom area code hugged by a feeling of fat and one day they will meet in Colorado and equal the same thing as a bath towel.

The whole is greater than the part. Things which coincide with one another equal one another. To construct an exhortation use three sheets of plywood and a stick of gum. Accelerate it into the stratosphere and explode it. If in a triangle the square of one of the sides equals the sum of the squares on the remaining two sides of the triangle, then the angle contained by the remaining two sides of the triangle is right. If not, it isn't wrong, but it will not resemble Kentucky. It will go naked and cut itself on an oyster shell. It will be a dragon of invention, a process of thinking, a thrash, a thread, a translucence. It will be abstract, geometric and lavish. It will be a radius, a diameter, a chord. It will be fragile. It will be strong. It will be full of contradictions. It will serve nothing, achieve nothing, symbolize nothing. It will be words on a page. It will be a splendor of volatility whose heat is not for the herd but heard by the ones at home in their solitude. It will cauterize the blood of meaning. It will drift through space. It will break apart and fall across the surface of a raging sun.

This is just a rumor, but I heard that there is a trombone so extreme it can create powerful insights and relationships. It can create veins through solid metal, and a wide range of molecules including France and mulberry. Beef gravy. Insoluble rickshaws. Unicorns. Unlawful sex. Flickering chins. Enormous pharmacies. Hypnotic real estate. Bubbles of soapy dream.

If such a trombone exists, may it extend the bistros of faith. May it varnish the zygotes of Neptune. May it ripple through my being sweetening everything with the stir of its vibrations and the trembling of its tone.

PORT TOWNSEND

Look out! Ronnie shouted. I flinched. The car to my immedi-ate right had tried to enter the lane with me in it. I glanced at the woman who was driving, a middle-aged lady in a busi-ness suit. I didn't make out the model she was driving, just that it was a big sedan of some sort and was painted gold. She gave me an angry look, and said something I was certain was hostile and unflattering, and behaved as if it were my fault she had nearly broadsided us by doing something stupid. Like enter a lane of heavy traffic without bothering to look.

That was close, I sighed. Driving rental cars makes me ner-vous. We had insurance, but I knew that an accident would be a complicated affair, a major headache that would go on for a year and maybe even require a lawyer. I have never known any-one to come out of an accident that they caused and assumed full responsibility for without an argument.

I started talking about Kerouac, for no particular reason. I'd been reading *Lonesome Traveler* the night before, one of my favorite books. I've lost count of the number of times I've read it.

You know, it's weird, it's a very personal book, totally autobiographical, and he talks about a lot of people, and never, and I mean never, says anything mean about anyone. I admire that, but I also find it frustrating. I wish he'd bad-mouthed people a little more. I wished he sounded more like Larry David at times and did some complaining. Kerouac's complaining has a way of turning into something sublime and Buddhist and full of dharma. One minute he's hungover and hungry and out of a job or he's just been read the riot act for being late on the job and the next minute his head is in the cosmos and he's kissing God or something.

Hey, look, said Ronnie, *The Pirates of Penzance* is playing at the Fifth Avenue Theater.

I saw that, back in the early 1980s. Peter Noone played Frederic. Jim Belushi played the Pirate King. Remember Peter Noone? Herman's Hermits?

Is he the guy that did the song about being Henry the Eighth?

Yup. That's him. And the other song, about Mrs. Brown having a lovely daughter.

I made a right turn on Madison and we headed for the waterfront. I was relieved to find a sign for the ferry, but lost sight of the entrance.

That's our turnoff. There. Turn! Turn!

Where?

There! Can't you see it?

Ah, I see it.

I made the turn and drove up to the ticket window behind which sat a very heavy Black woman with an affable and rather pretty face.

We're going to Bainbridge today, I said.

That'll be $24.

I handed her $30, and she gave me the change and smiled. I handed the change to Ronnie, who put it on her lap.

Where's the lane for Bainbridge? I asked Ronnie.

Don't go there, that's the line for Bremerton.

Ah, I see it.

We passed the sign and a man wearing a yellow vest waved us into the appropriate lane. I put the rented Camry in park and set the brake and turned the engine off.

It felt good to make it to the ferry dock and park and relax. I rolled the window down on my side. The other windows seemed to be stuck. We each tried to work the levers that electronically activated the windows to no avail.

There was a Harley-Davidson motorcycle parked to my immediate left.

Ronnie pulled a yellow note out of her pocket. It was from some guy who had taped a note to the window of our old Subaru Justy asking if we might want to sell it. We didn't know at the time that it would be breaking down on us about a month later.

Minutes later we could hear the toot of the ferry horn. Ronnie looked the ferry up on her smartphone. The schedule app used the term *fetching*.

Look here, said Ronnie. I looked. It did: it used the term *fetching*. We're being fetched. How fetching is that?

A team of women and men in yellow vests guided us onto the boat and the proper lane and we parked and got out and went topside to get a view of Puget Sound as the ferry churned the salt water and left the dock for Bainbridge. I love the vibrations on the ferry. These ferries are big and the engines must be terrifically powerful to vibrate through all these decks and cars like that. I watched a small ship with a crane of some sort on its deck pass in the opposite direction. The white railing below the window showed the patchy discoloration of rust.

I love to stare at waves. Waves fascinate me. The way they move, roll through the water. You never know where one wave starts and another wave begins, or why one wave will suddenly turn white and spit fume or dimples and whirls will appear or a flock of seabirds will gather over a certain zone of water.

We returned to the Camry when Winslow came into view. We passed an old woman fast asleep in a red Taurus, and a setter who gazed at us mournfully from the window of a Ford Explorer.

The drive seemed longer than I'd remembered it. I was also surprised at how lush the foliage was on both sides of the road, except for a long stretch through Poulsbo. The forest seemed to be a mélange of evergreen and deciduous trees, birch and ash and western red cedar. The cedar was particularly useful back in the days of the clipper ship. The trees made a lightweight durable timber.

We passed through junctions where a casino or roadhouse, post office and convenience store gave a sense of rural life and community. I saw a lot of trucks, vans, trailers and now and then a man or a woman going to a mailbox or standing in a doorway sipping coffee.

After Port Ludlow, houses and stores began to thicken and eventually we found ourselves gliding down Water Street in Port Townsend. It was 2:30 P.M.

I'd forgotten how rural and old and dreamlike Port Townsend is, how the old brick and stone buildings that line Water Street at the base of a high cliff seem to permanently gaze into the dreams and aspirations of the late nineteenth century, when high-masted ships like the *Glory of the Seas* or the *Susie T. Plummer* lay at anchor in the waters by Union Wharf and bars and bordellos provided entertainment for the sailors and bolstered the booming economy. Port Townsend is quintessentially Western, but salt air and fresh breezes blowing in from the Strait of Juan de Fuca ruffle the puddles and invigorate the nerves, imbuing everything with a distinctly marine character. Even if you don't sail or dive or do much in the water except drink it and look at it occasionally, the vastness that is the ocean reddens the brick and makes the glass shine harder.

We were both quite hungry but our dinner with Valerie wouldn't be until around five or six o'clock. Ronnie said she was feeling a little nauseated and faint. She needed food.

We parked in a lot outside a promising series of shops, the largest of which was quaintly named Quimper Mercantile, on Water Street, which is a community-owned company. People of the Quimper Peninsula own shares in it. Quimper Mercantile didn't have the kind of snacks we were looking for, but they seemed to have a colossal miscellany of everything else: shoes, bed linens, towels, fishing gear, jack knives, fat woolly socks, climbing carabiners, boots, raincoats, frying pans and gardening supplies. It served the purpose of an old-timey general store.

Outside, while we were standing on the curb wondering where to go next in our search for snacks, a friendly woman who had overheard our request for beverages and snacks gave us directions to a small deli called Getables, a few doors down past Taylor, offering cheese and pickles and baked goods and a variety of beverages. I fished out a concoction of mandarin orange from a barrel-shaped container full of ice while Ronnie nabbed some water and two sandwich halves stuffed with lettuce and turkey. We paid for our "getables" at a beautiful counter of wooden laminate. I remarked on the counter to the owner who told me he'd bought it at IKEA and then added that he'd coated it heavily with polyurethane, which gave it a high gloss. It looked new, but it was over a year old.

We'd made reservations online at the Washington Hotel, which we located between a dealer in rare books on the north side — RARE AND ANTIQUE AND COLLECTIBLE BOOKS — and a boutique of vintage clothing to the south which wrapped around the corner. The boutique was aptly named the Wandering Wardrobe. We found the address and sign for the Washington Hotel, inscribed in modest black letters on a white background, but no grand entryway, not even a lobby. Ronnie punched in a code and the door opened. We walked up a long flight of beige carpeted steps at the top of which a giant fleur-de-lis reposed on a small table. Our room was toward to the back. Classical music played on the radio/CD player adjacent upturned wine glasses and coffee mugs. An abstract painting of white and black hung above the commode. From a distance it looked like zebra skin, but upon closer examination it looked more like black water moving sinuously among chunks of pure white ice. A blue vase with a bouquet of cattails reposed on an endtable to the north of the bed. I looked out onto the graveled parking lot, where our rental car was parked in front of an old wooden door upon which was written, "OVERWEIGHT

MERMAIDS," underneath which a large white arrow pointed to the south, ostensibly to another cellar door that was hidden from view. It was odd not seeing anyone as we got situated in our room. It felt as if the hotel were run by fairies who chose to remain invisible.

It was, as advertised, a quiet room. I wasn't sure whether the adjacent building of antique cars was intended as a warehouse, a garage or a parts shop dealing mainly in retail in which old men with crinkly faces and white hair sprinkled astute queries with colloquies of helpful advice. However, I could not see any human activity, just murky silhouettes of what appeared to be machinery, oil cans or transmissions. I tried closing the blinds, but the cord wouldn't budge. I fussed with it a little, pulled the valence out a little and tried to peer through the little hole through which the cords ran, but couldn't see any switch or gear or toggle I could try to loosen. The cords remained as frozen in place as if they'd been nailed to the window sill. Well, I thought, why worry if there's no one in the antique car building? It was a continuing frustration, however, to look at those cords and not believe that there was probably something very simple I was overlooking, some little switch or button, and so bring the slats down with a mild clatter and bring shade and privacy into our room. Ronnie speculated it might even work by remote, like the radio and TV, but there were only the two remotes one for the radio and one for the TV. No wand or doodad that might be connected with window blinds.

I have trouble with gadgets. I have trouble with icons. I don't understand what they're intended to mean. The windows on our rented Camry were electronic, and all but the windows on the driver's side refused to go down. I thought the wiring had gone awry, but discovered later, while we were waiting for the Seattle ferry that the two little icons representing padlocks that were indented in white on the two little buttons above the small levers that maneuvered the windows up and down, locked and unlocked the windows. Locking car doors made obvious sense, but windows? What was the purpose of locking windows? Ronnie surmised that it had to do with keeping little kids from playing with the windows and falling out of the car. I found the lack of a manually operated window and all this electronic gadgetry maddening. I was used to muscling the windows up and down on our old Subaru, not to mention every car I'd owned in the past. This dependency on electronics unsettles me. I like levers and buttons. I like things you can push and pull. I like dexterity. I like engagement. I like the joy and sensuality of a well-designed object. I am especially perturbed, as in the case with our new dishwasher, when even the buttonness of the buttons goes missing and there is only the mere implication of a button on an otherwise smooth surface of shiny plastic. Pressing a sign or an abstract image instead of a tangible device is disquieting. I need physicality. I need solidity. A world of pure signage makes me nervous. I know how slippery signs and symbols can be. Here, at least, was something tangible to press. I clicked the "off" icon and Ronnie's window rolled down with a gentle hum. Sea breezes wafted through the car. I could hear the ruffle of paper as the white-haired woman in sunglasses read the Sunday paper in the white Lexus parked in the lane to our left.

It felt good to walk around Port Townsend. The pace was decidedly slower than Seattle, and the people appeared to be normal people, not the zombie-Android-smartphone addicts I see on Seattle's sidewalks and streets staring fixedly in hypnotic trances at a smartphone or iPad. And they were friendly. People offered information with gladness and zest. There were no homeless people, no one cadging money. Everyone seemed to feel very much at home. I counted at least five bookstores, high glass windows in Victorian buildings of brick and stone revealing the spines and tantalizing covers of hundreds of books, including stacks of Priscilla Long's *The Writer's Portable Mentor: A Guide to Art, Craft, and the Writing Life*. I felt simultaneous ascensions of joy, nostalgia and loss in seeing all these bookstores and living testaments to the enduring invention of the book, colophons and vellum and luscious Moroccan binding inviting the eyes and fingers for communion with the word, the beautiful printed word. Not the word behind the cold corporate plastic of a computer screen, but words embedded in paper. Fully committed words. Printed words. Words in frigate cohesion creaking with topgallant ideas. Words between visions and propositions. Between funny feelings, heady sensations and radical speculations. Between firm, tangible covers. Between tender buttons. Between fables and caves.

Port Townsend appears to be a remarkably literary town, which may be either a cause, or side effect, of Copper Canyon Press and the annual arts festival called Centrum. Centrum, unlike Seattle's Bumbershoot, where the literary arts have all but disappeared and have always been treated like the poor bedraggled cousin to the pop music acts that now dominate the fair, continues to showcase the literary arts.

Ronnie dialed Valerie's number and handed the smartphone to me. These objects always feel strange and awkward. Valerie's phone rang and I waited for the beep to leave a message. I left a message. I said we had arrived and were getting situated in our hotel room and that we'd be over at about four. The phone rang back a few minutes later and Ronnie handed it to me again. Hi, said Valerie. You've arrived. Come on over. Which way are you going? I'm right across from Fort Worden.

You must be well-protected, I joked. I don't know which way we're coming. I'll ask Ronnie. She's able to Google a map. What way are we taking to Valerie's house?

I thought we'd go up Jackson to Monroe.

Jackson to Monroe, I said into the air with the phone at my ear. It's a puzzle to me how one's voice enters into a smartphone. I missed the standard telephone receiver with its little holes. I felt more like I was pouring my voice into a machine and a network of wires than talking to phantom friends. The phone receiver had weight, too. The telephone conferred weight to your words. A conversation could weigh eight pounds and squeeze itself into the phone like a homunculus of words crawling into a cave. The voice coming out of the phone emerged shiny and light like a bubble that popped in your mind shedding light and information. Unless it was your father, work supervisor or bill collector. There were as many voices in the world as people. Some voices had warmth and other voices were cold as Montana granite.

Cherry is better, Valerie said. Valerie's voice was soft, like that of a young woman, although she was in her early seventies. She also seemed genuinely eager to hear from us.

Ok, we'll check out Cherry. See you in a bit. Bye.

I handed the phone back to Ronnie.

It felt odd to be going to Valerie's house for dinner. We'd only met her the one time, when we read together at Elliott Bay Book Company in Seattle. We seemed to have had a rapport, a mutual love of French literature and culture. Valerie had lived in France for eighteen years. She'd married a French sculptor. They lived in a small village surrounded by vineyards in the Loire Valley called Le Puy-Notre-Dame. Valerie had loved living in France, but when the marriage went south, she had to return to the United States, where she taught creative writing at a number of universities. She'd lived in New Orleans and Marfa, Texas, and Boulder, Colorado.

It was no problem at all finding Valerie's big black mailbox and house. And it was, indeed, right across the street from Fort Worden. It looked like a scene from *An Officer and a Gentleman*. I wouldn't have been surprised to see Louis Gossett, Jr., marching a company of men in front of the barracks.

Fort Worden had ceased being a military base in July 1957, and became a diagnostic and treatment center for troubled youths. The Washington State Parks and Recreation Commission reopened Fort Worden as a state park on August 18, 1973. The bunkers were still there, and it was fun and interesting to explore them, and imagine the artillery whose ten- and twelve-inch barrels poked from the walls. The guns were never used. They were dismantled and sent to the fronts in Europe during World War I.

Valerie was gardening when we arrived. She was dressed casually in a loose-fitting dress of dark purple velour. Her hair was long and thick and black. Her eye twitched in the sunlight and she said she'd been having occasional problems with the eye since bumping her head on a door in Paris.

Her house was enormous. She led us into the dining room which flowed into a sunroom where a number of books were stacked and a chair faced north, toward the fort. I envied her quiet and solitude. I had to contend with noisy neighbors on a daily course, doors slamming, feet pounding, power saws screaming, grinders grinding, people shouting and the strange noises emerging from the upstairs bathroom when Terri and Rocco were going through their hygienic ministrations. Some days it sounded like Snoqualmie Falls and Lake Sammamish were in a wrestling match.

She invited us to sit at an enormous dining table. There was a gigantic shell reposing at the far southern end. It seemed like the kind of table where people drink a lot of wine and burst into lusty German songs.

Valerie poured some of the Chardonnay that Ronnie purchased to bring with us into two big wine glasses and set them down on the table. I reached for mine then suddenly realized it was wine. I'm sorry, I told Valerie, I forgot to tell you I don't drink. She gave Ronnie a second glass and poured me some grape juice, which she was having herself for some reason.

Valerie presented us each with artichokes and earthenware saucers of melted butter. I tore off a leaf and dipped it in the butter, put it in my mouth and slid the leaf between my front teeth, scraping off the flesh.

Valerie joined us at the table and told us about the number of animals she'd seen in the neighborhood, mainly raccoon and deer. The neighborhood was full of deer. She told us about going outside one morning to find a female deer looking at her very imploringly and Valerie discovered a fawn trapped in her window well. The animal was in a panic and struggling hard to get out. Valerie got down into the well and helped the fawn out and the mother deer made an odd humming sound and headed for the woods with the fawn following close behind. I remarked on animal intelligence and in particular Graham, who constantly astonished me with his ability to jump from the floor to the arm of a chair and then onto the table cluttered with books and pens and notebooks without disturbing a single thing. He is able to map out a plan in a split second before he jumps. I couldn't do that. If I were his size and attempted to do the same thing I'd make a mess. It's a type of intelligence that I don't possess. Michel de Montaigne has an essay, "An Apology for Raymond Sebond," in which he praises the intelligence of animals. "What aspects of our human competence cannot be found in animals," he inquires. "Their very movements serve as arguments and ideas."

I can see myself killing an animal if I were driven by hunger, I confessed. If I was desperately hungry and I was in the possession of the necessary skills to bring an animal down and dress it and prepare it for eating, I would. I can see myself doing that. But it pains me to think of doing that. What boggles my mind are people who hunt for sport. For the sheer pleasure of it. I can't wrap my mind around that. Where is the pleasure in killing an animal? Especially these tough guys like Ted Nugent who go hunting with a bow and arrow, as if this were performing some benefit for the animals, honoring them in some way. That's absurd. Because you're far more liable to miss and wound an animal with a bow and arrow, in which case the animal will most likely get away long enough to die slowly and painfully.

I was astonished at how fast Valerie and Ronnie ate their artichokes. I'd only managed to dip a few leafs. Most of the artichoke was still sitting conspicuously on my earthenware plate.

We told Valerie about our upcoming trip to Paris, and our growing worries over pickpockets. Valerie said it was a valid concern. Her son had gone to Italy shortly after he graduated from high school, he was only seventeen, and some Italian youths distracted him while another came up from behind and sliced off his money belt and ran off with everything he had. He somehow made his way to the American consulate, who sent him back home to the United States. This did little to alleviate our worries, but underscored the need for caution.

Ronnie remarked on the beauty of the Indonesian shadow puppets that seemed to occupy all the nooks and crannies of the house, their finely chiseled features lending an otherworldly aspect to the space. Valerie said she just liked them. She hadn't actually seen any plays done with them, or been to Indonesia. I commented on how much Antonin Artaud loved these figures and the shadow plays. He said that out of their angular and syncopated modulations, the sounds produced at the back of the throat by the men operating the puppets, the thrum of insects, the hush of the ocean wind through jungle leaves, the beating of the gamelan, the intricate gestures and attitudes, emerged the sense of a physical language based on signs rather than words.

That's fascinating, said Valerie. Signs rather than words. I like that. It brings so much possibility to writing. It opens everything up. There is no single meaning but a play of meaning. Like those shadows behind the screen. Those rickety little puppets animating ancient stories. And with the jungle animals and sensations all around. Wow. That must be something. I'm glad I have them. I just feel strangely drawn to them. I always have.

I noticed one of the books lying in the floor in the sunroom. I could make out the title. It was poetry by Georg Trakl.

You like Georg Trakl?

Oh yeah, I think he's great, said Valerie.

I picked it up and carried it to the table and opened randomly to some lines in a poem titled "De Profundis," which I read out loud: "I am a shadow far from darkening villages / I drank the silence of God / out of the stream in the trees. / Cold metal walks on my forehead. / Spiders search for my heart. / It is a light that goes out in my mouth."

Wow, that line, "cold metal walks on my forehead," I love that, I said. Reminds me of some of the hangovers I used to have.

How long has it been since you stopped drinking? Valerie asked.

It will be twenty-three years in a few days.

Do you miss it?

Yes, I said. A lot. It's such an unimaginable luxury to be able to change your mood with a single glass of wine, or whiskey. Jesus, I loved whiskey. Trouble is, once that twenty or thirty minutes of euphoria dissipates, I had a tendency to try and keep it there by drinking more. And, of course, it doesn't work. You can't lure that chimera back into your being with booze. I remember those nights passing out in front of the TV and waking up at three in the morning to see Simply Red singing "Holding Back the Years" or Billy Idol doing "Eyes Without a Face." I remember hangovers so bad I couldn't appease them with codeine. The malaise was intense. I felt like death warmed over. Cold metal walked on my forehead a lot back in those days.

Valerie brought the freshly grilled salmon to the table and served it with blueberries and mashed sweet potatoes. I normally don't care for salmon, it tastes like cardboard, but this salmon was very tasty, quite remarkable. I ate it heartily. I did less well with the sweet potatoes, which I've never liked very much. My taste in food is plebian. I've tried refining my palate over the years, and have occasionally succeeded, discovering food in some French restaurants that was more like music than food. But gourmet activities like that cost a pretty penny. Ronnie did all of our cooking, and she was quite good, but she cooked on an electric range that has serious limitations. We mostly ate pasta, fettuccine Alfredo and gnocchi and linguini carbonara. I washed the dishes. That was my specialty. I wasn't particularly good at it, Ronnie always fussed over the kitchen after I finished, but I did it with gratitude and diligent fluency. I loved the little brush. It was such a handy little thing. And the sponge, too, which had a rough side and a soft side. But the most amazing element was water. Water never ceases to amaze me. Running water especially. That's what worried me the most about the fall of capitalism. The loss of running water. The loss of any kind of water. Potable water especially. It pained me every time Lyle brought out the power washer and wasted all those gallons so that the sidewalk and parking lot looked pristine and pretty. Christ, I hated that thing.

After dinner, I asked about some painting Valerie had mentioned earlier. Her studio was below, in what used to be a garage. I asked if we could go down and see it.

Sure, she said.

We followed her down the steps and as we approached I could smell familiar odors, paint and thinner and adhesives and liquid acrylics I associated with my father. The basement of my father's house always smelled of those things.

Valerie's paintings featured simple shapes with intricate geometric patterns. They reminded me a lot of aboriginal art, especially an object called a *tjurunga*. The *tjurunga* is a sacred object of stone or wood, quite often bearing intricate patterns of mythological significance. Each person is considered to have a personal bond with a *tjurunga*, whose energy has cosmic scope and connects mortal beings with the great mythic beings of the universe. It serves as a kind of connecting rod between the material world and the transcendent world of spirit.

We went back upstairs and Valerie made some mint tea. We continued talking about Paris. I described my last visit there, forty-one years ago, and a very sad day at the Gare du Nord, where my first ex-wife first told me she wanted a divorce. I don't know why she waited until that particular moment. I wasn't really expecting it. And a *clochard* was cadging money from me at the same time. He was kneeling in front of me and going on in French. I didn't know what to tell him. I wanted to push him over, whack him in the face, but I also felt like crying, and felt the mad naked terror of my own being rushing in on me once the illusion of the marital bond popped before my face. I was so naïve then. I really believed in loves that lasted forever.

I saw her for the first time in some forty years, I continued, right after I'd been in the hospital for a skin infection. I repeated the whole story of swimming in Lake Washington, getting sick, the quarantine, the morphine, the steady replacement of the IV bag changed every hour or so with yet another antibiotic.

So what was the deal? Valerie asked. A microbe?

Yup. They told me that there had been a spike in infectious diseases. They said it was global warming. The pathogens have grown stronger and more populous. They took cultures, but never told me what it was. I still don't know. I picture a series of Petri dishes in the hospital basement, some spooky lab with white tile walls and fungus-like H. P. Lovecraft organisms growing out of the Petri dishes, weird pink vines entangled and squirming their way across the floor.

Wow, said Valerie. Global warming. I believe it. I've got some friends who are climate scientists. They just shake their heads and say it's over. The coming apocalypse is irreversible.

Ronnie said she envies our cat, Graham. He lives totally in the present.

That would be nice, I agreed. I wish I could live outside chronological time. Be in the now, as the wise ones say.

Anyway, I continued, I'd been out of the hospital one day, which also happened to be my birthday, when the ex called to say she was in town with her new partner. They'd been visiting some friends on Whidbey Island. We met at a coffee shop in Pioneer Square, Seattle's oldest business district with red brick buildings and high stone archways, and sat outside on a patio at a small white table with three white chairs. She introduced me to her partner, a man about my own age with a deep tan and white hair, who graciously excused himself to do some work. I felt like asking him to stay but wasn't sure if his excuse was for real or not and didn't want to impose if he really did have some work to do. He seemed like a nice guy. I really had nothing to say that invited privacy, although I did want to apologize for being such a lousy husband those three years we'd been together. I'd been given to ridiculous insecurities and jealous tirades. It had also been evident that I was rather inept at making money and had had very poor prospects in the bread-winning department. My ambitions ran toward Kerouac's monastic attics, not John Cheever's Westchester lawns. It's a good thing my ex-wife had disembarked early in our marital voyage. She had done quite well for herself. Nevertheless, I couldn't bring myself to tell her how sorry I felt. I still regret that a little now. We spent most of our conversation talking about old friends, what had become of them, where they were now. I couldn't help but wonder how much our paths had diverged. All the people she talked about seemed to be quite well off financially. I was the one who went to college, but she's the one who got all the great jobs, like hosting a cable TV show. I know she meant well, and didn't really seem boastful, she was never like that, always fundamentally a good person, but when I left that meeting I felt like a loser. That whole thing about money and property being equivalents for success in our culture goes deep. It's hard to purge that from our system. It's another kind of infection. As an antidote, I went home and wrote an essay about losers in the movies. Beginning with my hero, Jeff Lebowski.

I've never seen that movie, said Valerie.

Oh, it's great, I said. It's one of my all-time favorites. I've seen it so many times I've lost count. *Bridesmaids* is another good loser movie. Kristen Wiig is terrific. She plays a woman whose bakery has just gone bankrupt and her best friend is about to marry this unbelievably rich guy. Everything goes wrong for her. She even gets kicked off a plane on the way to a bachelorette party in Vegas.

I've heard it was good, said Valerie. Have you been to the Rose?

The Rose was an historic little movie theater, which the poet James Broughton had invested in. It opened in 1907 and showed movies featuring the big names of the era, people like Tom Mix, Mary Pickford, Douglas Fairbanks and Lillian Gish.

Not on this trip, I said. We went to see a movie last time we were here, back in 1995. *Cry the Beloved Country*, with James Earl Jones.

Valerie provided us with a list of places to see in Paris, the Gallery of Paleontology and Comparative Anatomy, the Museum of Mineralogy, the Museum of Zoology and advised us to get a Michelin Guide.

We said our goodbyes, and drove back to the hotel in our rented Camry. It was still light out, and the cliffs on Whidbey Island across the bay turned gold.

Ronnie got up early on Saturday morning. She made coffee and read Colin Jones's *Paris: The Biography of a City*, making herself comfortable on the gigantic leather covered daybed in the spacious sitting room. The bedroom was filled with sunlight. As soon as we got dressed we went out to have breakfast at Sweet Laurette. Ronnie looked it up on her smartphone, which gave her a Google map in diminished size. Only one of the streets was named. The restaurant looked farther away than I'd imagined. We walked south on Washington Street to the Haller Fountain, a half-naked young woman in dark bronze strides gracefully forward above two cherubs riding monstrous fish, an apparent hybrid between dolphins and demonic goldfish, water arching from their snouts, the cherubs blowing into conch shells from which water also jets in spritely arcs of fountain classicism. The woman holds a swatch of thin drapery above her head, her right arm in a graceful upward curve, her left arm descending gracefully to her hand, her fingers extending delicately in feminine charm. The fountain was the donation, in 1906, of Theodore N. Haller, and it was intended to honor his deceased father and brother. Haller's dedication speech included a poem about the Greek sea nymph Galatea. The statue first appeared in 1893 at the World Columbian Exposition in Chicago. It is said that a local bar owner in Port Townsend named Charlie Lang placed trout in the pool at the bottom of the statue and trained them to jump through hoops. The Taylor Street stairs behind the fountain lead to the uptown business district, where Sweet Laurette is located.

We found Sweet Laurette easily enough, but it was about 7:15 A.M. and restaurant didn't open for breakfast until 8:00 A.M. We sat on a bench in front of the restaurant but it was too shaded and chilly so we got up and walked around. Ronnie noticed a crow pecking at a freshly killed mouse. The crow picked up the mouse and flew to the corner of the building across the street.

We visited an old yellowish clapboarded building that looked like a Grange hall but was in fact a movie theater. Today's feature was *Man of Steel*. The agitations of the crow we'd seen earlier caught our attention and we saw a young gray cat playing with a dead mouse, which the crow must have dropped from his perch on the corner of the building. We wondered if it was sheer carelessness on the part of the crow, or if the crow had seen the cat and dropped the mouse in order to get her teased and agitated. The crow hunched down and let loose a barrage of squawks at the cat while the cat pranced around the mouse not quite sure what to do with it. She eventually surrendered the mouse and the crow flew it to the top of another building.

The Rose movie theater was close to our hotel, but we hadn't time to see a movie there this time around, which didn't matter, as we'd already seen the feature film, *Mud*, with Matthew McConaughey, which is a damn good movie. The main character is none other than the Mississippi River. *Mud* is an appropriate title for this movie. The imagery is so visually intense you can smell the water and catfish, you can feel the current and the pain and bewilderment and joy in the voices of the people. You can feel what it's like to start an outboard motor and the complex emotions of being betrayed and loved by a woman simultaneously, in very much the same way a river brings sweetness and bounty but can also kill you.

Sweet Laurette opened its doors where a small group of hungry people had gathered. A young woman led Ronnie and I to a table in the center of the small restaurant and gave us some menus. I was leaning toward pancakes when we first entered, but started worrying about calories and being stuck in a car all day and gaining weight, and written in small letters beneath the three offerings of pancake (lemon ricotta pancakes, lemon and blueberry Dutch baby, apple and pear Dutch baby) was the warning that it may take a little extra time to get these dishes made. I decided to go high protein and ordered a Croque Madam, "all natural honey baked ham, gruyere cheese, two fried eggs and mayo-dijon spread on griddled sourdough, served with griddled potatoes." Ronnie ordered the Farmer's Market Scramble, which consisted of griddled potatoes and toast and whatever the "season dictates" in the way of fruit and vegetables. June was dictating cantaloupe and honeydew melon. Ronnie said the potatoes weren't quite crispy enough for her taste, and the coffee could have been a little stronger, but everything else was fabulous.

The waitstaff at Sweet Laurette were all women and were liberal with the coffee, which I thought was strong and tasty. I noticed some odd scripture tattooed on the wrist of a young woman refreshing my mug of coffee and asked her what language that was. I thought it might be Hebrew. She said it was Sanskrit, and was a prayer from the Bhagavad Gita meaning, roughly, oh lord please remove all illusion so that I may see the truth. I told the waitress that we may be illusions and she cracked up laughing.

THE PULSE OF
EXPERIENCE

I can see agitations of air rustle the plastic in the windows of the apartment in the house next door. Someone no doubt left a door open, so that it is full of cross-currents, and dialogues of air, but it looks like the house has filled with a spirit that isn't so much trying to get out as to spar with the soul of interiority. None of this is real, of course, but is a perception gone awry on a summer afternoon, filling in those spaces formerly occupied by logic and watercolor. Don't ask what your perceptions can do for you, ask what you can do for your perceptions.

The woman who lived in the lower unit moved. We never got to know her, but liked her. She had a quiet manner. She was tall and heavyset and middle-aged and seemed to have a profession that paid a lot of money, which you would most certainly require for the high rents Bronson charges, but lived humbly, graciously, serenely. Bronson has been working in the apartment, burnishing the floor, painting, patching, redoing the moulding. It's hard to imagine why so much work is needed. The woman was so quiet. It's not like she had wild Holly Golightly parties every weekend.

Ronnie hopes the new tenants, whomever they turn out to be, will also be quiet. I am not that hopeful. I tend to fear the worse. I run narratives through my mind that involve bratty kids, barking dogs and meth dealers. Loud professionals who like throwing big shindigs on the patio. This is my tendency, my curse. I try not to do it. I try to keep my mind empty, clean, void of silly, telescoping worries that tire my brain with the weight of their doom-laden postulates and limitless capacity for mayhem. I long for a state of *mushin*, the term Zen masters use to designate no-thought or no-mind. *Mushin*, a Japanese word, means "mind without mind," and refers to a state in which the mind is not fixed or occupied by thought or emotion and thus open to everything. I think of the apartment next door in its empty state, free of furniture, bills, occupancy, the floors freshly burnished, the breezes blowing through willy-nilly. I imagine a mind, my mind, free of furniture, overstuffed chairs with broken springs, worries tossed through the window and carried away by truck to a landfill of vexations and torments.

It's harder than I ever imagined to keep an open mind. Suspending judgment is difficult. I feel the hammer of an inner malaise. I am continually constructing patterns. The drive to make sense of things is irresistible. This in itself isn't a bad thing, but my tendency is to veer toward the dark and calamitous. The compulsion to make forecasts based on barometers of gall and isobars of bile is obsessive. The eye swallows a landscape and a pattern stumbles out, a danse macabre or "Garden of Earthly Delights."

Not always. The patterns are sometimes just that: patterns. Neutral as a logarithm. Impersonal as an improper fraction. The process, as Alfred Whitehead described it, is a composite of changeable entities considered in term of singular causality, about which categorical statements can be made. Each experience is a synthesizing process of feeling this wide environment and bringing its factors to a new head, self-enclosed and privately enjoyed. He borrows William James's phrase, "drop of experience," to describe this phenomenon as a cause with observable effects. He also uses the phrase "pulse of experience," because experiencing is an active process. A capacity for the spontaneous introduction of something not present in the environment is part of the structure of every experience. Each pulse of experience occurs as an atom of process, integrative or confluent in shape. Added to this is an internal principle of self-creation. Our experience derives from a natural world of throbbing actualities, into which we put our individual paddle.

The central hypothesis of cognitive science is that thinking can best be understood in terms of representational structures in the mind and computational procedures that operate on those structures. But this isn't what happens. What happens is the concentration of emotional energy upon some object or idea. A nude woman swims with a beluga whale near the Arctic Circle and I strain to feel what that feels like. But can't. Not entirely. The main problem isn't imagining myself in that situation, but in imagining the sensations coursing through my body. I find that it's easier to do that if I empty my mind of other distractions. Ideas. Assumptions. Suppositions. And leave a bare, open space. A flock of grebes. A biology of attraction. A nude woman swimming with beluga whales near the Arctic Circle.

How did the Arctic get to be a circle? The present tense has an unshakable certitude. It is raining. It is not raining. It is everything motivated by a carefully maintained illusion. Wild toads pull me to Oregon. There is a chair that talks and a chair that flutters its wings. Once an openness of mind is achieved, everything wants to be in it. Everyone wants a starring role. Objects suddenly assume character. The dim interior light of an airplane at night becomes a theory of rain dripping from the mouth of a gargoyle.

I decide to go for a run. To walk is to swim in the mind, but to run is luminous. I go up McGraw. There is always that splotch of white paint on the sidewalk that resembles the head of an extraterrestrial. I get to Fifteenth Avenue West and notice that the statue of the former brown bear and her three cubs has been replaced by a fully erect grizzly bear, fierce and imposing, with claws of gold. It's huge. I wonder if it's built to scale. Are grizzly bears that big? There's one cub, which the grizzly is ostensibly protecting as she claims her position on the rock.

I get to the Myrtle Edward trail and smell the unmistakable odor of Puget Sound at low tide. The smell consists mainly of rot but also desire, turmoil and the pull of the moon. There are two huge cruise ships moored at Pier 91, one of which is called *Celebrity Solstice*. I Google it later and discover that it has over a thousand cabins and staterooms and ten specialty restaurants, basically a floating city.

A container ship glides into Elliott Bay. The water is quiet this afternoon, hardly a wave on it. It has a deep blue color and complements the blue of the sky with an occasional flash of white or squiggle of foam.

I run past Michael Heizer's *Adjacent, Against, Upon*, a dramatization of words in four giant granite slabs.

Chrissie Hynde sings "Brass in Pocket" on an acoustic guitar in a crowded Manhattan bistro, but that's going on in my head, and is not in external reality. It was in external reality, but now it's a memory. It is the mental residue of an event that took place earlier in the day when I was watching YouTube.

I arrive at the Seattle Center's International Fountain and see hundreds of children playing around the central hemisphere bristling with spigots. Water shoots out at different intensities at different intervals while music plays. Today a Middle Eastern song is playing with a male singer who sounds astonishingly like those calls to Mecca heard from the towers of Amman and Baghdad. It is as if the Kaaba of Mecca had been replaced by a bright silver hemisphere shooting arcs of water out of an array of nozzles, the white-robed worshippers of Mecca replaced by hundreds of screaming children.

When completed, this paragraph will weigh 55 pounds and will house an olive grove and have very little to do with anything else other than its own internal drive to exist, to be a paragraph, an organism of words, a translucent membrane teeming with words, living forms, thought-provoking thought into infinite ramification, pretzels and zippers ironic as pharmaceuticals apologizing for all the pain of existence, ameliorating the ache of existence, ideas of paradise percolating through the sediment of its sentences as it continues to grow, like The Blob, into a pulsing gelatinous entity of alcoholic predicates and lambent nouns.

Meanwhile, life goes on, *ob-la-di ob-la-da*, the pipes behind the kitchen sink are making loud clicking sounds and the refrigerator is leaking. I had to put a pan in the fridge to collect all the water dripping beneath the freezer. I suspect it's a frozen drainpipe. I suspect more than that. It's as if the apartment somehow sensed that we were saving money and preparing for a trip overseas and didn't want us to go. No, you have to stay here and take care of me, buy me a new refrigerator, rip out the kitchen wall and give me new pipes, new sink, new faucet, new *ob-la-di ob-la-da*.

Here comes a new paragraph: there is a string dangling from it. If you pull the string, it begins to grind into motion, little pulleys and gears creating a fern whose fronds are inundated with golden summer light. A towering cypress sags into meaning. Black tentacles surround the Wine World & Spirits boutique and pull it into the water. A giant squid gets drunk and listens to The Beatles. A Viking *drakkar* glides past the base of a high rocky cliff in dead silence. Elevators graze in a public square. A shattered perception turns moody and enters the paragraph, penetrating its syntax and becoming a large cumulus cloud on the verge of thunder. An eyeball drags itself along eating words. The play of light and shadows congeals into a meaning. A philosophy of fern. The dreams of a gluttonous king. The ghost of Brian Jones. And I can't help but feel that if I pull the string again something new will form, something large, something sublime, something bold and approaching from the distance under a huge blue sky beautiful as an open mind.

PREPARING FOR PARIS

How do you prepare for something like Paris?
You don't. You just go.

A lot of people go: according to *Forbes*, Paris is the third most visited city in the world. My emotional craving for that destination seemed almost supernatural because of my infatuation with its literature, primarily Rimbaud, Baudelaire and Mallarmé. It is difficult for me to accept that for thousands of others Paris is just a great place to go for food, romance and wine. A kind of Disneyland for adults.

So when I say, how do you prepare for something like Paris, it means how does one prepare to enter into a dream? Or a drug-induced hallucination? Or another planet?

Paris, I reminded myself, is a place, in the same way that Las Vegas, Pittsburgh and Crater Lake National Park are places.

There are, however, a few things I thought it might be prudent to pack in my viaticum.

I bought a compass, a guidebook and a map. Then we visited the bank and got set up with a no foreign transaction fee credit card account.

Ronnie bought an adapter for her smartphone. France uses a slightly different electrical system.

We already had passports. We got passports after George W. Bush was handed the presidency by the Supreme Court, during an election won by Al Gore. We wanted to be ready in case things became desperate. I'm not sure what is meant by desperate, but apprehensions about the U.S. border shutting down would be one identifiable anxiety. We wanted to get while the getting was good. That worry still exists. Civil rights have been shredded to nothing and homelessness is on the verge of criminalization at a time when the real culprits who caused the loss of so many pensions and foreclosures not only remain free, but have a solid grip on the levers of power. The lockdown of the United States was scary, but too large to digest. When worries become too large to resolve, the mind battens on smaller issues, particulars closer to home. Trivial problems trump catastrophe. They offer a semblance of control.

We worried about pickpockets more than anything, innocent-appearing girls who might push past you while getting onto a crowded Métro car and pluck your wallet out of your pocket simultaneously, and with such dexterity, you won't notice it missing until it's too late. We Googled all sorts of information about ways to prevent such things from happening, from money belts to making a copy of your passport to being especially on the alert near the more touristy areas. Basic common sense. It's amazing how much worry you can invest into a problem before the occasion actually arises. How many different scenarios can you run through your head before you're actually occupying the reality you've been worrying about?

My most prominent memory of France was visiting Saintes-Maries-de-la-Mer during a gypsy festival and meeting the journalist Jerry Hopkins who was in the south of France to describe the festival for *Rolling Stone* magazine. My ex-wife and I spent the day with Jerry and his wife and in the evening they bought us dinner. I remember visiting their hotel suite and seeing Jerry's article still in his manual typewriter, an article I would actually read in *Rolling Stone* some weeks later. Jerry would go on to write a biography of Jim Morrison, who had died mysteriously in Paris the previous summer, in July 1971. What stands out in my memory of that day is its astounding vividness: the humidity, the shades of green and gray, the weathered faces of the older gypsy women and their black shrouds and golden earrings, the shanks of the white horses as Camargue gypsy horsemen carried a doll of the gypsy patron Saint Sara (or Sara la Kali, as she is known to the gypsies, Sara the Black) into the Mediterranean to receive benediction. According to legend, the three Marys (Saintes Maries de la Mer) — Mary Jacobe, Mary Salome and Mary Magdalene — were put to sea in a boat to escape persecution by the Romans. The sea grew rough and threatened to capsize the boat. Sara la Kali, having spotted the imperiled crew, had risked drowning in order to help the three Marys to shore. May 24 has been set aside for the gypsy pilgrimage and re-enactment of the landing. We happened upon the festival by sheer coincidence, and had hitchhiked to Saintes-Maries-de-la-Mer from Arles. I can't remember what drew us there. We were unaware of the pilgrimage until we arrived. Perhaps we'd merely followed all the gypsies, just to see what was up. Shortly after arriving, I'd descended into the fortress-cathedral that houses the sacred doll in a subterranean vault and felt the heat of thousands of lit candles. The doll was still in her niche, where people made offerings in the form of scribbled notes and incense and children's clothes. Sara la Kali is known for her powers to heal and give success. The heat penetrated me to the bone. The sensation was exquisite. I can still feel it.

Forty-one years later I sit at the computer with a map of Paris at my side Googling all the bookstores that French poet Claude Royet-Journoud had emailed me. One of the main reasons I wanted to go to Paris was so I could stand in a real bookstore once again before I die. The bookstores in the United States have deteriorated into something little better than a gift shop, or those book and magazine shops you sometimes see at the airport. Trashy titles. Nothing of any real interest. Books by Dan Brown, Suzanne Collins and Stephanie Meyer. It was disheartening. But at least these were books. Most people were "reading" on electronic devices now. Literature had become digitalized. True readers know that you cannot truly read on an electronic screen. So if somebody held an actual book in their hands, even something as inane and mawkish as *Angela's Ashes* or *Extremely Loud and Incredibly Close*, I felt some gratitude toward that person.

Seattle had at least two really great bookstores, Elliott Bay and Open Books. Open Books was really interesting, since they specialized in poetry, and somehow made a success of it. The store always felt bright and vibrant. Elliott Bay had lost some of its former glory when it moved from its historic lodging in Pioneer Square to a dingier neighborhood on Capitol Hill in a strange, indeterminate zone that had once been full of machine shops and warehouses and was now in the process of metamorphosing into a neighborhood of million-dollar lofts, waxing spas and chic boutiques but was still at a very ambiguous stage of development. It wanted to be Greenwich Village but was still mired in a recent past of greasy machine parts, mismatched nesting tables and busted manikins. It was harder for me to get to Elliott Bay. Pioneer Square had been a short bus ride downtown, and full of art galleries and other interesting things, so I tended to visit it much more frequently before its move to Capitol Hill, where there was little else except pricey boutiques and tattoo parlors. Also, my visits had been to attend or give readings, not for browsing books. I hadn't been able to tell if the new digital media had made inroads into the number of titles they carried.

Not that it really mattered. My tastes were now almost exclusively French. This wasn't because I was a Francophile, but simply because the writers I most admired tended to write in French. Elliott Bay did not carry many foreign titles.

As soon as I Googled an address within Paris city limits and located it on the map, I'd mark it on my paper map and try to orient myself in terms of our hotel. Several were within easy walking distance. One was way out toward what the Parisians called the Boulevard Périphérique. The Périphérique is the generally accepted boundary between the city proper of Paris and its suburbs, or *banlieux*, and consists of one of the busiest highways in Europe. I wanted to stay clear of that area. It was dangerous. That's where the bulk of the riots occurred and cars were burned and rocks and cobblestones hurled at the police *à la* any of France's notorious revolutions. It also had a reputation for nefarious drug trafficking.

There were things at home we needed to do as well that were far less exciting. Entropy showed us no mercy. The apartment somehow sensed that a huge outlay of money was going toward a foreign country and got jealous. It countered by falling apart, and costing us money.

First, the refrigerator began leaking and making odd whining sounds. It was nearly twenty years old, which is probably one hundred and twenty years old in refrigerator years. We bought a new refrigerator online after carefully measuring the space in which it would fit. I felt nervous about shopping for something as formidable as a refrigerator online, but a few days later two large Mexican-American men appeared with the new Whirlpool we'd ordered, black straps around their bodies, and moved the old one out and the new one in.

The blinds also reached their terminus. They were old and hideous. They'd been in the apartment when Ronnie first moved in, some years before she met me. They looked dismal and dingy, like a prop out of a film noir murder mystery in the 1940s starring Humphrey Bogart. So we got new blinds as well. They looked much lighter, and the ones for the front window came in sections, so that we could lower the main set of blinds and leave the one set up where we opened the window. It felt much more private and yet allowed more light into the room. Our apartment is ground-level and very dark. I joked with the man who delivered the blinds when he entered our bedroom, which is as chronically tenebrous as a story by Edgar Allan Poe, that you needed to be a speleologist to negotiate the rifts and stalagmites of our bedroom. The bats. The dead. The scintillating minerals. The shining crystals. The sharp obsidian curves. The Hindu dancers. The dust and tarpaulins. The joists. The indigo revolutions. The melting emotions. The accordion eyes glaring out of abysses of patched time and stretches of engaging lacuna.

The jukeboxes lactating ancient rock 'n' roll in silences denser than jungle rain.

The ceremonies of ghostly metals.

The paradisiacal tremors of calamitous perception.

The hardware of crocodilean late-night apothecaries whose overhead lighting buzzes like strontium buzzards raising their wings to the god of the intrinsically anomalous.

He didn't laugh.

He looked at me with his mouth open and eyes jack-knifing into slobbers of decimated logic.

Maybe he didn't know what a speleologist was.

I wasn't sure myself. I had to look it up later. I got the word right. It just wasn't funny, I guess.

The man who installed the blinds was a bit odd. He was a big man, about six foot five, two hundred and seventy-five pounds, who appeared at our door promptly at 10:00 A.M. as promised with the set of blinds in his arms. He was stunningly efficient and went to work immediately, removing the old blinds, then bringing in the new ones. He said he'd have to come back on Sunday to do the bedroom blinds. I wasn't sure what to make of this, then he said he was joking. I felt foolish for falling for this ruse so easily, but then explained how the guy who installed our new dishwasher was unable to remove a screw because of a manufacturing defect and had to bring the entire dishwasher back to the warehouse where it took a team of five men to remove the screw. He'd had to come back the following week with another dishwasher. So these things happen. It is, in fact, what I have come to expect. SNAFUs. Glitches. Cluster-fucks.

I generally appreciate an attempt at humor, even if the joke in question doesn't work, or come off as truly funny, which was the case here. It wasn't funny. But I didn't really relish his attempt, either. It left me feeling embarrassed and bruised my self-esteem.

I was embarrassed about the window well, as well. The window in the bedroom is narrow and when the blinds are up it reveals a view of a concrete wall, a well approximately five or six feet deep. It had been painted at least once before and some of the paint had begun flaking off and drooped in thin shreds of leaden gray despondency. I'd often had fantasies about scraping those shreds away and repainting that sad desolate surface with flowers or clouds or maybe a duplication of *The Garden of Earthly Delights* by Hieronymus Bosch or Salvador Dali's *The Persistence of Memory.*

I was going to make a joke about my future mural-making plans for the embarrassing window well but the blinds guy got to it first. You should get an artist to paint something here, he said.

You're right, I said. I was thinking something along the lines of *The Garden of Earthly Delights* by Hieronymous Bosch, but it got no laugh. No response. Nada. I remained embarrassed about the window well.

Maybe it would have been funnier if I'd said *The Creation of Adam* by Michelangelo.

Or *Luncheon on the Grass* by Édouard Manet.

Damn salesman, the blinds guy muttered.

Pardon?

I can never get these guys to use lasers for their measurements.

My heart sank. I assumed these two segments weren't going to fit and that his joke about having to come back to redo it was going to come true.

The two sections were off by a fraction, but the blinds guy knocked off a tiny cap on one of the units and it all dovetailed together with a nice crisp click.

Do you have a dumpster where I can put the old blinds?

No, you'd have to leave it off to the side for the garbage crew to pick up. But they'll charge extra for it.

At which point Ronnie swiftly came to the rescue: we paid an extra thirty dollars to have the old blinds taken away. It's on our bill.

I drove my car, the blinds guy said. That situation was not our problem. We said nothing.

Well, he said, I guess I can fold them or saw them in half. I'll work it out.

Great, I said.

The blinds guy removed the old blinds and left. The new blinds were wonderful. I felt a sense of privacy I hadn't had before. And the light had a new bright flavor.

Then there was the matter of shoes. Ronnie needed shoes. I was pretty much set. I had my running shoes and another pair of relatively new running shoes that I could wear for walking around and going to restaurants.

We took a bus downtown and went to a high-end shoe store near Westlake, where months ago we'd gone to donate a sleeping bag, raincoat and forty bucks to the Occupy movement.

We told the young woman helping Ronnie that she needed shoes for travel. The young woman asked where we were going. Paris, said Ronnie. Cobblestones, said the saleslady. You'll need shoes for cobblestone streets.

Wow, I said. You know the streets of the world. That's really cool.

I've never been overseas, said the saleslady, I get my information through hearsay.

How about London, I asked, or Beijing?

The owner of our store is from Beijing, said the young woman. But I'm not sure about the streets there.

China's doing pretty good these days, I said. I would imagine the streets are in pretty good shape.

Ronnie decided on a pair of Dansko sandals with wooden soles.

Later at night, still thinking about streets, and sitting in front of the computer, I looked up rue la Pérouse on Google for a street view. This is the street where Odette lives in Proust's *Du côté de chez Swann*. The street runs roughly north to south in back of the Arc de Triomphe at what is now called the Place Charles de Gaulle. It's a narrow street in which all the buildings are meshed together without any space between, so that it has the feel of a narrow canyon. I can imagine how Swann must have felt when he first began taking Odette home after their night at the Verdurins. Her interior life must have been charged with mystery. Proust describes the touches of nature that seemed delightfully incongruous: "the snow which remained in the garden and on the trees, the untidiness of the season, the proximity of nature, gave something of greater mystery to the warmth, to the flowers which he found at the entrance."

It was odd to think that there was a specific, physical location from Proust's novel that I could visit, touch, smell, experience, though my chances of meeting either Swann or Odette were negligible at best.

The really important thing was to figure out what book I was going to bring with me to read aboard the plane, a ten-hour flight. There would be movies, I was sure, but would there be movies for ten hours, and could I watch movies for ten hours? I was going to make sure I'd bring enough lorazepam to zone out when I needed to sleep, but what book?

I bought a used copy of *La goutte d'or* by Michel Tournier from Magus Books in the University District, one of the best, if not *the* best, used bookstore I'd ever been in. But I couldn't resist reading it. My curiosity got the better of me and I was, frankly, a little worried about the very Middle Eastern look of the front cover, which depicted a young man wearing a turban playing a flute as he watched over a herd of goats. I didn't want anything Middle Eastern about my person as I jumped through the various hoops of the Transportation Security Administration and allowed myself to be frisked and humiliated in exchange for security.

I thought about *L'air et les songes* by Gaston Bachelard, I liked his warm, philosophical touch, but didn't feel secure reading about air while I was in the air. It was also one of my favorite books, and although I was certain I could find another copy, I preferred to bring a used book that I could more easily afford to lose.

A friend had given me a copy of *Connaissez-vous Paris* by Raymond Queneau, which was full of fun facts and statistics about Paris, such as the one place in Paris where there was still a trace of the old Gallo-Roman line when Paris was still known as Lutetia (rue de la Colombe), or the pharmacy at 115 rue Saint-Honoré that was Marie Antoinette's favorite pharmacy and was where her lover Alexis de Fersen purchased the invisible ink with which he communicated secretly with Marie, but would not hold my attention for long. My brain can take only so many factoids before it grows unwieldy and my head tilts to the side with the weight of it.

So I would wait until we were within a few days of our departure and pay a visit to Magus for a small but engrossing book to stimulate and buoy my mind for ten hours of travel through the stratosphere.

BEING AND NOTHINGNESS

Breakfast has become a test of endurance with the toaster. It's slow. It's the slowest toaster of all time. It has outlasted empires. It occupies regions of the space-time continuum with the obstinacy of a barnacle on a Santa Monica boardwalk piling. It measures chronological intervals in terms of geological formation. Its slowness gives the structure and topology of time a voluptuous shape. Its slowness is a curse and a blessing. I have learned how to adapt. I have learned how to maneuver through conceptions of immediacy and sensory experience. I have widened my embrace of the universe. I can smell the burning of distant suns. I can smell the electrical coils of a kiss in the fourth dimension.

Here is what I do while I wait for the toaster: earn a Ph.D. in astrophysics, AstroTurf and ataraxia. Enter marathon poker games in Las Vegas. Raise turkeys. Watch trees cycle through seasonal changes in terms of sap flow density, leaf stomatal conductance and leaf transpiration. Write letters to dead poets. Invent participles. Disassemble and reassemble the refrigerator.

I finish breakfast and go online and try to fix my YouTube problem. It may not be strictly speaking "my" problem. The forums indicate that everyone is having problems with You-Tube. The frame keeps freezing anywhere from ten to thirty seconds into a video. It would appear that Google is having a spam war. I wonder if there is a connection between the frames freezing up and the shitstorm of penis enhancement ads I've been getting and endlessly deleting in my spam file. I can't believe how popular these penis size enhancement pills are. People must actually be purchasing them online. Why would anyone want to increase the size of their penis? It occurs to me that some penises out there might be truly petite. But how is a pill going to increase the size of someone's member? How would that work? What obscure chemical in the jungles of the Amazon has been discovered to increase the size of a man's penis? You don't find women wanting to increase the size of their vagina. I think in that case the situation might be reversed. Reducing the size of a vagina, perhaps, rather than augment its volume. Why do I not see pills for that? Women seem to be better adjusted to whatever nature has given them.

I go for some coffee, but there's only enough to fill not quite half of my Beatles mug. I decide to make more. The lid is stuck. This is a porcelain lid Ronnie recently discovered in our cupboard. She likes these lids. I'm content with the cone reposing on top of the pot. Ronnie prefers to put the cone aside and put a lid on the pot. It's more aesthetic. But I can't get it off. I think it was intended for a different pot and doesn't quite match the size of this pot. It's really stuck. I go for a pair of pliers but then realize I can't use pliers on a porcelain handle unless I can figure out how to cushion the pincers of the pliers. And why is pliers plural? It's really only one tool. Why is it called a "pair of pliers"? I return to the problem at hand. Maybe a butter knife. I get a butter knife and work the tip of the blade under the lid and begin wiggling it a little. I hear something break. There are two small lobes on the underside of the lid to keep the lid from falling into your coffee when you're pouring more coffee into your mug. One of them has broken. But now I can get the lid off. We keep the lid. A lobeless lid fits better than a lobed lid.

I am a reading a page from *Vie de Joseph Roulin* by Pierre Michon, a fragment of which has been read by French actress Alexia Stresi on a program on France Culture radio called *Je déballe ma bibliothèque,* when I hear a knock at the door. I get up to go see who's there. I hear footsteps going up the steps and figure it must be the mailman. It is. I open the door, and there is a package. I open the package. It's a copy of *Being and Nothingness* by Jean-Paul Sartre, a gift from James Heller Levinson and his partner Mary. I happened to mention to him in an email that my copy is lost somewhere in our storage bin and I had to check a copy out from the Seattle Public Library, which someone called back before I could renew it. That was kind of them. I open the book randomly to page 544 and read the beginning of the paragraph at the bottom:

> The "master," the "feudal lord," the "bourgeois," the "capitalist" all appear not only as powerful people who command but in addition and above all *Thirds*; that is, as those who are outside the oppressed community and *for whom* this community exists. It is therefore *for* them and *in their freedom* that the reality of the oppressed class is going to exist. They cause it to be born by their look. It is to them and through them that there is revealed the identity of my condition and that of the others who are oppressed; it is for them that I exist in a situation organized with others and that my possibles as dead-possibles are strictly equivalent with the possibles of others; it is for them that I am a worker and it is through and in their revelation as the Other-as-a-look that I experience myself as one among others. This means that I discover the "Us" in which I am integrated or "the class" *outside*, in the look of the Third, and it is this collective alienation which I assume when saying "Us."

Man, does that bring back memories of every job I've had. I remember one incident in particular with astonishing clarity. I was working for the University of Washington mailing service in a building with three floors. We, the drivers and mail processors doing the actual grunt work, worked on the lower floor with the loading docks and pallets and Pitney Bowes machines. The administrators and program assistants and other more highly esteemed office employees worked on the third floor. The breakroom for the workers was a tiny space that had formerly been a storage closet. It stank so badly I could not go in there. I took my breaks out on the loading dock, even in the cold of winter. The breakroom on the third floor was huge, and had a spectacular view, big tables and comfortable chairs. It was available to me, but the janitor always seemed to be there doing his work during my break. I dated for a short while a woman in her early thirties who worked on the third floor as a program assistant. I was in my early forties. It was quite obvious that although I was fully committed to my writing during my off-hours, I was not enjoying the success of a Tom Robbins or Sherman Alexie. My position was somewhat of an embarrassment to her. I went to visit her during one of my breaks and waited for her in the reception area on the third floor. The big boss strolled in. He was a tall man, probably the same age as me, maybe younger. I still remember his look. He barely looked at me at all, but when my presence there caught his attention, his look was identical to that of someone who had just seen a cockroach, or unidentifiable insect.

Later in the afternoon, I go for my usual run. Puget Sound is very serene. There is a turquoise mist obscuring the Olympic Mountains to the west and four big cargo ships waiting to get loaded with grain at Pier 91.

Water is magical, I think to myself. Everything about it is magical, especially the way it evaporates. Vaporizes, and becomes clouds and columns of turbulent reverie. The reverie is in my head, not in the vapor, but it still seems like reverie, a form of reverie performed by an element. Heat and moisture teased into a Bohemia of wild slippery shapes, elusive apprehensions of invisible forces that blossom into prominences of fleeting convocation.

The snowman in Zen philosophy is a symbol of transcendence. The snowman is water. Water in the form of crystalline ice particles, fine symmetrical flakes that compound into a being made of snow. Which, when the temperature rises, melts and evaporates. Perfect metaphor for the ephemerality of carnal existence. The Nothingness that is at the core of Being.

UNDER THE DOME

There was one other book I felt compelled to read because it captured something essential about Paris. About poetry. About survival. About consciousness and suffering and joy and friendship. About fascism and death and the black milk of daybreak. About wrenching and twisting and recreating language. "Dreamproof skiffs" and "Artpap" and "nightbile knitted behind time." This was *Under the Dome: Walks with Paul Celan*, by Jean Daive. Ronnie had read it and said it was a remarkably beautiful and moving book. It had inspired her to begin reading Paul Celan's *Breathturn*. It was full of references to Paris, and especially the neighborhood in which we'd be staying.

To hear Ronnie talk about Paul Celan was like hearing of an exotic country where a lot of painful and beautiful things have occurred, a place at once alluring and frightening, hellish and paradisiacal. A place where opposites are commingled in a blush of twilight air, where quivers of the ineffable glimmer among the debris of the literal. She said that Paul Celan was from a Jewish family living in a remote part of Europe called

Bukovina, which at the time of Celan's birth in the 1920s was part of Romania and is now a part of the Ukraine.

That Paul Celan's parents had been interned in a concentration camp after the Nazis occupied Cernauti.

That Paul Celan had tried persuading his parents into leaving the country but that his parents had insisted on staying at home and that he'd gotten so angry that he went to spend the night at a family friend's house and it had been on that very night that his parents were arrested and sent by train to an internment camp in Transnistria where his father died of typhus and his mother, exhausted by forced labor and no longer able to work, was shot dead. Paul, who had later been arrested and taken to a labor camp in the Romanian Old Kingdom, learned of their deaths during an exceedingly cold winter. That, partly as a result of immense survivor's guilt and the pain of these events, Celan had developed a highly ambivalent relationship with the German language. His mother had loved the German language and insisted on speaking it in the house. The language became imbued with conflicting emotions, conflicting values. German became a subject of joy and torture, a thing to bend and distort, a hell and an illuminating energy, a monstrous obstruction and an engine of deliverance.

Ultimately, the pain would prove too overwhelming, too enduring. Paul Celan ended his life by suicide, entering the Seine from Pont Mirabeau about April 20, 1970, around Passover. A strong swimmer, he drowned unobserved.

Shortly after Ronnie finished reading *Under the Dome*, another book appeared in our apartment: *Breathturn*, poems by Paul Celan. This was a small book I would often see on the marble surface of the end table on Ronnie's side of the bed on which Paul Celan's face smiles amiably, his eyes peering out deep and dark and penetrating.

I decided to begin with *Under the Dome* in order to get a clearer sense of Celan before reading his work, and get a sense of the neighborhood in which Jean and Paul met and walked and stopped for coffee or shared a dinner. They lived in the same neighborhood and so their encounters were sometimes the product of chance. Sometimes Jean would see Paul from a distance, walking with his hands behind his back, the way he'd seen the poet Edmond Jabés do.

Under the Dome is presented in fragments. There is no narrative chronology beginning with their first meeting and continuing till his death in 1970. Paul Celan appears and disappears at different times on different occasions so that there is a feeling of a continuous present, a period of time roughly from 1965 to 1970, Paul Celan's last, increasingly dark years, recollected from a distance of twenty years in a different part of the world, a Greek Island "amid the still green pears of a café set back from the sea..." Daive identifies the Aegean with an elusive, intangible pain. "The Aegean Sea is in front of me. Against my table and beyond my book, pines, waves breaking on the sand. The Aegean is a wound. I never talk of it. It is blue, transparent, I see it. I don't see the wound."

Always nearby is a donkey whose immobility serves to underlie a spiritualistic distance of some testimonial, unconquerable mass of time. "He does not eat. He does not work... The donkey is all I think about. He augments a distance... In the solitude of the island, the donkey's presence sometimes rends the air. He cries, he weeps, he brays. I hear him. And I hear within me a still living mass fall into the sea, into the Seine."

The donkey is a medium, a meridian collapsing the barriers of time, the past from the future, the future from the past. The donkey is assertively there, occupying space, yet seems to be outside time, occupying a zone similar to that of a fundamental plane marking an imaginary sphere of the present (a café on a Greek island) to its counterpart in the past (Paris in the late 1960s) and so creating the hemispheres of an imaginary zone where events in the past appear to be projected on the inside surface of a celestial sphere, lucid and phantasmal, like images in a camera obscura, as if the mind were a lens and the sky was the underside of a dome. Jean Daive peers across this horizon at events that continue to occur in a living tableau of the past, in which chestnuts thud to the earth and he and Paul Celan "walk side by side, the Seine black on our right...

We step over ladders, tables, chairs, cross bridges, walk along façades, railings, more façades, walls, more walls. Two voices. We are two voices. One low, the other toneless. Many juvenile gestures. Complicit looks. Smiles. Lots of complicity. We linger under the mass of a paulownia, then make for the chestnut trees farther on. Night. Moon. We talk. Jubilantly. The 'Aufklärung.' 'Hung up on the inner corpse,' Paul Celan quotes Artaud. 'There are two ideal states for man: extreme simplicity and extreme culture.' A remembered poster: 'THE ONE ALONE EXISTS.' We look down on the moist leaves. Rustlings that we interpret. We advance into the swinging night. The invisible."

"Syntax torments the narrative that words cannot untangle," writes Daive. "A story means progression, means torment." Daive's fragments oppose progression. Each is a dreamscape, a dream place, phantasmal and outside the limits and torments of time. "The poet's room is full of words," observes Gaston Bachelard in *The Poetics of Reverie*. "Words which move about in the shadows. Sometimes the words are unfaithful to the things. They try to establish oneiric synonymies between things. The phantomalization of objects is always expressed in the language of visual hallucinations. But for a word dreamer there are phantomalizations through language. In order to go to those oneiric depths words must be given time to dream."

The news of Celan's death is trauma. It leaves a scar, a tear in the membrane of time, and causes a break with the grounded and literal, with everything in fact. Even language: "My distress afterwards. Lasts and lasts. A month of emptiness, of anguish. Of no solid ground. Days absolutely empty. I feel his death in me as a break with the human world. With language."

The incidents related in fragments are marked by the kind of vividness, the kind of lucidity that accompanies a heightened sense of the transitory. "I may know that our travels on earth are a dream. They must be. Interrupted by the flash of an encounter."

It is these sudden bursts, these *éclats* of lightning-bright insight, the rush of lucidity into the shadows and vague apprehensions of our consciousness, these profound experiences of the unsayable, the ineffable that take our breath away. That give a start. We pause. We reflect. We resume our breathing. But with an augmentation. With an inhalation of fumes from an abyss, which we call inspiration, a magnitude of excitement characterized by an acute sense of otherness, particularly the inaccessible other in oneself. It is a species of awakening that Celan termed *Atemwende*, or *Breathturn*, and provided as title to a collection of poetry published in 1967. "Poetry... holds its breath before the problematic legitimacy of submitting the question of life to the question of Being, of life to Being," observed Jacques Derrida in his book on the poetics of Paul Celan, titled *Sovereignties in Question* in English, *Schibboleth* in French.

One imagines the color red as a whisper emanating from jagged tear in the canvas of time. Followed by silence. A deep, impenetrable silence, aphorisms of frost on the bump of being. Furrows imprinted with the hooves of deer, which may also be the dance of stars.

"Moderation is never obscure, and excess is always captive of knowing," Celan tells Daive on one of their walks in Paris's Contrescarpe. The Place de la Contrescarpe, with its little chain fence and fountain, is in the Faubourg Saint-Médard and is situated at the junction between the rue Mouffetard and the rue de Lacepede. The open-air market of the square Saint-Médard unfolds to the south, and to the north the rue Descartes attracts the thirsty *flâneur* with its small, trendy bars. This vicinity is notorious for its outlaw bohemian poets and colorful authors. François Villon frequented its streets and caroused in its taverns, the most popular of which, the Maison de la Pomme de Pin, sold cheap, untaxed wine. It was not uncommon to find Rabelais drinking there. The Place de la Contrescarpe is a crowded area, crowded not just with people but a huge variety of shops and markets teeming with window-shoppers and buyers — spirited, colorful places selling everything from wines and baguettes to hookahs and handmade pastas, ancient maps and almanacs, a stuffed yeti or the skeleton of a tiger, alluring vials of mandrake oil, miniature magnetic Eiffel Towers and snow globes galore for what the French call *les chionosphéro-*

philes, people with the uncontrollable urge to collect snow globes. The Faubourg Saint-Médard is a heaven for the incurable chionospherophile.

Daive writes: "By his side, I feel enclosed in a dark knowing without unease, hence without irritation. He is aware of it: no stranger to anything in the world... A world as in a dream, nocturnal, unraveling around the paulownias of the Contrescarpe. Crates stained with peach juice, crates full of half rotten tomatoes, black hands eating almost liquid pears and bluish hearts of lettuce... We walk down rue Mouffetard... The clouds scatter in the distant sky and beyond the sky."

"There are two worlds," Celan tells Daive, "the world and the world of the star. And I haven't yet mentioned the world of the shoelace."

There is also the world of the shell.

"Toward the end of winter," Daive writes, "Paul visits me on rue Coquillière... He crosses the footbridge and notices the three leaves carved in lead. He comes in, charmed by the place. 'Your place is a place of poetry. A poet's place.' Too taken aback to reply, I wait for him to finish his praise to announce: 'You know, the meal will be just as simple.' 'Ah.' 'Tomatoes with shrimp.' 'Ah.' 'Tomatoes with shrimp, the shrimp have been shelled one by one by...' 'Like my poetry, in short: every verse has been shelled, every word.' 'Yes.'"

Daive is also a photographer, has the eye of a photographer. "A first portrait," he writes midway into the book, "[Paul Celan] is waiting for me on the sidewalk of rue d'Ulm. Against the light, I surprise him with his head inclined, listening, his ear glued to an invisible wall: time. He is auscultating time."

My intrigue mounts. I ask Ronnie if I can see her book of Celan's poetry. She brings me *Breathturn,* Celan at his densest, the poems published in 1967, translated into English by Pierre Joris, and published by Green Integer in 2006. I flip to one of the poems: "When I knead the lump / of air, our nourishment, / it is leavened by the / letters' shimmer from / the lunatic-open / pore."

The brevity, the multilayered density, the freakish syntax, the intensely metaphorical language carried to an extreme of imaginative wildness, is characteristic of Celan's remarkable sensibility. This is the first time I have encountered a poetry of such startling originality and energy since my first discovery of Rimbaud in 1966, or *Les chants de Maldoror* by Comte de Lautréamont that same year. The poems are triumphs of the creative spirit over psychological pain. It is unfortunate for me that they are written in German, as I've spent the last several decades trying to learn French, and haven't mastered that language sufficiently to move on and learn another language. Celan's magnificent adventures in German, however, may tempt me to wade into the language just a little bit. I do know that one of German's more droll and wonderful characteristics, and certainly a pull on my attention, is an openness to neologism, the creation of new words by welding two or more nouns together. The result is often a shiny amalgam of semantic juncture.

One of the more remarkable words I have encountered in *Breathturn* is *wortdurchschwommenen,* which Joris translates as *worddrenched.* Worddrenched is quite wonderful, which is how it came to catch my attention, for one can imagine a being — a poet — dripping with words, or envision the work itself sodden with linguistic possibility. I do have a pocket German dictionary, and access to any number of online dictionaries and translation services, and so I did a little more research into this word and arrived at a clunkier, more literal translation as "word thoroughly swum through."

It is a concept that can be experienced, felt, perceived, explored as a pool of syllables, as a stream rippling with semantic possibility, as a medium to engage physically, bodily, and in which might also be found a deep silence. The poems do not move fluidly. Quite the contrary: they halt, they stumble, they collide. If there is swimming, it is that of the person who has waded into a rough stream, balancing themselves very carefully over a series of jagged, slippery rocks until coming to a deep interruption in the stream, a tranquil depth in which to immerse themselves.

The word for *swim* in German, *schwimm,* is very close to English. *Water,* in German, is *wasser. To drink, trinken.* One can hear glass in that word, a toast being made, glasses clinked. Reading Celan one almost immediately begins sewing associations. One could also say sowing associations. Scattering seed. In German, *samen*. Almost the same as English *semen*. Because of his conflicted feelings about the German language, Celan's poetry imparts a visible agitation, a struggle that stresses and strains his language as much as he plays with and inseminates it, impregnates it with the capacity to dream, imagine, set oneself adrift in reverie. As soon as we seem to connect with the sense of otherness the poem incarnates, it slips away, disappears with a flick of its vowels. And we must plunge deeper into that sea to find it again.

An Attempt at Exhausting a Place in Paris

We arrived in Paris at about 10:30 A.M. on a sunny Wednesday morning in late August. I pulled my black leather carrying bag out from the overhead baggage compartment and one of the carrying straps broke. I would have to carry the bag with the main shoulder strap, which I didn't like doing, as the bag was heavy and cut into my shoulder muscle. But what the hell, we were in Paris. We'd made it. Flown over Greenland and glistening chunks of arctic ice and a sliver of Ireland and landed in France. Who cares about a lousy strap? I hoped the rest of the bag would hold together, at least long enough to get to our hotel room.

We waited in the aisle for the flight attendant to open the door and the people in the aisle to begin their slow awkward bag-carrying movement to the front and out the door and into the airport gate at Charles de Gaulle Airport.

We entered into a cordoned labyrinth, one of those lines that double round and round and compress like an accordion, then noticed it forked and that there were two windows available. I chose the one to the right arbitrarily, only to discover that it was the line for French residents. The official pointed to the window to our left and said, *là-bas*. But the line for that window was still quite long. Did he intend for us to go immediately to the window, or to return to the end of the line? I erred on the part of courtesy and we headed for the end of the line. But then another official came our way and directed us to the window. So we went to the window and avoided the line. Our passports, which had not yet been stamped in the twelve years that they had been in our possession, were deflowered at last. *Whack! Whack!* Our passports now had the official stamp of France in them.

We entered a large room where people gathered to meet passengers and spotted our driver, a casually dressed man in his early fifties holding a sign with our name on it. *Nous sommes arrivé*, I said, eager to begin trying my French out on an actual French person. Can you wait here a minute? he responded in English, I have to take a piss.

He returned and he led us to his car. He was an affable man named Guillaume.

Comment a été le traffic? I asked, eager once again to get a French conversation going.

It's been very quiet, he responded in English. Everyone is on vacation.

So it's true, what they say, I said, giving up on speaking French with the driver, everyone does leave Paris during August.

Yes, he said, about seventy percent of the city leaves.

I was disappointed to hear this. I'd been hoping, first, that the whole thing about people making a mass exodus from Paris in August had been an overly exaggerated rumor. But it wasn't. It was evident as soon as we entered Paris's streets that it was unusually quiet. This would mean that a lot of the cafés that were off the beaten track and not so overtly directed toward tourism but whose bricks and candles and leaded windows reposed in gentle obscurity and the thousands of French faces and bodies speaking and gesticulating French would not be there. Instead, it would be German, Italian, Russian, English and Chinese peppering my ears.

Guillaume gave us a little tour of the neighborhood around Place Saint-Sulpice before depositing us at our hotel, the Hôtel Récamier. We drove around le Jardin de Luxembourg, rues Médicis and Vaugirard and Boulevard Saint-Germain. I spotted L'Écume des Pages, the bookstore I wanted to visit on Boulevard Saint-Germain, and the Luxembourg Palace and Café de Flore and Les Deux Magots and Musée d'Anatomie. All the stonework seemed to have a yellow cast to it and contrasted nicely with the black filigree of fences and balcony railings.

Guillaume helped us into the lobby of the Hôtel Récamier with our bags and I slipped him a five euro note. He introduced us to the concierge, a young woman in her early thirties named Carole with a warm smile and sandy hair who greeted us with a musical, *bonjour, bienvenue à l'Hôtel Récamier*. But then she reverted to English and explained a few of the hotel amenities such as where and when breakfast would occur and handed us an enormous key with a knobby black handle of fringed material. I was a little puzzled with the size of this thing. How would I fit it into my pocket with all my other paraphernalia? Would Ronnie be able to fit it into her purse? We found out later after we got situated in our room and came downstairs to go to the Boulevard Saint-Germain and Carole shouted, *pardon, vous devez laisser la clé à la reception*, you must leave the key with me. You did not read ze literature.

Pardon, we said, and Ronnie handed her the key, which was a relief to be rid of, though I felt a little embarrassed about not doing our homework about hotel protocol. The key would be left with the concierge each time we left and picked up again on our way back.

A young man with black hair and glasses had led us to the elevator that took us to the second floor where our room was located. I handed him a five euro note, which was the smallest denomination I had (it had come from a packet of euros we'd bought at AAA so that you'll have a little cash in hand when you arrive and don't have to traipse around looking for a bank or automated teller), and he smiled and left.

It was a fairly large room with a huge shower stall that had a glass door and two thick white bathrobes hanging on the door and plenty of other towels folded neatly and arranged in voluptuous stacks. There was a sign encouraging guests to use towels more than once to save on water and make less of an environmental impact and the thick chrome bars on which the larger bath towels had been hung were heated so that the towels would be nice and dry again after use.

There was a long tube-shaped device in the shower that squirted water horizontally when I shut the overhead shower valve off. I was puzzled by this device. I surmised that it was available for anyone who wanted to shower without getting their hair wet, but in order to activate it the overhead shower would have to be turned on first, in which case your hair would get wet. I never did find out what it was for, or if it could be removed from the wall for portable use.

There was a huge armoire of wood with a black veneer that offered plenty of space for clothes and laundry and whatever items might find repose there, and a bottom drawer that opened to a refrigerated wet bar that (happily) also contained Perrier and orange juice, the two most prominent non-alcoholic beverages that Paris appeared to offer.

The bed was huge and firm with a tall headboard upholstered in a durable fabric and upon which a generous array of pillows that spoke to us mutely of rest and relaxation. I understood their language immediately.

No bed, of course, can equal one's own bed, the bed that has conformed to the contour of your body, the bed in which you've made love, suffered a long illness, the vehicle by which one enters each night into oblivion, the bed that knows every particularity of your movements and skin, the bed where everything is placed within convenient reach, which includes most importantly in my case a radio/CD player where we play audiobooks, George Eliot and Shakespeare and James Herriot and Virginia Woolf, a headlamp for reading while Ronnie sleeps, and a table lamp with a dimmer so that I can look for things in gentle luminosity.

"The bed," observes Georges Perec in a personal essay titled "*Le lit*" ("The Bed"), "is the very best type of individual space, the elementary space of the body (*le lit-monade*, the bed-monad), the one that even the man most peppered with debts has the right to keep: the bailiffs do not have the power to seize your bed; that means — and one can verify this easily in practice — that we have but one bed, which is *our* bed; if there are other beds in the house or in the apartment, one refers to these as guest beds, or extra beds. One only sleeps well in one's own bed."

This is not quite true. I agree that if a bed is not one's own bed, it remains weirdly, ineffably foreign somehow, a soft slab for repose, but not the chrysalis of deeply personal fibers and silks in which one heals from the injuries of the day in the soft embrace of Morpheus and emerges the next morning rejuvenated, reinvigorated and swings one's feet to the floor like an astronaut leaving the ship-cocoon for the first expedition of a foreign planet. But our bed — sublimely familiar as it was — squeaked and quaked whenever either of us made a shift or change in position. It was small with a metal frame that Ronnie had paid an antique dealer $3,000 to refurbish and paint. It had sentimental value, which meant that we were doomed to sleep in it for some time to come.

The bed at the Hôtel Récamier was so big that I couldn't feel Ronnie's agitations. Once asleep, it was difficult to wake her. Her problem was attaining sleep, coaxing sleep into her body. Her sleep was patternless. It could be deep or shallow, depending on a broad array of circumstances. It was her relationship with the bed that seemed most consistently difficult. It is one thing to "fall asleep." It is an entirely different matter to search for sleep on a piece of furniture designated for that purpose. As soon as the need for sleep becomes purposeful, one is doomed. And this doom is taken out on the bed with flip-flops and punches. At home I was constantly disturbed as she thrashed and thrust about trying to get comfortably situated. The harder she tried, the less satisfying it became. It was a vicious circle. But here, the bed was so large and the mattress so firm, I hardly knew she was there. I fell asleep almost instantly, and this without the aid of the radio, which I could not do at home. At home, if I didn't hear voices coming out of the radio, I could not be distracted, and without being distracted, I was left with the carnival of nonsense in my head, a macabre Coney Island of worries and funhouse mirrors.

Ronnie slept better, too. The bed was more comfortable. There was no cat waking up her at all hours of the night, and she didn't have to go to work the next day.

The bed at the Hôtel Récamier faced a wall on which hung a plasma TV, mirror and a large print of a beautiful, impeccably groomed woman with a thick mane of blonde hair, fur coat, long eyelashes and flawless complexion who held a sponge to her check with a hand enveloped to the elbow in a blue rubber glove. An overhead lamp illumined this mysterious figure. Why such elegance paired with the implements of household chores? I liked the disparity. There was something quietly provocative about it. It was definitely better than the usual artwork one finds on hotel and motel walls, the usual moored sailboat and attendant seagulls, the alpine mountain, the herd of horses running in sea foam at the shore's edge of some idyllic coast.

The light switches confused me. There were two switches, side by side, in the entry hallway. They needed to be on for anything thing else in the room to be on. This meant that if I got up during the night to go to the bathroom, I had turn on both switches for the bathroom light to come on, and all the other lights, too, came on. We were sure we weren't operating them correctly, we were missing something, some detail, that allowed us to just turn on the bathroom light and nothing else, but we never did solve that mystery.

The window was tall and opened out onto the Place Saint-Sulpice, a quiet square that complemented the great façade of the church that is Saint-Sulpice, a massive structure of stone whose west façade overlooking the square is a balustrade close in spirit to the severely classical lines of the east front of the Louvre. It originally featured a pedimented façade designed by Giovanni Niccolò Servandoni, who had been inspired by the entrance elevation of Christopher Wren's Saint Paul's Cathedral in London, but lightning destroyed the pediment in 1770 and it was replaced with the balustrade, in which a double colonnade of Ionic order over Roman Doric with loggias behind them help bring more unity with the bases of the corner towers.

The massive church, in which the Marquis de Sade and Charles Baudelaire had both been baptized, enlarged my sense of being, my sense of occupying a deeply historical space, and connecting me with the actuality of figures who had once walked and stood and dreamed in that same space.

There was also a huge fountain, The Fountain of the Four Bishops as it is sometimes called, which became the subject of some of my first photographs.

I bought a digital camera — a Canon Elph 330 — a few days before we left. I wasn't eager to own another digital camera (I've never gotten along well with that technology), but didn't want to find myself in Paris surrounded on all sides by gorgeous architecture and curiosities and not be able to photograph it. I've always had an ambivalence for photography, it can get in the way of experiencing something since you're spending all your time fussing with buttons and settings and icons rather than just breathing in the general sensorium and mentally and spiritually digesting it. I refer to this process as "the darkroom of the mind." The mind, shall we say, as a form of camera obscura, a place (if one can think of the mind as a place) where images are developed and arranged and coaxed into virtual being. Eidolons of past experience float and flesh into meaningful narrations. Creaking ships. Flowers and scents. Challenges met. Turbulences spun into glistening reflection. Cameras can get in the way of this. Cancel out the deeper registrations of experience.

But I bought one anyway. I decided to err on the side of regret. If we arrived in Paris and I saw things that screamed to have a photo taken, such as César's very strange centaur at the crossroads of rue de Sèvres and rue du Cherche-Midi.

We had no end of problems the first night we brought it home. There was a dizzying number of options, directions, schemes, diagrams, formats, menus and an accompanying language of indecipherable acronyms intended for a priesthood of digital geeks. I couldn't get the camera to do anything I wanted, or stop doing things I didn't want it to do. I didn't understand the icons. I didn't understand the sequences. I didn't understand the rationale or its many other technological perversities.

I did manage to get two pictures of Ronnie playing with Graham before we left. It was painful to see them in the camera screen in Paris, Ronnie on her knees, Graham sitting beside his favorite toy, a white ball that spun round in a groove. I worried about Graham. I knew how lonely he'd be, utterly perplexed by our disappearance.

But now, in full sunlight, I stood before the Fountain of the Four Bishops, and I had to have a picture of it.

I get a shot of Ronnie sitting beneath a lion. A very big and powerful lion. A marble lion. The lion is one of four lions situated in rough symmetry on the lower portion of the Fountain of the Four Bishops. The water comes down in sheets. Bright, glimmering sheets that sprawl and bubble at the base into a rippling pool.

The four bishops crowning the fountain and reposing in alcoves of beautifully sculpted stone are François Fénelon (facing west), Esprit Fléchier (facing east), Jean Baptiste Massillon (facing south) and Jacques-Bénigne Bossuet (facing north).

Bossuet was court preacher to Louis XIV of France and a strong advocate of the divine right of kings.

Masks splitting water on two sides of huge stone urns look demonic and disgruntled, as if vomiting water in a trance of otherworldly preoccupations.

I hand the camera to Ronnie and she takes a picture of me sitting on the lower lip of the fountain, squinting in the sunlight, a stone lion roaring behind me.

The fountain was designed by Louis Visconti, who also designed Napoleon's tomb at Les Invalides. It was constructed between 1844 and 1848.

I love fountains. It's a wonderful way to experience water. You experience water in all its various forms. You experience water white and agitated. You breathe it. It has a smell. It has an aroma of air and humidity and earth and stratosphere. Sometimes a breeze carries it to your skin and it tingles there. The water toward the bottom of the fountain turns calm and green and reflects the sunlight splashes at it or elopes with it to some secret Mediterranean bay riding bareback the entire way, wedding gown spreading out in a fury of escape.

I was eager to check out the Jardin du Luxembourg, since that would be our primary place for early morning runs, and as we entered rue Férou we encountered a colossal printing of Rimbaud's *"Le bateau ivre"* on a wall. All of its one hundred lines, its twenty-five Alexandrine quatrains, covered a length of approximately seventy-five feet. It was monumental. There was some information about its history to the side that stated that Arthur gave his first public reading of the poem to a gathering of friends at a café that once occupied the same place. The mural poem had been printed there by a Dutchman named Jan Willem Bruins and unveiled on June 14, 2012, as part of the annual Marché de la Poésie that occurs at Place Saint-Sulpice.

We strolled a little through the Jardin du Luxembourg then headed for the bookstore I'd seen on the way to our hotel, one which the poet Claude Royet-Journoud had listed in an email months ago for me. It was called L'Écume des Pages, *écume* meaning foam or froth. It was a terrific image, that of the pages of a book being like sea spume, the froth of a tumbled wave. Mallarmé's shipwreck came to mind, the flotsam and jetsam of his long poem *"Un coup de dés jamais n'abolira le hazard,"* "A Throw of the Dice Will Never Abolish Chance."

I hungered for a real bookstore. It was one of the primary reasons I wanted to come to France. The book industry in the United States has been trashed by an industry obsessed with profit. Marketability is everything. Consequently, the mass-marketed titles were usually written (or ghost-written) by celebrities, or favored topics with a high emotional charge to appeal to the voyeuristic impulses of the public. There were stacks of self-help books and novels such as Dan Brown's *The Da Vinci Code* or Suzanne Collins's *The Hunger Games*, novels of romance and intrigue with sometimes a veneer of intellectual sophistication. I could hardly stand to go into an American bookstore anymore. It was just too demoralizing.

I was not disappointed in L'Écume des Pages. There was an abundance of titles on an infinite array of fascinating topics, ranging from essays such as Eric Dussert's *Une forêt cachée: 156 portraits d'écrivains oubliés (A Hidden Forest: 156 Portraits of Forgotten Writers)*, or his other equally intriguing title *La littérature est mauvaise fille (Literature Is a Bad Girl)*.

Ronnie discovered titles by Raymond Roussel, including *Locus Solus* and *La doublure (The Valet)*, as well as books by Georges Perec. She bought me a beautiful edition of Perec's *Romans et récits (Novels and Stories)* for my birthday and a copy of Perec's *Espèces d'espaces (Species of Space)*, for both of us, which she began reading immediately.

It was here that I tried out again my feeble French. I'm good at reading French, less good at writing French and awful at speaking French. But I had to give it a try. It so happened that the question I wanted to ask was fairly complex. It had to do with a literary project Georges Perec performed involving Place Saint-Sulpice, in which he had made a collection of observations occurring at Place Saint-Sulpice during the month of October 1974, focusing his attention on the kind of events that generally go unnoticed.

I approached an attractive, thirty-something woman behind the front desk and launched myself into French: *Pardon, je cherche le titre d'un livre de Georges Perec dans laquelle il a observé de petits incidents à la Place Saint-Sulpice et les a recueillies dans un livre.*

The words came out haltingly and slow and I felt like someone struggling with a speech impairment following a stroke, but she understood what I meant, and rather than respond in English the way Parisians usually do when an American attempts to speak their language, she continued our conversation in French and directed me to a man, also in his thirties, seated at a desk in the middle of the store. He was also kind enough to endure my French, and knew what book I was looking for. He went to look for it on the shelf, but there was no copy available. He wrote the title on a slip of paper (*Tentative d'épuisement d'un lieu parisien*), and handed it to me.

Merci, I said. I had done it. I had successfully conducted a conversation in French. Though, to judge by the disparaging facial expressions of a middle-aged man browsing through a nearby section of books, my foray was not an entire success. The man had a pained expression on his face, as if he were quietly suffering a hernia, or slipped disk, as he browsed the books. I'm sure he felt better as soon as we left the store.

NOTRE-DAME DE PARIS

We returned to our room, stopping by the little office in the lobby to pick our key up from Carole, still at the desk, she had a terrific smile and tolerated my French, I told her, we've just seen "*Le beateau ivre*" around the corner, how wonderful is that, *c'est merveilleux*, you can go on a drunken journey during your break, what is French for break?

C'est, «pause.»

Huh? Same as in English, I said, somewhat disappointed.

Carole handed Ronnie the large black key with its hula-dancer fringe and we mounted the spiral staircase passing busts of Madame Récamier (there was a bust of Madame Récamier reposing in a tiny alcove at each landing and each one was painted in whimsical colors or patterns) and went in and deposited our books and thought about what to do next. Although, technically, we were at the end of a day, a long ten-hour flight involving all the stress and complications that go with an airport and a flight and people crowded together for an absurdly long time and flight attendants dragging carts of booze and food up and down the darkened aisles as the jet crossed the

Arctic wastes of Greenland, the day was yet young and we were excited about discovering Paris.

What do you want to see first? Ronnie asked.

Notre-Dame, I answered. No question about it. Notre-Dame.

So we went down the stairs and dropped the key off once more with Carole and opened the door and embarked on our first long walk in Paris.

I got my compass out and held it flat in my palm and watched as the needle found north. Notre-Dame de Paris was approximately one mile distant from our hotel. We headed north on the Rue Bonaparte and passed several bookstores, one of which had the letters of various well-known writers and philosophers and dramatists taped to the window. There were letters by Georges Bizet, Henri Bergson and Stéphane Mallarmé. There was a letter by Jean-Paul Sartre to Wanda Kosakiewicz dated July 27, 1939, and a letter from Louix XVI dated October 15, 1791, written in a very flamboyant hand to the Marquis de Bouillé, expressing his deep gratitude for his assitance in his and Marie Antoinette's failed attempt to flee Paris ("You have done your duty, Monsieur, stop blaming yourself; you have dared all for me and my family and have not succeeded"), and a manuscript by Alfred Jarry dated 1901.

The bookstore was closed, as were many other fascinating boutiques and bookstores since this was August, the month when the Parisians make a mass exodus out of Paris to the shores of Biarritz and the Côte d'Azur and Baie d'Audierne on the west coast of Finistère. Nevertheless, I could have spent the rest of the day reading the letters taped to the window.

We discovered another bookstore a few doors down that featured the work of Guy Debord who, as I would discover later, was the focus of a generous exhibit at the Bibliothèque Nationale de France.

We exited onto the Quai Malaquais and headed west, where Notre-Dame had come into view. We could see from that distance that it was surrounded by a huge crowd of tourists. I took Ronnie's hand since I tend to walk a little faster and worried about losing her as the crowd thickened. I began hearing snatches of other languages, chiefly Russian and Chinese, laced with some Italian and English.

As we approached the cathedral, we saw that its view was partially blocked by a huge plywood structure that covered the parvis and offered a row of bleachers on the other side, as if there were a high school track event in progress, or tennis match or basketball game. It looked utterly incongruous. It had been erected in observation of the cathedral's eight-hundred-fiftieth birthday (construction began in 1163) in anticipation, no doubt, of the hordes of tourists who would come to visit and want to sit in view of its western façade and wait for the cathedral to perform some athletic miracle or dunk or free throw.

A tall middle-aged man from Los Angeles who was there with his family, his wife and two teenage kids, a boy and a girl, asked me to take their picture. Sure, I said. When I finished taking some shots of the group I asked if he could take a picture of Ronnie and me, which he gladly did. We stood in front of the western façade and tried to smile through our jet lag and confusion. Behind us, the three majestic portals of the cathedral displayed their ongoing tales of judgment, mercy and chaos and horror. In the central portal (enlarged in 1771 by the architect Jacques-Germain Soufflot so that processions with canopies could pass through), a majestic Christ sits in judgment upon the sinful and good. Saint Michael weighs souls in the upper lintel where horned and scaly demons take hold of the sinners in the lower of the two pans of the scale, and two angels stand beside Christ holding the nails, lance and cross of Christ's crucifixion. A little lower, Mary and Saint John kneel before Christ to pray that mercy be shown the human race. On the left side of the lintel, the saved ascend to heaven under Christ's upraised hand, and on the right the damned are dragged down to hell. These figures were not the originals but sculpted by Eugène Emmanuel Viollet-le-Duc and his students.

The left portal, the only one with a gable above the tympanum, was devoted to the Virgin Mary who, to the thirteenth-century mind, provided a link between human frailty and divine majesty. The tympanum shows Mary's burial and assumption. At the center, Mary is in Heaven, seated on the same throne as Jesus. She is being crowned by an angel while Jesus blesses her and gives her a sceptre. It is interesting to note that at the time of this sculpture, two women held unprecedented power in Europe: Eleanor of Aquitaine and her granddaughter, Blanche of Castile, the mother of Saint Louis of France.

Ronnie and I entered the cathedral through the Portal of Saint Anne, which features the oldest sculptures of the cathedral. The lintels of this portal depict scenes from the New Testament: the Annunciation, the Visitation, the Nativity, King Herod and the Magi, Saint Joachim and Saint Anne. The great heavy door, which was open, partially hid in shade the fabulous wrought iron work of Biscornette. The arabesques and metalwork of Biscornette's hinge (which is so much more than just a hinge) border the miraculous. No one ever saw Biscornette constructing the hinges for the two portals (he did not do one for the center portal), which generated rumors that the devil was helping him, and that he had sold his soul to the King of Darkness in order to enlist his supernatural assistance. Whatever the truth happens to be, the hinges on each portal door are testimonies to tremendous skill and passion, the delicacy of their arabesque patterns strong in the confidence of transcendent emotion ringing in the pound of a hammer on molten red iron. Why, as in the case of Biscornette or Robert Johnson or Bob Dylan, when an artist achieves such seeming preternatural beauty or power is it to be assumed a deal with the devil was involved? I find it curious. As if there some inherent quality in art that gave it a subversive edge even, as with Biscornette's hinges, the artistry was employed toward something sacred.

We left the hot August sun outside and entered a different world. People were encouraged to be silent, as there were worshippers who had come to the church for prayer and confession. It was, after all, not merely a tourist site, but a functioning church, a holy domain.

It was like walking inside a mountain. I gazed up at the vaults and found it difficult to imagine how someone could create such a remarkable feeling of lightness and grace amid such pressures, such prodigious forces and gravity of stone. It gave one a feeling of giddy transcendence, as if it had been the very intention of the stone to ascend into the sky and this contagion of exaltation, of sublimity, carried your spirit with it.

Auguste Rodin wrote: "To understand Cathedrals one must be sensitive to the moving language of their lines, amplified by shadows and reinforced by the graduated form of the adorned or unadorned buttresses. To understand these lines, tenderly modeled and caressed, one should have the good luck of being in love."

I agree.

We walked back to the hotel and rested a few minutes before deciding to get something to eat. We pondered the possibility of ordering something from the kitchen, but the awkwardness of receiving food in the privacy of one's room dissuaded me. As tired as we were, we decided to go out once more.

We headed toward the streets on the other side of the square, and were drawn to a small street called rue des Canettes. We didn't walk far before the Café Six with its two doors open wide seemed like a very informal and inviting place. It seemed to be more bar than restaurant. Early rock 'n' roll (Little Richard, Eddie Cochran, The Beatles) played loudly from the speakers, which made me fall in love with the place immediately. I caught the attention of the bartender and asked, *peut-on s'asseoir à l'arrière?* He nodded matter-of-factly, as if to say *bien sur*, and we found a table and sat down. The light was dim and soothing. A waitress appeared with two menus. I said *bonjour* and she immediately identified us as Americans, which I always disliked, because of all the usual stereotypes that go with being an American. This would include George W. Bush and his daffy grin and armadillos and wars. And John Wayne and Daffy Duck and Jack Kerouac (well, I hope Kerouac!) and bravado and gusto and all that good stuff, which was nonsense. And was mostly in my head. The waitress, whose name was Cécile, really liked Americans, and wanted very badly to come to America and was eager for information on how she might be able to find work in the United States. She asked where in the States we were from and I said, Washington, which she naturally assumed was Washington, D.C., and I said, no, not the capital city Washington, the state of Washington, it's on the west coast. We live in a place of mountains and lakes. Seattle. It's where Microsoft is, and Amazon and Starbucks. I didn't know about the green card stuff or getting paid under the table but I was pretty sure she could find work as a waitress. That's what's so great about waiting tables or working for a restaurant, you're pretty much qualified to find work anywhere provided you can speak a smattering of English. We Americans I must say are far more tolerant and encouraging of people trying to learn and speak English and accents and grammatical mistakes are often charming. The French always gave me the feeling I was tossing a fine crystal wine glass from the eighteenth century into the air and were nervous about whether I'd be able to catch it. I often didn't and if I mispronounced a word, as I often did, people would wince. Or speak in English, as Cécile did, thus avoiding the whole crystal wine glass metaphor circumstance. As long as the conversation occurred in English I could piss my pants for all they cared. Just please, *je vous en prie, monsieur*, please don't break our language.

Ronnie ordered the *escalope de dinde au sauce normande et tagliatelle*, and I was happy to discover they offered one of my favorite dishes from home, tagliatelle carbonara. I was also extremely happy to discover that they offered some very tasty non-alcoholic beverages (which the French delightfully term *boissons fraîches*), which is unusual for a bar, in France or America. I ordered a Bora Bora, which was a mixture of coconut, mango, grenadine and carbonated water. Ronnie was happy to discover that Parisian wine was not only cheaper than it is in Seattle but that the Parisians are much more generous in their pours.

Cécile was a delightful waitress, prompt, spirited and cheerful, but when we finished, and were waiting for the bill, it felt like we had fallen into an interminable limbo. We waited a long time before I caught her attention and asked *pour l'addi-*

tion, s'il vous plaît. She seemed surprised, as if she had counted on us staying much longer. Maybe that's what the French do. We were accustomed to getting a bill almost immediately after declining a dessert, or finishing a dessert, so the management could clear the table and get ready for a new set of diners. Not so in France. It seemed that wherever we ate, you had to wait a long time for the check, or catch the waitperson's attention and request *l'addition, s'il vous plaît.* People were used to lingering there, I guess. I was once quite good at lingering after a meal. But that's when I drank. Now that I'm sober, and finish a meal, I get antsy to leave. I get restless leg syndrome. Energy builds. A table becomes an obstruction. Is that American? Hi-ho, Silver, away!

A Vermeer of Shoes

We got up early the next morning and went for a run in the Jardin du Luxembourg. It was a lovely place to go for a run, except for the gravel. I wasn't used to running on gravel. And my black running shoes, which I brought because from a distance they could almost pass as dress shoes, and did in fact fool a shoeshiner in Seattle once down on Pike Street, I had to point to them and tell him they were running shoes, now turned a light beige from the dust. But apart from that it was one of the most delightful and peaceful venues for running I have ever experienced. And the strangeness of walking past Rimbaud's giant, mural-sized "*Le bateau ivre*" both on the way to and the way back from the Jardin du Luxembourg was pleasantly anomalous. It was a monumental fillip to the bounded, the restricted, the matte satisfactions of the sound and sedate. It triumphed in the lure of delirium, the underlying torrent and Bacchanal of existence, and I loved it. It reminded me, on those crisp constitutionals in the Jardin du Luxembourg with its stately palace and guards in their light blue uniforms, of drinking whiskey and tequila late into the night and listening to George Thorogood or Tom Waits as glimmers of dawn excused the night's extravagances and one began to drowse into the next day's rest and hangover.

I tend to sweat a lot when I run, and it was already a pretty warm day, so my shirt and shorts were soaked. I had to figure out a place to put them where they could dry. Ronnie suggested the wrought iron railing in front of our window, which I'd thought of before but had worried about the management getting upset about somebody's laundry hanging out of the window, especially since it was on the side of the hotel that faced the square. But there was nowhere else. It was the most logical choice. So I hung my shirt and shorts over the railing. They dried pretty fast and the hotel didn't say anything, so I was glad of that.

We decided to visit the Louvre this day. It was an easy walk. I looked forward to it. I loved walking in Paris. This was a little different for me as I usually don't enjoy walking. I love to run, hate to walk. I find walking boring. But it was never boring in Paris.

We showered and went down for breakfast in the hotel dining room, which was small but luxurious, with thick white tablecloths and rolled cold cuts and a big bowl of fruit and a large basket of chocolate croissants and another of baguettes and some of the best coffee I've ever had, and then headed north once more, toward the Pont du Carrousel.

You cannot take in the Louvre in a single day. It would take a solid month to even get close to viewing, and I really mean absorbing, digesting, mulling all the art within its walls. The place is huge. Colossal.

The Louvre has over a million works of art, about which 35,000 are on display.

The Louvre is overwhelming. It's gigantic. You don't know where to start. There is such an infinite number of things to look at, angels and cherubs and devils and gods. Clouds and ships and flowers and mysterious aristocratic women. Sirens contorting in marble. Chariots floating in heaven. Sad kings and happy kings. Tragic queens and haggard old women carrying burdens of children and wood. Peasants dancing. Peasants sipping soup in hovels. Bowls of fruit. Vases of flowers. Eyeballs of dead fish gazing into eternity. Everything artfully, skillfully represented. So beautifully represented that in all honesty you don't know which is the real world, the true world or the idealized world. Are these courtiers and hunters and card players and weeping women a world doctored by an early Renaissance master, or the world seen clearly, vividly, and rendered with such skill that it is a world more real than the world it represents? Are these lute players and merchants and tables and fruit the world as it is, the world as it truly existed five hundred years ago, or the world sublimated into eternal beauty by a skilled Dutch artist using pigments crushed in a mortar? Is this eye of lapis lazuli a true blue eye or the result of aluminum silicate with sulfur?

You can take pictures in the Louvre. This grosses out some people, some true art lovers, I know, I'm aware of that. I get it. Taking pictures of paintings in a museum is gross. Why would the Louvre allow such a thing? I can't speak for the Louvre, but I can tell you that I won't do it again. I promise. I will also tell you that what I ended up with was a lot of pictures of my shoes.

My flash kept going off. The museum officials are strict about such matters. *Sans flash! Sans flash, Monsieur!* Ok, dude, I get it. *Sans flash*. But I can't get this new fucking camera to cooperate. I had a tough time understanding all the mysterious little icons and was weak with option fatigue from clicking through menus I didn't fully grasp, if I understood them at all. I was dizzy with incomprehension. I tried to find the automatic flash function and disarm the damn thing. But I couldn't find it. Sometimes I thought I had it and then *pop!* another frigging flash and a museum official staring daggers at me. What was once Vermeer's Lacemaker of luminous yellows and reds and greens is now a faded replica of curly hair and fingers and pale concentration.

I got the bright idea of testing for the flash by taking pictures of my shoes. If the flash went off, it would harm nothing, and more importantly, the museum official would see that I was taking pictures of my shoes, either because I was enamored with my shoes, or because I was trying to gain control of the flash function on my camera, which would have been the correct assumption, though it would also be accurate to say that I was, indeed, enamored with my shoes, they had been the best running shoes of my running life before I retired them to the more sedate function of walking. And so what I have now are magnificent photographs of my shoes. My wonderful running shoes. My wonderful black running shoes.

For the Louvre of my feet.

For whose feet are not a Louvre of bone and cartilage and elegant muscle?

If there were a Vermeer of shoes, this is what the painting would look like: a leg of denim leading downward to a black running shoe lightly dusted with the yellowish dust on the paths of the Jardin du Luxembourg, where I had run that morning, before entering the Louvre, and discovering what art, what skill went into the production of my shoes.

For what shoes are not also a Louvre?

What shoes are not also a Musée de l'Orangerie of nylon, gel and rubber? A Georges Pompidou Centre of eyelets and nails? A Musée d'Orsay of plastic weave and leather overlay?

Apart from my shoes, I was focused on one exhibit in particular, Georges Braque's painting of birds on the ceiling of the Etruscan gallery, which I had written about in my novel *The Seeing Machine*, but had not actually seen for real. In person. In the flesh, as it were. I was eager to see the entire room, how the paintings felt and looked and operated within that room, what the interplay was like, the whole phenomenon.

It was hard to find, but I had a good time looking for it because most of the museum officials I asked either didn't speak much English or were especially accommodating of my French. So when we arrived at the room, I felt good because we'd arrived there via the French I spoke, and the directions thusly received.

I must say, the paintings really do stand out. The colors are strong. The shapes are strong. There are three panels altogether.

Normally, people tend not to look up at a ceiling, particularly high ceilings, such as the ceilings in the Louvre, many of which reveal gorgeous paintings by Romanelli, Fragonard and Tiepolo, the panels beautifully carved, but which make their presence known and draw the eyes upward, the head leans back, and — *voilà!* — angels and cherubs and scepters and kings embody the mythologies of otherworldly realms amid panels of gold and delicacies of mallet and chisel.

Braque's panels peer out into a night sky of the imagination. Giant black birds outlined boldly in white spread their wings over a well-lit room of bronze goblets and ivory centaurs. I was surprised by how thick the paint had been applied and the intensity of its color. The black was really black, the white was terrifically white, and the blues were enormously blue. There was an energy of light in the room that dazzled the eyes with reflections, subtle plays of glint and sparkle that trapezed through your eyes and pegged its visions of Saharan stars and warm Mediterranean winds to your mind and put mystic scents of myrrh in your nose and ancient Etruscan luxuries in your subterranean musings.

I lifted my troublesome camera and began taking pictures of Braque's birds on the magnificent ceiling. The panels were framed in beautiful wood carving that had been done many years previous to Braque's work.

I never quite resolved my ambivalence over the camera. There was something indefinably irreverent about taking pictures, but there was another aspect to it as well. I didn't it want it to get in the way of my experience, particularly art. Aside from all the little technical complexities, a camera has a way of tyrannizing one's senses by concentrating all of your attention on everything that has a strong visual presence. It does this to the exclusion of the other senses, touch and smell and hearing and taste. The camera monopolizes your attention. You miss the sound of birds, the way a breeze felt when it blew across the Seine, the smell of a street full of fish and sausage and freshly baked bread, the feeling of a scarf across your hand.

So why, then, did I bring a camera? For starters, I have a terrible memory. I knew there would be things I would later struggle to remember and having a strong visual cue would help stimulate an enfeebled memory. Nor did I want to buy a giant museum book or book on Braque's art and have to lug that back to the States and the pictures on the internet would seem faded and commercial. This was a pilgrimage. I wanted a record of my pilgrimage.

I also tried taking pictures of the other objects in the room so that I'd be able to describe and refer to them later. This proved much more difficult. I waited for a tall black man to finish cleaning a glass case filled with bronze goblets and plates and cups that had been found near the slope of Vesuvius and had once belonged to a Roman villa buried during the volcano's eruption in 79 A.D., and when he finished I took several pictures but the images were blurred by reflection from the glass. I also tried taking pictures of two shrine-like mountings in what appeared to be frames of marble, one a narration of Bacchus and Ariane in cameos of ivory on a deep blue background and another titled *The Triumph of Bacchus* with the backs of two centaurs facing one another and the busts of two people above the heads of the centaurs, turned to view one another and the couple above. The frame was supported by two golden lions and at the center a plump, ivory-colored fish of glass flipped his tail up on a rocky seabed. The pieces were fairly recent, relative to the antique statuary in the adjoining room that featured a ceiling painted by Cy Twombly, and were done by an Italian goldsmith named Luigi Valadier between 1780 and 1785.

Ronnie and I continued to view the rest of the exhibits in the Sully wing, which included a marble statue of a boy about five or six in a wrestling match with a huge goose, the kid with his arms around the neck of the poor bird, which was the work of Boéthos de Chalcédoine, and had been discovered amid the ruins of the Villa des Quintili, a rich Roman family favored by Marcus Aurelius.

The Portrait of Plato sculpted in marble circa 175–200 A.D., the philosopher looking eminently sedate, as deep in enduring thought as the stone in which he has been given form and identity, the nose broken off, the hair in wavy curls.

Pan, sculpted in marble, sitting on a rock with strong furry goat-legs partly spread and revealing a very large and weighty scrotum. He holds a bunch of grapes in one hand a flute in the other.

Certainly one of the more jarring things to catch my attention was Michelangelo Pistoletto's *Venere degli stracci* (*Venus of the Rags*), a shapely nude female rendered in marble pressing against a huge pile of rags. Pistoletto is representative of an Italian art movement called Arte Povera, in which he wanted to contrast classical statuary against the presence of so-called common things and so tear down the imposed and imaginary division between hierarchies of high art and the muck and mufti of the everyday.

As I mentioned before, I was also eager to see some Vermeer. The last time I'd been to the Louvre, forty-one years ago, the Vermeers had not been available. This time I wanted to be sure to see them. I loved the work of Vermeer. I loved his detail and subtleties of light and how he made everything in a room object or human glow with an inner, numinous grace and beauty.

We got lost and found ourselves on a lower level, but our misdirection proved serendipitous as we discovered an exhibit of Roman mosaics dating roughly from the third century A.D. that were exquisite in pattern and detail. Three large panels mounted on the floor depicted various birds, fish and wild animals (lions, an elephant, a giraffe, a tiger and a bull) that were often featured during gladiatorial games. We were both very much charmed by the ducks. But the fish were tremendous, some of them (they appeared to be largemouth bass) open-mouthed and open-eyed and alive and moving.

Vermeer was located at the opposite end of the Louvre, in the Richelieu section, on the second floor. We climbed a high escalator that had broken down and entered into the domain of the northern Dutch painters of the seventeenth century. My attention was immediately taken with a painting by Valentin de Boulogne, a seventeenth-century French painter who was very much taken with Caravaggio and whose canvases bore similarities. In this canvas, titled *Concert à huit personnages*, eight people are involved in a musical production in what appears to be an inn, or tavern. A woman plays a spinet, gazing down in concentration at a musical score off to the side (half of it hanging from the edge of the table), a man plays a flute, three boys and a bearded man are singing (one of the faces is barely visible, hovers in the background darkness, and so the age is difficult to discern), and a soldier, still in his armor, leans against the table and listens. The energy of the painting was splendid with chiaroscuro plays, the soldier stands with his back to the viewer and his armor gleams and contrasts its hard metal light against the softer luminosity of a band of cloth crossing his opposite shoulder. He appears to be holding a blunderbuss, a gigantic firearm, while a man deeper in shadow plays a cello, his arm coming down in a billowing sleeve of soft bluish brown and moving a bow against the strings of the cello. The young boy at the center of the canvas opens his mouth wide to let the song out and the other boy, slightly older, presses the musical score to the table with the back of his hand while singing with a calmer expression on his face. The man playing the flute (it's a long flute which graduates to a flare at the end), wears a plumed helmet and a plush silken shirt with a big puffy sleeve printed with a floral design of merry arabesques rendered in a lighter tint of green than the overall emerald green of the fabric, and the hilt of a sword sticks up from the rear of his leg where he sits on a bench shoved up to the table, the flute just above the table, so that there is a blend of music and war, the voices of everyone in harmony and this suggestion of imminent battle, the blast of the horns of war and the clash of metal. Valentin de Boulogne's blend of beauty and violence must have had strong appeal.

I had a hard time finding the Vermeer paintings. I stopped and asked a young female museum official. She said the Vermeer was closed that day. I was aghast. I tried to explain I'd come to see it forty-one years ago and had traveled again from the United States to see it. She said to come back tomorrow, preferably at a later hour, when there wouldn't be so many tourists.

We made rather a quick journey through the gallery of Italian masters (all that art is fatiguing) but stopped to take in a powerful scene of violence by a sixteenth-century Tuscan artist named Daniele de Volterra titled *The Battle of David and Goliath*. It is a two-sided painting depicting the same scene in which David, having felled Goliath with his slingshot, is about to behead him with a huge sword. David straddles Goliath. The musculature of the two figures is taut with brutal energy. The colors are intense. The painting is mounted in a gold frame on an elaborate pedestal that allows viewers to go round and see the scene from two angles, giving the painting a sculptural quality. It's rather stunning to see such naked violence rendered in such voluptuous beauty while all around you are the murmur of voices all in different languages and the swirl and turbulence of a crowd in motion.

We passed the room in which the Mona Lisa is kept and it was just plain weird. We couldn't get close. The crowd facing the painting was too thick to negotiate. Everyone's arms were raised, holding smartphones and digital cameras similar to the one I carried, robotically and frenziedly taking pictures of the celebrated painting. There was a feeling of desperation about it. It spooked me. It didn't seem to be about art but all about fame and celebrity. Was anyone really looking at the painting? It was mindless. Lemmings falling off a cliff.

It felt good to get out of the museum and back into the light of day. We headed down the long dusty courtyard toward the Place du Carrousel and passed a group of black Senegalese men strategically placed at different spots jangling chains of miniature Eiffel Towers.

WE PADLOCK A BRIDGE (AND LATER FEEL SORRY)

We visited the Musée d'Orsay the following day. I got shots of the big clock and William Bouguereau's *Les Oréades* before I was told you couldn't take pictures at all in the Musée d'Orsay. This suited me fine. I was tired of letting the camera get the better of me. Now I could just enjoy the paintings.

I was delighted to discover a room with some canvases by Odilon Redon, particularly his luminious seashell, *La coquille*, and his *Bouquet de fleurs des champs dans un vas à long col*, and *Le char d'Apollon*, a heavenly display of color and nuance that I had on my computer desktop at home. I studied Arthur Rimbaud's adolescent disdain a long while in Henri Fantin-Latour's *Un coin de table* and Proust's poised and elegant portrait by Jacques-Émile Blanche. Proust wears a white orchid in his blazer and his eyes peer at you piercingly, a little sadly and wearily and his mustache seems a little prissy, but hey, this is Proust, he is allowed certain aristocratic touches. He suffered. He labored hard to bring his marvelous, largely unread prose into the world.

We spent a great deal of time in the Musée d'Orsay. By late afternoon, we were hungry and tired and barely had any energy left, but I was eager to see the Vermeers, so we returned to the Louvre. I was happy to find that the escalator was working and we rode once again to the second floor of the Richelieu wing and eventually found two works by Vermeer, *The Lacemaker* and *The Astronomer*. I was surprised at how small they were. I had expected them to be so much bigger. A young woman came by and put her digital camera as close to *The Lacemaker* as she could get and took a picture. It seemed wrong, somehow, as if she were desecrating the work. But I felt compelled to photograph these paintings, too. I don't know why. I guess that's why you call a compulsion a compulsion. Something is driving you to do something, something contrary even to your set of values, and you can't define it, you can't identify its nature, the character of it, if it has anything like character. It mostly feels like greed. The lust to possess something. Drag it home to your cave and gnaw on it. Study it. Feel it become part of you. Because that's ultimately what we want when it comes to art. We want it to become part of us. We want to be elevated out of the mundane into a zone of acute perception, the work of amphetamines, the neurotransmitters humming with reality, boiling with it, sublimating our lower natures into ethereal clouds of golden angelic vapor. And I know I will find many people who will argue this. And I think that's great, whoever you are, wherever you are. Because there is no single answer for anyone when it comes to art. I cannot say anything with certainty and do not pretend to say anything with certainty, anything I say is a line tossed out there into the water of the river and if I get a bite, I get excited and if I don't, I go home with an afternoon's worth of reflection under my belt and none the wiser. But I do know desire, I do know the impulse of greed. That's what these little cameras do to us. Make us go crazy in a museum.

I took a photo of *The Lacemaker*, then went to take a shot at *The Astronomer*, a young man with a long, straight nose (quite possibly Antonie van Leeuwenhoek, the first man to observe and record spermatozoa and bacteria and blood flow in capillaries, painted the year he qualified as a surveyor, 1669), long flowing hair and what I originally assumed to be funny round cap but is more like a band keeping his hair in place, his hand moving over a globe swarming with mythological creatures, his other hand resting on plush fabric flowing down from the table. There is a small book just below his head, *On the Investigation or Observation of the Stars* by a Dutch astronomer named Adriaan Metius, the volume open to Book III, a section recommending the knowledge of geometry and mechanical instruments and inspiration from God. My flash went off. I couldn't believe it. I was horrified. Had I just destroyed a priceless painting? Had I just effaced a major work in Vermeer's rather modest oeuvre? Did I just cause those marvelous colors to fade a little?

How the fuck did the flash go off?

I was glad a museum official hadn't caught me. I checked the camera. My understanding of all the little icons and doodads was poor. I pressed little metal things and formats changed without my understanding how they came to be there or make the camera go back to the screen I wanted before it changed into the new set of options it was now presenting, most of which meant absolutely nothing to me. I went back to taking pictures of my shoes. It was the only way I could make sure the flash was off, but even that didn't work. The camera had a mind of its own. I would check to make sure the flash was off, then take a picture, and the flash would go off.

Ronnie assured me that a camera flash wouldn't hurt a painting. It would take a gazillion cameras flashing before the painting would be hurt or faded in any way. I tried to believe her but vowed to look into it later, which I did. It turns out she was right.

Small digital cameras are frequently used by people who do not know how to turn off the flash that automatically fires in low light. This worries museum curators. How much damage, in reality, might these camera flashes cause? Most incorporate a small xenon flash with a GN value (Guide Number, sensitivity to light based on a numerical value) of about six to nine candela (the light produced by a pure spermaceti candle weighing one sixth of a pound and burning at a rate of 120 grains per hour). In other words, it exposes the object to about the same quantity of light as what would fall on it every one-eighth of a second in a 200 lux (ca. 18.6 footcandles) gallery, or every half second in a dark 50 lux (ca. 4.6 footcandles) gallery.

There are also copyright issues, and the unpleasantness to other viewers when distracted by a flash or crowds are slowed up by people fussing with their cameras. There are good reasons for prohibiting photography in art museums, though damage caused by the flash of a digital camera is not one of them.

The rules of the French museums are utterly inconsistent. This led to problems further on.

We left the museum, hungry and tired as the day before. I felt the kind of frustration with being exposed to such a huge quantity of art and feeling like I'd only gotten a tiny taste of it.

We entered the Pont des Arts and noticed a group of men selling padlocks. I'd seen the padlocks before and assumed that they had had something to do with bicycles, but didn't bother to connect any dots. Now I got it. There was a tradition here, called the love lock.

We bought a padlock for ten euros (they were going for three euros back on the Quay), which came with three keys and the loan of a red marking pen. We used the marking pen to write our names and the date. It was my birthday, August 23. I turned sixty-six. We each made a wish, then tossed two of the keys into the Seine. We used the third key to lock our padlock to the railing with all the other padlocks (of which there were so many we had a tough time finding room for our own), and brought the key home with us. It now reposes in our kitchen drawer.

So do images of all the keys tossed into the Seine, lying there in the muck and sand of the river bottom. I was sorry we'd done that afterward. One can only imagine the weight of those things on the poor bridge. Not to mention all the keys in the Seine. There was something about the Seine. Something in its green-tinted waters. It was the water of all rivers, the same water, the same water that months previously may have been the waters of Lake Washington, or a cloud over Missouri, or a ripple in the Danube, or a cresting wave in the Black Sea, or a puddle in London, or a pond in Bucharest, or a bead of water trickling down a window in Yokohama. But here, walled in by the yellowish stones of the quays, churned into glitter by the propellers of the *bateaux mouches*, wakened into gentle swells by the hulls of the barges and river steamers, surrounded by gargoyles and palaces and the echoing voices of long dead poets, the water seemed enchanted.

We decided to go somewhere special to have dinner, since it was my birthday. I'd pretty much given myself Paris as a birthday present. The hard part was unwrapping it.

I'm still unwrapping it.

Earlier that day, on our way to the Latin Quarter, we'd passed a restaurant called Pouic Pouic on rue Lobineau which Ronnie remembered seeing praised in *Bon Appétit* for its service and quality of food. We rolled on over to rue Lobineau at about seven and were given a table inside, though near the sidewalk, which was completely open. The entry wall to the restaurant slid open and the manager, a man in his early forties with a great deal of brio, had set up some tables across the street in the roofed but open area on the sidewalk leading to the entry of the Saint Germain market. It was a marvel to see him carry about four plates of food across the street, balancing it all effortlessly, all the while regaling his guests with information about the preparation of the food and his pride at not serving anything that had been frozen. Everything was fresh. He made a point of letting you know that. And I had no reason to doubt his word. Everything I tasted there that night was a gustatory revelation.

We each ordered a salad. Ronnie ordered the *carpaccio de betterave au fromage de chèvre* and I ordered a *sable de Parmesan* with *légume confits*. They were really, really great, everything crisp and fresh and screaming with flavor. For our main meal we each ordered an *entrecôte* with red wine sauce. I was a little worried about my digestion going awry as it invariably does whenever I have a steak in the States, or any kind of meat for that matter. My theory is that it has something to do with antibiotics, or the hellish way the livestock is treated. In any event, I did not get sick. I had no digestive problems whatsoever that evening. And the steak was delicious, moist and tender and subtle as a thread of thought in meaty texture and flavor.

For dessert, we each had the *millefeuille vanille* with caramel *beurre salé* that was sinfully, exquisitely good.

A LITTLE SCIENCE

The man who picked us up at the airport had strongly recommended a museum called Musée des Arts et Metiérs,
which is housed in the priory of Saint-Martin-des-Champs. I
had some interest in science and had even written a book about
Joseph Priestley and the discovery of oxygen.

The museum opened at 10:00 A.M. and we arrived at about
9:45. It was overcast, but warm, and the pavilion in front of the
museum was a pleasant place to linger. There were two large
posters on the wall of the museum, one depicting a strange
contraption which looked like a hybrid between a bat and a
tropical plant and said *"premier avion de Clément Ader."*

Clément Ader, whose grandfather had fought for Napoleon, was a French inventor remembered for his pioneering
work in aviation.

How is it I'd never heard of this guy? In the United States,
the quintessential pioneers of aviation have always been the
Wright Brothers. They are as ingrained in my mind as the
fathers of flight as the yolk in an egg or grain in a slab of oak.

And it's wrong.

How many more of the ideas nailed down hard and tight in my brain as ensigns of fundamental truth and fact are wrong?

Ader's first contraption was a bat-like design similar to the one on the poster that was powered by a lightweight steam engine of four cylinders capable of producing twenty horsepower and which drove a four-blade propeller. The wings had a span of forty-six feet, which is pretty impressive, but had no elevator for pitch control. The pilot sat in front of a boiler. Ader attempted a flight with this machine, which he christened Éole (after Aeolus, ruler of the winds in Greek mythology), in October 1890. The Éole left the ground, attained an altitude of eight inches, and traveled roughly one hundred and sixty-five feet before touching down on the earth again without incident or injury. This was thirteen years before the Wright Brothers.

The French unequivocally claim Ader's experiment as the first human flight in a heavier-than-air craft. But according to other authorities, particularly in the United States, three criteria must be met: it must be powered, sustained and controlled. It is extremely doubtful that Ader was in complete control of his craft. But to my mind these are pesky technicalities. Ader's machine flew. He landed it without injury. As he put it, during those few seconds of flight, "I was suspended in a state of indefinable joy."

I wondered what he would have thought of several hundred people riding in a heavier-than-air-craft at 35,000 feet watching movies and snoozing and nibbling cookies for ten or eleven hours.

Ronnie took my picture in front of an adjoining poster, this one depicting a contraption that looked like a giant disk with a huge woofer attached. This was the "*première télévision de René Barthélemy (1931)*."

René Barthélemy, son of a tailor in Nangis, became at age twenty-two a radio telegraphist at the Eiffel Tower and in 1929 chief in charge of a laboratory doing research into television. Using a receptor called a Nipkow disk and a specialized camera, Barthélemy produced the first public demonstration of television in France in the ampitheater of L'École Supérieure d'Électricité before eight hundred guests. The show was called *L'Espagnole à l'éventail* (*Spanish Woman with a Fan*), starring Suzanne Bridoux.

A tall, heavyset German man appeared and chatted with us for a while. He said he taught applied physics in Munich. I mentioned that the poet Rainier Maria Rilke was from Munich, but this did not lead to much in the way of conversation. I speak no German, and his English was quite good, but I suspect his interests leaned more heavily toward science than poetry. He was an affable man, though somewhat guarded, and spoke with pride about Munich. He said it had long been a center of learning and culture and that Richard Wagner's operas had had their premieres under the patronage of Ludwig II of Bavaria.

We were let into the museum and began immediately with an exhibit featuring the work of Enki Bilal, a French comic book creator and film director. He is best known for the Nikopol trilogy (*La foire aux immortels, La femme piège* and *Froid équateur*).

I found it to be a fascinating show. It reminded me in many ways of the Museum of Jurassic Technology in Los Angeles.

I was also quite thrilled a little later to discover objects on display from the laboratory of Antoine-Laurent de Lavoisier, including his pneumatic trough, which I had written extensively about in that book I tried selling in the late nineties and early part of the millennium. I had concentrated my efforts on the work of Joseph Priestley, the man credited with the discovery of oxygen, and who was a contemporary of Lavoisier, and visited him in Paris where they exchanged ideas and conducted similar experiments. A literary agent had represented my book but had been unable to sell it, mainly because I lacked credentials. I should have done the smart thing and followed a scientist around *à la* John McPhee. Hindsight is 20/20.

Our main reason for visiting this museum, however, was to hear French. Our driver told us that they only conducted lectures and tours in French at the museum, which I was very happy to hear. It is more difficult than one can imagine to hear French spoken in France. Apart from brief conversations with a hotel concierge or waiter, unless you know someone French who only speaks French and does not insist on answering you in English the way most French people do, it's difficult to find means in which to practice French conversation, or even overhear snatches of conversation amid the fast-paced activity of the streets and subways. This was an opportunity to hear a nice large chunk of uninterrupted French.

Which we did.

We arrived in time for a lecture on Foucault's pendulum, a specimen of which hung in the choir of Saint-Martin-des-Champs. The original Foucault's pendulum, which Foucault introduced to the world at the Universal Exhibition in Paris in 1855, had originally hung there, but had to be replaced in 2010, after the bob snapped and damaged the pendulum and floor.

A young man in his late thirties or early forties, thin and dapper with black shaggy hair and the stylishly knotted scarf I saw all the Frenchmen wearing, gave a spirited talk on the pendulum, describing how it worked, how it demonstrates the rotation of the earth by swinging in free rotation clockwise in the northern hemisphere over a circle marked with little slabs of metal or wood that the bob knocks over as the planet rotates. The brass bob weighs about sixty-one pounds and hangs from a roughly two-hundred-and-twenty-foot-long wire from the dome in the choir.

I only managed to hear a little. The acoustics were bad and the man's voice echoed. I was quite glad he didn't call on people.

We finished our tour of the exhibit in a dimly lit room where the original droid from Star Wars series, R2-D2, stood on exhibit, ready to go into spinning motion at any moment, and a replica of C-3PO. R2-D2 would be the only celebrity with which I would come this close to on our trip to Paris. Unless, of course, you include the lacemaker in Vermeer's painting of the same name in the Louvre, or the headless Winged Goddess of Victory, her robe billowing in Hellenistic stone, blasted from Aegean winds in the prow of a ship just as she had when she still had a head and occupied a niche in the rock wall overlooking the Sanctuary of the Great Gods on the island of Samothrace, everyone's cameras and smartphones raised in clicking veneration.

ZAP! POW!
BANG! SHAZAM!

The next day we decided to stay out of museums and go to Montmartre. But when we got outside and discovered how hard it was raining, we changed our minds and decided to walk to the Pompidou. We borrowed an umbrella from the hotel and headed north to Boulevard Saint-Michel, which became the Boulevard de Sébastopol on the right bank of the Seine. The Pompidou was a stone's throw from Sébastopol.

The museum didn't open until eleven. We arrived about thirty minutes early. A long line had already formed. There was a small group of young men and women behind us speaking what sounded like Russian. Another small group of young men and women in front of us spoke French. The group behind us asked us if this was the line for the Roy Lichtenstein exhibit, or for the museum exhibits in general. We'd been wondering the same thing.

Pardon, I interrupted the group in front, willing once again to put my smattering of French on display and struggle like a stroke victim relearning vowels and consonants, *qu'est-ce que c'est la ligne pour le Roy Lichtenstein exposition seulement, ou pour le pièces de musée en général? Tous les deux*, they cheerfully answered.

Both, I told the Russians.

We chatted with the Russians a little more, and I gave them my heartfelt thanks for taking Edward Snowden. They laughed heartily.

The line began to move. Inside the museum, we stood in another long line to check our hotel umbrella. The last time a hotel had lent us an umbrella, we'd gone to the Joseph Cornell exhibit in San Francisco and put the umbrella in a slot provided for umbrellas that allowed people to bypass the check-in line. We returned to find the umbrella stolen. We were accompanied that day by the poet Andrew Joron, who valiantly helped us find a replacement umbrella, traipsing all over Berkeley until we found a rough facsimile at a Walgreens. The ruse appeared to have worked, as the hotel said nothing.

This time we weren't taking a chance.

We found our way to the tubes outside the building upon which escalators take you as high as the fifth floor, which is where the Lichtenstein exhibit was housed.

Ronnie was not eager to see Lichtenstein. She thought of him mainly as the artist of highly enlarged comic book images, women crying on telephones, superheros going *pow* and *shazam*. We were both in for a big surprise. Lichtenstein had created a huge variety of work, culminating in some imitations of early Chinese scrollwork dedicated to Buddhist thought.

It was on one of the lower floors, in a huge exhibit of work by Simon Hantaï, that we suffered an unfortunate collision with a museum official.

The Pompidou had the weirdest, most inconsistent rules of all concerning photography. It was OK to take pictures of some work, but not others. What made it complicated was that often it was permissible to photograph most of the work of the same artist and in the same gallery, but not all; there may be one or two with the small icon of a camera with a line slashed through it just to the side and below the canvas or sculpture to indicate that pictures were prohibited. Ronnie did not see the icon and raised her smartphone to take a picture of a huge canvas by Hantaï when a French middle-aged woman came screaming out of nowhere like an avenging fury and explained in rapid-fire French that we could not take a picture if there was a slashed camera telling you that pictures were prohibited. I tried to communicate that we understood, but the woman kept jabbering away. She was seriously aggrieved. Had I said, *calmez-vous, madame, calmez-vous,* I feel certain that she would have slapped me.

We continued to view the rest of the canvases, which were pretty amazing, highly textural surfaces that seemed almost volcanic in their intensity. Hantaï develops his images by folding blank sections of canvas, scrunching and squeezing it and dousing it with color, then unfolding the canvas. The result is startling. The images are strong, vibrant, alternating patches of blank canvas with sections of color, red and green and orange and blue, sensual, eruptive and electrically charged.

Hantaï was, in many ways, a revelation for me because he was new to me, I'd never heard of him before, and then as I came to discover more about him I realized that his art, the production of art, was a resistance to the commercialization of the art world. There was a long fifteen-year period in which he did not make art. Hantaï objected to the art market and identified it as the greatest danger that modern art has had to face. In the early days, he observed, society contested and rejected the values of modern art, which made the situation of artists difficult. Now it pretends to support them by creating a market where money decides what art gets made. I see the same thing happening in the literary realm, where the academic institution, the MFA programs, and the provision of awards and grants such as the National Endowment for the Arts, heavily impacts the kind of poetry that gets written and published. The monetary rewards in the literary realm are slight and not nearly what they are in the visual arts, and certainly not what they are in music. But they're there. Hantaï urged that the only defense was to refuse to participate. He told Paul Rodgers that "if I get involved with them, I'll be finished. We cannot join on these terms. We have to stand outside."

The question that often plagues me is, why did art feel the need to separate from society, regardless of the commercial aspects? What's going on in society that makes it appear toxic to artistic consciousness? When I hear reports on NPR and elsewhere about the so-called innovations going on in Silicon Valley that lead to billions of dollars and mega-wealthy entrepreneurs still in their twenties, such as Mark Zuckerberg, I feel depressed, I feel a sickening and sinking of the spirit. There is nothing artistic or spiritual involved with what these people are doing in Silicon Valley. They're simply making products that people don't need. Products that are in many ways eroding society, eroding human contact, eroding the human imagination. By far, the most dispiriting thing I saw in Paris were the posters for the biopic about Steve Jobs. Fortunately, except for a little boutique in Saint Germain selling stylish covers for smartphones, technocracy was not much in evidence in Paris. People still conversed at the outdoor restaurants, they did not gaze trance-like into digital screens ignoring one another.

This begs the question: Is art necessary? Do people need art? Why do people buy art? Why do people pay so much money for art? Why are so many books of poetry published when so few people read poetry? What's going on in our world? All I know is that we create ourselves in the process of experiencing. Perhaps it was this that made Hantaï's canvases so compelling, yet so hard to describe. I had no vocabulary for them. When an experience becomes this immediate, language — which is a discriminatory medium, laden with conjugations and prepositions and nouns and nougats and nuggets and discrepancies in meaning — is paralyzed. Only when it moves through stages of disintegration and re-integration in a fresh perspective does it begin to find life and movement in a concrescence of feeling. Language as act rather than thought about the act. Thought about the act can come later. Language as act is where it's at.

A hole in the skin called a mouth out of which sound out of which talk out of which parables and prongs.

The immense canvases on display at the Pompidou were not only visually startling, but were the direct result of a process. Hantaï brought process to the forefront of artistic activity. He was not the first. Pollock was arguably the first to bring process into art. It is process that gives art its vitality. It is process that allows the materials of art, the colors and fabrics and volumes and shapes to combine synergistically to create a pulse of experience, an immediate existence, that is to say a pure existence with mediating filter.

Ronnie was especially eager to view Brancusi's *La muse endormie*, a smooth brass head lying on its side in a glass case, the lids closed, the forehead large, the nose and lips thin. The room was bright and light reflected from the head. I also took a picture of myself taking a picture in the knob protruding at the end of Brancusi's *Princess X*, which is a sculptured rendering of the French princess Marie Bonaparte, the great-grandniece of emperor Napoleon Bonaparte, created between 1915 and 1916. It was originally displayed at the Salon des Indépendants in Paris, but removed after complaints over its obscene content, in that it strongly resembled an erect penis with a pair of shiny brass balls. And it does, I could see that. But I wouldn't reduce it to that, even if I didn't know its history. It was obvious that Brancusi was seeking the expression of an essence, a fundamental reality that transcended the merely literal and one-dimensional grasp.

Brancusi defended himself. "A Lady from Paris," he said, "a princess, insisted that I carved her bust. You know the horror and miserably low opinion I have about bust sculpture. She did not understand. She coquettishly asked me to make an exception. She had a beautiful bust but ugly legs and was terribly vain. She was looking in the mirror all the time, even during lunch... discreetly placing the mirror on the table looking furtively. She was vain and sensual. I did not intend to model the embodiment of her hidden desires. Do you think that this phenomenon happened unconsciously? I have a very low opinion of psychoanalysis... My statue you understand, is the woman; the very synthesis of the woman, it is the eternal feminine of Goethe reduced to its essence... And I believe to have finally won a victory by overtaking the bounds of the material. Besides, what a pity it would be to spoil this beautiful material by digging into it little holes for eyes, hair, ears. And my material is so beautiful in its sinuous lines which shine like pure gold and which embody in a sole archetype all the feminine effigies on this earth."

The room of pieces by André Breton was closed. *C'est pas vrai, c'est pas vrai*, I whined to the young man museum official, sitting in a chair and yawning. He seemed barely awake.

A New Correspondence

The poet Clayton Eshleman had urged me before we left to get in touch with the French poet Michel Deguy, now eighty-three years old. I was daunted by this, but thought I'd give it a try, partly because I was still so hungry to speak and hear French, particularly with someone with whom I had something in common, but also because I'd been reading his poetry and really liked it. The poetry was intense and had a certain rough quality to it, a fullness of being as gravelly and deep as his voice. Deguy's poems are the kind of "high energy constructs" to which Charles Olson referred. They were kinetic, they kept in movement, they were muscular and twisted and turned ideas like shapes of hot metal, still red from the fire. They were openly philosophical, the prose poems especially, wrestling with ideas in the same manner as his old friend Jacques Derrida, going deep into word etymologies and seeking the full dimensions of a word as well as its current range, sounding it for everything it was worth, beaming his light into veins of Greek and Latin to determine the history of this strange, metaphorical ore called language.

Deguy had oft been saluted as the "French *Dichter-Denker*," or *poésophe*. He was a thinker poet of the first order. "Deguy redefines the art of poetry," his friend Jacques Derrida observed in his essay on Deguy, "How to Name": "in a performative and irruptive gesture, he gives it a new definition, a new name (he rebaptizes it) and thus, in another space, from his invention of a new cartography, he assigns it a new task. He assigns one to it, that is to say, he signs a new concept of the art of poetry, a new correspondence to its ancient name, and a new responsibility."

His poetry resembles oak: it is hard-grained, enduring, complex and pushes its roots deep into the abiding earth. There is a roughness to its bark, its outer husk, the heave and tumble of its syllables, what Baudelaire called *l'élastique ondulation*. The sacred oak of the sanctuary known as Dodona, located in a mountainous region of limestone folds and thrust fault blocks named Epirus in the ancient Greek world, had oracular significance; it was the favored tree of Zeus. Priests divined the pronouncements of Zeus in the rustling of its leaves.

Oak trees are large, spreading their branches in a pyramidal profusion of radial prodigality, catching the wind in wonderful agitations of give and take. Oak is able to do this because its internal structure consists of cells that stretch inward from the bark to the pith and stabilize the framework, keeping the vertical fibers from splitting. It is the constant buffeting of wind that brings the oak tree to life, that causes it to shake and bob, chatter and convulse.

"There is no inertia in consciousness," observed Jean-Paul Sartre. Agitation is the life of the mind in its exertions toward meaning, those rare and wonderful encounters in the more delicate, exquisite region of one's Being where Being encounters its own Nothingness.

Poetry speaks to that region. It is where consciousness, to quote Sartre again, "makes itself, since its being is consciousness of being; it sustains being in the heart of subjectivity, which means once again that it is inhabited by being but that it is not being: consciousness is not what it is." So what is it? We must look to comparison. The eyeball cannot look at itself, but only through itself. We need a mirror in order to see the very eyeball that permits us to see.

Deguy's poetry is generous, generative and germane: it burgeons in analogy, flourishes in comparison. Reading Deguy is an intellectual adventure. The spirit of inquiry is immediate and strong and boundless in ramification.

I thought of Deguy whenever I rushed into a room and forgot to turn on the light and had to feel my way in the darkness for familiar objects, a desk, a bed, a bureau and eventually a lamp. Illumination, too, is immediate. Phenomenal. As in, Latin *phaenomenon* ("appearance"), from Ancient Greek φαινομενον (*phainomenon*, "thing appearing to view").

It wasn't the light coming on that made the poetry great. It was the groping around the dark part, feeling the shape and texture of things, the confusion, the stumbles, the gambles, the slowness of movement, the carefully considered movements, the palpability of the darkness. It was like pressing a stethoscope against the chest of the universe and hearing an actual heartbeat.

I bought a copy of *Comme si comme ça* at a bookstore called Gibert Joseph on the Boulevard Saint-Michel in Paris, which was a collection of Deguy's work from 1980 to 2007.

Later, when we returned home, Deguy would become a compulsion. His work had what I'd been looking for in poetry and found lacking, particularly in the more recent American poetry, which was full of snotty irony and a distancing of fragment and collage. I liked fragment and collage, but used solely as a technique they left out the voice of the poet. This was deliberate. I got it. I understood. There was a time when I championed that position. But now it seemed brittle and dry, the dusty purview of college courses. You saw it proliferate like kudzu on the internet. It seemed as if no one really wanted to commit to writing anymore, writing as a product of the hand and arm and brain, the teeming brain, the boiling blood, the eyes rolling in delirium.

Deguy's *À ce qui n'en finit pas (To That Which Does Not End)*, which was included in its entirety in *Comme si comme ça*, would, in the coming months after our return to Seattle, prove to be one of the most moving collections of poetry I have ever read. It is a threnody, written shortly after the passing of Michel Deguy's wife of forty years, Monique. I find it remarkable that he not only had the strength to write, but to explore his pain and this universal sorrow with such remarkable articulation, depth and frankness. Its honesty and openness to experience is breathtaking. It grapples with issues I find difficult in the extreme to come to terms with: the loss of a loved one, mortality, the pangs of solitude, the daily effort to dress, work, bathe, feed oneself, maintain a social existence and locate whatever meaning one can in a universe of stunning indifference.

À ce qui n'en finit pas was first published in 1995. It consists of short prose fragments, each a deep reflection on the experience of loss, on the nature of existence, on coping with the absence of a partner, and the dynamics and sometimes harsh reality of marriage itself: *"Je relate que la vie conjugale fut contentieuse, violente, impossible. J'ai souffert du marriage comme personne, comme beaucoup comme tout le monde?"* ("I relate that conjugal life was contentious, violent, impossible. Have I suffered in marriage as anyone else, as much as everyone else?")

The original book was unpaginated because, Deguy remarked, "each page, or almost, could be the first, or the umpteenth. There is no ordinal series. Everything begins with each page; everything ends with each page." He had, in fact, originally wanted the book to come out as a roll, a forever unrolling scroll of paper.

"Non-being is a euphemism," Deguy remarks within the work. It is impossible to conceive of non-existence. As soon as we begin to imagine non-existence, it recedes. It cannot be imagined. Imagining non-existence is to give it a conceptual being. To give it a name, such as "non-being," is to give it an identity and mask its stark reality. *Non-being* is a term, a philosophical abstraction, an entity of sorts. The finality of death is so utterly beyond human imagining that its impact on the living must be filled with something, anything, flowers, prayer, shrines, graves, tombstones. There must be devised a substitute, a proxy, a recognition that acknowledges death as a fact but not as a reality. Who hasn't felt at home in a funeral home? What a wonderful (albeit expensive) fiction.

I would come to find, when Michel signed my copy of *Comme si comme ça* and wrote that very phrase at the top of the frontispiece and began to talk about it, try to explain it in a combination of French and English, the immense importance that word *comme* had for his work.

"*Comme*" was a vehicle by which Deguy was able to give a living presence to the "eloquent silence" of the unknowable, its fullest possibility as appearance in perceptual consciousness. It is the logic of one hand touching the other. Comparison brings the unknowable — that which resists perception, eludes even a thematic framework — within perceptual range, particularly when the objects of our consciousness are altered, inverted, converted, reconstructed. "Death," remarked Deguy in a piece titled "*Il et ratures*," "is that 'unknowable,' immeasurable thing whose event comes to transform all life, perhaps 'giving all things the status of figure.'" It is a haunting. An obsession. Deguy elaborates further: "We are *haunted*, to pick up on that saying by Mallarmé, which is also a saying by Merleau-Ponty (one of those imaginatively charged terms whereby philosophy gets ventriloquized by poetry); obsession: an intimate, cure-less mode of the two-in-one relation... if at every point in language 'the union,' the sound-sense crease has already always occurred. To this obsession, which is indivisibly 'obsession with the world' in its figures or 'rich postulates enciphered' (Mallarmé), poetry devotes itself, tearing language away from this *usage* that lessens it through univocalities, but also dialectics that restrains play itself."

He was fascinated by the phenomenon of comparison. The poet, he said, must find the real, and must do so using figures that may themselves be mistaken for the real. This was part of the phenomenon of writing. It had to cut the air, ring in the air like a hammered blade, hot from a furnace. But in order to do that it was necessary to slide things around, make grafts, hybrids, dress them in steel or stuff them like puppets and dangle them from strings. The real was not necessarily that dull, monotone empirical rock Samuel Johnson talked about kicking but something far more intense, something far more imaginative. In order to learn how to experience one had to free oneself from the technical interpretation of thinking. Remove it from the service of doing and making and let it be a living creation, a feather, a flutter, a panache brilliant as butter and conformable to nothing.

"Reality becomes a nightmare when the 'dream' invades the real," Deguy observed in one of his prose poems.

The poet must go in the opposite direction, urging the full apprehension of the eternal present.

He discussed the Münchhausen paradox in one of his prose poems, presumably the tale in which the Baron Münchhausen pulls himself and his horse out of a swamp by pulling his own hair. The story stresses the impossibility of proving any truth, in part because all things change as their relations change and we see them from different points of view. This is especially pertinent to language, which is inherently metaphorical and powerfully evocative, generating chain upon chain of association. The poem goes in quest of the energies that will feed it by first immersing itself in a swamp of metaphor, then pulling itself out of this epistemological muck by pulling on its own metaphorical hair.

"Language is hostile to the particular and nevertheless seeks its rescue," tugged Theodor Adorno in another like-minded contradictory pull of the hair.

I bought another of Deguy's books at Gibert Joseph on the Boulevard Saint-Michel, called *Spleen de Paris*.

I loved reading *Spleen de Paris*. I began reading it as soon as we returned to our hotel. We were in Paris, so I had already become familiar with some of the things he talked about. The swarms of pedestrians like the atoms of Lucrece, the repose of Père Lachaise and its implicit ceremonies of *adieu* to the other side, its fourteen universities and throngs of students, its many ethnicities and immigrant population, *le Maghreb, l'Afrique francophone, les exilés successif de Chili, de l'Iran*, the ongoing conferences and colloquiums and visiting colleagues, noises near and distant, the crows of the squares, the gulls of the Seine, the rain, the soft plummeting of the rain, the fragrance of cheese and oysters, crêpe and caramel in the green Paris air.

Clayton had given me Deguy's telephone number a few weeks before we left Seattle, and I'd emailed Deguy earlier in the month to let him we were going to be in Paris, and sent him a copy of my prose poetry and essays, *Larynx Galaxy*. That the hotel where we'd be staying, the Hôtel Récamier in Place Saint-Sulpice, was very near to where he lived, and that it would be wonderful to meet him. I was nervous about calling him, but I had written out a script to read into his voicemail, assuming that he was like most people who would not answer their phone. I couldn't remember the last time I phoned someone and they answered their phone. So I dialed the number, heard the phone ring several times, and the deep, rough voice of an older man came out of the phone receiver: Michel Deguy.

Bonjour, I said, *c'est John Olson. Je suis l'ami de Clayton. Ça va?*

Oh hello, he said kindly. Are you in Paris? My English, it is not very good.

That's ok, I answered, *j'ai beaucoup de mal à parler français.*

He laughed. No, your French is good. Where are you staying ?

The Hôtel Récamier.

I have to3 visit my daughter today. But perhaps we could meet tomorrow? Are you familiar with the Café de la Mairie? It is directly across the square from your hotel.

I looked out the window. Yes, I can see it.

How about if we meet there tomorrow at eleven?

Sure. *Onze il sera.* Café de la Mairie.

We decided to go look for a place to eat on rue Mouffetard. I'd remembered rue Mouffetard from my visit to Paris in 1972 as a place of quirky energy and curiosity and romance. One of Paris's most colorful neighborhoods.

It had stopped raining. We left the hotel and headed east. We had a hard time finding rue Mouffetard. It was represented on the map, but none of the surrounding streets were indicated on the map.

I stopped a young woman with black hair and asked if she knew where the rue Mouffetard might be.

Do you speak English? she asked. I'm English.

It was nice hearing an English accent.

She pulled out a map that was more detailed than ours and provided three-dimensional representations of Paris's monuments. I watched as her finger drifted from street to street until she came to rue Mouffetard. It must be in that direction, she said, pointing to a tangle of streets and cafés and kiosks and statuary.

Thank you, I said. I guess we'll head that way then.

Good luck, she said, and continued on her way.

We wound our way up and down the rue Gay-Lussac, the rue Saint-Jacques, the rue Soufflot, until we arrived at the Place du Panthéon and from there made our way to rue Mouffetard, which was as I remembered full of crowds and little cafés and bizarre little spectacles such as two adolescents racing by on mountain bikes dressed up in tinfoil helmets with propellers and long flowing scarves.

We ambled up the rue du Pot-de-Fer and decided on eating at La Petite Provence. There were plenty of tables available and we skipped inside as a man at the adjacent café was hosing down the street. A young woman arrived with menus and left us for a while to study them and when she returned I told her that we'd both decided to start with the *salade de pâtes fraiches au basilic* and that I would like a *jus d'orange*. I made the mistake of pronouncing the 's' at the end of *jus* and the waitress corrected me, *le 's' ne se prononce pas, monsieur, c'est du joooo d'orange. Il me dérange d'entendre le 's' dans le jus, il me dérange!*

I thanked her for helping me out with my French because, truly, that's what I'd been hoping for all along, for the French to help me out with their language as I maneuvered my way through it, though I could have done without the melodrama.

For dinner I had my regular tagliatelle carbonara, which was ok but not quite as good as the Café Six and Ronnie had something involving cream sauce and chicken.

Shortly before our dinner arrived I smelled something odd, a strange combination of steam and tobacco. And I noticed the reflection of a black man in the window on the other side of the street with a long golden tube in his mouth puffing smoke with great vigor and concentration. He spent a full half hour smoking the shit out of a hookah. There was a small breeze in the narrow street that tended to keep the smoke away from our open window (the man was sitting right around the corner within inches of our table), but occasionally the breeze shifted and carried wisps of the strange moisture-laden smoke into the restaurant.

When we finished eating and paid our bill and re-entered the rue du Pot-de-Fer I noticed that the man had been sitting at one of several outdoor tables at a hookah boutique called Chicha Shop. *Chicha* is a slang word in French for *nargile*, or hookah.

I took my compass out to find an eastern direction but didn't put my reading glasses on and the needle, although pointing north as always, indicated south because I was holding the compass upside down. Consequently we headed farther west rather than east. When we reached the Jardin des Plantes I became aware of my mistake and we reversed our direction and enjoyed a short walk through the Jardin des Plantes.

We were just a few blocks from our hotel when Ronnie spotted a plaque on a building that identified it as the residence of Paul Verlaine for eight years at the beginning of the twentieth century. I thought of that curious old man with his fuzzy goatee and bulging brow and if he wondered as I do daily about the exploits of his old buddy Arthur Rimbaud. Did Verlaine even know Rimbaud was in Yemen and Ethiopia? Did he still feel the rain falling in his heart as it did in the city?

The morning of the following day we headed over to the Café de la Mairie. It was about 10:45, sunny and warm. It was a short walk across the square in front of Saint-Sulpice cathedral to the Café de la Mairie.

I had heard that Michel Deguy smoked cigarettes so I looked for a table and some seats outdoors, on the patio. There were several rows of chairs, but they were tethered so that they couldn't be moved around. Everyone would have to sit forward in a row looking at the square as if it were a movie, or stage set. We found a table and three chairs closer to the restaurant in an area that was still outdoors, although with a roof to provide shelter from the rain. Ronnie and I ordered coffee, which arrived in the form of espresso. This is normal for France. Coffee, unless otherwise specified, comes as an espresso. Our form of drip coffee is called American coffee. We preferred the espresso.

I saw Michel arrive on a bicycle. I got up and went to greet him as he dismounted. He was wearing a green blazer, white striped shirt and a burgundy scarf which he knotted stylishly and loosely around his neck in the manner typical of the way French men wear their scarves.

Bonjour, I said. *Je suis John. Mon épouse est là-bas*, and pointed to Ronnie at the table we secured.

Do you mind if I have a cigarette? he asked. He must have realized that smoking was prohibited in the area where we were sitting. I hadn't realized it, but apparently the extension of the roof technically qualified that area as an interior space where it would be prohibited to smoke.

Sure, I said.

He took out a package of Marlboros and fired one up.

He took a few puffs and as I explained how long we'd been there (five days) and that this was our last full day and how happy I was that he was able to come and meet us.

He only smoked about half of the cigarette, held it out front to look at it as if it were a living creature, tossed it to the cobblestoned ground and said, *adieu.*

We joined Ronnie and the waiter appeared and we ordered another round of coffee.

Michel did not seem at all like an eighty-three-year-old man. He was spirited, spry and completely charming. He immediately began telling us about the area, pointed to a building and said that Man Ray had lived there, pointed to another building and said that Jean-Paul Sartre's magazine had been headquartered there. He pointed south, and said that at 8 rue

Férou, where the mural-sized *"Le bateau ivre"* next to our hotel had been printed, resided the publishing house Éditions Belin, which had been in business since 1777, and once published the work of Pilâtre de Rozier, the French chemistry and physics teacher who had attempted a fatal balloon flight over the English channel on November 21, 1783, and was the publisher of the literary review he edited, *Po&sie*.

Michel remarked on the bizarre architecture of Saint-Sulpice, particularly the ungainly, rococo façade and two mismatched towers, its weighty double colonnade and loggias, and revealed that the poet Louis Aragon had so despised the ugliness of Saint-Sulpice that he'd composed a poem lamenting the architectural pomposity of the church that Michel recited in French. I can't remember the poem, but I remember that it involved urination on the church, and rhyming Sulpice with piss.

I tried conveying my appreciation of Deguy's work in French, and held out two books I'd purchased several days before and asked if he would sign them, which he most graciously did.

He asked several times if I knew German, hoping, I think, for a more fluid conversation than we were managing with English and French. I don't, I told him, feeling a little crestfallen that my French was still so bad after years of reading it (which I did quite well) and attending classes at Alliance Française, trying hard to get my mouth and vocal cords to make the sounds as I knew they were supposed to sound but never getting my lips and tongue to cooperate. I was also slowed by having to grammatically construct the sentences in my mind before uttering them. It was like constructing a boat out of syntax and reeds and putting it into the water and hoping that it will float. Or that it will even be recognizable as a boat.

Ultimately, I found myself falling back into English.

Michel complained of the tourism ruining Paris. I agreed, although I did point out the fact that Ronnie and I ourselves were tourists. But I knew what he meant. People had begun coming to Paris just to say they had gone to Paris, or because traveling to Paris was considered chic. Paris was becoming a theme park, a kind of haut couture Disneyland. I remembered the swarm of people in the Mona Lisa room at the Louvre, all robotically taking pictures of that dimly smiling lady, a celebrity trapped in oil behind glass. It could have been Madonna, or Lady Gaga or Kim Kardashian for all they cared.

Michel kindly posed for several photographs, smiling broadly, and after we finished our coffee, Michel took us on a short walk around the neighborhood, showing us the space formerly occupied by the *Village Voice*, where a reading series had been conducted, and suggested that I buy the space. I told him I wish I could, but was quite certain the lease for that space exceeded my financial reach. However, if he wanted to go in on it with me…

We led Michel back to his bicycle and said goodbye. He gave Ronnie some vigorous *bisous*, and I got a vigorous handshake.

That night, we began packing for our return flight home. I went downstairs to ask the concierge if there might be some tape available with which to fix the strap on my valise. A man with thick black hair was manning the desk. I asked, *je me demandais si vous pourriez avoir un peu de ruban adhésif, la sangle sur ma valise est cassé*, hazarding my awful French once more. He responded to my request, however, which made me feel wonderful. However much I mutilated those syllables, he had understood them. He brought me a roll of very shiny tape, which I brought back to our room. I tried tearing it but it was much stronger than I thought. I wondered if we had anything sharp in our possession. My razor was the disposable kind, so I could not extract a razor. Ronnie held the tape outstretched while I hacked at it with one of my keys and managed to tear it. I wrapped the tape several times around the tear in the leather strap and tested it. It held. The tape worked. I brought the tape back and gave the man a sincere *merci*.

The next morning we paid our bill and the concierge, the same man who had lent me the tape the night before, complimented me on my French.

The driver greeted us. He drove a Mercedes-Benz van. I was surprised to see Mercedes-Benz made vans. I assumed this fellow, a very young man, was running a pretty lucrative business. The driver was nice, and kindly carried on a conversation in French on our way to the airport, talking about his fish and aquariums and how hard the aquariums were to clean and maintain, but how much he loved his fish. *Je dois être très prudent avec le poisson que j'achète,* he explained, *certains poissons vont attaquer les autres poissons. C'est très, très important de faire des recherches.*

The flight home was a duplicate of our flight to France, except this time the right speaker of the earphones didn't work. I could hear the movies well enough with the one speaker pressed hard against my ear so I decided not to bug the flight attendants about it. They seemed busy enough already and you had to keep an eye out to catch one of them if they weren't already maneuvering a cartload of drinks or food down the aisle.

Light flashed into the compartment as Ronnie lifted the window shade to get a look at the sights below as we crossed what must have been Greenland. We saw craggy mountains jutting through ice and auras of gold among wisps of cloud. The Russian woman in the seat across the aisle rolled her head to the side and gave us a nasty look. Ronnie shut the window, and I went back to watching Tom Cruise battle drones in *Oblivion*.

PARIS AS PROZAC

Sad thing is, it's not a joke. Paris was an effective antidepressant. And there were no side effects. It did not deaden your
emotions or impede you sexually like a lot of antidepressant
medication. In essence, what buoyed our mood in Paris were
very specific things, values that we lacked in the United States.
People read books. There were bookstores everywhere. Good
bookstores. Not like the ones in the United States that had caved
so easily to Amazon and let their inventories dwindle down to
Harry Potter or the Twilight Series or *Fifty Shades of Grey*,
but books on an infinite assortment of eccentric and outland-
ish topics, philosophical perspectives that had never occurred
to me. And it wasn't merely bookstores; once at a kiosk to buy
a postcard in order to get some change, I saw a few journals
on philosophy. I nearly fell to my knees. Imagine standing in
line at the supermarket in the States and seeing magazines of
philosophy instead of the usual tabloids. People still conversed
in Paris, talked to one another face to face. They weren't Lud-
dites. The French loved science. The French loved novelty. The
technology was there; I'd seen a boutique that specialized in

covers for smartphones and could easily imagine one of the women from Proust's *À la recherche du temps perdu* shopping in one of them. But it was rare to see anyone walking down the street in a zombie-like trance staring into their smartphone, or people at an outdoor restaurant patio gazing into a laptop. We saw people engaged in vigorous conversation everywhere. Voices and facial expressions were lively and vivid. It was still a physical universe. Philosophers and writers and poets were still lauded far and above the technocrats and business magnates like Donald Trump. How much longer would this last before the values of the United States and its crazed love of technology and money would seep into Paris and corrode those values we treasured so much? Time was of the essence. A return was inevitable. We began saving our money.

One night as I was idly Googling, I looked up the Site du Centre Pompidou. There was to be a monograph exhibition devoted to the painted work of Marcel Duchamp running from September 24, 2014 to January 5, 2015. This I had to see.

I told Ronnie. She liked Duchamp, too, but was eager to return to Paris no matter what. Duchamp gave us a target, a date. Ronnie said she wouldn't be able to get off during December because of Christmas and New Year's Day, but that she could most likely get time off right after New Year's Day because the grocery business was extremely slow then. If we left on January 2 we would arrive in Paris on January 3 and be able to see the Duchamp exhibit on January 4.

I worried about Graham. He is very attached to us. There was no way to tell him that we would be away for six days and that we would return. He was only about one and a half years old the first time we left him alone on a trip to New York. We were away five days. When we returned, we found that all of his toys had been chewed to smithereens. Years later, even as a much older cat, his behavior had not much improved. Things did not go well on our first trip to Paris. The cat sitter, a warm, middle-aged woman named Elaine, had had difficulty just getting into our apartment. Graham growled and hissed at her. He could be formidable. How much of Graham's anger was territorial and how much was fueled by the anguish of our absence one cannot say. This pained me. I felt very bad about leaving him. There was no way to tell him how many days we'd be gone and assure him that we would be returning. I don't know what goes through the mind of cats, but I had to assume that when we didn't return home in the evening to go to bed, he didn't have a clue as to what was going on. Did he think we got lost? Eaten? It was the one thing that plagued me whenever we went on a trip. If it hadn't been for Graham, we would've made arrangements to stay in France for a much longer time. We have often thought of moving there, but that is outside our financial ability.

Or was it? Would it be possible to find an affordable house in a rural area? Was there any chance of becoming a citizen? What kind of bureaucratic hoops did one have to jump through in order to stay there longer than six months? Would we have to schedule a trip to Germany or Belgium every six months?

On New Year's Day 2015, Ronnie printed out our boarding passes. And on January 2, at 9:30 A.M., we said goodbye to Graham and headed down to catch the bus for downtown Seattle and the light rail train that would take us to the airport.

Our seats were in the middle of the plane, next to the wings. I liked gazing at the wings. It reminded me of *The Twilight Zone* episode in which Bob Wilson, played by William Shatner, thinks he sees a gremlin on the wing. I also liked to imagine other things: standing on the wing, having a picnic on the wing, playing piano on the wing, painting a watercolor on the wing.

Opportunities to look out of the window were limited an hour or so after takeoff because the shades came down so people could sleep or watch movies or read. The interior of the plane felt like a cross between a bedroom and a theater. Those who weren't sleeping were immersed in movies or iPads or books. The quiet was pervasive, but could be shattered by a single sudden streak of light.

I also liked following the flight path on the little screen on the back of the passenger seat in front. I was fascinated by the flight data. Somewhere over Greenland, I copied down the flight data: ground speed, 534 mph; 59 mph tail wind; temperature, −67 degrees Fahrenheit; altitude, 35,014 feet; distance to destination, 2,026 miles; distance from origin, 3,054 miles; longitude 45° 34″ West; latitude 60° 3′ 47″ North; heading, East.

I watched three movies: *Boyhood*, *A Trip to Italy* and *Lucy*. All three were disappointing, and the quality was bad since there was something wrong with the download and the movies didn't run correctly but were jerky. The flight steward tried rebooting but it didn't improve much.

The sound, however, was fantastic. I decided to bring my Bose earphones on this trip so that I could lie in bed and listen to radio broadcasts on my Galaxy tablet while Ronnie slept. I was also able to use them aboard the plane. I went to REI and bought a strap for the Bose carrying case and wore the earphones around my neck, along with my camera.

Across the aisle an English woman read a book by Alain de Botton while her husband slept and her three-year-old daughter watched cartoons on a tablet.

A Catholic priest sat behind us, a young man in his thirties. It occurred to me to make a joke about the convenience of his being there in case the plane had trouble I could make a confession. But then, I didn't. It seemed in bad taste, and I'm not Catholic. I'm not even religious. Though I'm not entirely without religious feelings. I'm religious about a few things. Toast, for instance. I have a reverence for toast. Is there anything more welcoming and reassuring and spiritually fulfilling than a slice of toast slathered with butter and strawberry jam? It is like a stained glass window for eating rather than gazing, or studying a parable from the Bible. The parables of jam are venerations of sugar, allegories of goop.

Édouard LeFevre, a quiet-spoken man with a love of jazz, met us at the airport and drove us to the hotel. It was a wet, gray, gloomy morning similar to those in Seattle. The trees and houses along the road looked familiar. We wondered if the plane hadn't circled back and landed in Seattle again by mistake.

It hadn't. It wasn't long before we saw the Paris skyline, Sacré-Coeur Basilica atop Montmartre, Eiffel Tower and

Notre-Dame. It felt like returning home, especially when we arrived at the Hôtel Récamier.

I peeked around the corner to make sure *"Le bateau ivre"* was still on the wall overlooking rue Ferou. It was.

It was still morning and the couple occupying the room we had chosen had not packed and left yet so we left our luggage with the hotel concierge (the same young lady who had been there in August 2013, Carole) and struck out to get some coffee or something to while away the time. We went to the Café de la Mairie. I wondered if we'd see Michel Deguy there. We didn't. We sat down at a small table and when the waiter appeared Ronnie ordered a hot chocolate and I ordered a *café viennois.*

When a sufficient amount of time had passed we returned to the hotel and were happy to find that our room was ready. We got situated and spent several hours resting and then decided to go out somewhere for dinner. It was a bit early, four in the afternoon, and we weren't terribly hungry after eating several meals earlier on the plane, but hungry enough to be in search of a restaurant that was open during the day. Not many were. Most of the restaurants on the main boulevards that catered to tourists stayed open all day but the really good restaurants didn't open until 7:00 P.M. at the earliest.

We opted for Les Deux Magots. This restaurant was famous for being the rendezvous of the literary and intellectual elite, people such as André Breton and other surrealists, André Gide, Simone de Beauvoir, Jean-Paul Sartre, Ernest Hemingway, Albert Camus, Pablo Picasso, Bertolt Brecht and James Joyce. It was now a highly popular tourist destination.

I didn't expect to see James Joyce or André Breton or their twenty-first-century equivalents, if such creatures existed, but the bright lights and energy emanating from the establishment on the corner of Boulevard Saint-Germain and the rue Bonaparte were most welcoming, and we were two tired travelers.

We sat at a small table. All French restaurants seem to have a plethora of small wobbly tables. Is it the small wobbly table that inspires so much creative writing? Or the energy and noise of so many people convening in one place? Or the incredible variety of food and wines on the menus?

All of the above, I would suspect.

I gave Ronnie my hat and she put it on the bench next to her where I continued to worry about it. What if someone sat on it? It was an expensive hat, a wide-brimmed fedora with a pretty black ribbon for a band. Wherever I went I had to find a place to put and protect it, which often turned out to be my left knee. It was like having a small pet.

The restaurant hummed with energy. It was like sitting in an electrical substation where you can hear the voltage humming in the transmission lines.

There is no spectacle as intimidating as a French waiter. These people, men and women alike, moved with such splendid efficiency as to dazzle even the most jaded spectator.

We each ordered a *jambon de San Daniele* and a Coca-Cola. The ham was very thinly sliced and spread over the plate like a pancake. It was tasty but not very filling. After dinner, a young lady came around with a pastry tray. Ronnie ordered ice cream. I ordered a *"2000 feuilles"* by the legendary master of pastry Pierre Hermé. *Feuille* means leaf in French. The *"2000 feuilles"* was a multilayered affair of caramel, praline puff, Piedmont hazelnuts and crème de mousseline. It knocked me out. Ronnie, who normally loves ice cream, wished she hadn't settled for something so prosaic.

We struck up a conversation with a young woman from Argentina who was eating alone. The waiter took her picture. She was in France to do a study on snapping turtles. She was headed to a place called La Vallée des Tortues in the Pyrénées, but wasn't due to go there until the spring. Meanwhile she pursued her research at the Muséum National d'Histoire Naturelle. Her husband worked for Exxon Mobil. I didn't comment on that.

After dinner, we returned to the hotel. This was the night of Ronnie's swollen eye and our trip to the Hôtel Dieu. We awoke tired the next morning, but eager to go for a run in the Jardin du Luxembourg. Ronnie's eye had already begun feeling better, and was less swollen. I could see her actual eye now instead of folds of puffy, discolored skin, to which she referred to as her "Elephant Man eye."

It was stranger than ever to jog past Rimbaud's poem about drugs and delirium. The air was brisk and biting. My interest in Rimbaud's poem had become strictly literary. I no longer drank alcohol. But there was a time in my life when I did drink and drug and attain ecstasies of drug-induced mania and the poem had a more visceral connection. I lived the poem. I knew exactly what Rimbaud meant when the haulers — nailed naked to colored stakes and used as target practice by yelping Peau-Rouges — let the boat drift to sea on its own accord, and "from then on I bathed in the Poem / Of the Sea... where, like a pale elated / Piece of flotsam, a pensive drowned figure sometimes sinks." This sentiment clashed interestingly with my new athleticism, which made me feel more like Teddy Roosevelt than a decadent French symbolist.

We began our run and almost immediately my shoelaces came undone. I'd decided to bring the same pair of running shoes that I used to walk in at home. These were running shoes that I'd retired from running but the shoes were still in good condition. I didn't want to bring my new running shoes. I don't know why. I soon regretted that decision. The laces of my shoes kept coming undone. Why was this happening? It didn't happen at home. Was it because the air in Paris was slightly less humid than the air in Seattle? Or did it have something to do with Rimbaud's subversive poem?

We enjoyed running in the Jardin du Luxembourg. Normally, I hate doing laps. When I run I like to do a circuit that in no way repeats ground that I've already run over, or through. It keeps things interesting.

This wasn't true of the Jardin du Luxembourg. I never tired of repeating the course. The hard part was trying to figure out when I had completed a course. At the beginning, as we entered through the gate on rue de Vaugirard, at the north end of the park, near the Musée du Luxembourg. I took in the immediate surroundings, noting as many details as I could: buildings, trees, the configuration of the trails.

It didn't work. You would think the museum would serve as an important and obvious marker, but it didn't. There were several other structures in the park that resembled it.

I began looking for something notable, something really remarkable. I couldn't find anything remarkable. Everything was remarkable. No single thing stuck out, no particular building, no particular statue or historical plaque. The entire environment was crowded with phenomenal architecture and history.

At last, I found a tree. It was a highly unusual tree. It was extremely old and gnarled with a huge branch that ran horizontal to the ground and had a supporting iron bar beneath it and a spot within its gentle curve worn by thousands of people sitting there over the years, lovers holding hands, old men smoking pipes, young boys pretending to stand at the helm of a war ship.

I liked the trails, particularly the trail that followed the outside rim of the park, which has a rectangular shape. The gravel had a yellowish tint as did most of the buildings in Paris due to the preponderance of limestone in the region, and the mixture of pebbles and sand was fine enough to provide sufficient traction.

There were many other runners, runners of all ages and ethnicities.

I kept having to stop and tie my laces every half mile or so. One morning, as two old men passed by in the fog and looked down at me, I looked up and smiled and said *bonjour*. They smiled and said *bonjour* in return. It was a small thing, but made me feel connected.

READY FOR THE READYMADES

We showered and dressed and left to go see the Duchamp exhibit at the Pompidou. We took the Métro. I let Ronnie figure out the ticket dispenser while I froze and turned into an icicle. The wind getting sucked into the tunnel was bitter cold, the kind of cold that burns the rims of your ears and penetrates to the bone.

I'd made a mistake in wearing my spring jacket instead of my winter coat. I checked the forecast before we left and according to their predictions (I'm assuming a bureau of French meteorologists) temperatures in the 40-degree Fahrenheit range were predicted. These are generally the temperatures in Seattle's winter months. Consequently, I thought I could get away with wearing my spring jacket over a thick, woolen cardigan sweater, a shirt and T-shirt. In fact, I thought, what with all the walking we'd be doing, I'd be sweating under that.

Wrong.

Oh, how wrong. I longed for my winter coat.

Ronnie handed me my ticket and we entered the bowels of the Métro with its colorful, enigmatic destinations: Boulogne-Billancourt, Tuileries, Varenne, Trocadéro, Villejuif, Sèvres-Babylone, Montreuil, Neuilly-sur-Seine, Saint-Denis, Mabillon.

We arose at Châtelet, near the Tour Saints-Jacques, which André Breton had loved so much (I loved it, too), and walked the short distance to the Pompidou on Rue Saint-Martin.

There were two long lines. We got into the first, but found out minutes later that this was a line for the Bibliothèque Publique d'Information du Centre Pompidou.

We went to the other line and were standing there when two gypsy girls approached with clipboards. I was asked to sign a crudely drawn petition that had something to do with supporting the deaf, though no organization or goal was specified. I began writing a fictitious name when the woman behind us with two boys told us not to sign, it was a scam. They were there to hit us up for money. The gypsy girl shot an angry look at the woman and she and her companion left in a huff of indignation, clearly not deaf.

I thanked the woman behind us. She didn't have to do that. It was nice that she felt protective toward two American strangers. Though, in some way, I felt bad for the two gypsy girls. Maybe one of them was Carmen.

There were two more lines inside the Pompidou. One was for checking items that you didn't want to drag around in the museum, umbrellas, coats, hats, canes, shopping bags, purses, backpacks, camping gear.

I was glad, now, I didn't have a big winter coat to check. It was the one benefit to my wearing a thin spring jacket over a cardigan sweater.

The Duchamp exhibit was remarkably crowded. This surprised me. I didn't think Duchamp would be such a huge draw. How many people got this guy? Duchamp was a peculiar artist, highly intellectual, somewhat hermetic, more apt to withdraw from society than to become an iconic figure like Picasso. Duchamp seemed utterly immune to celebrityhood. He was too enigmatic, too cerebral, too mysterious. He didn't fit any of the usual categories. He didn't fit any category. He was vigorously anti-categorical. Not a public figure at all.

And yet here were all these people.

Well, they were French. That explained it.

Duchamp became an important, influential figure to me in the mid-1970s. I'm not sure how this happened. I had always been passionate about art and my stance had always been one of romantic transcendence. Duchamp was not. He professed indifference toward art, toward the found objects he called *readymades,* such as his bottle-rack and bicycle wheel.

I never completely believed his professed arbitrariness when it came to choosing a readymade. The objects he chose were unusual and beautiful. Signing them and mounting them as *objets d'art* was both funny and transformative. They became art. They truly did. The project seemed to backfire on Duchamp. Instead of exhibiting a philosophy of detachment to the oft-fraudulent nature of the art world and its pseudo-intellectual bullshit, they called attention to the fact that any object in the world had a certain inherent beauty, a certain unfathomable mystery.

I jotted down in my notebook a statement made about this issue on the museum wall: Duchamp surrounds his figures with an aura, sign, for him, of his "subconscious preoccupations toward a metarealism," a painting of the invisible. This was a new narrative for me.

I was awestruck. The bicycle wheel on the kitchen stool with the heart-shaped shadow in the corner was nothing less than sublime. I also noticed that the wheel didn't have a tire. It was just a bare rim. I hadn't noticed that before.

Duchamp had begun his career as a painter. His paintings were intensely colorful works influenced by the Fauve movement. There was a collection of female nudes, most of them red, an alluring, hot, sexual red.

Nude Descending a Staircase, No. 2, a print of which hangs in our bathroom at home, shocked me with its astonishing beauty. The real painting glows with diamond-like precision.

The show was made all the richer by including work that had influenced Duchamp, paralleled Duchamp, resonated with

Duchamp or belonged somehow in the same suitcase. There was *La danse à la source*, a painting by Francis Picabia with a lot of reds and oranges and browns in square and triangular patches; *Anémic cinéma*, a movie Duchamp made in collaboration with Man Ray; *Le déshabillage impossible*, a film by Georges Méliès in which a man attempts to get undressed and as fast as he gets his clothes off more clothes appear on his body; *Portrait de Marie Laurencin, Four in Hand* by Francis Picabia in which there is no recognizable face at all but instead a group of mechanical parts; a first edition of *Un coup de dés jamais n'abolira le hasard* by Stéphane Mallarmé; and a copy of *L'eve future (The Future Eve)* by French author August Villiers de l'Isle-Adam, a symbolist science fiction novel published in 1886 best known for popularizing the term *android*.

First editions of *Impressions d'Afrique* and *Locus Solus*, by Raymond Roussel, were also included. Roussel was brilliant at using language to invent some of the most fabulous machines imaginable. In his introduction to Michel Foucault's *Death and the Labyrinth*, a monograph on Roussel's writing, John Ashbery summarizes *Locus Solus* thus:

> A prominent scientist and inventor, Martial Canterel, has invited a group of colleagues to visit the park of his country estate, Locus Solus. As the group tours the estate, Canterel shows them inventions of ever-increasing complexity and strangeness. Again, exposition is invariably followed by explanation, the cold hysteria of the former giving way to the innumerable ramifications of the latter. After an aerial pile driver which is constructing a mosaic of teeth and a huge glass diamond filled with water in which float a dancing girl, a hairless cat, and the preserved head of Danton, we come to the central and longest passage: a description of eight curious tableaux vivants taking place inside an enormous glass cage. We learn that the actors are actually dead people whom Canterel has revived with "resurrectine," a fluid of his invention which if injected into a fresh corpse causes it continually to act out the most important incident of its life.

There were also some fascinating machines housed in bell jars by anonymous artists. The inclusion of all these machines suited Duchamp's sensibility, particularly since his enormous *La mariée mise à nu par ses célibataires, même (The Bride Stripped Bare by Her Bachelors, Even)*, consists of imaginary mechanical parts. There was a replica on display in order to give some idea of Duchamp's invention. This included the two divisions, the upper section known as the Bride's Domain and the bottom division representing the Bachelors' Apparatus. The entire structure looks like a window into the fourth dimension. The images in the glass, as Duchamp stated, are a "Delay in glass... not so much in the different meanings in which delay can be taken, but rather in their indecisive reunion," a "delay in glass" as you would say "a poem in prose" or a "spittoon in silver."

The Bride hangs above the Bachelors "fat and lubricious" in an "apotheosis of virginity." She has reached the goal of her desire and emits a "cinematic blossoming... the sum total of her splendid vibrations... and the orgasm which may (might) bring about her fall." The cinematic blossoming consists of lead wire and dust and looks like a cloud upon which hang three sheets of paper. These are the three "draft pistons" and were made by hanging a curtain above a radiator, then photographing it as currents of warm air disturbed the material. The Bride is a mechanical apparatus driven by "quite feeble cylinders, in contact with the sparks of her constant life (desire-magneto)," which explodes "and makes this virgin blossom who has attained her desire."

The Bachelors consist of a Chocolate Grinder, Glider, Malic Moulds and Capillary Tubes. Pigment, chocolate brown in color, is used to create an "apparition of an appearance." The pigment does not merely represent the metal frame of the Glider, but is the substance itself. Oxides of lead and cadmium compose the metal framework of the Glider, or Chariot. The Chariot, Duchamp wrote in his notes to The Large Glass, "should be made of rods of emancipated metal; the chariot would have the property of giving itself without resistance of gravity to a force acting horizontally upon it." The Chariot produced litanies. These were: "Slow life, Vicious circle, Onanism, Horizontal, Round trip for the buffer, Junk of life, Cheap construction, Tin, cords, iron wire, Eccentric wooden pulleys, Monotonous fly wheel, Beer professor." The Glider, upon which ride the Nine Malic Moulds (who represent the bachelors), and which is powered by an imaginary waterfall (not visible in the Glass), goes back and forth onanistically emitting a doleful litany: "Slow life, Vicious circle, Onanism, Horizontal, Round trip for the buffer, Junk of life, Cheap construction, Tin, cords, iron wire, Eccentric wooden pulleys, Monotonous fly wheel, Beer professor." There is a Hook, which is a "sort of fork," and "which falls between the Grinder and Glider and which makes the glider glide, is made of a substance of oscillating density."

The malic forms, according to Duchamp's notes, "are provisionally painted with red lead while waiting for each other to receive its color, like croquet mallets." The job of the Nine Malic Moulds is (upon receiving a signal from the Bride) to convert an "illuminating gas" produced by the Chocolate Grinder into "spangles of frosty glass" which, being lighter than air, are dazzled upward at a terrific velocity into the "splash area" of the Bride.

I'm providing only a crude overview of *The Large Glass*. It's important that nothing in this work be taken too literally. That would deflate the performance of the bachelors, dessicate the bride's "cinematic blossoming," and run contrary to Duchamp's "adage of spontaneity," which wisely states "the bachelor grinds his chocolate himself." Each viewer must reinvent the Large Glass by one's self. It takes time to immerse oneself in a perpetual exchange that never achieves consummation but blossoms forever into unreachable displays. Masturbation wasn't built in a day.

We were exhausted after show. We went to the restaurant within the Pompidou for some water and juice and rested a bit before catching the Métro and returning to the hotel. Ronnie also needed some time to apply some eye lotion.

JE SUIS CHARLIE

On Monday we visited the Basilica of Sacré-Cœur atop the butte that is Montmartre and on Tuesday — the day of epiphany — we visted both Notre-Dame and stood in a long line to view the interior of Sainte-Chapelle.

I nearly keeled over from sheer awe at the interior of Sainte-Chapelle. Its towering stained glass windows were immensely beautiful, almost supernaturally so, as something that stood outside and above the natural world, a gem of heavenly illumination. People stood in awed stupefaction looking up at this marvelous configuration of color and stone lacework.

On late Wednesday afternoon, after spending hours wandering the galleries of the Hôtel de Cluny which houses the Musée National du Moyen Âges — Thermes et Hôtel de Cluny (National Museum of the Middle Ages — Cluny thermal baths and mansion), and viewing the incredible tapestries allegorizing the six senses (the sixth sense being that of the heart) in the series known as the *Lady and the Unicorn*, we returned to our hotel for a little rest and then went out again hoping to find a modestly priced restaurant on the Boulevard Saint-Germain.

The previous night we'd enjoyed an early dinner at the Bouillon Racine, a restaurant with an art nouveau interior. We loved this restaurant and hoped to have dinner there again before we left but meals there were a bit pricey, so this particular night we thought it would be better to be a little thrifty. Thrift is a hard quality to come by in a city like Paris where extravagance seems to be embedded in its walls and monuments, a drug that quickened the appetite for food and intellectual stimulation while simultaneously creating a universe of infinite possibility in which money was always a nagging, secondary consideration, a sour note in a symphony of ineffable refinements.

We were approaching the intersection at rue de Condé and the Boulevard Saint-Germain when I saw four French soldiers in camouflaged battle fatigues walk by carrying machine guns. That seemed strange. We'd also been hearing a constant chorus of sirens wailing all that afternoon.

We had dinner at L'Avant Comptoir. I ordered the steak *hachée* that came with an egg on top and asked the waiter for a non-alcoholic beverage, *un boisson sans alcool*. He said, Buckler. I said, what? Buckler, he repeated. Ronnie ordered wine. When our drinks appeared, I saw that Buckler was a non-alcoholic beer. This gave me pause. Really? How could it be non-alcoholic? I sipped some, trying to detect alcohol. I hadn't had any alcohol in almost twenty-five years. I could definitely taste the beer, but couldn't detect any alcohol. I figured if they didn't get all the alcohol out, what was left would be so minimal as to hardly make a difference. And, in fact, after drinking the beer I felt nothing, not the slightest buzz. It was the taste of beer that got me. It brought back memories, strong memories, of a time when I would drink and smoke with abandon, and it felt wonderful. I loved being drunk. I was a happy drunk, laughing and friendly until my later years, when I began falling off bar stools and picking fights.

I pictured the steak *hachée* as being something like, I don't know, the thinly sliced ham I'd had at Les Deux Magots, only all mixed up in a nice pile of tasty protein. It turned out to be hamburger. It wasn't bad, but the salad that came with it was lousy, wilted bits of lettuce. In Paris, it doesn't pay to go cheap. That is to say, if you have to eat thrifty, it takes a little more expertise to find out the good places from the more tourist-oriented places.

We went next door to a snack shop and ordered a couple of large cookies to go and returned to our hotel. Ronnie lay down to take a nap and I got out my tablet to check our mail and see if the cat sitter wrote anything about Graham. She hadn't. I checked Facebook and pressed the like button a couple of times and then turned it off and put it away and turned the TV on, a large black plasma screen attached to the wall. French television is so extremely different from American TV. The French have a lot more documentaries and reality shows in which people talk about cooking and plants and architecture. The ads are always funny: mischievous pebbles strategizing different ways they can tumble into people's windshields on the freeway creating dings, or two bearded young men in office attire rolling through an office building in swivel chairs until they crash joyfully out of one of the windows and roll off into the sunset. The ad was for a lottery.

When the news came on, I saw what had happened not more than three miles away from our hotel. Two Islamist terrorists, brothers Saïd and Chérif Kouachi, armed with assault rifles and other weapons, forced their way into the offices of the satirical weekly newspaper *Charlie Hebdo*. They fired up to 50 shots, killing eleven people — most of them journalists and cartoonists — and injuring eleven others, all the while shouting, *Allahu Akbar* (Arabic for "God is greatest") during their slaughter. More shooting followed in the Île-de-France region, also by Islamic terrorists, in which five others were killed and another eleven wounded.

Ronnie awoke to hear gunfire and see men in the streets firing machine guns at one another. Where is that? she asked.

Here, in Paris, I answered.

What? she responded, shocked.

We continued to watch the news. It was deeply unsettling. We both loved Paris and it was dreadful to see it under attack like this.

It was hard to get to sleep that night. The next day, Thursday, we stayed close to the hotel, choosing to spend our time shopping for snacks and water at La Grande Épicerie on the rue de Sèvres and going to have dinner once more at Bouillon Racine.

We left early on Friday morning. After showering and getting dressed and packing I went down ahead of Ronnie to pay our hotel bill. The concierge was a middle-aged man with thick black hair and horn-rimmed glasses and a very gentle manner that I remembered from our trip in August 2013, the man who went into the back to get some shiny tape with which to repair the strap on my bag, which has since been retired, and replaced with my red "spinner."

I joked that I would have to go back to our room and try and pry Ronnie's hands loose. She didn't want to go.

I hope, he said, that you had a pleasant stay despite what happened yesterday.

We did. Very much so, I said. It was terrible what happened. Unthinkable to see gunfire in the streets of Paris.

And then I added, *Je suis Charlie.*

Merci, he answered.

quale [kwa-lay]: *Eng.* n 1. A property (such as hardness) considered apart from things that have that property. 2. A property that is experienced as distinct from any source it may have in a physical object. *Ital.* pron.a. 1. Which, what. 2. Who. 3. Some. 4. As, just as.

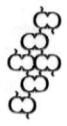